WINGING IT

EMMA MURRAY

Boldwood

First published in Great Britain in 2021 by Boldwood Books Ltd.

Cover Design by Alice Moore Design

Cover Illustration: Everyday People Cartoons

A CIP catalogue record for this book is available from the British Library.

Paperback ISBN 978-1-83889-495-5

Large Print ISBN 978-1-83889-494-8

Hardback ISBN 978-1-80280-980-0

Ebook ISBN 978-1-83889-496-2

Kindle ISBN 978-1-83889-497-9

Audio CD ISBN 978-1-83889-489-4

MP3 CD ISBN 978-1-83889-490-0

Digital audio download ISBN 978-1-83889-493-1

Boldwood Books Ltd
23 Bowerdean Street
London SW6 3TN
www.boldwoodbooks.com

For my husband Sam, and our daughters Ava and Anya who are frankly growing up too fast.

1

It's six months since my husband David announced on New Year's Eve that he had been offered a job in New York and I am still awash with a heady mixture of excitement and nerves. I have been on work trips to New York before and I fell in love with it instantly, but that was when I was single and in my twenties.

Don't get me wrong – it is, of course, an opportunity of a life-time and on paper, it seems like a dream. David's new company is pulling out all the stops to make the transition from London to New York as smooth as possible. They are putting us up in a flat in Manhattan, paying for our five-year-old daughter Anna to go to a fancy school a couple of blocks from Central Park, not to mention flying us over business class, all for the sake of a year's contract with an option to extend if all goes well. But I can't think that far ahead.

When I told my mother the plans, she thought it all sounded too good to be true and so has started calling David's new company 'The Firm' and saying things like: 'They'll be wanting their pound of flesh,' and 'There's no such thing as a free lunch!'

She's similarly unimpressed that we're flying out in late July: 'You'll be boiled out of it going there in the summer; you'll drown in the humidity!' followed by constant reminders that 'The grass is never greener, Saoirse,' which doesn't help settle the nerves.

Still, I know I have to go easy on her. She's far from happy that we're taking her only grandchild across the Atlantic, and I know those little digs are her way of letting us know that she is going to miss us terribly.

She's not the only one struggling with our departure. Bonnie, David's birth mum, has openly shed tears. Bonnie has just reunited with David after years of separation since his adoption, and she has formed a close bond with him and Anna already. I am hoping she will visit us in New York, but every time I ask her, her eyes take on a faraway look and she changes the subject. I don't want to pry but I get the impression that financially it could be a struggle. Bonnie works as a 'rent-a-friend' – someone who gives support to people who are lonely or in need of a kind word. I have no doubt that anyone privileged enough to be in her company leaves with a lighter heart than when they arrived. But as worthy as her job is, I don't think it pays very much.

David's adoptive mum, Rose, is taking a slightly more stoical approach, making it very clear that she is 'too old' for long-haul flights, and '*those* types of Americans' (whatever that means) and that she will be more than happy to use the telephone to stay in touch.

Jen, my best friend from Ireland, is more excited than I am, judging from her texts:

The shopping, Saoirse!

And:

The nightlife!

And:

The BUZZ!

Dee, my other close friend from Ireland, is working a more jealous angle, her texts peppered with vomiting emojis and things like:

'Big Apple' my arse.

Today is Friday, the last day of school before it breaks up for the summer, and my final school run in London. I give the head teacher, Mr Russell, a wave as I walk through the school gates, and he waves back with a neutral smile. We have come a long way, Mr Russell and me. I'm sure it's not easy to work at a school when one of the mums (me) has given you a blowjob after a boozy night out (over a decade ago!). But time is a healer, and now we have reached that ideal stage where we both pretend it never happened. The Organics, on the other hand, the insufferable, judgemental, self-proclaimed 'supermums' who have recently started a Facebook group called Mums Against Screentime (they also constantly berate other mums on everything from working full-time to not buying organic food) have not let blowjob-gate go as easily. Even though I have taken myself off the unbearable class WhatsApp group, I am still subject to their whispers, narrowed eyes and behind-the-hand smirks, all enthusiastically encouraged by Organics' kingpin, Tania Henderson.

At least they are not brave enough to say anything to my face, especially with Bea around. Like pretty much everyone else we know, the Organics are terrified of my best mum friend, Bea, and her pull-no-punches attitude. To my absolute joy, Bea has taken her son, Harry, out of his posh private school and sent him to Woodvale

Primary School. Even better is that Harry has ended up in the same class as my daughter, Anna, and the pair have been inseparable ever since.

As I round the corner to the playground, I feel the corners of my mouth twitch. There's Bea, standing straight-backed, blonde hair tied up in an impeccably high ponytail, arms folded, in her usual spot, right outside the classroom, just in front of the Organics' territory. Despite the simple, knee-length, pretty, patterned blue summer dress she is wearing, paired with plain white flip-flops, her stance still screams *don't fuck with me*. I marvel at her nerve. Before Harry started at the school, I always lounged against the back fence as far from the Organics as possible, not daring to encroach on their space, pretending to tap on my phone as if I was absolutely fine being friendless, but Bea has no such hang-ups. She has refused to join the class WhatsApp group and none of the Organics have dared approach her to rope her in to help out at school events.

I walk towards my friend, picking my way through the litter of adult scooters (the Organics' preferred mode of transport), ignoring the disapproving sighs and headshaking, led mainly by Tania.

Bea breaks into a smile as soon as she sees me, and she wraps me in a big hug.

'Last day of school!' she says, laughing.

My stomach gives another jolt as I draw back from her.

'How are you feeling?' she says, giving me a playful punch on the arm.

'A bit nervous,' I admit.

I'm sick to my stomach.

'Well, I think that's a perfectly normal way to react when you're moving to a different country for a year!' she says, in that schoolmistress way of hers. 'What time are you leaving for the airport?'

'It's an afternoon flight – leaving at 2.30 p.m.,' I tell her.

'Well, I shall be around to say goodbye properly before you go,' she says.

'Don't!' I say, the word shooting out of my mouth before I can stop it.

Suddenly, more than anything else, I can't face the thought of saying goodbye to her, even if she has promised to visit. Ryan, Harry's dad, a management consultant, will be working in Connecticut on and off for the next six months, which is enormously convenient as Bea plans to bring Harry to see Anna in Manhattan before dropping him over to stay with his dad. I'd be lying if I didn't say I had a bit of 'a moment' when I heard Ryan was going to be only a couple of hours' drive away from our new accommodation. Let's just say Ryan and I have a bit of a history, one which I'm at great pains to forget. After all, it's been almost a year since he kissed me in the park and eight months since I bumped into him (hammered) at a concert at the O2, and I've managed to successfully avoid him every time he has flown over for a visit with Harry. I'd rather not come face to face to him in New York if I can help it, and the thought of David bumping into him doesn't bear thinking about. Not that I'm still attracted to Ryan – because I'm not. Even if he looks a little too like Ryan Gosling for my liking...

Besides, Ryan is seeing someone: Adriana, a make-up artist, who is apparently a dead ringer for the Brazilian supermodel, Gisele. The thought of seeing two fabulously good-looking people together makes my stomach heave.

Bea raises an eyebrow.

'I mean, Harry has football on a Saturday afternoon and you can't be missing that,' I babble, desperate to give some explanation for my earlier knee-jerk response.

Bea shoots me another look and I cave.

'I'm shite at goodbyes,' I say miserably, fighting to blink away the tears.

Bea looks away, as if to gather herself, and folds her arms across her chest.

When she turns to me again, her eyes glisten.

'Fine – no goodbyes then,' she says, nudging her glasses up her slender nose. 'But you must text me when you're on the plane and send me some smug photos of the free champagne in business class.'

I laugh, and hastily brush away the tears in my eyes.

Bea's expression hardens.

'Incoming,' she hisses, narrowing her eyes at a point over my right shoulder.

I turn around slowly, and there she is – Tania Henderson in her summer Lycra gym gear of a hot-pink tank top and calf-length, shiny black leggings emblazoned with a brand that is too exclusive for me to recognise.

'I hear you're off to New York!' she says, in a falsely bright voice.

There's no point in asking how she knows we're leaving, mostly because she makes it her business to stick her nose into everything. And Anna has told the entire school by now, so it's not exactly a surprise.

I take a deep breath.

'Yes, we're off tomorrow,' I say, keeping my voice steady.

'Wow!' she says. 'How fabulous!'

I eye her suspiciously, waiting for the sting in the tail.

'I mean, I'm happy for you but I just don't think *I* could uproot my children at this age, to haul them halfway across the world, you know? Just when they're so settled in school. Seems a bit selfish, doesn't it?'

There it is.

The cow. As if I haven't worried myself to death about how Anna is going to adjust to a new school in a different country, thousands of miles away from everyone she knows.

Bea steps in before I have time to compose a barbed response.

'That's the problem with being handed the opportunity of a lifetime. There are always jealous people around to try and put you down.'

'Oh, I'm not jealous,' Tania says, with a nasty, tinkling laugh. 'Far from it! I could never leave London. I suppose I'm the type of person who worries about my kids too much.'

Bea shakes her head, catches my eye, and gives me a nod as if to say, *it's your turn*. She's right. I can't let her fight my battles for me. I've put up with Tania's shit for too long.

'The problem with you, Tania, and all your friends,' I say, deliberately keeping my voice measured and silky smooth, 'is that you're nothing but parasites, feeding off the insecurities of other mums because it makes you feel better about your own shortcomings. I fervently hope your children don't end up like you, because we seriously don't need any more of your poison in the world.'

Tania's mouth drops open and then closes. It's the first time I've seen her speechless and it feels glorious. Her mouth opens again but before she can say anything, the school bell rings.

She gives Bea and me a filthy look before whipping around and striding angrily towards her Organics bubble. No doubt she will find the comfort she needs from her minions, who will go to great lengths to reassure her that I'm the arsehole, not her.

'Nice,' Bea says, giving me a little nudge.

'Thanks,' I say, a little shakily. I've never been good with confrontation but I am proud that I stood up for myself – and I didn't even swear!

Then a little hand slips into mine and a feeling of warmth travels all over my body. Anna is here and she is beaming so widely that it's hard not to smile back.

'We're going on a plane tomorrow!' she says, swinging my arm up and down.

'We are!' I say, just as enthusiastically.

After all the efforts we have made to prepare Anna for the big move – showing her pictures of the Empire State Building (which I am determined to get to the top of) and the Statue of Liberty, not to mention images of her new school and the apartment building where we will be living – it's the plane journey that she is most excited about.

She shouts the same thing to Harry, who is busy tucking into a bumper-sized bag of crisps, and he says, 'I know – you've told me a zillion times,' through a mouthful of crumbs.

Bea and I start to laugh. It's so funny to see a five-year-old act like a grumpy teenager. As the four of us walk out of the school gates together, Mr Russell shouts 'Safe trip' to me and I give him a smile and a wave in return – I have to say he looks rather relieved to see the back of me. I squeeze Anna's hand and try to ignore the legion of butterflies in my stomach.

Time for a fresh start.

2

There's nothing quite like walking into a business-class lounge with a small child to make you feel like a social pariah. I can almost hear the collective intake of breath as we make our way towards the seating area. Look – I get it. People pay thousands of pounds for the luxury of flying in the executive classes and the last thing they want to see is a young child who might disrupt their precious experience. But I try to ignore all the hard stares and rictus smiles as I settle Anna into her seat in the waiting area with her iPad. Fair play to her, she's being very well-behaved, given that the entire morning has been a maelstrom of last-minute packing chaos. But since closing our front door, I have to say that, at the risk of cursing us, the whole experience has been seamless. The Firm sent a car to pick us up, and check-in was also smooth – no endless queuing and pushing through crowds. Business class – how the other half live.

David wanders off to make the most of the free snacks. It's hard to believe that just last year he was tearing his hair out over being made redundant. Financially, we were in trouble and the lucrative ghostwriting job I took on to help fell through spectacularly. The advance I got paid for the book on motherhood that I had written last year ran out months ago, and we have been relying on our savings and payments from a few small writing jobs to get us to our big move to New York.

If it hadn't been for The Firm, swooping in to save us by offering David a great job in New York with a fabulous salary, I dread to think what might have happened. I've told my agent, Harriet, to keep an eye out for some writing work for me in the US but she is more keen for me to promote my book when it comes out in January next year, although I get butterflies even thinking about it. How do I promote a book in a strange country where I have no contacts?

Then there's David. Although we've talked about the move inside out and upside down, I still worry about him. He was so happy playing chef, househusband, and spending more time with Anna for all these months of not working, that I do worry that this is going to be a huge adjustment for him. But he has reminded me, time and again, how much he loves New York – that he has been there dozens of times over the years and that technology is his passion. This was a role he really couldn't turn down and I just hope my mother is wrong, and they don't work him to death.

My phone starts to buzz in my bag and I don't even bother checking the screen before I answer.

'Hi, Mum,' I say.

Twenty pairs of eyes in the row of seats opposite me immediately shoot me looks of disapproval, even though I am speaking very quietly. Clearly, I have been tarred and feathered by virtue of the fact that I have a small child with me.

'You're at the airport so,' she says with a sniff.

I don't bother asking her how she knows we're here – she's had mine and David's phones tracked for years.

'I am,' I say.

'And have you checked in your bags?'

'I have.'

'You didn't bring the kitchen sink with you, did you?'

I tell her no. In all honesty, for a family that's moving to a different country, we don't actually have a huge amount of stuff. Three large suitcases, and one of those cases mostly consists of Anna's stuffed toys. Her doll, Rose-Bonnie (named after David's adoptive mother and David's birth mother), has been awarded the privileged position of flying with us in business class.

'And have the cleaners come yet?'

I tell her they're due a bit later. We're having our house cleaned before the new tenants move in. Another bonus of moving away – not only do we get free accommodation for the year but we also get rental income from our place.

'I hope that fella looks after the place now,' Mum says for the millionth time.

'It'll be grand,' I say, trying to keep the impatience out of my voice.

I don't know why she's so worried. David has vetted our new tenant, Caleb, thoroughly, practically asking for his dental records and inside leg measurements. Caleb is a quiet, dignified-looking man in his sixties, recently divorced and looking for a modest house in our area of London. He's definitely not the type to throw wild parties and annoy the neighbours. Nevertheless, David, who is known for his domestic fussiness, has left the poor man a clear set of dos and don'ts for every single part of the house, including the 'right' way for the dishwasher to be stacked, and how to clean out the black bins in the front. I have told him not to leave the list – not everyone is a neat-freak like him – but I might as well have been talking to myself because I saw him slip it under the door as we were leaving.

'Now listen – don't be drinking champagne on the plane. It'll go right to your head. It's the cabin pressure that does it.'

'Mm hmm,' I mumble.

Champagne is the first thing I'm having when we get to our fancy seats.

'You don't want to be making a holy show of yourself,' she adds. Then her voice softens. 'How's my beautiful grandchild?'

'She's grand,' I say. 'Sitting here beside me glued to her iPad.'

'Ah, I won't disturb her then.'

Wise.

'Give her a big kiss from me, and text me when you arrive.'

'I will, of course,' I say, although I wonder what the point of texting her is when she knows exactly where I am at all times.

'That's it so,' she says. 'You're off.'

I try to ignore the wobble in her voice. If she cracks, I'm a goner.

'See you on the other side!' I say brightly.

'Bye, love.'

And she's gone.

I take a few deep breaths and do my best to blink away the tears. This is why I hate goodbyes.

David comes back, arms full with an assortment of snacks for Anna, and she dives on them like she hasn't eaten in weeks.

'Everything OK?' he says, sitting down beside me.

'Mum just called. I think she was a bit emotional towards the end,' I say, blowing out some air.

'It's hard on her,' David says, taking my hand. 'And you.'

'It's hard on everyone,' I say, thinking of Rose and Bonnie.

'Still, we're doing the right thing,' he says, his voice steady.

I nod and try to ignore the little voice inside that says, *Are we?*

3

I think it's fair to say that the worst-behaved passenger on the business class flight is not Anna – it's me. Feeling overly emotional after the call with my mum, I have gone to town on the free champagne to numb the reality of moving an entire time zone away from her. Bea's text doesn't help either – she has written me an unusually heartfelt message saying that I am her best friend in the world and she's going to miss me to the moon and back. However, she does make me smile through the tears by ending the message with:

Now send me that smug photo of the free champagne, you bastard.

So, I live up to my promise with gusto. Not only do I send her the photo of me sipping champagne, little finger up, in a faux-upper-class way, but I also make David and Anna pose with a glass in their hands (orange juice in a posh glass for Anna). After the hilarity is over, and Anna is settled in an airplane seat twice the size of her, I try to settle down and focus on take-off. Usually, I love this part of flying – the noise of the engine, the gentle tilt of the aircraft as it rises gracefully into the sky, but this time I have a knot in my stomach that the champagne just won't shift. I keep coming back to the thought that this is no two-week holiday to Ireland – this is a whole year living halfway across the world.

Anna, of course, is too immersed in Danny Dare, her favourite YouTuber, to do so much as glance out the window, so I ask the air steward for more champagne. After I polish off the second glass, I decide that this is the perfect time to interrupt David's movie to quiz him about exactly why we're going to New York and leaving all our loved ones behind. I have done the same sort of thing after a few drinks over the last few months but have hastily backtracked as soon as I've sobered up, going to great lengths to allay his concerns about cold feet. Now I can tell by his tired expression that this sort of chat is wearing a bit thin.

'To earn some real money so we have a future to come back to,' he says shortly.

Fair point.

Then his expression softens.

'Are you *sure* you're OK about the move, Saoirse?'

Jesus – bit late now.

'Of course, of course!' I tut. 'It's just that now that the moment's here, I'm a bit nervous.'

'Me too,' he says, stroking my arm.

I smile back. We can be nervous together.

The air steward – dark olive skin, flashing brown eyes, gelled-back hair – comes over with a basket of fabulous-smelling bread rolls, and more champagne. Now that both David and Anna are firmly plugged into movies, I decide this is the perfect time to make friends. I peer closely at his name badge – Lorenzo – and use that as a starting point. He is indeed Italian and has been living in London for ten years. No, he does not miss Italy that much and has never been to Rome. He answers politely and patiently, which I take as a sign to continue the conversation.

I tell him all about moving to New York and I ignore the impatient head-twisting from the puffy-faced, suited, middle-aged man across the aisle until Lorenzo tells me, not unkindly, to keep my voice down, as I am disturbing other passengers. Despite his soothing tone, I am affronted nonetheless, and decide to stand up and announce to the cabin that I have *every right* to talk in business class because like them, I have spent thousands of pounds on the tickets, which is bullshit obviously because The Firm paid for it, but *they* don't know that.

My announcement clearly alerts David to the fact that his wife is making an ass out of herself, and he quickly jumps up from his seat, gives me a calming hug, and immediately turns my seat into a bed. The fight goes out of me as soon as my head hits the soft pillow. The last thing I hear before I pass out is David whispering, 'Everything will be OK, Saoirse.'

* * *

Anna shakes me awake after what feels only mere minutes asleep. I try to raise my head, but the pain is too much. Why did I drink so much champagne?

'We're almost in New York, Mummy!' Anna says, tugging my sleeve.

I attempt a smile and my lips crack.

Then David's head appears over Anna's.

'Well, how are you feeling?' he says, with a smug grin.

'Absolutely fine!' I say, determined to style it out.

I reach for the button and bring my seat into an upright position.

'Water?' he says, waving a little bottle at me.

I grab it and drink it within seconds.

Anna settles back with her iPad.

'Everything OK with Anna?' I mouth over her head, feeling horribly guilty that her mother has been too pissed to check in with her for most of the flight.

'She watched movies all the way here,' David says. 'Perfectly behaved,' he adds with a wink.

The subtext is loud and clear: *unlike her mother*.

4

The two-hour queue at customs is more than enough punishment for overdoing it on the champagne, not to mention the one-hour wait at baggage claim, and I'm cursing myself for not packing any paracetamol for my thumping head. It's almost 8.30 p.m. by the time we haul our last suitcase onto the trolley. I follow David grumpily as he thrusts our suitcase-laden trolley through the doors to arrivals, but cheer up when I spy David's name printed neatly on a board, held by a stout man wearing a smart uniform of white shirt, black tie and black trousers. Thank Christ The Firm has provided a driver to pick us up, especially as Anna started to wilt about half an hour ago. After the day she's had, I can't say I blame her.

I tug Anna gently by the hand to urge her to walk a little more quickly but she drags her feet at a snail's pace, so I pick her up and carry her towards the driver. With any luck she'll sleep in the car. The driver greets us with a curt 'hello' and takes over the trolley and I'm relieved he's not the chatty type because I'm really not in the mood.

A wall of heat hits me in the face as soon as we step through the glass, sliding doors to the waiting car outside. Although I've been to New York before, I've never visited in late July and I can't believe it's still so hot this late in the evening. The added warmth from Anna, whose head is buried into the side of my neck, does not help to soothe my prickling armpits. I can feel my hair springing up – I'd forgotten how badly behaved it can be in high levels of humidity.

Carefully, I settle a dozing Anna into a car seat in the back of the limo that's a million times more plush than our car at home, pluck Rose-Bonnie off the top of the trolley and into her arms, climb in beside her, and strap myself in, grateful for the air con. David sits in the front with the driver and then twists around.

'Is she asleep?' he says quietly, casting a doubtful glance at Anna.

'On her way,' I whisper back, noting her falling eyelids.

'It's 1.30 a.m. in London,' he says, frowning at his watch. 'I'm surprised she has lasted this long. I wonder if we should try and keep her awake until we get to the apartment? Then we can just pop her into bed straight away.'

I scrunch up my face in disbelief.

'Are you taking the piss?' I hiss quietly. 'Have you ever tried to stop a child from going to sleep? If you want her to stay up, then I suggest you get back here and try it for yourself.'

He takes one look at my folded arms and hard stare and does a sort of *OK, OK!* motion with his hands before turning around in his seat again.

I lie back against the headrest, enjoying the quiet hum of the car as it moves slowly through the traffic-logged roads leading to Manhattan. Despite the months of conversation and endless discussions about what we'd be leaving behind and what we'd be gaining, I can't believe we are actually here – in New York – to live. For a year.

The usual voice rises to the surface. *You don't know anyone in New York*, it whispers.

My stomach turns over.

I have had this same conversation with David and Bea on several occasions, and they have both reassured me – at length – that it will all be fine: 'You'll make loads of friends when Anna starts school.'

And on the face of it, they're probably right. Anna starts school in September, less than six weeks from now, and, of course, I am bound to meet other parents. But the voice says, *Don't they say it's harder to make friends later in life? What if they don't like you?*

I am so engrossed in my thoughts that I lose track of where we are until much later, when David twists around in his seat again.

'You're missing the Chrysler Building!' he says delightedly, gesturing towards the window.

David has always been a city boy. He loves the bright lights, the crowds, the buzzy atmosphere, the big buildings. This sort of environment suits him down to the ground – it's his happy place. I'm just not sure that it's mine.

Anna stirs.

'Anna!' says David before the poor child even opens her eyes. 'To the right of us is the Chrysler Building. Remember? The one from your book?'

Anna opens her eyes and yawns.

'Are we there yet?' she says.

'Almost, sweetheart,' I say, stroking her soft, brown hair away from her forehead.

'I can't wait to go up the Empire State Building,' I say to David, trying my best to match his enthusiasm.

David gives me a thumbs up before facing front again.

'Now, we're just heading up towards Times Square – the Empire

State Building is to the left,' he says, staring at his phone; he sounds like one of those guides on a tour bus.

Then after a few minutes, he turns around again, his face bright with enthusiasm.

'Anna! Do you remember Times Square with all the lights?'

'Do you mean the one from my book?' Anna says, her eyes suddenly wide.

'Yes!' David claps.

Anna squeals.

A sudden rush of adrenalin flows through me as I see their faces lit up with excitement. Why am I feeling so apprehensive? We're in one of the most exciting cities in the world! There is nothing quite like the bright lights of New York dotted on every surface, the flashing billboards of Times Square, and the sheer life of the place to make your heart sing.

The car moves snail-like now, not just because of the traffic congestion but to avoid the dozens of people jaywalking right in front us. It's Saturday night and it's buzzing. I grab Anna's hand.

'We're in Times Square, baby!' I say, my eyes watery with emotion.

We're here – we made it. It may be daunting, but I just know everything is going to work out. It has to.

* * *

Despite our new accommodation being located a mere five-minute drive away from Times Square, the traffic is not kind. If it wasn't for our luggage, I would have got out of the car and walked. Anna, who has finally cracked under the strain of being on her best behaviour for so many hours, has started the whinging but to be fair, the driver doesn't show any sign that he's disturbed by her – no tutting, or turning the music up to drown out the whines of 'But *why* is it taking so long, Mummy?' I pledge to give him a big tip when we finally arrive. The man is a total pro.

I put my arm around Anna and pull her close to me – I can tell by her reddened eyes that she's way beyond bribery or reason. Now she just needs a big cuddle.

Finally, gloriously, the car pulls up to the side of the street and comes to a halt.

'We're here!' I say, quickly unstrapping Anna from her car seat. I pop Rose-Bonnie into her arms, and flash a grateful smile at the driver, who has kindly opened the door for us. I lead Anna onto the pavement (or sidewalk, as I should probably start saying) and wait for David, who is busy checking the car for anything we might have left behind.

The driver heaves our luggage out of the boot (trunk!) and takes two of the suitcases into the building while David follows him with the third. As I wait for David to come back, I pause a moment to take in the building, which will be our home for the next year.

Of course, The Firm has sent us tonnes of information about it, including a glossy brochure, but nothing has prepared me for the sheer size of the building. I crane my neck as far as it can go and I still can't make out the top, despite all the city lights around us. It's brown-brick, more like an office block and would be fairly nonde-script if it were not for the huge, ostentatious entrance with an impressive revolving door – giant gold columns stretching up to meet a chunky, gold sign emblazoned with the name of the build-ing: Ashton Tower.

My heart skips a beat – I can't wait to see our new apartment. It's been years since I've experienced apartment living and I used to love it. Not as much to clean, less space means less clutter (which means fewer rows with my neat-freak husband) so there's the added thrill of being able to lay your hands on everything.

David comes back for the hand luggage and we both thank the

driver, handing him a tip before he drives away. We approach the building and enter the revolving door. Once for David and, thanks to Anna's fondness for this sort of thing, twice for me. There would have been a third time (or more) had Rose-Bonnie's plastic arm not become stuck halfway around the second time, sending Anna into a bout of near-hysteria.

Once we're safely inside the lobby, Rose-Bonnie rescued from the perils of death, I dig frantically in my bag and find a packet of chewing gum I have been saving for emergencies. Anna has been asking to try gum for months, but I haven't caved until now. I hand her a piece and her eyes brighten.

'We have just enough time before the flavour runs out,' I mutter to David, who has been waiting for us patiently to exit the revolving door. 'Go ahead and get the keys, pronto. I'll deal with Anna.'

'On it,' David says, walking briskly towards the expansive, black, circular, marble-topped reception desk that forms a centrepiece to the whole area.

Anna and I follow at a slower place. I take a moment to marvel at the sheer majesty of our surroundings. Giant, brown and cream-streaked, marble columns stretch high to meet the white ceiling, which is dotted with dozens of spotlights. The floor picks up the same colours as the marble but is less fussy in pattern with cream and brown squares covering the entire surface, giving it the effect of a retro chessboard. The whole décor scheme is a luxurious mixture of modern and old-style New York grandeur.

Anna and I reach the desk and stand next to David, who is talking to a short, wiry man with grey, curly hair clinging to the sides of his head, but nowhere else.

David says, 'We've just flown in from London, and my company has booked an apartment here.'

'Name?' the man says in a heavy New York accent, without looking up.

David tells him and the man starts violently banging the keys on his computer.

The phone on his desk rings, and he snatches up the receiver with a curt, 'Yeah,' cradling it between his neck and shoulder.

David and I exchange a look. Not exactly a welcome party.

Then he slams the receiver down and rises with a sigh. It is then I notice the name badge on the top, right-hand corner of his dark grey shirt. My heart lifts – he may not have given the best first impression but now I have seen his name, I am positive we will be best friends.

'I see your name is Patrick!' I say, in a highly exaggerated version of my own accent. 'You must have an Irish connection.'

'Nope,' he says, head down, rustling through some papers.

I feel a jolt of disappointment. 'Not even half Irish?'

'No,' he mumbles.

'Or a quarter?'

He doesn't answer me.

David raises in his eyebrows in a *don't waste your time* sort of way, and I sigh. He's probably right, but for a brief moment, I had pictured myself winning over the surly receptionist through the simple exchange of lively stories about our shared Irish heritage.

Patrick hands David a sheaf of forms to fill out and sign and I bend down to check on Anna, who's happily trying to feed Rose-Bonnie some of the gum from her mouth. I leave her to it, and text my mother quickly to tell her we've arrived safely. She texts back within seconds.

Drink plenty of water after all that champagne on the plane.

How does she know? But before I have a chance to reply, another text pops up.

I'm your mother – I can read you like a book.

I shake my head and put my phone back into my pocket. I'm in no mood for my mother's smugness. There's no way I'm telling her she was right about the brutal humidity either.

David hands the pile of forms back to Patrick, who gives them a cursory look before handing David two key cards for our apartment. Then he waves towards the elevators and turns back to his screen.

As it doesn't look like Patrick will be giving us a hand with the bags or indeed doing us any favours at all, David grabs two cases and I take the other, balancing our hand luggage on the top of each bag, and we enter an enormous lift. Anna immediately presses all the buttons so we stop at each floor on the way up, which wouldn't be too annoying had our apartment not been on the fortieth floor.

Despite the lingering dull ache of a hangover and the underwhelming greeting from Patrick, I am excited to see our home for the next year. The elevator finally pings and the doors hum smoothly open. We roll our cases along a worn but clean-looking, dark red carpet, passing three doors on either side before we reach our apartment.

The feeling of anticipation grows as David inserts the key in the door.

'Are you excited, Anna?' I say, beaming down at her.

'I need the toilet,' she says, wiggling her hips.

'Excellent timing,' I say, as the door springs open.

David tells me to go ahead and sort Anna out while he brings in the cases.

I hurry into the apartment and try the first door to the right of the entrance, relieved that it leads to the bathroom. I switch on the light and take Rose-Bonnie from Anna while she fiddles with her leggings. She glances at the toilet and jumps back with a little 'Oh!'

'What's wrong, Anna?' I say, leaning over to have a look, half-expecting to see a stray poo floating in the water, but it's perfectly clean.

'The water is going to come out!' she says, lip trembling.

Oh god, I'd forgotten that the toilet water levels are way higher than our loos in London. I explain this to her and she looks at me, chewing her gum sceptically, but in the end, her tiny bladder overrules any further suspicions, and she finally jumps on to do a wee.

While I'm waiting for her to finish, I give the bathroom a quick once-over and I'm immediately impressed. For starters, it's about twice the size of our biggest bathroom at home, and fifty times better decorated. A pinky-beige marble surrounds the oval-shaped sink and one entire wall is covered in mirrored cabinets. There is a bath for Anna with a shower attachment for us and the whole area is sparkly and clean. My spirits lift even higher as I see the neat stacks of towels lined up on a little shelf next to the sink.

I step out of the door, dying to tell David how cool our new bathroom is but my heart slows when I see the expression on David's face.

'What's wrong?' I say.

'I've had a look around. There's only one bedroom,' he whispers, looking at Anna, who is busy opening and closing the bottom cabinets in the small kitchenette to the left of us.

My stomach falls.

'There can't be,' I say in a panicky voice.

He runs his hand through his hair and shakes his head slowly.

Shite.

Anna tugs on my hand.

'Can I please see my bedroom?'

David and I exchange horrified looks. Anna has been talking about her new bedroom since the moment we told her about the move.

'Well, you can see *a* bedroom,' I say carefully.

With David leading, we begin our short walk towards the only visible door off the living area, which I barely take in, my mind clouded in panic at the thought of the bedroom situation. Unable to contain her excitement, Anna dashes past us both and flings open the door.

David and I quickly follow only to find her star-fished on a super-king-sized bed that takes up most of the room.

'I love it!' she says, staring at the ceiling with a wide grin on face.

I bet she does.

Then she springs off the bed and rushes out of the room, shouting something about Rose-Bonnie.

'Jesus Christ, David, what are we going to do?' I hiss. 'Are the three of us supposed to sleep in that bed for the year? I know it's massive, but it'll be a nightmare with Anna and all her acrobatics.'

David nods, pressing both sets of fingers against his eyes.

A wave of sympathy rushes over me. He hasn't slept for most of the flight like I have. He must be absolutely shattered.

'Listen, there must be some mistake,' he says, his hands dropping to his sides. 'I'll go down and have a word with Patrick on the desk.'

I calm down a little. He's right. Of course, there has been a mix-up. All this will be resolved soon.

David walks out of the bedroom just as Anna marches in, her little arms full of as many soft toys as she can carry. Clearly, it hasn't taken her long to find the right suitcase. I watch her with trepidation as she lays each toy out on the bed, one by one – her favourite ones closest to the pillow on her chosen side, near the window, with the other less important cuddlies thrown carelessly towards the end of the bed.

I debate whether I should break the news to Anna that this is not going to be a permanent situation – but I decide to hold off until David comes back.

Leaving Anna chatting happily to her teddies, I decide to take the opportunity to explore the apartment further. I know we will be moving to a bigger place, but I imagine they will all have a similar layout. I am relieved to find the cupboard-lined kitchen well-stocked with enough crockery and utensils for the three of us, and a small but adequate dishwasher for David to stack just so. It has all the basics, yet I can't help thinking I'm missing something. I drum my fingers on the kitchen island, fold my arms and stare around the space again but my poor befuddled mind isn't working properly. Giving up, I walk out of the kitchen, my eyes landing on a round, wooden dining table and four chairs positioned just to the left.

Perfect.

From there, it's a mere ten Anna-sized steps to the living area, which contains a comfy-looking, squashy, leather two-seater sofa and a chunky armchair arranged around a dark brown, oval coffee table – each piece of furniture far too big for the space it occupies. I climb over the coffee table to take a peek out of the window but aside from the lights in the anonymous-looking building across the road, I can't make out much.

A wave of exhaustion washes over me. I step back over the coffee table and sink down into the sofa. I'm not sure what to do next. I'm loath to start unpacking when we're moving to another apartment. Anna comes wandering over, her mouth working slowly, her eyes glazed with jet lag. I pat the couch and she climbs slowly onto my knee.

'Are you hungry, sweetheart?' I say, kissing the top of her head.

Her hair still smells like the plane.

She shakes her head, reaches into her mouth, takes out her gum and hands it to me.

Lovely.

Apart from all the sandwiches I took for her for on the plane –
there was no way I was going to chance her rejecting the airplane
food – and dozens of snacks, she's had nothing decent to eat in
hours, although come to think of it, neither have I. But all I really
want to do now is get into my pyjamas and go to sleep.

I shift Anna gently off my knee, where she flops sleepily onto
the couch, and go to the kitchen to dispense of the gum in the lined
bin under the sink. The front door clicks just as I'm emerging from
the kitchen and David walks in, looking more dejected than when
he left.

'What's the story?' I say, but his dark expression says it all.

'Computer says "go fuck yourself",' he says, massaging his
temple with one hand. 'According to Patrick, there is no mistake.
But as soon as I get to the office on Monday, I'm going to call HR
and sort this out.'

I take a deep breath and try to remain calm. There's no point in
adding any more stress to the situation. David will sort everything
out next week. It will be fine.

With foggy heads, we unpack just enough to get ready for bed.
Apart from one brief burst of desperate energy investigating the
couch to see if it turns into a bed (it doesn't), we are mostly lethar-
gic, wordlessly moving from bathroom to bedroom in slow motion.
Even Anna is quiet, barely making a sound when I help her with
her pyjamas. All three of us climb into bed with Anna tiredly
directing us towards our sleeping positions – she is in the middle at
her insistence. Frankly, I'm surprised she's allowing us in 'her bed'
at all.

Exhausted as I am, I am filled with that unsettled feeling that
comes with staying somewhere new. Even up this high, the contin-
uous wailing of police sirens accompanied by the odd bit of blaring
music, not to mention the cacophony of honking cars, penetrate my
can't-sleep-without-them ear plugs. I tell myself that city noises are

comforting – signs that we are not alone – and determinedly close my eyes. After all, it could be worse – at least there are no foxes around waking me up with their seriously disturbing sex noises like they do back in London. I drift off into a sort of half-sleep, which is pretty much the only sleep anyone can get when a small child is continually doing somersaults and kicking them in the ribs.

* * *

I must have drifted off because the next thing I know, Anna is shaking my arm, whispering, 'Wake up!' into my right ear. My head feels woolly, and my eyes are sticky with sleep. I groan and reach for my phone on the side table, forcing myself to check the time. It's 3.33 a.m. – 8.33 a.m. in London. No wonder she's up.

Christ.

I fall back on my pillow and try to persuade Anna to doze with me, but it's no good. She's far too sprightly. I glance at David's side of the bed, harbouring a vague hope that he will somehow stir, take care of Anna, and let me go back to sleep, but judging by his peacefully sleeping figure, I am on my own.

'I'm hungry, Mummy,' Anna pouts.

Resigned to my fate, I gingerly step out of bed and follow Anna into the kitchen. I rummage in one of the suitcases and find a Tupperware of Anna's cereal, which I packed in anticipation of this very moment. I even have a small carton of milk to go with it... which I have forgotten to put in the fridge. Praying fervently that Anna won't notice the distinctly warm temperature of a liquid that has been flown across the Atlantic, I grab a bowl from the kitchen cupboard and pour it on top of her cereal. With a confident, 'There you are now!', I bring it over to the table and put it in front of her. Anna looks at it suspiciously, as if she knows something's wrong but can't quite put her finger on it.

I leave her to it and go back to the kitchen to get her a glass of water. Just as I'm reaching into the cupboard, I hear a scream and a crash. I whip around to find Anna covered in milk and cereal, the bowl upturned on the table.

'I'm sorry, Mummy!' she says, heaving hysterically.

I take a deep breath and carry her quickly to the bathroom to take off her sodden pyjamas. Even though I tell her over and over again not to worry, that it was just an accident, she still cries and cries. Still David sleeps and sleeps.

It is only when Anna is in her fresh pyjamas munching a fresh bowl of cereal, her iPad resting next to her, that she calms down. I rinse her milk-drenched pyjamas in the kitchen sink to remove the cereal, and spin around holding the sodden material with the intention of firing everything into the washing machine. After flinging open every single cupboard door in every possible area of this tiny apartment, I come to the horrific realisation that there is no washing machine. Or dryer.

That's what's missing.

5

If there was a prize for giving the least amount of shits about anything, Patrick would win it hands down.

'So now you're missing a bedroom *and* a washing machine,' he says, tapping repeatedly on his mouse. He hasn't made eye contact with me once since I approached the reception desk.

'And a dryer,' I add.

Not that we have a dryer at home in London but at least I have the washing line in the garden.

Anna lets out a huge yawn beside me, showing the fresh piece of gum on her tongue. It's the only way I can think of to keep her happy while I'm trying to sort our accommodation issues. I glance at my watch. It's just after 7 a.m. We've both been up for hours. My head feels fuzzy and my mouth seems permanently dry no matter how much water I drink. David is still asleep and although the temptation to wake him up is mighty, I am aware he is starting a new job tomorrow and he needs to adjust to the time zone as quickly as he can. So, I have decided to tackle Patrick about the washing machine situation by myself.

I place my elbows on the desk and lean over a little, willing Patrick to look me in the eye.

'I just need to know if there is going to be washing machine in the two-bed apartment.'

Patrick finally looks up, crosses his arms, and shakes his head. 'But you're in a one-bedroom apartment.'

I take a deep breath to stifle my impatience. 'I am aware of that, Patrick, but as we will be moving to a two-bed when this mix-up is sorted out, I'm asking if there will be a washing machine there.'

'But you're not moving to a two-bed,' he says.

I have never wanted to punch someone in the face more.

Patrick shrugs and makes eye contact for the first time – his expression is pure boredom.

'Like 80 per cent of buildings in New York City, there is no washing machine in this one either, lady.'

He says this like I'm thickest person he has ever come across, and then he turns away and starts bashing his keyboard as if it has wronged him in some way.

My head starts to throb. Wearily, I step back from the desk, take Anna's hand, and drag my feet back towards the lifts. I am at the stage of jet lag where even pressing the button seems like too much effort. The lift pings and I enter it, fuming. How could someone in the service industry be so bloody unhelpful? I raise my middle finger in Patrick's direction just as the lift doors close. He won't have spotted it but it makes me feel a bit better.

* * *

My wifely consideration for David wears off at 8 a.m. Besides, Anna needs to get a decent meal into her and I'm also getting hungry, which isn't helping with my general levels of crankiness, so I turn to Anna and tell her to go and wake up Daddy. I am aware that there is a distinct edge to my voice, which, if she was older, would probably translate as *go hard or go home*.

I go into the bedroom when I hear the second yelp. Anna has achieved her goal, and Daddy is very much awake, his arms wrapped firmly around his knees.

'She got me right in the—'

'Anna – sweetheart, go grab your iPad and I'll be out to you in a second,' I say.

She rushes out and I sit down on the bed beside David.

His face is pale and his eyes are swollen.

'What time is it?' he yawns.

'It's just after 8 a.m.,' I say. 'Anna has been up since 3.30 a.m.'

David positions himself gingerly to an upright sitting position. Clearly Anna has done one of her 'special jumps' on him.

'How are your bollocks?' I ask, cringing.

I may be grumpy and jet-lagged but I'm not without sympathy.

'Getting there,' he says, wincing.

'Anyway, Anna has been up since 3.30 a.m., spilled her cereal, ruined her pyjamas, and if all that isn't bad enough, I've discovered something else missing in this apartment, and, in fact, just about every apartment in this city according to my best friend Patrick, that you're not going to believe.'

David, who is never impressed by my tendency to build up to a crescendo, sighs and says, 'What is it then?' in the type of bored voice that would rival Patrick's.

Undeterred, I take a moment to maximise the suspense. Drum roll please...

'There. Is. No. Washing. Machine,' I say, punctuating every word for dramatic impact. Then I fold my arms and wait for his explosive reaction.

David scratches his head and sighs. 'I know.'

What?

'What do you mean, you know?' I say, waving my hands in the air.

'I know there's no washing machine here,' he says. 'Over 80 per cent of buildings in New York City don't have them,' he adds, as though this is the kind of fact that everybody knows. Everybody except me, evidently.

'And you didn't think to tell me?' I say, my voice reaching a dangerously high squeak.

'I thought you knew!' he says, slapping the quilt in frustration. 'The details the company sent over – none of them listed a washing machine as an appliance.'

Jesus Christ.

'So, what are we supposed to do?' I say, wringing my hands.

I have no problem going to a laundromat but I can't image Anna sitting through endless washing cycles without throwing one of her special meltdowns.

'Just go to the dry cleaner's,' he says. 'I checked before. The nearest one is about a block away.'

Oh right. That actually sounds sensible.

David starts to laugh.

'I can just picture you marching down to Patrick – the least helpful receptionist on the planet – all indignant because there is no washing machine in this place.'

I feel a hot blush rising from my chest up to my cheeks. God, I must have sounded so entitled.

Anna walks in, headphone-less and iPad-less. This is a bad sign.

'No more jumping!' David shouts, covering his crotch area with both hands.

She glares at him, hands on hips and says, 'I'm hungry' in a pouty voice.

* * *

You can tell by the sticky humidity that's it's going to be another scorcher and I'm relieved we are all dressed in shorts and T-shirts. We're on our way to Times Square to hunt for something to eat. It's less than a twenty-minute walk from where we're staying but Anna is already starting to flag. She perks up the minute the colourful lights come into view and I'm relieved to see that it isn't particularly busy – last night's revellers are probably still in bed sleeping it all off.

David whips out his phone.

'First family photo in Times Square!' he says, grinning madly.

Anna and I let out a simultaneous groan.

David has an annoying habit of taking photos when you least feel like posing for them.

But clearly the death stares don't put him off as the next thing I know he has produced a selfie stick from his backpack. He might as well have taken his cock out.

'Jesus Christ – would you put that thing away!' I say, mortified.

David's face falls.

'Everyone else is using one,' he says sulkily, pointing towards a group of baseball-capped and *I Heart NY*-T-shirted tourists huddling in the centre of the square.

Anna tugs my hand. 'I'm starving!'

Knowing where his priorities lie, David sulkily packs up his selfie stick and we start looking around for restaurants. The only problem is that it's Sunday morning and quite a few of the proper restaurants don't open until noon, which is still three hours away. But it turns out that it's not a problem because Anna soon finds exactly what she wants.

'Look, Mummy!'

It's a hot-dog cart.

And that's how our first full day in New York begins – each of us happily gobbling down giant hot dogs slathered with oodles of ketchup and yellow mustard – and all before 10 a.m.

After we've finished licking our fingers – God, I love a New York hot dog – David looks at me with wide eyes and says 'Family photo?' in a pleading voice.

'OK, *fine!*' I say. 'But no selfie stick.'

A random guy dressed in board shorts and a *Suck This* sleeveless T-shirt shouts, 'Right on!' as he walks by. 'Selfie sticks are for assholes!'

I double over with laughter and give the guy a thumbs up. I'd forgotten how direct some New Yorkers could be.

David shakes his head, and we huddle together so he can take his snap. He shows us the photo and frowns. I still have the giggles, so my face appears all screwed up in the photo. Anna is raising her eyes skyward, and has ketchup dribbling down the right side of her mouth, and David just looks a bit cross. It's the most real, in-the-moment family photo we've ever taken. I love it.

I tell David this and he says, 'Are you going to post it on Facebook, then?'

'Jesus no! Facebook is only for fake, happy family photos. The state of us – I'd be morto.'

David sighs and looks at his watch. Then his eyes brighten.

'Since we're all fed and happy, will we go for a wander? Take in the sights for a bit?'

I immediately look at Anna. She's been up for hours – and she has dark circles under her dark circles.

'What do you think, Anna?' I say, cheerfully swinging her hand. 'Shall we explore our new home?'

'OK!' she says happily.

Great! We have been granted a rare licence to explore.

David starts tapping on Google Maps to find places to go.

'The Rockefeller Center isn't too far from here,' he says cheerfully.

I smile at this enthusiasm. He really does love a new city.

We make it about two blocks before Anna begs David to give her a piggyback. David scoops her up in his arms and lasts about another block before his back starts to twinge. He goes to put Anna down, but I stop him. She is fast asleep.

We take it in turns carrying her back to our apartment building and she doesn't wake up once – not when a fire engine goes screaming by, or even when Patrick cackles, 'Found the washing machine yet?' as we walk through the lobby.

When we finally get back to the room, I lay Anna on 'her' bed and close the door quietly.

Facing an hour or so of uninterrupted peace, David begins to get his work clothes ready for his new job, while I flop on the couch – my eyes stinging with exhaustion. David insists on waking Anna up after an hour to try to get her adjusted to the new time zone and it's like a wildcat has entered the apartment. She is beside herself with the injustice of it all. We finally calm her down by ordering her pizza (tactical, because neither of us can face the supermarket yet) and she huffily sits down on the couch with her iPad. By the time 7 p.m. comes along, I am desperate for sleep. Ignoring David's warnings of 'It's too early!' and 'You need to stay up longer to beat the jet lag,' I climb into bed beside Anna and cuddle up to her warm, already-dozing body. David can feck off with his stupid time zone advice. I know exactly what my body needs.

6

I wake up at 4.02 a.m. At first, I try to kid myself: this isn't jet lag, I just need the toilet! But after my loo trip followed by long minutes of gentle tossing and turning, lest I disturb Anna, I know it's no use. At least Anna is still asleep. I just hope she stays like that until David gets up at 6 a.m. That's another new thing we have to get used to: David starts work earlier here and needs to be in the office for 7.30 a.m. every day. I have spent months dreading that alarm going off so early, and now with all three of us in the bed, it's going to wake up Anna too.

I ease myself out of bed, grab my phone off the bedside table, pad into the living area, and flop onto the couch. It's just gone 9 a.m. in London but I might catch Bea if she's working from home.

I text quickly:

Greetings from the Big Apple!

The dots appear immediately and my spirits lift.

You're up early! Jet lag?

Plus green-with-illness emoji. I send a vomiting one back in response. I text:

Are you off to work?

Running late. Harry up at dawn nagging me to help him upgrade his avatar online. Couldn't get the little fucker back to bed.

I giggle. Despite Bea's best efforts, Harry has become sucked into the gaming world and has created a virtual community with his pals, even sneaking down to log on in the early hours. Harry has begged Anna to join him slaying creatures in whatever magical land he has created, but she has refused, telling him curtly that she's not into 'boy' games. To be honest I'm relieved she's not bothered about gaming just yet – her YouTube obsession is bad enough.

Bea texts:

How's the swanky apartment?

I fill her in quickly on the missing bedroom/washing machine situation.

It's New York City! Can't believe you expected a washing machine in your apartment!

Plus crying laughing emoji.
I send her the only obvious one back – the middle finger.
We go back and forth for a bit before she signs off with:

Horrific post from Tania Henderson on Vale Mums if you fancy a nose.

Ha! I didn't fly hours across the Atlantic just to check Vale

Mums, our smug local Facebook group – I have left all that behind. No more Organics. I put my phone down with a firm pat on the couch. But my fingers start to twitch. Damn it, Bea!

I pick up my phone, and log in quickly to Vale Mums. Oh god, Bea's right. This one is particularly odious – *even* for Tania.

I've just found out that Heath is gifted. I really don't know what to do. I knew he was bright but... SUCH a responsibility for his mummy and daddy.

Ugh.
I type a quick message to Bea:

Humble bragging at its finest.

She replies with more vomity emojis before wishing me luck on the extra bedroom front.

My eyes prickle with irrational tears. I miss her. We would have had such a laugh slagging off Tania for that horrific post. Jesus – I can't be homesick already! I swipe a hand roughly across my eyes – it's just the jet lag.

* * *

I must fall asleep on the couch at some point because the next thing I know David is shaking me awake to say goodbye. I reach my arms up to give him a kiss, inhaling the lovely fresh scent of aftershave.

'You look lovely,' I say, bleary-eyed.

He always looks great in a suit.

'Good luck on your first day.'

And then he's gone.

It strikes me then that it's just me and Anna now in an unfamiliar city where I know absolutely nobody. My stomach swirls with butterflies but I squash them immediately. It's time to get organised. We have nothing in the place to eat, for starters. I peep in at Anna, who is still sleeping blissfully, and take an opportunity to have an uninterrupted shower, basking in the big, warm drops of water, luxuriating in the strong water pressure – in our house in London, we're lucky to get a thin stream. Just as I'm switching off the tap, Anna wanders in, hair tumbling all over her face. She sits on the toilet – no mention of the water levels this time, thank goodness – gets up and staggers out again without wiping herself or washing her hands. I could give her the benefit of the doubt and blame her lack of hygiene on the jet lag, but I bet she does this all the time at school too.

'Anna!' I call. 'Come back here and wash your hands!'

She appears again, feet dragging on the ground. I step out onto the cool marble tiles, wrapping a towel around me.

'Let's get ready and head to the shops!' I say brightly.

I reason that we can buy the essentials locally and then I'll do an online shop just like we do in London. Anna hates a supermarket as much as I do but at least it's only a couple of blocks away. I dig out some clothes for Anna and myself and we dress quickly. Let's do this!

* * *

'That'll be 111 dollars and 38 cents,' the dead-eyed teenage cashier with a blonde buzz-cut says flatly.

My breath catches in my throat.

'Erm, I think there must be some mistake,' I say, my hands clenching tightly around my wallet.

'111 dollars and 38 cents,' he repeats.

It's as if I haven't spoken. For a mad moment, I wonder if he's related to Patrick.

I hear some impatient muttering from the long line of customers behind me and feel the hot heat of humiliation rising to my cheeks. It hasn't been the most peaceful of shopping trips. Despite what would have been considered an off-peak time to hit the shops in London – Monday morning at 10 a.m. – it seems to be the opposite here. The place is packed with people moving at speed, all of them knowing exactly what they're looking for. I am completely at sea and the frenetic energy of the place leaves no room for browsing or hesitation. I have spent less than twenty-five minutes in the place, but my heart is already thumping and my breath is short. Beads of sweat run down my back even though the air conditioning is at sub-zero temperatures.

I breathe slowly to calm the beating in my chest, and try to focus on the items spread across the conveyor belt, feeling totally mystified: apples, milk, bread, cheese, cereal, pasta, a dozen eggs, a giant bag of cheesy puffs (bribe for Anna for being good in the shop), a couple of steaks for myself and David tonight, and a couple of paper bags (because I had completely forgotten about the new NYC no-plastic bag rule). Between my anxiety to get out of there and an impatient Anna, I haven't checked the price of anything.

'Come on, lady!' a male voice shouts behind me.

I can't hold up the queue any longer or I will be lynched. Defeated, I hand my card over to the cashier. I pack the bags hastily and walk a little way towards the entrance before setting the bags down again, much to Anna's dismay. Desperate as I am to get out of there, I can't leave without looking at the receipt. I dig out the cheesy puffs and give them to her to stop the whining and scan the receipt quickly. My heart starts to thump even more wildly. Have I just paid $25 each for two steaks? And $5 for a half gallon of milk?

'Jesus Christ,' I breathe.

'What's wrong, Mummy?' Anna says, through a mouthful of luminous orange crumbs.

'Mummy has just paid $50 for two pieces of meat,' I say, trying to keep the panic out of my voice.

A woman in a smart, fitted, pink shirt and a black, knee-length skirt catches my eye, raises her giant Starbucks cup at me, arches an eyebrow and says, 'Welcome to Manhattan.'

7

At 6 p.m., David walks in the door after his first day of work. He called at lunchtime to tell me that he hadn't been able to get hold of the right person in HR regarding the apartment, but would do his best to sort everything out before the end of the day. I'm hoping he has some good news, but judging by his shifty expression I'm not holding out too much hope. It's been a long day so I'm not feeling optimistic about much at the moment. Between the world's most expensive shopping expedition, the rising heat and the lingering jet lag, Anna and I have spent the rest of the day in the flat. We managed scrambled eggs for lunch but have felt too drained to do anything more adventurous.

'How was your first day?' I say, going in for a quick kiss, and then recoiling at the sight of the shimmering pearls of sweat on his upper lip.

'I've only walked home eight blocks and I'm drenched,' he says, taking out a handkerchief and dabbing his face impatiently.

I nod sympathetically. I only walked two blocks to the super-market with Anna this morning and, even then, I had to change my sweat-soaked knickers when I got home.

He takes off his shoes and suit jacket and I notice that his shirt is stuck to his body.

'I'm going to have a quick shower,' he says, heading for the bathroom.

Not so fast.

'Are we moving to a two-bed place then?' I blurt out.

The slump of his shoulders tells me everything I need to know.

'We're *here* for the year, aren't we?' I say miserably.

He turns around and shoots me a hopeless look.

'I had a chat with HR. It's no mistake. Apparently, this is pretty normal for small families, especially for people desperate to live in Manhattan. I was told that we were very fortunate that the company was paying for us to live in such a great location, and to basically shut the fuck up.'

I open my mouth to protest and then close it again. It's not great news but I understand where The Firm is coming from. They have forked out tens of thousands of dollars to move us over here and put us up in free accommodation for a year in one of the most desirable cities in the world. If it had just been David and me, then it would have been ideal, but having Anna in tow makes the situation harder. Then I have an idea – one that could solve everything.

'How about if we cover the difference in cost between a one-bed and a two-bed apartment ourselves?' I say, flushing with excitement. 'That way we get to move and the company doesn't lose out.'

But David tells me he has already looked into it and the cost to move to a two-bed is double the rental of our house back in London. That's that, then. We can't afford it and given that I paid $6.99 for a small bag of Granny Smiths earlier, we'll be lucky to go back to London with the shirts on our backs.

David comes over and puts a hand on my shoulder.

'It'll be all right Saoirse, OK?'

I pat his hand and attempt a smile. It's not ideal but I have to stop comparing our lives here to what we have in London. Maybe we can set up a blow-up bed somewhere, although I'm not sure the cramped space would allow it.

David goes to have a shower and I wander back to the kitchen and take the most expensive steaks ever out of the fridge, thoughts of the year ahead swirling through my mind: the three of us sharing a bed; Anna kicking the bejaysus out of us every night; no sex; and worst of all, no space for visitors.

But determinedly I snap out of my reverie, grab the salt and pepper from the cupboard and start seasoning the steaks vigorously. I need to make the best of this, for all our sakes.

* * *

'Savour every bite,' I say to David later that evening, watching him with narrowed eyes as he shovels pieces of steak into his mouth with alarming speed. Anna has been fed earlier with pasta-with-cheese-on-top, her usual delicacy, and is now cuddled up on the couch with Rose-Bonnie and her iPad. It's almost 8 p.m. and she hasn't fallen asleep yet, which is a good sign that she is adjusting to the jet lag.

He shakes his head impatiently at me.

Although I have accepted the one-bedroom situation, I can't help myself from ranting about the exorbitant shopping trip from earlier, especially when he's eating as if he barely tastes his expensive steak.

'Look, Saoirse,' he says, swallowing quickly, placing his knife and fork down with a clatter. 'We're living in the middle of Manhattan – it's always going to be expensive here, just like it would be in any sought-after location.'

'I know, David!' I say, tutting. 'But Anna and I had scrambled eggs for lunch at practically a dollar per egg. Those chickens must be raised in the lap of luxury to justify those prices.'

David forks another bit of steak into his mouth and, noting my glare, chews more slowly.

'I mean, how do people live here?' I say. 'How do they eat when everything is so expensive, especially healthy food. Did I tell you how much the apples were?'

David nods and partially closes his eyes as if he is just about clinging to his last strand of patience. He takes a deep breath.

'People eat out more here, I guess. They get takeaway more. This is the city that never sleeps, right? You can get food whenever you want.'

'Well, I'm not having Anna living on takeaway pizza for a year,' I say huffily.

And I'll be as big as a house.

David, probably wisely, changes the subject and fills me in properly on his first day at work. Aside from the snippy exchange with HR, it seems that everybody has been really welcoming. The office is enormous, and like many tech firms these days, offers a load of perks such as on-site table tennis, pool tables, and free food served from a very cool food hall packed with every variety of food you can think of. It even offers free cooking classes, which is right up David's street.

Despite my glum mood, I am happy for him. After being made redundant last year, a new job in a company that treats him well is exactly what he needs to boost his confidence.

Our big year away may not have got off to the greatest start, but we are here to build our future and I need to make more effort to enjoy this opportunity. Besides, even I have to admit the steak is absolutely delicious – which it really should be, given the price of it.

8

'I ONLY want to go on the swing,' Anna says, arms folded determinedly across her sparkly, unicorn-patterned T-shirt.

I rub a hand over my burning scalp and wonder for the millionth time why I thought it was a good idea to take her on the twenty-minute walk to Central Park, during one of the hottest days of the year with no sun hats or water bottles. Despite the crushing heat, I'm not the only one who has made this mistake. The playground is rammed with kids of all ages, parents and nannies looking as hot and bothered as I do.

Why do we do it to ourselves? *Because,* a little voice answers, *if you don't get Anna outside at least once a day, she will follow you around saying 'I'm bored' for hours until your last nerve is shredded.* Now that I know we are in the apartment for good, I spent the morning unpacking before registering for an online shopping account, figuring it couldn't be as pricey as the local supermarket. Then I managed to tie myself up in knots choosing between eight different types of bananas, and working out if I was choosing one bag of potatoes or just one potato. By the time I finished, it was time to grab a quick lunch for myself and Anna before taking a trip to the park.

I gesture hopelessly at the massive queue for the three tyre swings.

'Anna, we're going to be here all day,' I say, impatiently tugging my damp white T-shirt out of my armpits. I had intended to take her to see her new school, about a ten-minute walk from here, but now I just want to get back to the air-conditioned coolness of the apartment.

'Swing!' she says, her cheeks flushed with both heat and temper.

Suddenly, Anna tilts sideways and falls against my waist. I catch her just before she hits the ground and immediately kneel down to her eye level, propping her up with both hands.

'Jesus, Anna, are you OK?' I say, sweeping her hair back from her eyes. Her skin is flushed and feels hot and dry.

'I just feel a bit dizzy, Mummy,' she says, and promptly bursts into tears.

Bloody heat. I have to get her back to the apartment. A mixture of adrenalin and guilt rushes through me as I pick her up, feeling her hot forehead sear through the thin fabric of my T-shirt. Short of breath and feeling light-headed myself, I battle through masses of people to get back to the exit, struggling with the weight of Anna, trying to shield her from a torturous white sun at its strongest.

I make it out of Central Park and set Anna on the ground, but her legs immediately give way and I know I'm going to have to carry her home. 'It's only twenty minutes,' I mutter to myself, saying it repeatedly like a mantra. But it might as well be fifteen miles because I don't even manage to make it five minutes before I'm gasping for breath. At this stage, I can barely see for the amount of sweat dripping into my eyes. Little splashes of yellow moving slowly in the traffic catch my eye. Fuck it, I'm getting a taxi.

Balancing Anna with one arm, I stick my thumb out, gesturing wildly to any car that looks yellow. But nobody stops for us. Tightness floods my chest and my eyes fill with panicky tears. How the hell am I going to get her home? I stumble along the pavement for a few more minutes, battling against throngs of people, feeling the anxiety rising in my chest. I fight the claustrophobia that threatens to engulf me and focus on getting her home.

Then a miracle happens. A taxi pulls to a stop right alongside me. Saved! A middle-aged, balding man, with the sort of dark stubble that starts growing seconds after he has shaved, sticks his head out of the window and shouts, 'Where ya goin'?'

I heave Anna to my other shoulder and give him our address in midtown. He shakes his head impatiently, and says, 'I'm going uptown only.'

My stomach drops.

'Please take us. My daughter isn't well and I have to get her home.' I'm almost in tears now.

He shakes his head and revs the engine.

'Please don't go!' I sob desperately.

'Hey, what's going on here?'

I whip around and almost collapse in relief when I see a heavy-set woman in a dark blue uniform emblazoned with impressive-looking gold and silver badges. Her jet-black hair is scraped back into a tight ponytail and her dark brown eyes are filled with impatience.

'He won't take us and my daughter isn't well,' I say in a pleading voice that I hope will melt her tough exterior.

'I'm going uptown only,' the taxi guy says, glaring at the cop defiantly.

The cop steps forward, leans right into his face and says, 'You take this lady and her little girl home right now – you understand?'

The exchange goes from zero to one hundred in the space of a couple of seconds and before I know it, the pair of them are shouting and swearing at each other while I stand awkwardly clutching a very quiet Anna, not really knowing whether I should stay or go.

Then the shouting stops and the cop opens the car door and nods at me.

'You go home now, ma'am, and take care of your daughter,' she says, her mouth firm but her eyes soft.

I have a sudden flashback of Bea years ago when she shouted at some grumpy passengers on the bus who tutted at me when I was trying to manoeuvre Anna's pram down the packed aisle. My eyes start to water. I want to throw my arms around this strong, take-no-shit woman, and beg her to be my friend. But instead, I choke out a simple 'Thank you' and bundle Anna into the back seat of the car.

The taxi driver, clearly still furious, hits the gas before I have time to put a seatbelt around Anna, and shouts the whole way back about 'asshole cops', braking hard at every red light.

Anna, more alert now that the cool air has hit her, looks at me with big eyes and for her sake, I know I should try to calm him down given that technically he is responsible for our safety. He doesn't seem the type to respond to 'Excuse me, sir, but there's a child in the car so I would appreciate it if you could slow down,' so I take a different tack and tell him (with a seriously prickling conscience) that all cops ARE assholes in the hope that by agreeing with him, he will get us home in one piece.

To my relief, my attempt to pacify him works and the rest of the drive goes smoothly. As soon as he pulls up outside the building, I unbuckle Anna quickly and step out onto the sidewalk, hurriedly giving him a pile of dollars, including a big tip because I'm too much of a wuss to make a point about his shocking customer service. He drives away with a screech that makes me pity the next unfortunate person to get in his taxi.

I take Anna by the hand, grateful that she has recovered enough to walk by herself, and we walk through the blessed coolness of the lobby towards the lifts. It's barely 1.30 p.m. and I feel like I've run a marathon. Once back in the apartment, I give Anna a big glass of water and settle her on the couch. Then I call David for a rant, figuring that he should be on his lunch now and free for a call. He picks up on the first ring.

'That's weird,' he says. 'I was just about to call you.'

Is it just me or does he sound nervous?

'Is everything OK?' I say, hoping he says 'yes', so I can go full throttle on the Central Park outing debacle.

'Did you take Anna to see her new school today?' he says.

'No, I didn't because—' I say.

But he cuts me off. 'It's just that—' Then he stops.

'Jesus, David, spit it out!' I say.

I'm in no mood for pussy-footing.

'HR have just called to tell me that Anna won't be going to that school.'

What?

'Er, apparently there's been some sort of scandal, so they have put Anna into a different school instead.'

I try to quell the rising panic. OK, so Anna will be going to a different school but it's not the end of the world. Maybe this school is even better.

'Right, so where is this other school?' I say, as calmly as I can.

'That's the slightly awkward part,' David says.

I can almost see him grimacing.

'It's in Battery Park City.'

What? That's miles away from here, right at the bottom of Manhattan. My head starts to spin. I'll need to get the subway there and back every day – at rush hour. No more walking to school like we do in London. People crushing against us on a moving train every day for a year. I would have felt the same way if I'd had to take Anna across London on the Tube in rush hour.

'I checked it out – it's not so bad if everything runs on time – twenty minutes, no changes, and then a ten-minute walk the other end,' he adds, trying to sound positive.

My thoughts whirl – twenty minutes rammed in like tinned sardines with hundreds of other commuters twice a day. With Anna.

'I can't.' The words pour out of my mouth before I can stop them.

A voice in the background calls his name.

'Listen, Saoirse, I have to go to a meeting but let's talk about this later,' he says, using his 'professional' voice.

I whisper an 'OK' and hang up.

I rest my head on the cool tabletop, trying not to cry. I know I'm being ridiculous. Loads of people take their kids on the subway to school here. Plenty of people would kill to be in my position – a free apartment in a fabulous city, husband with a great job, daughter experiencing a new country – and I do appreciate it all, I really do, but the thought of battling the swarming masses every day elevates my anxiety to new heights. Maybe it would be different if I had a fellow mum with me to help me through it, but I have nobody.

Without even bothering to check the time in London, I pick up the phone and call Bea.

'Saoirse! How are you?' she says, sounding surprised.

I open my mouth to tell her my fears about the school run and promptly close it again. I can't do it. It just sounds too pathetic. Besides, she wouldn't blink if she had to do it – she'd have all the commuters scared out of their wits for starters. So, I gulp back my anxiety and tell her that everything is fine apart from sharing a bed with Anna every night.

She doesn't buy it for a second.

'Are you sure you're all right? You sound a little wobbly,' she says.

Her voice is so compassionate that I almost cave.

'Ah, I'm grand,' I say, blinking back the tears. 'Just knackered from Anna kicking the bejaysus out of me every night.'

A male voice mumbles in the background. Bea tells him to piss off but in an affectionate voice that I've only ever heard her use with Harry, so despite my anxious mood, I'm curious to find out who has managed to bring out her warm and cuddly side.

'Who's that?' I say.

'Oh, it's just Tom badgering me for a report,' she says, casually enough, but I'm pretty sure I can sense some excitement in her tone.

'Do you mean Tom the cream cracker thief?' I say.

'The very one,' she says.

Bea developed an addiction to cream crackers when she was suffering from morning sickness last year. Much to her annoyance, Tom, one of her work colleagues, used to nick them from her desk. Bea lost the baby at ten weeks and I know, despite Bea's 'take the bull by the horns' attitude, there is still sadness there. Maybe a bit of romance is just what she needs. Besides, I am delighted to focus on something other than my fears over the school run.

'Do you think Tom nicking your cream crackers is the equivalent of a little boy running off with your schoolbag in the playground?' I say, hoping to coax something out of her.

She tuts.

'Honestly, Saoirse, as if I would mix business with pleasure,' she says, in her signature strident tone.

Bollocks. She once told me after a few drinks that in her early twenties, when she was on a break from Ryan, she had shagged her boss in the toilets during an office party.

'Oh, go on a date with him. Give the poor guy a chance!' I say.

She deserves some proper fun after everything she's been through. Besides, the only 'dates' I've ever known Bea to go on have been via Tinder so maybe it would be good for her to go down the traditional route for a change.

She's just in the middle of telling me to (justifiably) mind my own fucking business when Anna pipes up with 'I'm hungry.' Time to go.

As I prepare yet another round of scrambled eggs for Anna – the online shop is arriving tomorrow – my spirits lift a little. Although I've been too much of a wuss to tell Bea about how I'm really feeling, just hearing her voice has given me a boost. I throw back my shoulders and decide to do a practice run to Anna's new school tomorrow. I have been trapped in my comfort zone for too long – working from home, living an off-peak life, not straying very far from Woodvale. It's time I burst out of my bubble.

I can do this.

9

Jesus, I don't know if I can do this. I'm at the entrance to the subway with Anna and I'm fighting with a voice in my head that's demanding I turn around immediately. Despite deliberately heading out at 10.30 a.m., during off-peak time, one of the subway entrances has been blocked off for renovations so Anna and I have been stuck sweating in the middle of a giant swarm of people, many of whom are just as frustrated as I am and aren't shy about airing their grievances.

'Move it along, people! Are we all fucking dead here?' a voice shouts behind me.

I grip Anna's hand tightly, breathing in and out deeply to calm the nervous butterflies in my stomach. Anna clutches an entire packet of gum in her other hand – I figure it's enough to keep her occupied on the subway ride to Battery Park City and back.

After ten torturous minutes, people finally start to shuffle forward down the steps into the dark interior of the subway station. I clutch the train tickets David handed me earlier, relieved that I don't have to queue at the kiosk.

We arrive at the crowded platform to wait for the next train. It's so hot and humid in here that even the shiny, white-tiled walls look like they're sweating.

The countdown clock tells me that the next train is two minutes away but even that short amount of time seems too long to bear. I dig in my bag and take out a small bottle of water for Anna. She sips it through her chewing gum and asks me when the train is going to be here. I open my mouth to answer her but I'm cut off by the crashing sound of the train barrelling into the station. Anna immediately covers her ears. We follow the flow of people into the carriage, and miracle of miracles, I manage to find a couple of seats for the two of us at the end of a row of hard, plastic seats. I release the air that seems to have been trapped in my chest since I left our building and feel a tiny glow of achievement. I have made it onto the subway with a small child and everything is OK. This is a good start.

Stops go by and people pile in and pile out, but the carriage doesn't get much busier. There is room to breathe and I try to focus on the positive and not dwell too much on what it will be like at rush hour.

'I need a wee,' Anna announces.

My chest fills with panic. We're a few stops away yet, but Anna only ever tells me she needs a wee when she is just about to wet herself. There's absolutely no point in telling her to hold on.

'You need to pee, honey?'

I look up and lock eyes with an elderly lady sitting next to Anna, her grey hair wound in impressive dreadlocks tightly woven across the crown of her head; she is dressed in a fabulously bright-yellow and pink patterned dress.

Anna stares at her and nods.

'No problem,' she says, rooting in her bag.

I stare at her, wondering what kind of magic she has in there to make this problem go away. Then she comes out with a pink plastic bag, reaches across Anna and drops it on my knee.

'She can pee in there.' She smiles, patting my arm.

Desperate as I am for Anna's bladder to be relieved, I'm not entirely sure it's a great idea for Anna to be weeing on public transport.

Then the woman looks at me with kind brown eyes and points towards the door.

'She can do it on the platform, Mom.'

I thank her, so grateful for her kindness that I feel tears springing into my eyes. I count the seconds until the train shudders to the next stop. Thankfully the platform in the next station isn't too busy and I am able to hide Anna behind one of the big steel columns at the very back of the station where she can wee in privacy. Thank goodness I have a load of wipes with me for her hands. I have managed to conquer another challenge in a strange city and now all I have to do is figure out how to get rid of this bag of wee when there doesn't seem to be any bins. I can't put it in my bag because I'm afraid it will burst and I would feel awful about leaving it on the platform.

In the end, I take Anna's hand and climb up the stairs in the hope that there will be a bin on that level. There isn't. The only option is to leave the station. Anna and I emerge into the hot, stagnant air to the glorious sight of a bin just outside the station entrance. I drop it in and turn back towards the entrance.

'This is quite an adventure isn't it, Anna!' I say cheerfully as we clamber down the stone steps once more.

This may be the most convoluted journey, but the most important thing is that I am persevering. We reach the platform once again only to find that our next train has been delayed and my positive mood starts to fade. More people start piling onto the platform, complaining noisily to each other about the delay. A fresh coat of sweat trickles down my back and the energy drains out of me. Between the crowds, the humidity, and the unplanned wee stop, I just don't have it in me to keep going. By the look of Anna's pained expression, I'm pretty sure she feels the same way.

* * *

We don't make it to the school. I get a taxi back to the apartment, trying not to feel like a total failure. Why is it that other people can cross whole cities without even thinking? Jesus, it's not like I'm a stranger to travel. Before I met David, I used to travel loads and I didn't even think about navigating my way across different countries. Since when have I lost my confidence?

My stomach lurches and my head starts to thump. The thought of going through all this again tomorrow with Anna and every school day for a year fills me with dread.

10

David is chuckling. I have deliberately put a humorous slant on the aborted subway journey to disguise my anxiety at the thought of having to do it again. If I voice my fear then I won't be able to do it, and I *have* to do it. I have no choice.

'Fair play on sorting out Anna's wee emergency on the train – I would have lost it completely,' he says through a mouthful of mashed potato. We're all having mashed potato. In fact, we'll be having it for a long time to come thanks to the online shop. It turns out that ordering six potatoes means that you get six bags of potatoes. Still, it's comforting to have a full fridge of food, and for a lot less cost than our local rip-off supermarket.

Anna wanders over to the table and puts her head on my shoulder.

'I miss Harry,' she says miserably.

David and I exchange a glance. This is the first time that Anna has mentioned home since we got here. Clearly the novelty of moving to a new country is wearing off along with the jet lag.

'I know, sweetheart,' I say, smoothing her hair away from her eyes.

My eyes start to water. I miss my friends too!

Anna wanders off, shoulders slumped, and my heart aches for her.

'You know, we should really set Anna up on Zoom so she can chat to Harry from her own iPad,' David says thoughtfully.

It's a good idea – I have Zoom on my phone but she could do with having some kind of contact on her iPad with her best friend. I'll have to educate her on the time difference, though. Bea will murder me if she starts calling Harry at all hours.

David jumps up from his chair.

'Oh! I almost forgot,' he says. 'Anna, I have something that will cheer you up!'

He walks off towards the bedroom and beckons Anna to follow him while I remain at the table, curious and apprehensive to see what he has in mind for her. In a minute Anna comes running towards me, squealing, waving two small pieces of silver paper.

'We're going to the world's biggest toy shop!' she says, jumping up and down.

Oh, bloody hell. Much as I love to see Anna so happy, I tend to steer clear of these types of shopping expeditions, not just because they are hectic, noisy affairs but also because I don't want to totally bankrupt us.

I give Anna a great big hug and frown at David over her shoulder.

David tuts at me. 'I know what you're thinking but this is a private tour – for employees of The Firm only. There's even a goodie bag at the end so we don't need to go overboard.'

A rush of relief washes over me. The shop won't be chock-full of wailing children and stressed-out parents and we won't have to spend all our money. I lift Anna onto my knee so I can get a better look at the tickets. The tour starts this Sunday at 10 a.m. Even better, David is coming with us so I won't have to deal with Anna's inevitable Veruca Salt moments by myself. Hurrah! Finally, we get to do something together as a family in New York.

11

A couple of days have gone by since we told Anna about the visit to the toy store, and I'm seriously regretting telling her so soon. At her insistence, we have looked it up online, walked past it several times (amusingly, she refuses to cross the threshold until her VIP status kicks in) so she can peer through the giant glass windows, and debated endlessly what may or may not be included in the goodie bag.

As it's Friday today, I decide to splash out on a bottle of red wine (a snip at $20 from a local wine store) to celebrate surviving our first week.

It also helps that the jet lag has finally worn off, so the days begin to have some sort of rhythm. David and I have accepted that sleep will never be the same again but we are adjusting to Anna's bruising somersaults. And now that she is finally going to bed before us, we at least have some time in the evenings to spend together.

We whisper about sex – exactly how and where we're going to have it in such a tiny apartment with Anna so close by. David reckons the only option is to get a babysitter for Anna and check into a hotel for a night of passion. I'm more interested in getting a full night's sleep. Still, I know what he means. We're never going to get some proper time together the way things are now. We need to settle in properly – make friends, find recommendations for a babysitter, build a life.

I haven't made any further effort to get back on the subway to see Anna's new school. In fact, I've been actively trying to find another way around it, but I haven't been successful so far. The only other option is getting a taxi there and back twice a day, but at $120 for the daily round trips, it's just not practical. Eventually, I do what I always do when faced with a complex problem: I push it to the back of my mind and pretend it doesn't exist.

Aside from the toy store, Anna and I haven't ventured too far. She seems happy enough with our morning walks and screen-filled afternoons, but as we walk back together from the wine shop, I feel like I should be doing more with her.

Maybe it's the shock of the fabulously cool air conditioning as we step into the lobby that messes with my judgement, but I find myself asking Patrick if he can recommend any indoor play areas for children nearby. He raises his eyebrows and answers me by way of a two-worded question:

'Got Google?'

Arsehole.

As soon as Anna has eaten a bowl of pasta for her lunch – 'No more eggs, Mummy!' – I pop her in front of the telly. I don't know why but for some reason I feel better about my parenting when she watches TV rather than her iPad. Then I pick up my phone and call my mother. We have been texting, but we haven't spoken since I got here, mostly because I can't bear her inevitable reaction to everything that has gone wrong since we arrived. She has always been suspicious of The Firm and I can't cope with the 'I told you so.' Still, I can't dodge her forever.

She picks up and I listen carefully before greeting her. No tell-tale echo or the sound of dribbling liquid.

Good.

She's not on the loo then.

'So, it's only the one bedroom, then,' she says.

'It is,' I say, drumming my fingers on the table with impatience.

'And no washing machine?'

'That's right.'

She huffs for a bit and says things like, 'If it looks too good to be true, then it probably is.'

'And have you been to Anna's school yet?'

This is the one I've been dreading and honest to God, I can't face telling her yet.

'No,' I say. 'The weather's been too hot to be dragging her to see it.'

So, it's not exactly a lie. The weather has been too hot. Thankfully, she jumps at this with the enthusiasm of a puppy being rewarded with a biscuit.

'Well, didn't I warn you about the heat!' she says in her most self-righteous tone. 'We wouldn't be used to that now, Saoirse.'

And by 'we' I'm guessing she means 'the Irish'.

'Do you know what temperature it is here in Dublin today?'

I do a quick calculation in my head. It's the first week in August, the hottest month of the year in Ireland.

'Around sixteen degrees Celsius?' I guess.

'It's eighteen degrees here, Saoirse, and sure, we're *boiled* out of it. Jesus, I'd *die* now if I was in New York. The perspiration would be *dripping* off me.'

Wonderful.

'Anyway, thanks be to God, it won't be that hot when we visit in December.'

Hang on.

We?

'I didn't know you were bringing someone with you,' I say, feeling a bit anxious.

'It'll be myself and Miguel,' she says, in the type of voice that suggests that this has been the plan all along.

I nearly drop the phone. I found out about Miguel, Mum's new friend, last Christmas when we were staying with her in Ireland, but I've never met him. All I know is that he's one of her students (she teaches English to 'foreigners') and accompanies her to Mass most Sundays. She's mentioned him casually over the months but although I'm pretty sure they are more than just friends, she refuses to be drawn into revealing their relationship status. Things must be getting more serious than I thought if she's bringing him to New York.

'Now, we won't be staying with you, Saoirse. Sounds like there isn't enough room to swing a kitten in there, never mind a cat.'

She's right, of course, but I do feel a bit sad. I had been looking forward to spending time with my mum and taking her to see the sights with Anna.

'Miguel has mentioned a hotel a few blocks away from you,' she says, with a sense of pride in her voice.

She tells me the name of the hotel and my mouth drops open in surprise. Miguel must have a few quid. I tell her this and she says that Miguel was a bit of a mover and shaker in his day and did well in the Spanish property market before moving to Ireland five years ago. This is as much as I've ever heard about Miguel and I'm desperate to find out more.

'What took him to Ireland?'

'He did a European trip with a few pals when he was in his twenties and fell in love with the place, and always wanted to live here. His English was all right but it's better now after coming to my class.'

'Does he have much baggage?' I say.

'Well, I'm sure he'll have a suitcase with him, but what difference does it make how much baggage he has if we're not staying with you?' she says indignantly.

Jesus Christ.

'I mean, has he been married before?'

Silence.

'Mum, are you there?'

Then her voice suddenly bursts through. 'Jesus, Saoirse! I don't like the look of those clouds – I'll have to dash, go and take the clothes off the line.'

Hasn't she just told me the sun is splitting the stones over there? There's something she's not telling me.

* * *

'I don't see why you think your mum is hiding something,' David says, shovelling a giant dim sum into his mouth. He has come home from work with a takeaway and we're tucking into it in front of the telly. Anna has guzzled a bit of rice and her weight in prawn crackers and is currently in the bedroom playing school with her teddies. I swig another gulp of my wine before carefully placing it back on the table. I've been drinking too quickly and my head is feeling fuzzy.

'There's something she's not telling me about Miguel,' I say, trying to organise my thoughts. 'If they are more than just friends, why wouldn't she just tell me?'

'Maybe Miguel has more baggage than she's willing to let on,' David says, taking a sip of his wine.

He might have a point.

David nudges me, his eyes playful. 'Do you think they're doing it?'

'Doing what?'

'You know, getting down and dirty in the bedroom.'

Oh, for goodness' sake.

I'd be lying if I said the thought hasn't crossed my mind, but the image is too much to bear.

'Feck off, David,' I say, giving him a much harder elbow back.

He bursts out laughing while I continue to give him the evil eye.

'Ah, good on her,' he says, his cheeks flushed with wine and merriment. 'She deserves a bit of happiness in her life.'

I know he's right. I just hope that Miguel is good enough for her.

I am halfway through topping up the wine for both of us when David's phone rings. He jumps up to grab it from the kitchen island, checks the screen and mouths 'work' to me. I sigh in annoyance – it's gone 7.30 p.m. on Friday night.

I grab my glass of wine and go to check on Anna to give David a bit of privacy.

'Great!' she says, eyes shining as soon as I enter the room. 'You can be Lia, the troublemaker in the class.' She throws me a brownish rabbit that would have been pink in its heyday, and thanks to the wine, I start playing my role with gusto. It turns out Lia doesn't like school at all, wrestles with the teacher (Anna's stuffed penguin) and tries to escape at every possible opportunity. Just as Anna is telling Lia off for her behaviour for the fifth time – 'I will put you in *prison*, Lia!' – David walks into the room, his face distinctly paler than the last time I saw him.

'Can I talk to you outside for a second?' he says, in a serious voice.

Anna whinges.

'Listen, I'll be back in a minute, OK? Put Lia in prison, and pick a teddy to guard her,' I tell her.

Seemingly satisfied with this plan, Anna starts her game again while I follow David out of the room and into the kitchen.

He takes a big gulp of air and blows it back out again. Then he runs his hand through his hair and looks at the ground.

'What is it, David?' I say, his seriousness cutting through my tipsiness like a knife.

'That was work. I have to fly to LA first thing on Sunday morning,' he says, looking at his hands.

'Oh bloody hell!'

'I know – it's shit, but they need me to present at an important meeting first thing Monday morning, so I need to fly out the day before.'

I've always known travel would be a part of David's new job, but I didn't expect it so soon.

'What time are you leaving?' I say.

He tells me and my stomach drops. Shite – the toy store tour; he's going to miss it.

'I feel awful,' he says.

He looks so wretched about it that I don't have the heart to vent.

'Look – this is what we signed up for. We knew you'd be doing more travel. It's just happening a little earlier than we thought,' I say gently.

He shoots me a grateful smile but then his expression darkens again.

'There's something else,' he says. 'I'll be away for three weeks.'

Jesus Christ.

My thoughts swirl. Three weeks just me and Anna. In the boiling heat. With no friends for her or me to hang out with. The only way I have made it through this week is the promise of David walking through the door every evening. The understanding wife mask slips and I tell him that The Firm is a *disgrace* for expecting him to just take off at the drop of hat when we've barely unpacked.

But what I don't tell him is how terrified I am of being left alone in a city with a small child without any friends to support me.

He waits until I have run out of breath and says quietly, 'Saoirse, you knew travel was going to be a big part of this job before you committed to the year away. You need to be prepared for the fact that it could be like this for the rest of the year.'

My stomach churns over, reality striking hard.

David pulls me into him and throws his arms around me.

'It'll be OK, Saoirse. It's only for a year. At least there'll be more room in the bed!'

I snuffle into his shoulder. It's going to be the longest year of my life.

12

The Firm must have invited every employee and their dog to the toy store because the queue outside the main door is enormous. I squint my eyes against the blazing sun, grateful that I have remembered to put sun hats on both of us plus a good lathering of sun cream. Anna chatters away to me about all the toys she might see and I smile back at her, but inwardly I'm feeling utterly shattered. I polished off the bottle of red last night while David packed for his trip and my head is throbbing. Saying goodbye to him this morning wasn't easy. I know it's important that this year goes well for him, and I know he's doing it to secure our financial future, but I still can't get my head around the fact that we might be apart so much.

Between the scorching heat and the crowded pavement populated with what seems like hundreds of families with high-pitched kids, I'm already feeling the butterflies.

The crowd starts moving forward and I breathe a sigh of relief. There is a time limit of an hour in the shop so all I have to do is last until then.

By the end of the hour, I feel like I've gone through the speed cycle of a washing machine. Anna dashes from floor to floor, while I try desperately to keep up with her. Admittedly, it's not as packed as it would be during normal opening hours but it's busy all the same. Everything seems to be a bunfight. Anna takes a couple of steps on the giant black-and-white piano based on the movie *Big*, and suddenly ten other kids are fighting for the same space. Then Anna reaches for a doll and a bigger kid snatches it off her. The staff look as stressed-out as the parents, desperate attempts to keep their jovial expressions weakening at every chaotic interval. Tears ensue (from Anna, but I'm not far off) until we move down to the basement, which is a bit less crazy. Overwhelmed with all the choice, Anna chooses a small teddy bearing the toy shop's logo.

'Let's go get the goodie bag,' I say, grabbing her hand and leading her firmly up the escalator to the main floor. My heart sinks as I spot the queue for the goodie bags. Despite the air conditioning, my hair is plastered to my head. Thankfully, Anna is so chuffed with her new bear that she doesn't whinge once during the long fifteen minutes of queuing. Finally, we leave the chaos and step out into the crushing heat, Anna delving into the goodie bag and squealing every time she brings out a new item.

'Look, Mummy!' she says, brandishing a small teddy at me, her face shining.

It's the same teddy that I bought for $30 minutes before.

'They can be twins!'

Fantastic.

She chats happily all the way back to the apartment building, while I drift along beside her, dazed by the surreal vision of the heat rippling off the ground. My phone rings just as we enter our street. I hurriedly root around for it in my bag, thinking that it might be David although he really should be on the plane to LA by now. Checking the screen, I see that it's Harriet Green, my agent.

Harriet doesn't call me unless she has some news. Curious, I answer while steering Anna out of the way of the fast-moving pedestrians.

'Hi, Harriet!' I say.

She greets me with her usual sigh as if calling me is absolutely the last thing she wants to do.

'Searcy, early copies of your book have been sent to your New York address.'

Despite my irritation at Harriet's persistent refusal to pronounce my name properly, my heart quickens. I have always dreamed of seeing my own book in print and now it's finally happening. My heart sings. I can't wait to see it.

'Great!' I say.

'As you know, it's not publishing until next January, so your job is to promote the hell out of it to build up a buzz before then,' Harriet says.

I'm with a very small publisher with zero budget for promoting books. I knew that when I signed the contract, but even so, I have no idea how to go about it.

'Any suggestions?' I say.

'Social media, *obviously* – connect with mummy influencers and book bloggers, but word of mouth is probably the most powerful way to promote a new book,' she says. 'And always carry a copy around in your bag to give to the people you meet.'

'But I don't know anybody here,' I say, trying to keep the whine out of my voice.

She says something but I don't hear it because a motorbike with two bikers has just pulled up alongside the pavement, right by where we're standing. I glance at it in annoyance and turn towards the wall, phone pressed closely against my ear, shouting to Harriet to repeat what she has just said.

But then suddenly, I feel a pressure against my hand. I spin around quickly as a tall figure, dressed head to toe in black, mounts the back of the motorbike behind the driver. And then they're gone.

I look dumbly at my empty hand where my phone used to be, unable to process what has just happened. Anna's chatter breaks me out of my reverie. She's role-playing with the twin bears and clearly hasn't noticed a thing.

A fear that I haven't felt since she was a baby breaks through the numbness and my legs start to tremble. In my rational mind I know that this is as commonplace and straightforward as a mugging gets. I know loads of people in London who've been at the mercy of the motorbike muggers. They are opportunists who will no doubt wipe my phone and sell it on.

But although I know all this, I can't stop the wave of terrifying thoughts churning around in my head. What if they had pulled a knife? What if Anna had been hurt? Who could I have asked for help? I am completely and utterly alone and solely responsible for this small human being, and the force of that thought makes me so utterly terrified that I almost lose my breath.

'Are you OK, Mummy?' Anna says, studying me.

I try to regulate my breathing and fight to control the trembling in my voice.

'Silly me – I think I lost my phone,' I manage to say.

'It's OK, you can get another one,' she shrugs. Then as if sensing a vulnerability, adds, 'Can I have the giant lollipop from the goodie bag?'

I start to laugh hysterically – later, I will learn this is a common reaction to shock – and with shaky legs, I lead Anna towards our building, the practicalities of no phone suddenly striking hard. No phone means no contacts, no photos, no way to call anybody, no email, no texting, no social media. Despite the blazing heat, I feel a shiver go down my spine. Jesus, I can't even let David know what's happened because I don't have his number any more. He's always teased me about not learning important numbers off by heart. How stupid could I be?

'Think, Saoirse, think!' I mutter to myself as I enter the lobby.

This is ridiculous. I managed to live for the first two decades of my life without having a phone; I'm sure I'll be able to sort this out. I spy Patrick out of the corner of my eye, tapping away at his keyboard as usual. I go to ignore him and then stop dead, much to Anna's frustration. Patrick has David's number. David might still be in the air but at least he will be able to contact me through reception when he lands if I leave a message.

'Come on, Mummy!' Anna says, tugging my hand with sticky fingers. 'I want to introduce the twin bears to Rose-Bonnie.'

'Just give me a minute,' I say, zoning in on Patrick.

I don't waste time on pleasantries or wait for him to stop typing. Time to channel Bea.

As soon as Patrick spots me, he lets out a huge sigh (honestly, he and Harriet would get on like a house on fire), glares at me with those dead eyes, and shakes his head.

'I need David's number and I need to use your phone,' I say firmly.

'Where's your phone?' he says impatiently, crossing his arms.

'I was mugged,' I whisper, worried that Anna might overhear.

His expression remains completely blank.

'What kind of phone?' he says.

I tell him through gritted teeth.

He lets out a huge yawn before imparting his next piece of wisdom. 'Happens all the time. They call it Apple-picking.'

Jesus Christ. Now is the time that Patrick decides to get chatty?

'Just the number please,' I say, giving him the classic Bea don't-fuck-with-me stare.

He swivels around in his chair, taps slowly on his computer in a way that is designed to make me burst into flames in frustration before scribbling David's number down on a Post-it and sliding towards me.

'Now I need your phone,' I say, reaching for the handset.

'No, you don't,' he says, covering the phone with both hands.

I can feel my neck start to prickle with rage. I swear to God...

'You have a phone in your apartment,' he says quickly, clearly picking up on my death stare. 'It's probably on top of your wardrobe. Just plug it in and away you go.'

I look at him through narrowed eyes. I've never seen a phone in our place and if I go up there and it's not where he says it is, I'm coming back down to tear him a new one.

Clutching the small piece of paper in one hand, I turn to Anna and tell her it's time to go back to the apartment.

'FINALLY,' she huffs, giving her lollipop an aggressive lick.

On the way to the lifts, she says something that catches me off guard.

'Mummy – I don't want to go outside any more. It's too hot and I just want to play inside with my new teddies.'

An instinctive response bubbles up into my head. What a preposterous idea! Of course, we have to go outside every day. How are we going to make friends if we don't start getting to know the area? But then a quieter voice counters, *Is it really fair dragging Anna around in such high temperatures? With no friends to play with and nothing to do? Doesn't it make more sense to stay inside where it's safe?*

Anna has hit the nail on the head. There's no need to go outside now – at least until David gets back. For the time being, we can have our own mini staycation and spend all day in our pyjamas and order food online. And more importantly, I'll be able to protect her all the time.

Fortunately for Patrick, the phone is exactly where he said it would be and I leave David a message, my voice steady for the first time since the mugging. I place the handset back with a sense of satisfaction. We will sit tight until David gets back: no more crowds, no more heat, no more dragging a reluctant child around a strange city. Frankly, it's the best decision I've made since we got here.

You're hiding, says the little voice.

But I ignore it.

13

David calls me from LAX Airport later that afternoon.

'I'm coming home,' he says in his decisive voice, shouting above the din of airport announcements in the background.

'Don't be mad,' I say, fiddling with the phone cord.

'You've just been mugged, Saoirse!' he says passionately.

'Shhhh,' I tell him, glancing frantically at Anna. 'Nothing happened,' I say quietly. 'Nobody got hurt. We're both fine.'

I do feel more calm about it, especially now I have crafted my plan to stay inside. David protests for a bit but I eventually manage to persuade him not to jump on the next plane home.

'You'll need a new smartphone,' he says finally.

My stomach plummets. A new phone could mean going to the Apple Store, which means going outside again. But then he says something that calms my beating heart.

'I'll get The Firm to messenger one over from head office, but it might take a few days before it gets signed off and delivered to you. Will you be OK?'

'Of course!' I say, happy now that my cocoon isn't under any threat. 'You can always call me on the landline anyway.'

He sighs. I can just picture him running his hand through his hair.

This is the last thing he needs after a long flight and an intense few working weeks ahead of him.

'We'll be fine,' I tell him brightly. 'Anna and I are going to chill out for a few days and treat ourselves to some more of New York's famous pizza.'

Then he asks to speak to Anna, who merrily tells him all about the toy shop and the bear twins before dropping the handset onto my lap.

I wish him luck for his first day in the LA office tomorrow.

'Are you sure you're going to be OK, Saoirse?'

'Of course I am!' I tut. 'I'm absolutely fine.'

No sooner have I replaced the handset than the phone rings again.

'Hi again,' I say, for who else but David would be calling me on this number?

My mother, that's who.

'Jesus, Saoirse! I've been trying to text you on WhatsApp all day. Then I tried tracking your phone and that didn't work either.'

'I lost my phone,' I say instantly.

There is no way my mother is going to find out about the mugging – I just can't cope with the drama, let alone the inevitable interrogation.

'How did you get this number?' I say, puzzled.

'I spoke to that *eejit* at the desk, Patrick.'

Thank Christ Patrick hasn't spilled the beans to her about the mugging.

'And how did you lose your phone?' she says.

I tell her that I must have dropped it in the street on the way back from the toy shop.

'And did you retrace your steps?' she says.

'I did,' I lie.

'And did you tell the NYPD Blue?'

I stifle a giggle. Trust my mother to confuse the NYPD with the long-running television drama.

'Ah, there's not much the police can do,' I say casually.

She huffs for a bit.

'I suppose the police over there have more important things to be doing than hunting for a lost phone,' she says.

I agree, relieved that she seems to have accepted my story. Then I tell her that David's company is sorting out a new phone, so I'll be back up and running by the weekend.

'And are The Firm paying for the replacement?' she says, in an accusatory tone.

Actually, I have no idea. Why should they? It's not their responsibility – frankly I think they're being generous enough to messenger one over. But I tell her 'yes' anyway.

'Hmm, well, you always have to pay the piper, Saoirse.'

Jesus, you can't win.

'Now, I wouldn't be too fond of that fella Patrick,' she says out of nowhere.

Oh, I'm dying to hear this one. 'What did Patrick say?'

'Well, first he said he couldn't give out your number for privacy reasons. But I told him that rule didn't apply to mothers!'

'And what did he say to that?' I say, grinning.

Patrick, unpleasant as he is, would be no match for my mother.

'He gave me the old "I don't make the rules" line so I told him that if he had any *balls* at all, he would forget about all the bureaucracy and give me your number.'

Jesus, I almost feel sorry for Patrick.

'Anyway,' she continues, 'after he gave me your number, I ended the call by telling him he could do with learning a few manners.'

I am bursting with suppressed giggles.

'So, then he started saying "yes, ma'am" to me, which I told him I hated because it makes me feel about one hundred and fifty. Then I hung up.'

'Sounds like you put him in his place,' I say.

'Well, someone had to, Saoirse,' she says, sounding pleased.

Then she asks about David and Anna and I tell her that David is in LA for a few weeks and she tells me that a *day* would be too long in LA as it's too full of vacuous celebrities with more money than sense (even though she's never been there).

After that she chats to Anna for a bit and when Anna finally exhausts her toy shop story, and flings the receiver back at me again, my mother says, 'Will you be all right on your own with Anna?'

'I'll be absolutely fine,' I tell her.

And I *almost* believe it.

14

Anna and I spend the next few days stuffing our faces with pizza, watching movies on her iPad and making up new plays with her abundance of soft toys. It takes two days before I get out of the habit of reaching for my phone every five seconds and I marvel at how dependent I have become on technology. There's something quite liberating about being cut off from the world. Apart from David calling me every day, and a call from Patrick (who, thanks, to a stern word from my mother, is being a lot more polite than he was before) to tell me the shopping delivery guy is on his way up, I don't have contact with anybody.

It has occurred to me to ask David to contact Bea and Jen (Jen and I have exchanged a few texts since I got here but haven't had a chance to have a proper catch-up) in case they're wondering where I am, but I reason that it won't be too long before I get my new phone, and I can fill them in then.

The early copies of the books arrived but when I opened the box, I felt flat. I had been so excited to see it in the flesh – my very own book – yet I didn't feel a thing; I simply piled them up in the corner in the living room and forgot about them.

15

It is 6.30 p.m. and I am on my second glass of red wine. After the altercation this morning, it has taken all my willpower not to inhale a bottle sooner to soothe my nerves. Instead, Anna and I changed back into our pyjamas and spent the day drawing pictures, watching movies and playing teddies. It has been remarkably peaceful. David has called to check to see if the phone has arrived and tells me to set it up straight away. I said I would but that was hours ago and it's still sitting in the box. I don't feel like being connected just yet.

The doorbell buzzes and the glass of wine jumps in my hand.

I eye the door suspiciously. I haven't ordered anything – we're still working through the online shop from last week – so I decide not to answer it. Someone's probably got the wrong apartment anyway. Although given that the place is like a ghost town – apparently it empties out over summer when residents escape the heat to bask in their homes in the Hamptons – it probably is for me.

The door buzzes again. Sighing, I heave myself off the couch and tramp grumpily towards the door, and fling it open, half-expecting to see Patrick's bulging eyes glaring back at me.

By the time Friday morning comes around, I'm feeling the effects of too much pizza and an overindulgence of wine. Gently unwrapping myself from Anna's grip on my arm, I get out of bed with shaky legs and make my way towards the bathroom. I run the tap and throw some cold water over my face. Then I look in the mirror and the image looking back isn't pretty. My face is spotty and bloated from too much junk food, and my eyes look bloodshot.

Christ, David has been gone less than a week and I'm a bloody mess already.

The phone jars me out of my thoughts, and I run to answer it before it wakes up Anna. Too late.

'It's Patrick,' she says sleepily, handing me the receiver.

'Courier delivery,' he says curtly.

'That's my new phone. Can you tell him to bring it up?'

'No – you'll have to come down for it.'

Then the line goes dead.

I stare at the receiver for a moment before slotting it back into place. Clearly the effects of the dressing-down from my mother have worn off. The knot in my chest seems to swell.

'We have to collect a package from downstairs,' I say to Anna as cheerfully as I can.

'Is the package for me?' she says, her big eyes brimming with hope.

'It is not,' I tell her. 'You've had enough toys lately!'

Reluctantly, I drag on a pair of jeans and a T-shirt, shamefully aware that they could both do with a wash. I haven't been to the dry cleaner's since we got here and the dirty clothes are piling up. I help Anna dress quickly and we step out of the apartment for the first time in days.

'The courier's waiting outside,' Patrick shouts as soon as we step out of the lift.

The knot jumps a little. Shite – I had been hoping to grab the package from the lobby before heading straight back to our cocoon. I tell myself to stop being ridiculous and walk as purposefully as I can towards the revolving doors.

A familiar rumble fills my ears as soon as Anna and I step onto the pavement outside. I blink fast as the glare of the sunlight hits my eyes, even more intense now that we haven't left the building in five days.

'Mummy, someone is waving at us!' Anna says, tugging my hand and pointing excitedly.

I look to where she is pointing, and freeze.

The person waving at us is sitting on a motorbike dressed head to toe in black leather, a helmet covering his head.

It's not the mugger, I tell myself, my heart beating fast. The helmet turns towards me.

I walk slowly towards him, focusing on putting one leg in front of the other. The knot in my chest begins to throb in time to the roar of the engine. I wait for a stream of people to pass before I cross the pavement. It's unsettling to be among so many others when it has just been me and Anna for the last few days.

He flips up his visor and says, 'Sign here,' handing me a small clipboard with a pen attached.

I scribble my name quickly, trying to stop the pen from falling out of my shaky hands. Then finally he hands me the package. I thank him and watch as he revs before driving away as I breathe deeply to calm my thumping heart.

I did it! I got the package.

I'm exhausted.

I turn to Anna and tell her that it's time to head back inside.

'Wait. I have something in my shoe.'

I do my best to stifle my annoyance.

'Well, let's just sort it out when we get back to the lobby,' I say sharply, desperate to get back to the safety of the building.

'It hurts, Mummy!' she says, screwing up her nose.

I sigh and bend down, take off her shoe, shake it (nothing comes out) and put it back on, hoping the action itself will pacify her until we get back to the apartment. I'm just straightening up when a nasal voice behind me says, 'Jeez – take up the whole sidewalk, why don't cha.'

I turn my head round and see a tall, heavy-set man, dressed in a navy-blue suit with gold buttons down the front of his jacket. The open collar on his shirt reveals a thick neck that looks as though it has swallowed his chin. His beady eyes glare at me as if daring me to answer back.

The tension from the last few minutes builds to breaking point.

I snap.

'Is the pavement not big enough for you?' I say, in the most sarcastic voice I can muster. 'Too much trouble for you to walk around us, was it? You can see I was helping my child. Do you think you actually take priority over her? How fucking arrogant are you?'

His mouth drops open and his eyes flash. He is momentarily speechless, but then he recovers.

'Nice language in front of your daughter,' he sneers.

'Well, maybe I wouldn't have to use bad language if arseholes like you could be a little more considerate and a lot less self-obsessed.'

'I don't have time for this,' he says, and starts to walk away.

'Yeah, walk away, you selfish prick!' I scream after him.

He doesn't turn back.

Then, ignoring the curious stares of onlookers, I grab Anna's hand, clutch the package in my other hand and march back to the lobby. The adrenalin wears off as soon as I reach the lifts. I've just screamed abuse at a stranger in the street. This is not me.

I am drowning.

'Surprise!'

My eyes are telling me that two fabulously dressed women are standing in the hallway, grinning at me, each of them waving a bottle of champagne, but my mind is too slow to catch up. I just can't believe they're here.

My two best friends.

Bea and Jen.

On my doorstep.

'Oh my god,' I cry out.

The knot in my chest starts to unravel with a force that bends me double. My body starts to shake with huge waves of unstoppable laughter and relief. Then before I know it, I am sobbing, crying so hard I can barely catch my breath. Two hands clutch my waist and gently ease me into an upright position, and I am encircled by the warm embrace of a friend who I've known all my life. I breathe in her floral perfume and cry messy tears onto the shoulder of her playsuit.

'Come on, missus, let's get you inside,' Jen whispers softly into my ear.

I nod and let her guide me.

Bea follows with the bags.

Anna runs out of the bedroom, her days-unbrushed hair forming a wild halo around her chocolate-streaked face. Her eyes grow wide as she spots Bea and Jen.

'Where's Harry?' she says instantly.

My eyes fill again. Poor Anna – she's as lonely as I am.

Bea immediately grabs her suitcase, looks at Anna and says in her most matter-of-fact voice, 'Harry is with his dad tonight, but he can't wait to see you soon.'

Anna's face falls. 'Soon' is clearly too far away.

'Now, come with me and help me find the presents I have brought for you.'

Anna lets out a squeal of delight and disappears into the bedroom with Bea. Jen steers me towards the couch and sits down next to me. She reaches over to the coffee table, grabs my wine and hands it to me.

'I'm just going to get a couple of glasses for myself and Bea,' she says, jumping up again.

I watch her graceful figure move towards the kitchen, immediately suffused in shame as I look at the state of the place through her eyes. Empty pizza boxes piled up on the kitchen island because chucking them in the trash disposal at the end of the hall has seemed like too much effort; a huge bag of dirty laundry dumped in the corner of the living area because I haven't been able to face taking it to the dry cleaner's; Anna with her wild hair and dirty face. And me in my filthy pyjamas, unwashed hair and expanding waistline, cocooning from the world, teaching my little girl that it's too scary out there. That it's normal to hide.

I gulp down my wine, craving the numbness it brings.

Jen returns, two empty wine glasses clinking together in one hand, and a big bag of tortilla chips (Anna's favourite) in the other.

Bea steps out from the bedroom, smoothing down her peacock-blue T-shirt over her simple, white cotton shorts. I am painfully aware of how awful I look in comparison.

'Now,' Bea says. 'Anna is settled with a bumper pack of duty-free jellies.'

I smile at her gratefully. Chattering comes from the bedroom and it sounds like Anna's back in role-play mode.

'She sounds very happy,' I say, the words catching in my throat.

'Oh yes, I set her up on Zoom so she's talking to Harry.'

Jesus. What's wrong with me? David mentioned it before he left for LA, but I had totally forgotten about it.

'Glass of wine here for you, Bea,' Jen says.

Bea takes the glass from Jen and squeezes in on the other side of me. I don't even know where to begin.

'Why are you here?' is about all I can manage. 'I had no idea...'

Bea exchanges a glance with Jen.

'David told us about the mugging, Saoirse,' Bea says softly.

My stomach drops at the word 'mugging'.

'He was worried about you – he wanted to fly back,' Jen adds. 'But he knew you didn't want him to do that, so he suggested that we fly over instead and cheer you up.'

'I'm so glad you're both here, but you know, the mugging wasn't such a big deal,' I say, waving my free hand casually. 'It's not like anybody was hurt.'

Bea tips her glasses to the end of her nose and gives me a hard stare.

'Being mugged, violent or not, is a big shock, Saoirse. It is a violation of your safety. You need to give yourself a chance to recover.'

'Oh, I'm fine,' I say.

'That's what I said when I miscarried,' Bea says. 'I didn't think I had a right to grieve because it was so early on in the pregnancy, but you were the one who told me that I needed to give myself time to recover. And you were right.'

I gulp my wine.

Jen places her glass carefully on the table.

'You've had a hard time, Saoirse,' she says, holding my free hand.

The force of that statement and her warm touch sends me into more gulfs of emotion and before I know it, I'm telling them everything through great sobs. The taxi incident when Anna almost passed out in Central Park from the heat, Patrick (for being Patrick), the school run debacle, even the altercation with the irritable man on the street this morning.

When I have finished my sad tale, Jen squeezes my hand and says, 'Stop being so hard on yourself, Saoirse. New York can be a tough city to live in.'

I've thought about this a lot. Why do I feel so threatened? Is it the relentless pace of the city that famously never sleeps? Is it the punishing heat? Or is it New Yorkers themselves? Are they all as rude, jaded and impatient as the stereotype suggests? But I know that's not true because I have experienced random acts of kindness from strangers – the woman on the subway; the cop who made sure the irate taxi driver took me home; the shopping delivery guy who helped me carry the bags to the lift the other day...

Bea chips in.

'You see, this is what I was worried about when you told me you were moving here,' she says, folding her arms across her chest.

'What do you mean?' I say.

'You're not a city person.'

'I've lived in London for twenty years – of course I'm a city person!' I scoff.

'Correction, you live in a quiet suburb of London,' she says, holding up one finger. 'Think about it, when was the last time you went into the centre of London? When I suggest we go clothes shopping in Bond Street, you make excuses. You did the same thing when I suggested we bring Anna and Harry to London Zoo. You're just not a city person, Saoirse.'

I stay quiet because I know she's right. My bubble has shrunk since I had Anna and I haven't made much of an effort to expand it again. And now I realise I am doing the same over here but a more extreme version – too scared to venture any further than my own apartment building. I am drowning in my own anxiety.

Jen adds, 'And you don't know anyone here, which makes it worse.'

'Saoirse, have you told David how you're feeling?' Bea says.

I shake my head slowly. What can I say? That I'm too much of a weakling to live in a big city? That I'm lonely? That I'm too scared to do the most basic things, like take the laundry across the road or get the subway across Manhattan? That I hate being away from him for long periods?

'I don't want to worry him,' I say in a low voice.

'I think David would want to know,' Bea says softly.

I bunch my fists in frustration.

'You don't understand,' I cry out. 'I *knew* all this before we came here. I knew he was going to be travelling loads and that I would be looking after Anna by myself. I also knew that if everything went well, we would be going back in London in a much better position financially. This is the trip that could set us up for years if we get it right. I can't be the reason this doesn't work out.'

Bea holds up her hands in a placatory way. 'I get it, Saoirse – I really do. But the two of you planned this trip, which means that both of you need to be happy. It won't work when you are this miserable.'

I wipe one hand across my eyes.

'What can David do, though?' I say. 'This is it for the year, and I just need to suck it up.'

Jen cocks her head to one side.

'You should still talk to David, though,' she says.

'Definitely,' Bea says, with a sharp nod.

I sigh and tell them that I'll think about it.

Jen checks her watch and springs up from the couch, clapping her hands.

'Right, we should be making a move to the hotel,' she says, looking at Bea. 'We need to check in.'

I try to arrange my features so my disappointment doesn't show too much. Of course, they have to go – they must be exhausted from the long journey over and there's certainly no room for them in this tiny space. I stand up on shaky legs and watch them grabbing their bags, packing the two bottles of champagne in their suitcases. Probably for the best, I think. Hardly anything to celebrate here.

Bea catches my eye.

'You might want to start putting some stuff in a bag for yourself and Anna,' she says, in her most commanding voice.

I look at her in puzzlement.

Jen bursts in.

'I've been DYING to tell you, Saoirse, but one of the US TV producers I've been working with recently has booked us into a swanky suite in a fabulous hotel on Park Avenue for the weekend. All expenses paid. And you and Anna are coming with us.'

Oh my god.

My first reaction is panic. Going there means leaving the cocoon and I don't know if I'm strong enough for that yet. But I desperately want to go with them. Then a second scary thought crosses my mind.

'The *state* of me,' I cry.

Jesus, I can't be going into a fabulous hotel looking like something the cat dragged in. My hair is in desperate need of a wash, and I'm pretty sure none of my nicer clothes fit me any more given that I have been binge-eating and drinking for days on end.

'Listen, Saoirse,' Jen says softly. 'All you need to do is get out of your pyjamas and into some clean clothes. We're going to stay in the suite tonight and order room service. Nobody will be looking at you!'

'I'll get Anna organised,' Bea says, striding towards the bedroom.

'Jesus, can I at least have a shower before we go?'

'Nope,' Jen says, shaking her head. 'Save yourself for the luxury bath experience in the suite instead.'

Following the squeals from the bedroom, I walk in to find Anna jumping up and down on the bed.

'Harry's coming too!' she says breathlessly.

I look at Bea.

'We're picking Harry up on the way; he's with Ryan and Adriana at her place not far from here. Ryan's been making a big fuss over not seeing him enough in the summer holidays, so I agreed to let him have Harry for a week. He's been in Ryan's place in Connecticut for the last few days, but I'll pick him up now and take him with me to the hotel. Ryan was supposed to fly back with him to London next week but when David told us about what happened to you, I thought it would be the perfect opportunity to pick him up and see you too.'

That does it. I might not see Ryan and his Gisele-type girlfriend but the possibility of running into two impeccably gorgeous people in this state is too much for my ego to bear. I spring into action and manage to dig out a floaty summer dress that I haven't worn since we got here. It's not posh hotel standard but it's clean and it still fits me, so it'll do. Then I race to the bathroom to plaster on some tinted moisturiser and a load of concealer to cover up the pizza and wine spots. I pull on a pair of gold, sparkly sandals to complete the outfit and pad quickly towards the living room to find a suitcase for myself and Anna.

Jen wolf-whistles the second she sees me.

'Mummy, you look pretty!' Anna says.

'You too!' I say, kissing the top of her head.

Bea has done a fabulous job of dressing Anna, who is now twirling around in a gorgeous, pale-green, frilly top and pleated, white skirt. Her brown, wavy hair has been brushed into a sleek, high ponytail secured with different coloured slides. She looks like a beautiful mini ballerina – her clothes a far cry from the chocolate-stained nightie she was wearing minutes before.

Just before we leave, Jen spots the pile of books in the corner by the television.

'Oh, Saoirse! You never said!' she says, grabbing a copy and stroking it lovingly.

'They're just early copies,' I mumble. 'It won't be out until next year.'

'Can I have one? I can't wait to read it!' she says, hugging it to her.

'Me, too!' Bea says, grabbing a copy.

I nod, feeling suddenly shy. Then Jen bends down and grabs another couple of copies. 'I'm heading back to Dublin after this, so I'll give one to your mum and send one to Dee – save you the postage.'

I open my mouth to protest but then close it again. Of course, my mum is going to read it. There'll be no stopping her.

Anna, clearly impatient at the delay, tugs my hand.

'Come on, Mummy,' she says. 'Let's blow this joint.'

Jen, Bea and I crack up, and a little light flickers inside my chest.

I think it's hope.

16

To be honest, I don't think 'swanky' does the hotel suite justice. We're in the type of room that you might see in a blockbuster rags to riches movie. Looking around the lavish space, I'm pretty sure our entire apartment could fit into it at least three times. I count three crystal chandeliers in the living area alone, twinkling above a mixture of blue and gold suede armchairs and couches. An enormous gold filigree mirror hangs above an equally ornate fireplace, highlighting the impossibly high ceilings. Two gigantic bedrooms are set off the living area – one triple room for me, Bea and Jen; and a twin room for Harry and Anna. Each bed is covered with crisp cotton white sheets and at least six blissfully cosy-looking pillows.

We're only a twenty-five-minute drive away from the apartment, but I already feel like I'm in a different world – somewhere fantastical where only good things happen. Patrick, who seemed to crumble when confronted with Bea's no-nonsense attitude in the lobby on the way out, ordered us a taxi, which is just as well as Anna turned into a jumping bean the second we all climbed in, such was her excitement at seeing Harry.

To my relief, I didn't see Ryan (although my stomach gave an annoying jolt just as we pulled up outside Adriana's building) – Bea ran in to fetch Harry and came out just as quickly. Harry and Anna hugged like long-lost friends and proceeded to chat over each other the whole way to the hotel. I can't even look at the pair of them now without breaking into a huge smile.

'This is amazing,' I say to Bea and Jen, who are sprawled on a bed each, both of them poring over the room service menu. Anna and Harry are in their room filling themselves with tech and sweets.

'Steak and chips all round?' Bea says.

Jen and I nod immediately.

'What about Anna?' Jen says.

'Just chips,' I say, wondering when the last time was that something resembling a fruit or vegetable passed her lips.

'Chips for Harry too,' Bea says.

'Why don't you have a bath now before room service arrives?' Jen says, smiling at me.

She's right – I seriously need to have a wash.

'Here, take a glass of bubbles with you while you're at it,' Jen adds, springing off the bed and over to a small table where a slim, elegant-looking bottle rested in an ice bucket – courtesy of the hotel.

I accept the crystal flute, slip off my shoes and pad towards the bathroom, taking a moment to admire the sparkling gold taps, and soothing grey-and-white, mosaic, porcelain tiles that cover the walls. The bath is an enormous, white, oval-shaped affair that stands tastefully in the middle of the bathroom. It looks like it should be in a museum. I rest my glass of champagne on the surface beside the sink before turning to run both taps.

Then I strip naked and explore the basket of irresistible toiletries. I pour a couple of bottles of liquid into the bath and breathe in as the calming aroma joins the steam permeating the air with its flowery scent.

I turn off the taps and put one leg gingerly into the bath, to make sure I don't scald myself. Then, with one leg still in the bath, I lean over to the sink to pick up my glass of champagne.

The door flies open.

'I'm bursting,' Harry mutters, holding on to his crotch and racing towards the toilet in the far corner of the room.

I jerk in surprise, spilling half my champagne onto the floor.

Harry starts to pee and I'm not sure he has even noticed me through the steam. Still, I worry that he is going to slip on the spilled champagne when he's finished so I gingerly step out of bath and grab one of the folded towels by the sink, shake it out and throw it on the floor. I also need to cover up my nakedness before I scare Harry half to death, so I desperately peer through the clouds of steam to see if there is a towel within reach. Suddenly, I spy a white, inches-thick, cuddly-looking robe, hanging off a hook on the door. As I reach for it, the door flies open for a second time and whacks me right on the forehead.

'For Christ's sake,' I groan.

So much for a peaceful, soothing soak.

It's Anna.

'Where's Harry?' she demands, hand on hips.

Bea races in seconds later, muttering apologies, and ushers the pair of them out.

Before she shuts the door, she says, 'Get back in that bath, Saoirse, and don't come out until I call you for dinner.'

I smile as I sink into the warm, fragrant water. I forgot how bossy she can be. I've missed it.

* * *

The rest of the night goes by in the happiest of hazes. All three of us adults are cuddled up in white bathrobes sitting at a huge, lacquered, black dining table, shovelling steak, chips and champagne into us like there's no tomorrow. It's like a really unhealthy spa weekend.

'Are you finishing your chips?' I call over to Anna, who is too busy giggling with Harry on the couch in the living area to notice that she has half a bowl of chips left.

'Nope,' she says quickly in a stop-interrupting-my-fun voice.

I give her a thumbs up and she beams at me and my heart fills. This is the happiest I've seen her since we arrived in New York.

I walk over and scoop her bowl off the polished, mahogany coffee table in front of her and bring it back to the table.

'More chips!' Jen squeals.

'Genius,' Bea adds.

'Honestly, how did you swing this room, Jen?' I say through a mouthful of carbs. 'I still feel like I need to pinch myself.'

'You're not shagging the producer, are you?' Bea says, giving her a cheeky wink.

Jen raises her eyes skyward, shooting us a mock-scolding look.

'No, no,' she says. 'It's a US channel that's keen to collaborate with our show on some kind of fashion project. The details are pretty sketchy at the moment, but with this treatment, I'd work with him in a heartbeat!'

I look at her with unabashed envy. My best friend from school has made it from personal shopper to fashion TV presenter and now, by the looks of things, she has a good chance of breaking into the US.

'Is he good-looking at least?' I say.

Jen could do with a bit of luck on the romance front. As far as I know, she hasn't met anyone since her long-term boyfriend (and mega-arsehole), Liam, left her out of the blue last year – he wanted children; she didn't. I know how hard it must be for her to trust again.

She dips a chip in some ketchup.

'He's good-looking if you like men who have about as much expression on their face as a Ken doll,' she says. 'I'd say he's 90 per cent Botox.'

Then she takes a deep breath. 'Well, anyway, it wouldn't make much difference if he was Adonis, because I'm already taken,' she says quietly.

Bea and I look at each other, eyebrows reaching our hairlines.

'Wow! You kept that one quiet!' we chorus.

Jen smiles at our enthusiasm but her expression grows serious again. For somebody in a new relationship, she doesn't seem too thrilled about it.

'Is there something wrong, Jen?' I say, grabbing her hand across the cool, polished surface.

She bites her lip. 'Listen, I didn't want to say anything before, because I wanted to be sure I was making the right decision.'

Then she fiddles with the stem of her champagne flute and says something that completely catches us off guard. 'He's asked me to marry him.'

What!

'And I've said yes.'

I don't know what to say. I know I should be covering her with hugs of congratulations but who is this mystery man? I notice that Bea is as frozen to her seat as I am.

'Congratulations,' I manage to squeak.

Jen throws me a nervous smile.

What's going on? Why is she being so cagey?

Bea suddenly springs into action, grabs the champagne bottle, fills up the glasses quickly, and holds hers aloft.

I match her by raising my glass too.

'To Jen and her mystery fella!' I say, with as much enthusiasm as I can muster.

Bea and I down the champagne like shots but Jen doesn't touch hers.

Then I look Jen in the eye. 'I want all the details. Right. Now.'

To my shock and mortification, her eyes start to fill up.

'You're the one I'm most worried about telling, Saoirse,' she says.

My mouth drops open.

'Why?' I say, my mind racing.

'Because you're not going to approve.'

I'm stumped. What's Jen's love life got to do with me?

She takes another deep breath. 'The man I'm marrying is Liam.'

I couldn't have been more shocked if she'd told me she was marrying the Ken-doll TV producer. Liam? Her ex? Who blind-sided her last year by dumping her? The first thought that enters my head is: *That fucker Liam*, closely followed by a lightning-quick assessment of the degree to which I have slagged him off ever since he broke her heart. Going by rough calculations, I'm pretty sure the answer is – a lot. Jesus, I hate when people get back with their exes after you've bitched about them at every opportunity. But she's my best friend and I have to make an effort to support her. So, I arrange my features into a big, fake smile and say, 'I'm delighted for you, Jen!'

She sees through me in an instant. 'Ah, feck off, Saoirse.'

Bea casts a wary look from Jen to me and jumps up abruptly, mumbling something about checking on the children. I flash her a grateful smile. Jen and I could do with a bit of space to talk this one out.

'Look, I'm sorry, Jen,' I say, biting my lip. 'Your news just caught me off guard. I had no idea you were even back in touch with Liam, never mind marrying the guy!'

She rests her chin in one hand and sighs.

'I know,' she says. 'And I'm sorry I didn't tell you, but after what happened last time, I wanted to make sure that our relationship was rock solid before we announced it.'

Apparently, Liam made contact just after New Year's Eve telling her he'd made a terrible mistake and was absolutely positive that he didn't want kids. He had spent 'too much time' with his baby nephew, who 'burned the ears off him with the crying' and couldn't handle it at all. Then he told Jen that although he knew he could live the rest of his life without kids, he couldn't live without her. Jen put him through the wringer by making him jump through many hoops, not to mention months of couples' counselling to rebuild the trust between them. A few weeks ago, Liam popped the question over dinner one night in Jen's favourite restaurant.

'What do you think, Saoirse?' she says, with a pleading look in her eyes. 'Do you think I'm mad to be marrying him?'

I am conflicted. On the one hand, I still want to kill Liam for hurting her so much, but on the other hand, I want her to be happy.

'Do you trust him, Jen?'

She nods instantly. 'I know it sounds crazy, but I think we've come a long way. I wouldn't even think about getting back together again, let alone marry him, if the trust wasn't there.'

'Well, there's your answer,' I say.

I'm still not totally convinced but I need to push those feelings aside because, at the end of the day, my best friend is getting married and the occasion needs to be celebrated.

I leap up to grab the champagne, and call to Bea, who has just emerged from the kids' bedroom.

'We have some celebrating to do!' I say.

A huge smile crosses her face as she walks quickly towards us.

'Amazing!' she says, bending down to give Jen a big hug.

I pour the champagne and we spend the next while grilling Jen. It turns out Jen hasn't made many wedding plans so far other than the appointment to pick the rings together in Dublin next week.

'Do you have any idea where you want to get married?' I say.

'In Ireland,' she says instantly. 'I travel so much already and I can't bear the hassle of having it abroad. I don't want any fuss,' she says. 'Just a small intimate wedding with my close family and friends. I know it sounds nuts because it will probably piss it down, but I've always imagined a spring wedding somewhere romantic and clifftop-y.'

Bless her. She *is* nuts. An outside wedding in Ireland is just begging for trouble, regardless of the seasons. Bea's forehead creases and she mumbles something about making a call. Then she walks off purposefully towards our bedroom. Jen turns to me, her eyes shining.

'And there will be only one bridesmaid, Saoirse – and that's you.'

My heart fills.

'I'd love to,' I whisper, now determined more than ever to push aside my doubts about Liam.

My excitement builds – I love a wedding and it's great to have something to look forward to after everything that's happened over here.

'I'd also love Anna to be our flower girl.'

Ah, for Jesus' sake.

Anna's moods are about as predictable as the sodding Irish weather. I'll have to make sure she is well prepped beforehand so she doesn't mortify me on the day.

Then we chat about wedding dresses for a bit – Jen wants something simple and elegant but realistically she could walk up the aisle in a brown sackcloth and still steal the show.

Bea appears again with an inscrutable look on her face.

'Everything OK?' I say.

'I think so,' she says, glancing at Jen before sitting down at the table. 'I've just spoken to my mother back in South Africa and although she wasn't best pleased that I've woken her up at an unforgivably early hour, she has agreed to my suggestion.'

Then she twists her hands a bit. I've only ever seen Bea nervous a handful of times so I'm desperate to hear what she has to say.

'Come on, woman!' I blurt out.

'Well,' she says, giving Jen a shy look. 'If you would like a romantic clifftop wedding, my mother has agreed to let you use The Cube as a venue.'

Oh my goodness! Memories race through my mind. Writing the pitch for my book from the kitchen of the stunning all-glass structure in Wexford, southeast Ireland, set high up on the wild clifftops with the raging sea in the background. The place where I escaped to when I (mistakenly) thought David was having an affair. The same place where Ryan and I almost kissed... but I push that thought out of my head. The Cube would be the perfect, romantic, outdoor wedding venue – if it doesn't piss it down – which it will.

I'm not sure how Jen will react, though – she knows The Cube from visiting me there, but Wexford is also the place she sought refuge when Liam broke up with her. It mightn't hold the best memories for her.

But I needn't have worried. Jen squeals, her champagne jumping out of her glass. Then she races around to Bea and wraps her in a tight hug.

'That would be amazing!' Jen says, her cheeks blushing with excitement.

Bea draws back, smiling, and holds up her customary one finger.

'That's not all. My mother is also going to make an appointment for you to try on wedding dresses tomorrow. Apparently, one of her biggest fans is a top New York wedding dress designer.'

Bea's mum is the hugely successful children's cookbook author Arianna Wakefield. She is an extreme Organic and regards any kind of junk food as the work of the devil. Last Christmas, when Bea took Harry back to Cape Town, Arianna insisted on giving him vegetable smoothies every day for his breakfast, which he unceremoniously flushed down the toilet, with Bea on lookout duty. Although Bea's child-rearing views may differ from her mother's, there's something to be said for having a mum with bloody great contacts.

More high-pitched squeals from Jen follow and suddenly we're all on our feet, swaying in excitement and chattering about wedding dress shopping.

Then Harry and Anna fly over to the table, demanding more sweets, their little faces streaked in ketchup.

'You've had enough sweets,' Bes says sternly, hands on hips.

Their faces fall.

'There are some crisps in the suitcase in my bedroom – have those instead.'

The pair of them light up and race off. No doubt their beds will be riddled with crumbs later. Still, anything for a bit of peace.

Then my mind jolts. We can't be bringing them to the wedding shop tomorrow – they'll run riot. When I say this to Bea, she just shrugs.

'Don't worry – I'll take them to McDonald's for lunch followed by the cinema. You and Jen can go shopping in peace.'

Jen and I immediately protest, but Bea folds her arms and shakes her head. There's no talking her out of this one.

Two hours later, both adults and children finally hit a wall, so we decide to hit the sack. After finally settling a protesting Harry and grumpy Anna into their beds, I settle into the glorious, soft cotton sheets, my head sinking into the soft, downy pillow. As my eyes start to droop, I can't help but smile to myself. I haven't felt this happy since we got here, and I can't wait to see what tomorrow brings.

17

As it turns out, tomorrow brings a crashing headache and severe dehydration. Why did I have so much champagne? You'd think I'd have learned my lesson by now. I open my eyes gingerly, and move my thumping head, hoping to find two allies who feel as rough as I do, but both beds are empty. I grab my watch, hastily thrown on the mahogany bedside table last night, and exclaim out loud.

It's 11.30 a.m.! I can't believe I've slept this long. What on earth has Anna been up to? She's probably been up since 7 a.m. I scramble out of bed as best I can given the extent of the hangover and throw on the robe I was wearing last night. One sleeve smells of champagne and I make a solemn vow never to drink it again. Stumbling out of the room, I make my way towards the living area, where I see Jen dressed in a pretty, floral, sleeveless dress sitting with her feet up on the coffee table, staring at her phone and sipping a cup of coffee.

For a moment, I genuinely hate her – she looks absolutely stunning. I don't get it. She's got to be jet-lagged, and I know that she gets bad hangovers like me, but there she is looking like she's just stepped out of hair and make-up. It's just not fair.

She spots me and a wide grin spreads over her face.

I tell her to feck off, and she laughs.

'Where are Bea and the kids?' I say. 'Have they gone to the cinema already?'

Jen shakes her head. 'No – Bea took them swimming. They should be back soon.'

'Does Anna even have a swimsuit?' I say, not remembering putting one in the bag when we were packing last night.

'Bea said she was going to pick up one from the hotel shop.'

My heart fills. The swimsuit is the easy part: anybody who is brave enough to take two hyper kids to a pool in a very posh hotel deserves a medal.

'Ready to go wedding dress shopping?' she says.

'I am but I need a big can of Coke and a bacon butty first,' I say.

'I'll sort out room service, while you get yourself together,' she says.

I shower and dress quickly, half-heartedly slapping on some make-up so I don't look like a complete hound next to Jen. Just as I'm finishing up the last glorious bites of the best bacon sandwich I have ever inhaled, Harry and Anna come tumbling through the door, wet-haired and rosy-cheeked with a fresh-faced-looking Bea (honestly, am I the only one suffering from last night?).

Anna throws herself into my arms, and I cuddle her close, not caring that her wet hair is likely smearing half my make-up. Apparently, she had the *best* time and she went underwater, *without* goggles. I kiss her and she wriggles off my knee and tells me she has to dash because she needs to get ready for McDonald's, and then she's gone. Harry follows her at great speed.

'Bea, there are no words,' I say, my eyes filling with tears. 'Thank you for the swimsuit and the lie-in. You must be jet-lagged too.'

She waves a hand in a *no bother* gesture and says, 'They had coloured marshmallow pieces masquerading as cereal for break-fast,' she replies. 'And, of course, it will be McDonald's for lunch.'

I tell her that I don't care if they sip from a chocolate fountain all day as long as they (and she) are happy.

Jen rises from the couch and stretches her gloriously tanned arms above her head.

'Shall we make a move?' she says.

Feeling a bit better, I kiss Anna goodbye and head down to the lobby with Jen, where the doorman hails us a taxi. My heart is bursting with the anticipation of seeing her in a wedding dress. This is going to be the best afternoon ever.

* * *

'Jesus, I look like the fairy on top of the Christmas tree,' Jen mutters through her teeth.

I spy Jen's phone peeking out of her handbag on the floor, grab it and take a quick snap of her reflection in the mirror.

'I swear to God, if you show those photos to anyone...' she says, growling in a distinctly inelegant way.

I giggle. To be fair, the dress is flouncy and very blingy, and not at all her style, but every dress Jen has tried on so far has been a massive, plumped-up affair and the twenty-something, thin-as-a-rake shop assistant, Allegra, who clearly lives and dies by her commission, won't tolerate any nay-saying. Whenever Jen subtly tells her that the dresses aren't really what she's looking for, she simply repeats the same stock phrase in the same flat, robotic voice: 'Anna Cho is actually the world's best wedding dress designer. Her dresses look good on anyone.'

'I think you could do better,' I whisper.

I'd like to be more candid, but I can hear Allegra breathing impatiently from the other side of the dressing room's gold brocade curtains.

Jen nods grimly at herself in the mirror and starts to slide out of the straps.

Jen's phone pings in my hand.

It's Dee.

SICK with jealousy that you're living it up in Manhattan without me!

Plus vomiting GIF.

I feel a sharp twinge of disappointment for her. Before we went to bed last night, Jen mentioned that she'd invited Dee on the trip, but she couldn't make it. Out of all of us, Dee could have done with a break, especially with kids that young.

I send her the photo of Jen in the ostentatious dress to cheer her up, and she replies immediately.

Jesus Christ, is she auditioning for one of the ugly sisters?

I read her message to Jen and she sticks her tongue out at me.

There is a rustling sound as Allegra sweeps back one of the heavy curtains and walks purposefully across the plush burgundy carpeting towards us.

'Well, ladies,' she says, her arms folded across her expensively cut, white tuxedo-style suit. 'What do we think of this totally awesome dress?'

Jen stays facing the mirror, her mouth in a hard line. It doesn't take a genius to know that she absolutely hates it.

'Not for me,' she says politely, but with an edge to her voice.

Allegra's unnaturally full lips transform from a fake smile to a pout, then back to a fake smile again. I watch this lightning quick alteration in fascination; it's like someone has just dropped a coin in her.

'Let me get you a couple of dresses from the Anna Cho 2021 Collection next,' she says, whipping around on her ankle-breaking, shiny black heels.

'No!' I cry out.

Like Jen, I've had enough. The hangover sweats are setting in and if I don't get out of this stuffy changing room soon, I'm in danger of vomiting all over those ridiculously grandiose curtains.

Allegra glares at me.

'Please unbutton the dress for Jen now,' I say, as evenly as I can. 'We will be leaving directly afterwards.'

I catch Jen flashing me a grateful look in the mirror and I give her a decisive nod back. I am her only bridesmaid, after all; my job is to protect her from any bullshit at all costs.

Half an hour later (I'm pretty sure a now-sulky Allegra unbuttoned that dress deliberately slowly), we're back outside in the steaming, humid Manhattan air again. The air might be stale and full of petrol fumes, but I still gulp it in greedily, relieved when the nausea starts to abate.

'Ah, sorry you didn't find the dress of your dreams,' I say to Jen, as we stand on the pavement trying to flag down a taxi, but she just shrugs.

'At least I know what I don't want.'

A taxi pulls up and we move towards it, but just as I'm reaching for the door handle, a woman dressed in denim short-shorts and a neon-pink crop top elbows me out of the way, climbs into the taxi, and shuts the door in my face.

'Jesus!' Jen cries, banging on the window. 'The cheeky cow!'

The woman casually takes out her phone as if we're invisible and the taxi moves off into the traffic. Jen makes to run after the car, but I clutch her arm.

'Listen, it's not worth it,' I hear myself say, and then pause a moment to wonder why I'm not as cross as she is, but, of course, the reason is that I'm with someone I love and trust. The throngs of people don't bother me as much and the heat doesn't feel as intense, which reinforces the fact that, if I'm going to survive this year, I'm going to have to build another tribe. I just hope I can find one.

Another taxi pulls up and we get in without any further incident. I check my watch and tell Jen we have another hour or so before Bea gets back with the kids.

'I'm in no mood to be traipsing around Manhattan,' she says wearily.

So that's how we end up back at the hotel at 4 p.m. on a Saturday, blatantly ignoring everything that New York has to offer. As Jen pours a hair-of-the-dog white wine back in the hotel room, we stick our feet up, making the most of the silence until Harry and Anna pile in, saying nothing, content just to be together.

18

It's Sunday morning and we're packing up our things, ready to check out. My heart feels heavy. I hate the thought of my two best friends leaving me by myself, but I am still blown away by the effort they made to fly all the way over here.

After the mayhem of Friday night, we took it easy last night, ordered room service again (more chips), and chatted, Bea and I giggling over the photos I took of Jen in her over-the-top wedding dresses, all the while sharing a mere two bottles of wine. It was Bea that ended up needing the booze the most. Apparently, Harry and Anna had decided against a movie and spent most of their afternoon in an arcade across the street feeding coins into machines that never yielded any prizes, and Bea looked broken.

As we get to the goodbyes in the hotel lobby, I try not to cry. Anna and Harry squeeze each other for a whole minute, while I try to look anywhere but at Bea and Jen. My eyes start to water and Bea steps in.

'Saoirse, you'll be fine,' she says in a voice that won't tolerate argument.

Then she leans in closer and gives me a quick hug and whispers, 'Zoom me *any time* for a chat, OK? Fuck the time difference.'

She releases me and walks over to Harry and Anna, muttering something about prising them apart.

Jen goes down the 'Sure, you'll be grand' route, followed by a brisk hug for her goodbye.

'The next time I see you, you'll be walking up the aisle,' I say, and I mean it to be light but then our eyes meet, and before we know it, the tears are flowing on both sides.

'Jesus, what's wrong with me?' Jen says, mascara running down her face. 'I'd better not be turning into one of those brides who gets all emotional about her wedding.'

Bea announces that it's time to go to the airport and Harry and Anna break free to give each other one final hug and clutch each other while we all walk out to the waiting car.

Anna and I say our final goodbyes and wave madly until the car disappears from view. Then the doorman magically appears and flags down a taxi for us. Anna is unsurprisingly subdued on the way home and my heart goes out to her. She needs her friends as much as I need mine.

*　*　*

Whatever euphoria is left from the weekend quickly wears off as soon as we walk into the apartment, which is even more of a shithole than I remember, and I am awash with shame. With Anna reunited with her teddies, I spend a couple of hours tidying up, chucking the pizza boxes into the rubbish disposal, stuffing laundry into black plastic bags with a vow to take it across the road tomorrow, and washing all the dishes piled up in the sink. Then I finally take my new phone out of its box and set it up. It's time I was connected again.

My phone pings just as I've put on the tiny dishwasher for a second time. It's Bonnie asking if she can Zoom with Anna. I feel a twinge of guilt – I have exchanged a couple of texts with her since we got here and she's had a few chats with Anna – as much as you can chat with a five-year-old with an attention span of a goldfish, but her contact so far has mostly been with David. I go into the bedroom and find Anna and a naked Rose-Bonnie playing 'newborns' together. She looks up at me and frowns.

'How does a baby get in your tummy, Mummy?'

'Bonnie wants to Zoom with you,' I say hurriedly.

'Great!' she says, diving towards her iPad.

Distraction successful.

I add Bonnie's details to Zoom and wait until she answers before leaving the pair of them to it. A chat with her warm, kind grandmother is just what Anna needs to cheer up her. I'm just in the middle of unpacking our weekend bags when Anna appears.

'Bonnie wants to talk to you,' she says, flicking back her hair impatiently, waving the still-naked doll in my direction.

'Did you have a good chat with her?' I say, stroking her little cheek as I walk by her to the bedroom.

'It was fine,' she says grumpily. 'She didn't tell me where babies come from either.'

Then she wanders off to the couch, grabs my phone off the coffee table and starts taking pictures of Rose-Bonnie. Confident that I might get at least a five-minute chat with Bonnie, I go quickly into the bedroom and sit down with my back against the head-board, balancing Anna's iPad on my hunched knees. Bonnie smiles back at me but I am taken aback by her appearance. She looks absolutely wrecked. Her white hair is as soft and cloud-like as ever, but her skin is pale and she has dark bags under her eyes. It's hard to tell on a screen but it looks as though she has lost weight too.

'Are you feeling all right, Bonnie?' I say, concerned.

'Och, I'm fine!' she says cheerily, in her gentle Scottish lilt.

But I'm not convinced.

'It sounds like Anna had a wonderful weekend!' she says.

'We all did,' I say.

I tell her all about the surprise visit from Bea and Jen and she laughs when she hears about Jen's misfortune with the overly fussy wedding dresses.

She tells me that she's been missing us terribly and is willing the year to pass quickly. After a short silence, she looks at me, eyebrows knitted, and says, 'And how are you coping over there so far away from home? David tells me you've not had an easy time of it,' she says, her eyes full of sympathy.

My first impulse is to brush her off with a 'grand, grand' but before I know it, I'm telling her everything – from the crowds, to the heat, to surly Patrick downstairs, to missing my friends, to Anna's painful school run, and finally to the mugging.

She waits until I've finished and tilts her head to one side.

'I'm sorry you've had to deal with so much. Have you thought about making some changes?'

I am perplexed. 'What do you mean?'

She takes a deep breath. 'Well, clearly you're not happy and a year is a long time to be miserable...'

'There's nothing I can do,' I say.

Bonnie shakes her soft curls and tuts. It's the first time I've seen her impatient.

'Saoirse – you are not a city girl,' she says, her voice stern.

If I hear that one more time! First Bea and now Bonnie... I must come across as some kind of recluse.

'Have you ever thought that you're at the wrong stage of life to be making this sort of drastic change? Maybe if you were in your early twenties, career-orientated and childfree, this would be the ideal place for you. But you were settled in Woodvale before you moved so it's not surprising you're finding Manhattan a difficult adjustment.'

My mind flickers.

She's right. If I was in my twenties, footloose and fancy-free, I would be having an absolute blast.

'The fact is that people change,' she continues. 'You were settled in London. Your friends and family were close by. Anna was going to a school up the road. It was the life you wanted, the life you and David created for yourselves.'

Jesus, what's she trying to do to me? I'm now more homesick than ever!

Then she leans closer to the screen, her eyes glinting in a way I've not seen before.

'I might have an idea about how things can improve for you and Anna over there.'

I don't see how but I'm intrigued at the same time, so I gesture for her to go on and listen intently while she tells me about an area called Westmont in the New York suburbs, about half an hour on the train from Manhattan. Apparently, it's a small, quiet town with a friendly community with great schools and a beachside location.

Wow, the thought of getting out of this hot, stuffy city to live by the sea is almost too much to bear. By the time she has finished talking, I am halfway there in my mind, strolling along the white sands with Anna, delighting in the shockingly cool water on my skin.

'It sounds lovely,' I sigh, 'but what does it have to do with me?'

'I think you should move there,' she says tartly.

What?

'I can't move to the suburbs, Bonnie,' I say through a nervous laugh. 'The Firm is paying for this place for the year and for Anna's school.'

'Well, then get The Firm to pay for a smaller place and a school in Westmont – it'll be cheaper than Manhattan rent. They'll probably be happy to save money.'

She makes it sound so easy and my head starts to swim.

'What about David?' I say. 'He needs to be in the city for work – he doesn't need a commute from the suburbs on top of all the travel he's doing.'

'Look, Saoirse – from what David has told me, he is going to be travelling for long periods at a time. He's going to miss you and Anna terribly, but he'll worry more if you're not happy. Besides, it'll be good for him to have a change of scene when he does get home for a break.'

Hope starts to flicker but I squash it immediately. This is crazy!

'I know it's been a bit rubbish, but I've been here less than a month, Bonnie! I should probably give living in the city more of a chance. Get back on that horse and all that.'

Bonnie shakes her head vigorously at this.

'Why do people think they should get back on that horse or that bike?' she says, throwing her hands up in frustration. 'Years ago, I was in a minor car accident. Nobody else was involved and I wasn't hurt. But it made me realise how much I hate driving, so I sold the car and haven't driven since. I have absolutely no regrets. You're in your forties now, Saoirse. Old enough to know what you want and don't want. Stop wasting any more time focusing on what you "should" do, and instead think about what's best for you, OK?'

She might be right, but I am drowning in guilt about seeming ungrateful for the opportunity life has handed me.

'But I'm not even working, Bonnie – here I am with all this free time, and I should be at least doing something.'

Bonnie throws up her hands in exasperation. 'Why should you feel guilty about having free time? You're not working – so what? At the moment, you're all at sea because you've ended up in a situation that doesn't suit this stage in your life. That is why *you* need to make some changes.'

My head bobs along with everything she is saying – she's like a powerful motivational speaker. But even if she's right, a change as big as moving out of Manhattan seems like a totally unrealistic prospect. As if sensing my resignation, Bonnie cuts in again.

'How about *I* go through a few rental listings in Westmont?' she says.

Why not? I might as well take a look. I have nothing to lose after all, even though it seems like a pipe dream.

It suddenly occurs to me that she seems awfully knowledgeable about Westmont, but when I ask her about it, her eyes shift and darken.

'I used to know someone who lived there,' she says. 'Long gone now, though.'

Something in her sombre expression deters me from asking more. I remind myself that Bonnie had a whole life before she met us and there's so much we still don't know about her. Maybe this 'friend' was a former lover – who knows? It's really none of my business anyway.

Anna scuppers any further conversation with the 'I'm hungries' so we both blow kisses goodbye to Bonnie. I lead Anna into the kitchen to find something to eat. She surprises me by choosing an apple from the fridge and I start to chop it to her exact specifications, my mind full of everything Bonnie has just told me. Is there a chance I could swap my life in the city for glorious beachside living? It sounds like a wonderful fantasy.

My phone pings just as I'm placing the apple slices onto a plate. I wait for Anna to start munching before I check it.

It's an email from Bonnie with a link to a rental property in Westmont.

My heart skips a beat as I click on the link.

The property pops into view and by the time I cycle through the photos, I'm already in love.

Maybe it could work. I just hope David thinks so too.

19

Hope builds every day as I'm waiting to talk to David about moving to Westmont, and by the time his return comes around, I've already mentally left Manhattan. In fact, I am so buoyed up by Bonnie's plan that I start to venture out with Anna, braving the crowds and the heat to take her on an open-top bus tour to see the sights. I wouldn't say it was a massive success – she preferred being on the bus than off it, so we ended up doing big circles of Manhattan while she waved and blew kisses at the people far below her on the street, like some sort of visiting queen. Still, the fact that I was out and about gave me a bit of confidence to do more; I even finally gathered the courage to drop the laundry off (while trying not to take it personally when the worker laughed at me for handing over ripped, black, plastic bags that had melted in the heat during the short walk from our building).

When Friday arrives I'm sick with anticipation. I haven't mentioned anything about Westmont to David. Instinctively I know that this is a chat I need to have with him face to face. I just hope he sees things my way.

* * *

'Jesus, Saoirse,' David says, his head in his hands. 'This is a lot.'

Anna's in bed and we have just finished an Indian takeaway and half a bottle of wine. I have waited until this moment to tell David about Bonnie's idea, figuring he will be a bit more open to it after some decent food and a bit of alcohol. To be honest, I feel guilty about raising it at all. He looks absolutely shattered after his time away, but I've waited all week to have this chat and I can't wait any longer.

'Let me show you the photos of the house Bonnie sent over,' I babble.

I find the link and pass my phone to David.

'It's a pool house,' he says, surprised.

'I know!' I say delightedly. 'It's so dinky and cute!'

The house is like something out of a fairy tale with its triangular roof, white Greek columns and tall, square-paned windows. It has three bedrooms (hurrah! A bed to ourselves at last! And room for visitors!), a laundry room (double hurrah!), a fully equipped kitchenette and a modest bathroom. But the best thing of all is the small pool just outside the front door. A pool for Anna, and the beach, the school and a local high street not more than a ten-minute walk away. We won't even need a car.

'But you'd be living in someone else's back garden,' he says, his eyebrows creased.

I've covered all my bases.

'Yes, that's what makes it so affordable,' I say. 'Look at the ad – female, single occupant, living in the main house. It'll be good to have the landlady so close by if something goes wrong.'

David taps the screen to see more photos.

'That's some house,' he says, when he reaches the page showing the homeowner's residence. 'I wonder why she's renting out the pool house?'

I've thought the same myself – the main house seems too big for an average-sized family, let alone just one occupant. Still, maybe she's a wealthy widower who just wants a bit of company around. An image pops into my head of sitting down with a kindly old lady by the pool, munching on homemade biscuits and listening to her stories of the past, Anna happily frolicking in the pool beside us.

David hands my phone back to me and shakes his head.

'I don't know if The Firm will go for it, Saoirse,' he says. 'They've been pretty generous flying us over here and putting us up. This might be a step too far – I feel bad asking them especially as I've only been working there for just over a month.'

I know. I would feel the same way, but if you don't ask, you don't get.

'I just don't know if it's a good idea to give up this place, you know?' he says, looking around our tiny apartment. 'Especially when it's only a couple of blocks away from the office.'

Thanks to Bonnie, I have that one covered too.

'David, realistically you're only going to be here on weekends and, depending on where you are working from during the week, you won't even make it home for some of them. JFK Airport is a thirty-five-minute drive from Westmont and if you do need to get into Manhattan, the train takes you there in less than forty minutes, not even as long as your London commute. This is all doable, as long as The Firm agrees.'

He nods his head slowly and my stomach flips over with excitement. Then he looks at me, the bags growing darker under his eyes, and says something that I haven't anticipated.

'Is this because you were mugged?'

My mouth drops open.

'Jesus, David!' I say. 'Being mugged was shite, but it has nothing to do with leaving the city. I could have been mugged anywhere! I want to move to the suburbs because I have no chance of making friends or experiencing any kind of local community the way things stand. I loved seeing Bea and Jen but seeing them for a couple of days and holding scattered conversations over Zoom isn't enough. I want to live in a place where the pace of life is a bit slower, to walk Anna to school, and have her friends over for a play now and then. And I need to make friends, too.'

He looks at me searchingly and takes my hand. 'Why didn't you tell me all this before?'

I start to well up.

'Because you're just getting to grips with a new job and I couldn't put that extra pressure on you,' I say, tears running down my cheeks now. 'Besides, anybody would kill to be in our position. Swanky flat, slap-bang in the middle of this fabulously buzzy city – I didn't want to come across like a spoiled brat.'

He squeezes my hand. 'Saoirse – if you're not happy, then I'm not happy. And Anna's not happy, and Christ knows Anna is hard enough work as it is.'

I nod dolefully. A permanently miserable Anna on top of her usual mood swings doesn't bear thinking about.

He releases my hand and gets to his feet.

'Besides, with more than one bedroom in this new place, we might actually get to have sex when I'm back from my travels!'

I was wondering when that particular penny would drop.

'No time like the present,' he says, reaching into his back pocket and producing his phone.

'You can't call The Firm now!' I say in shock, glancing at my watch. 'It's almost 10 p.m. on a Friday!'

'Trust me,' David says wryly. 'The Firm never sleeps.'

Although I desperately want to earwig on the conversation, I go into the bathroom to give him a bit of privacy and sit on the toilet.

The street sirens outside muffle any sound from the living room, so I just sit and wait, wondering how I will cope if The Firm says no. Long minutes go by before David appears again, a big smile on his face.

'Well, Bonnie was right. Anything to save a few quid. The school is on their approved list and the fees are much lower than the one in Battery Park City. They just need the rental agreement for the pool house and then they'll sign off on everything.'

I jump up and let out a little squeal and immediately clasp my hands over my mouth. Thankfully, Anna doesn't stir.

I can't believe this, I think, beaming at David.

Unless the pool house is gone, in which case we're not going anywhere.

20

The next morning David calls the estate agent to make an appointment to see the pool house, and as luck would have it, there's a space that afternoon. Anna is beyond excited during our walk to Grand Central Station. We've had to tell her about the pool house but we have warned her that it might not work out. After all, although it looks great in the photos, it could be a total hole when we see it in the flesh.

It's been years since I was in Grand Central Station and I pause to point out the celestial ceiling and showstopping brass clock to Anna. She humours me for about a millisecond before tugging my hand and telling me to hurry up. That child really has no appreciation for culture.

David is quiet on the train journey. I know if it was up to him, he would rather we'd stayed in the city. His willingness to compromise makes me love him even more.

The train comes to a shuddering halt at Westmont Station and we quickly clamber off. As we follow the signs to the high street, I am pleasantly struck by the temperature. The air is noticeably cooler and cleaner than in the city, breezy with the fresh smell of sea salt. My heart quickens in anticipation as we turn in to the high street. It's exactly what I'd hoped for. Brightly coloured awnings adorn every shop front, some of them named after their owners in charming alliteration: Sally's Sweet Shop, Carrie's Cupcakes, Bodie's Book Shop and so on. Boutique clothes shops form a cluster at the end of the street, advertising expensive-looking clothes in prices way beyond my budget, and a small grocery store takes the corner spot.

David doesn't notice any of this with his head stuck in Google Maps.

We turn in to a maze of meandering streets with names like Vanderbilt Place, Tiffany Avenue and Rockefeller Circle. Magnificent, French, Tudor-style houses with their steeply gabled roofs and gloriously elaborate chimneys line the pavements, towering over us.

'Well, the residents here have a few quid all right,' I mutter to David.

He nods, his eyes still focused on his phone. Then he looks up and points towards an impressive, three-storey, red-bricked building, with intricately designed white stonework cut into the brick. I recognise it immediately. It's Anna's new school.

'Look at the school, Anna!' I say, making every effort to stop myself from saying, 'Look at *your* new school!' Although the truth is unless something goes drastically wrong, I can picture her there already.

She gives me a look that says *I don't care.*

We round a corner and see the big house from the photos in all its glory.

'Here it is: 1282 Astor Avenue,' David announces.

As we move closer, I notice that all the shutters are closed. Maybe the owner is away.

A woman with distinctly feline features and shoulder-length, straight, brown hair, dressed in a sleeveless white blouse and black linen trousers, appears from a narrow lane on the left side of the house, a smile fixed on her heavily made-up face, her hand already outstretched even though we're metres away from each other. Unable to bear the social anxiety of waiting any further for the formal greeting, I drop Anna's hand and break into a semi-trot until I reach her.

'I'm Kelly,' she says, in a sing-song way, gripping my hand firmly. 'I'm guessing you're Saoirse?'

She pronounces my name so impeccably that I bet my life she's Googled it beforehand.

I smile and nod and wait for David and Anna to catch up, before introducing them to Kelly.

Anna squints and looks up at her.

'You look like a cat!' she says.

Oh god.

But Kelly doesn't miss a beat.

'Do you like cats, Anna?' she says.

Anna nods vigorously.

'Well, you're in luck because the lady who lives in this house owns a cat called Luna!'

Anna squeals in excitement and claps her hands.

Kelly's no eejit. She's already hoodwinked Anna and we haven't even seen the house yet.

Kelly leads us down the side passage towards a garden that is approximately ten times the size of our patch of grass in London. The pool house is set right at the back of the garden, the small swimming pool in front, the blue water glistening prettily in the sunshine. Anna squeezes my hand. I have warned her around a dozen times not to expect to get into the pool until we are sure that we're moving here, and I hope she has remembered.

As we near the pool house with its gleaming, steepled, white roof, I am delighted to see that it is as adorable as it was in the photos. The tall, white double doors are already open, so we all step through into the kitchen and living area with its cool, grey-tiled floors and off-white walls. The blue-and-grey patterned couch forms an L shape around a large, upholstered coffee table in the same design. David immediately checks with Kelly to see if it turns into a sofa bed (it does – hurrah!). The kitchen stands to the left of the living area with an oval-shaped island and white wooden glass cabinets. I give the washing machine and dryer a loving stroke.

'I will never take you for granted again, my angels,' I whisper.

David gives me a look.

When we enter the bedrooms, I am delighted to see that the beds are perfectly made up – the bed in the bigger room is covered with a white duvet sketched with vines, with four huge pillows, and what would be Anna's room is decorated with cheery blue-and-white stripes. The third bedroom is bright and airy and there are pictures of seascapes on every wall. There is a compact, but perfectly functional, white-tiled bathroom between our room and Anna's room with a small skylight letting in an extra cheery glow of afternoon sun.

Of course, we do not go around the pool house unaccompanied. Kelly gives us the sales spiel throughout the tour, and I presume it's because the place is so small that she feels like she has to extend the visit by pointing out local attractions and amenities in the area. She addresses each of us in turn, totally undeterred by our responses: 'David – there is a boating club by the beach. Do you sail?'

'No,' David says.

'Well, perhaps now's the time to start!' she responds, with a tinkling laugh.

Then she moves on to me, glancing me up and down.

'Saoirse, there's also a fitness class for moms in the Westmont Studio on the main street.'

The cheek!

She turns her attention to Anna.

'Now, Anna!' She claps. 'Do you like the beach?'

Anna nods vigorously.

Kelly smiles triumphantly and turns her attention back to me.

'It's a thousand dollars for beach membership to the beach club,' she says casually.

That beach had better have luxury sunloungers and a free bar.

'Where's the cat?' Anna says.

Kelly falters for the first time.

'I think the cat is with the lady in the big house!' she says brightly, in the same rhythm and cadence as a nursery rhyme.

I take it Kelly doesn't have kids.

'Can we please see the cat?' Anna wheedles, not remotely deterred.

I raise my eyebrows at Kelly. In all honesty, I don't give a shite about the cat, but I am curious to meet our new landlady, especially as I have already decided to move in here as fast as I can chuck everything into our suitcases.

Kelly narrows her eyes and shakes her head in a regretful way.

'Is she not home?' I say.

'Mmm, I'm not sure,' Kelly says vaguely.

I exchange a glance with David. Why has Kelly suddenly become so shifty?

'It would be good to meet the landlady,' David adds.

'Oh!' Kelly laughs. 'She's not your landlady. She's simply staying in the house for a few months. The owner lives abroad and he has instructed our agency to take care of any maintenance issues.'

Clearly noting Anna's disappointment, Kelly suggests that we have a little walk around the back yard to see if they can spot Luna.

Anna skips towards the front entrance with Kelly, while David and I hang back a little.

'What do you think?' he says.

'I've already mentally moved in.'

He takes a deep breath.

'So, I guess we're really doing this,' he says, taking my hand.

'I guess we are,' I say, looking into his soft-brown eyes.

The thought of being apart for such long stints makes me feel physically ill but I already know that I will have a better chance of making a life for myself and Anna here.

A loud shriek interrupts any further conversation.

I race out the door. My first thought is that Anna has fallen into the pool, but a quick, frantic glance tells me that the water remains mercifully empty. David taps me on the shoulder and says, 'Look!'

I turn around and gasp at the sight of Anna, stumbling towards us, a distinctly unhappy-looking, gigantic, ginger cat in her arms.

'Jesus, that cat is almost the size of her,' David breathes.

I walk towards Anna quickly, kneel down in front of her, and spend long moments persuading her to let Luna free, telling her that we can see Luna any time she wishes when we're living here.

Kelly pounces.

'I'll have the contract over to you this evening,' she says briskly.

Anna releases Luna, who skips away, her tail twitching irritably.

Then Kelly walks us back down the side alley and comes to a stop just outside the front of the main house.

'I hope the three of you will be very happy living here,' Kelly says, by way of goodbye.

David tells her he won't be here very often because he travels a lot for work.

Kelly shoots us both a look and says, 'Oh, you're a LAT couple.'

I have no idea what that means.

'You know, living apart together,' she prompts.

My stomach rolls over. I guess that's what we are now.

We say our goodbyes and I turn around to find Anna, intending to grab her hand, but something catches my eye. There is a sudden movement of the shutters in the downstairs window. I shield my eyes and raise my head in that direction, but the shutters close instantly. Someone has been watching us.

21

I really should have known that out of everything I have told her about Bea and Jen's surprise visit to Manhattan, the huge news about Jen's engagement, plus our big move to the suburbs, my mother would fixate on this one particular detail.

'I just can't get *over* that you need to pay for private membership to go to the local beach. Isn't that just as tight!'

She takes an indignant breath.

'And one thousand dollars too!' she adds. 'Sure, you can't expect The Firm to be paying for that on top of everything else!'

I let out a wheeze of exasperation.

'Well, of course not,' I say.

'Exactly!' she says self-righteously, as if she's just talked me out of making a ludicrous assumption. 'Didn't I tell you that your dollars wouldn't be going very far over there?'

Then I tell her that I agree it is expensive to join the beach club, but it's probably well-maintained, yet she just says, 'Well, I've heard it all now! If they charged to get into our beach, the whole place would riot!' Then she moves on to ask me more about the pool house, immediately finding the negative there too.

'You'd want to be careful with Anna around the pool. The news is full of stories about children drowning in pools.'

And: 'That cat sounds as big as a horse – mind it doesn't take Anna's eyes out!'

Time to steer her towards the positive.

'Well, the good news is that you and Miguel can stay with us over Christmas after all,' I say. 'You'll have your own room and everything!'

'Grand, but will you be all right if we stay the week? Usually, I wouldn't be staying any longer than three days with you, Saoirse,' she says. 'Fish and friends!'

Oh, for goodness' sake. I am well used to her trotting out this ancient expression about friends and fish stinking out the place after three days every time she comes over to London, but I tell her, of course, she can stay the week.

Now that's been decided, she starts on Jen's engagement and how she hopes to the great God that Liam doesn't jilt Jen again, and so on.

I'm only half listening – my mind is now channelled on packing up for our move to Westmont. Kelly sent the contract over last night but realistically, we can't move until The Firm signs off on everything, which hopefully will be done by the weekend. It's cutting it a bit fine since Anna won't have long to settle into her new home before starting school, but at least it will be Labor Day weekend, which means Monday is a holiday, so she won't be at school until the Tuesday.

In the end, I don't have to make my excuses to end the call because my mother gets there before me with an urgent announcement.

'I have to go, Saoirse – I can feel a poo on the way.'

Wonderful.

David walks into the bedroom, frowning, just as I'm hanging up.

'I've just had a text from Bonnie asking if we're free to Zoom.'

Shite. I've forgotten to fill Bonnie in about our visit to Westmont yesterday. I nod quickly and within moments his phone starts to vibrate. He hands it to me.

'Hi, Bonnie,' I say, smiling.

I am relieved to see she has a bit more colour in her cheeks this time. Even so, she still looks tired.

'Great news about the move!' she says.

'All thanks to you!' I say, blowing her a kiss.

I tell her a bit about the pool house and how lovely and quiet the area is, and she nods and smiles.

'Did you meet the woman in the main house?' she says, her eyes flitting away for a second.

I tell her what Kelly said but I don't mention that I'm pretty sure someone was watching us through the shutters yesterday. Mind you, even if the woman was there watching us, doesn't she have every right to be a bit nosy about who's living in her back garden? I would have probably done the same thing.

She nods slowly.

'You should introduce yourself anyway,' she says, turning back to meet my gaze.

I know she's right. I tell her I'll knock and introduce myself when we move in next weekend. Then I hand her over to David.

I take a moment to text Jen and Dee the big news about the move to the suburbs. I already texted Bea earlier and she sent back a load of party emojis. Then I head to the kitchen to cook some pasta for Anna.

My phone pings a few times just as I'm shaking the pasta out into the colander. I wipe my hands on the nearest towel and grab my phone from the kitchen island, keen to see the impact of my big news.

Jen:

Ahhhhh, amazing Saoirse! You'll be the queen of Wisteria Lane!

I smile – trust Jen to go for the *Desperate Housewives* reference.
I scroll down to read Dee's text.

Big Apple not good enough for ya, was it!

My smile drops. I know she's joking but I'm still feeling a bit
sensitive about not being able to 'make it' in the big city.

David walks into the kitchen, sniffing the air.

'How did Bonnie seem to you?' I say, curious to hear his
viewpoint.

'Good,' he says, pinching a bit of freshly cooked pasta from the
steaming colander, and popping it in his mouth.

'Do you not think she looked tired?'

'No.'

'Do you ever wonder about her past? Like how she knows so
much about Westmont?'

'No.'

'Did you ask her again if she'd accept your offer to fly her over?'

Every time David talks to Bonnie, he offers to pay for her flight
but so far she has refused.

'Yes.'

'What did she say?'

'No.'

'Do you think it's the pride that's stopping her?'

'Dunno.'

Jesus, I think as I scoop some of the pasta into Anna's bowl. *It's
like talking to a feckin' robot.*

Men are hopeless.

22

Saying goodbye to David on Monday morning doesn't seem as hard now that I have the move to look forward to. On Tuesday, David calls from Arizona to tell me that The Firm has signed off on the pool house and it's all systems go. By the time David gets back from his travels on Friday, we're all packed and ready to move out the next day.

As Westmont is a mere eighteen miles from Manhattan, we decide to treat ourselves to a taxi to our new home, dragging our suitcases along the smooth marbled floor of the lobby to hail down the nearest yellow cab.

Just as we reach the glass doors, a voice rings out.

'You leaving a tip or what?'

I drop my suitcase and turn around slowly to meet Patrick's glare. The cheek of this rude little man.

'A tip?' I say, my voice squeaky with rage. 'I'll give you a few tips, Patrick: learn some manners and treat people with respect.'

Then I wheel around and march through those glass doors with my family for the last time. And it feels fucking great.

* * *

The traffic is unexpectedly kind and we pull up outside the main house in Westmont around midday. I look closely at the windows as I help Anna out of the taxi, but the shutters remain firmly closed. I've been in touch with Kelly, the realtor, during the week to discuss the handover of keys and to ask a few 'leading' questions to get more information about the woman living all by herself in the big house. I mean, I know she's not the landlady but isn't there something weird about not meeting the person living in your back garden? But to my disappointment, Kelly hasn't met her either. Apparently, all correspondence has been on email and the keys for the tour were left in a secure lockbox positioned around the side of the pool house where they're also being left for us. She ended the call with, 'You know, Saoirse, some people just really like their privacy'.

David and I haul our three suitcases out of the boot while the taxi driver stays where he is, casually smoking out the window. I pay him and include a tip. He may not have been great with the heavy lifting but at least he got us all here in one piece. David wheels two of the suitcases down the side entrance towards the pool house while I follow with Anna and the other suitcase. David drops the cases by the door and walks quickly around the side of our new home, reappearing moments later with the keys.

And then we're in.

We have barely tugged our cases through the door when Anna announces in a voice that brooks no argument that she wants to get in the pool. This isn't such a bad idea – it'll keep her happy and out of the way while we're unpacking, but although she can swim, there's no way I'm leaving her in there without some sort of flotation device. I unzip one of the cases and rummage through it desperately, under pressure from the heat of her impatience. After a few tense minutes, I finally find her life jacket and make David inflate it. She shrugs it on, barely patient enough to allow me to do the clasps, and before I can accompany her, she runs straight out of the door and jumps right into the pool.

And screams.

I race out to find her trying to frantically climb up the side and I immediately lift her out.

'It's freezing, Mummy!' she says, teeth chattering.

I dip my hand into the water and it's cold, but not that cold. A year of swimming lessons back in London in an overly heated pool has clearly turned our daughter into a bit of a wuss.

I'm tempted to regale her with 'Well, if you think that's cold, then try getting into the Irish Sea like your mummy did last summer!' But I know she won't care. I dry her off, dress her again, pop a blanket over her and hand her the iPad. So much for blissfully peaceful balmy days, sipping cocktails on the patio while Anna splashes contentedly in the pool. I'll have to try to persuade her another time – that pool will not go to waste!

Usually, I'm not a huge fan of packing or unpacking but this time it's a joy. Unlike the Manhattan apartment, we now have three bedrooms to store all our clothes, and more importantly, David and I no longer have to share a bed with Anna. Despite the nightly thrashing, part of me will miss Anna in the bed – her angelic sleeping face, the rise and fall of her chest, the smell of her tousled hair when her eyes open in the morning. I say all this to David and he looks at me as if I've lost my mind.

'Saoirse, we haven't had sex since we got here,' he whispers, casting a furtive glance at Anna to make sure she's out of earshot. 'I've been counting down the days for Anna to have her own room,' he adds, wringing his hands.

'Oh, fine,' I say, sighing. 'We can do it tonight if you like. But we're having wine first.'

'Deal,' he says curtly.

A knock on the front door makes us both jump.

'Who can that be?' David says, frowning.

'Maybe it's the mysterious woman from the big house,' I say, walking quickly to the door, my heart beating in anticipation. I am dying to see what she's like.

I pull the door open and a shortish, stocky (or 'well-rounded' as my mother would say) woman who looks to be in her late forties stands there in casual beige shorts and an oversized, bright-orange T-shirt, holding a plate of biscuits. She has short, curly, blonde hair, darkened at the roots, and an unmistakeable softness to her pale-blue eyes.

'Hi! I'm Darcy, I live across the street,' she says, showing a mouthful of startlingly large, supremely white teeth.

I smile back.

'Here are some cookies to welcome you to the neighbourhood,' she says, handing me the plate.

I thank her, take the plate, and introduce myself.

Her forehead creases.

'Wait. I need to get your name right. Now teach it to me.'

I give her the phonetic version, 'Seersha', and she says it back. I give her a thumbs up and she beams.

'Now, I'm using cookies as a cover for coming over here. The truth is I'm nosy and I saw your family get out of the taxi earlier. I wanted to know the people moving into our mysterious neighbour's pool house.'

I laugh. I can't help but admire her honesty, although inwardly I'm disappointed that she doesn't know the woman in the big house. So, I give her a brief history about moving over from London, living in Manhattan, before finally moving here.

She listens intently and says, 'I think you'll like it here. You have the best of both worlds – a quiet, leafy suburb, and

Manhattan is only a short train ride away. The school is great too.'

She shifts from one foot to the other and I realise that I haven't even asked her to come in. But when I do, she shakes her head.

'Love to but I need to get back to the kids before they set the house on fire.'

I laugh and ask her how many she has.

'Five,' she says, holding up her left palm. 'Four boys and one girl.'

Jesus.

'What about you?' she says.

'Just the one,' I say, hating how apologetic I sound.

'Lucky,' she says drily.

I burst out laughing. I'm so used to the 'poor you' head tilts, and 'such a shame Anna doesn't have a brother or sister' (that one is an Organics special) that her comment comes as a refreshing surprise.

'I'm serious!' she says. 'Honestly, we should have stopped at the twins: a boy and a girl, right? Perfect. But no, my husband had some sort of mid-life crisis and wanted to go for one more, so we tried again and ended up with triplets.'

Holy God.

'That's some roll of the dice, right?'

'Wow!'

'I mean, I should have seen it coming,' she says, raising her eyes skyward. 'I'm a twin myself. It was hell in the beginning and we had a ton of help but they're a little easier now. The twins are eighteen and I barely see them. My daughter Mia lives and dies by her social media so she is usually in her room on some device or other. And as for her twin brother, Mason, he only appears for mealtimes.'

'What about the triplets?' I say, still not able to get my head around the fact that, help or not, this woman has managed two, and then three babies all at the same time.

'The boys are seven now and spend most of the time trying to maim each other. What age is your kid?'

I tell her that Anna is five and although there is a bit of an age difference, her best friend in London is a boy and maybe we could get them together, but she cuts me off with a violent shake of her head.

'No. The triplets are batshit crazy and if I expose them to anyone younger, I won't have any friends left. But I can certainly loan you Mia. She is a very popular babysitter, and she loves any young kids outside her own siblings. Fancy hairstyles are her specialty.'

My heart lifts. A babysitter is exactly what David and I need when he gets back from his travels. We haven't had any kind of social life since we moved here. And Anna would buy and sell us for a fancy hairdo.

I beam at Darcy and tell her that I would love to meet Mia and we exchange numbers.

Then she looks at her watch and tuts.

'I have to go, but just to let you know that I'm head of the PTA and a few of us are getting together tomorrow night at Westmont Tavern, just off the main street, for a back-to-school meeting. Maybe you'd like to come along?'

I do everything in my power to stop my face from falling. Just when you think you've found a new friend, she turns out to be in the PTA.

23

'You're being ridiculous,' Bea says, wagging a finger at me through the screen. 'Not everyone who joins the PTA is an Organic. From what you've told me, Darcy doesn't fit any of the criteria.'

It's Sunday morning and I'm sitting on the patio, making the most of the gentle, warm breeze while Anna ignores the good weather in favour of watching the latest update on YouTube Kids from her favourite influencer. David has gone for a run to explore, and I've told him to pop by the beach club to see what it's like. We're planning to treat ourselves to the beach membership today.

'Maybe I'm being groomed,' I say.

'Just because a stranger rocks up on your doorstep with a batch of biscuits, kindly offers her daughter as a babysitter, and then invites you to a PTA meeting does not mean you're being groomed,' she says, tutting at me. 'When did you become so paranoid?'

Since horrible, judgemental people came into my life several years ago, I think. But I can see her point.

'So go to the PTA meeting tonight and see what it's all about. If they turn out to be a bunch of Organics, then steer clear, but at least give them a chance.'

Oh fine.

'How are things with the cream cracker thief?' I say, deliberately trying to wind her up.

I try to find a sexual innuendo to go with 'cream cracker' but fail.

I, of course, tried to interrogate her about the same thing when she came to visit but she firmly shut me down. I'm not giving up.

'Have you gone all the way yet?' I add, in the most annoying American high school accent I can muster.

She tuts. 'If you must know, Tom and I are taking it slowly.'

God, it's a nightmare getting anything out of Bea.

'When do I get to meet Tom, then?'

'Well, I have asked him to escort me to Jen's wedding,' she says, almost shyly.

Wow! Jen's wedding in April is months away – things must be serious if she's thinking that far ahead already.

'Now go and fetch Anna because Harry wants to talk to her, and I need to keep him amused so I can get on with my laundry.'

I shake my head at her blatant subject change and she glares back at me. I can see I'm not going to get anything else out of her today.

Defeated, I call through the open doors to Anna, who is splayed on the couch with her iPad, oblivious to the beautiful sunshine outside. She scrambles to a sitting position when she hears that Harry is online and expertly logs into Zoom.

'She's all set,' I say to Bea.

Then we end the call.

I lean back in my chair and think about what Bea has said about Darcy. I know she's right – the PTA gathering tonight will be a good time to meet new people. I close my eyes for a bit, content to hear Anna chatting so happily to Harry.

No sooner have I closed my eyes than the distinct scent of man sweat hits my nostrils. I open my eyes to see David standing in front of me, panting heavily, his running T-shirt and shorts stuck to him, sweat dripping down every available surface. I have to say, even though I'm feeling quite affectionate towards him after some surprisingly energetic sex last night, 'sweaty jogger David' is not my favourite look.

'How was the run?' I say, rising from my chair and walking backwards a little to keep some distance between us.

'It was OK,' he pants, wiping a forearm across his brow. 'Beach was closed, though.'

What?

'Yep, there was a sign up. Something about bacterial contamination in the water. Shame it had to happen over Labor Day weekend.'

'And when does it open up again?' I say, in what Anna would call my 'warning voice'.

'Next summer. The beach always closes the day after Labor Day weekend.'

What?

David says it so casually that I feel like giving him a good dig in the ribs. Waves of disappointment rush over me: no beach walks, no swimming for me, no sandcastles for Anna – not until next summer, anyway.

'At least it saves us a grand in membership fees,' David says, plonking himself in the patio chair I have just vacated.

I stare at him for a minute, the realisation slowly dawning on me that the expensive beach membership was just for the summer months – not for the whole year as I had thought.

'David, I need you to promise me something,' I say, folding my arms across my chest. 'Don't ever, ever tell my mother about this.'

She'll have a fucking field day.

* * *

What with the bad news about the beach plus dealing with the inevitable tears from Anna, who had her heart set on a beach outing tomorrow, I am in absolutely no mood to be going to the PTA meeting tonight. Still, on the positive side, at least it's being held in a pub, so if all else fails I can drown my sorrows. I throw on a pair of calf-length, off-white cotton trousers and one of my more presentable summer tops – a pale-pink one with a bit of lace trim on the sleeves – slap on some tinted moisturiser, and head out of the bedroom to say goodbye to David and Anna.

'Have fun!' David says, giving me a kiss.

I make a face at him. He knows that after my Organics experience I am reluctant to attend anything remotely associated with a PTA.

'I'll be home in an hour,' I say grumpily.

Anna throws her arms around me in an *I'm never letting you go* way. This will be my first time away from her in weeks. Eventually, David comes to the rescue.

'Come on – let's go and find Luna!' he says, holding out his hand.

Anna drops me like a hot stone and shoots out of the door.

Good luck, I think, as I walk down the side passage towards the main road. There's been no trace of that giant cat since we moved in.

I follow Google Maps until I find Westmont Tavern – an inviting, red-bricked building with a smart red-and-white-striped awning – positioned just off the main high street. As I draw closer to the pub, I deliberately slow my walking pace, suddenly nervous at the thought of meeting so many new people at once.

I take a deep breath, throw my shoulders back and walk as confidently as I can through the heavy wooden doors. I spot Darcy sitting at the bar, sipping from a bottle of beer, so I pull out a stool and sit down beside her. She greets me with a wide smile.

'I have a tab going. Beer?'

'Yes please!' I say.

She signals to the barman, who deftly pops beer in front of me and I smile my thanks.

Darcy checks her watch.

'How many people are you expecting?' I say, savouring the delicious bubbliness of the beer.

She wrinkles her nose.

'It depends. Technically there are supposed to be ten of us, but it's always the same four or five people who show up. You know how it is.'

'Mmmm,' I say, nodding gravely, but in all honesty, I don't have a clue.

Her eyes shift away from me and she waves. I turn and see a couple of women, one tall, one small, around my age, coming towards us. Darcy introduces me and I smile and try to look friendly: Sakura, a divorce lawyer – dark eyes, her jet-black hair pulled back into a loose bun; and Nina, who runs her own beauty salon – a petite brunette, short hair, with bright-green eyes. Both of them are make-up free and casually dressed in shorts and T-shirts. I try my best to memorise their names even though I know I will forget them as soon as the others arrive.

'Come on – let's go to our table,' Darcy says, scrambling down off her stool.

I follow her towards the back of the pub where a large mahogany table has been laid out with ten placemats, cutlery, glasses, wine bottles on ice – the lot.

'Are we eating?' I say, surprised.

I didn't think it would be such a big do.

'First rule of PTA,' Nina says, giggling, pulling out a chair. 'No talking about school until we've finished eating and drinking!'

Wow! I doubt Tania Henderson and her Organics crew don't operate their meetings like this. I bet theirs is more like 90 per cent slagging off working mothers over huge pots of green tea and sugarless biscuits, and 10 per cent discussion about school matters.

I take a seat beside Darcy as the rest of the group flow in, full of chatter and smiles. I count seven of us in total: all dressed casually, most of them make-up free. Darcy goes around the room filling glasses with ice-cold, delicious white wine (hurrah!), introducing me again and a chorus of welcomes follow. I can't help but smile back in return. Then there is a flurry of ordering and I am gratified to see that everyone, without exception, has gone for classic pub grub – either a burger, chicken wings or battered fish. Not a green salad or watery broth in sight. Tania Henderson and her gym-freak minions would pass out.

I can't resist ordering a burger and fries even though I've already had a slice of pizza at home – and I field questions while we're waiting for the food to come. I fill them in without dwelling on too much detail, but honestly, they seem to be much more interested in the woman living in the big house than my background.

'So, what's her deal anyway?' Sakura says, her dark eyes flashing.

I shake my head.

'I haven't met her yet.' I shrug.

'All I know from talking to the local realtor is that the owner rents it out to people for short-term lets – most of them seem to come for the summer. Then this woman moves in late one night in mid-July and apart from taking out the trash, she never seems to leave the house,' Sakura continues.

'Really?' I say, covered in goosebumps.

'She gets everything delivered as far as I can see,' another woman with a short brown bob, who I think is called Nancy, says.

'I know, right? I never see her around town,' a woman with a hastily tied-up blonde ponytail and who may be called Madison, adds.

'As soon as I saw the lights on, I went over there with my cookies to welcome her to the neighbourhood,' Darcy says, 'But she never opened the door, although I'm sure she was there.'

'Fletcher in the flower shop is so over going to her house,' Sakura continues. 'Someone sends her flowers every week but when he knocks on the door to deliver them, she opens it barely a crack, grabs the flower box, and slams the door in his face.'

Wow. I'm not sure I fancy introducing myself now despite what I said to Bonnie on our last call.

Darcy tuts good-naturedly and says, 'Honestly, ladies, Saoirse will think we're a bunch of gossips.'

Any further discussion is disrupted by the welcome arrival of the food. I am now one large beer in and half a glass of wine down. I'm a little woozy and so welcome the carbs to soak up the alcohol.

The chat moves on to what everyone did over the summer and I am content to listen. Then, just as I'm polishing off the last delicious chip with a touch of regret, I find myself in the spotlight again.

It's short brown bob. 'Hey, what grade is your kid starting?'

I swallow quickly, and tell her kindergarten, and ask the table if any of their kids are doing the same, hoping for at least one ally and potential playdate in the class. The room goes quiet and I notice several looks are exchanged, but the moment passes before I can get to the bottom of this curious shift in atmosphere. Then suddenly the others pile in, talking over each other to tell me the grades their kids are in: it turns out that some are a couple of years above, but most are in the older years.

Nina refills the glasses, then Darcy gets out an iPad as the table is being cleared and starts the meeting by asking everyone for fundraising ideas. I inwardly groan, recalling the horrific bake sale that Tania shafted me with last year where all the kids ran riot and stole the money off the table. I still have nightmares about it. I take a large swig of wine, already thinking of excuses not to join the PTA.

But then Sakura says something that captures my attention.

'Let's get the fire truck to collect food donations from the school and deliver it again to the homeless shelter,' Sakura says.

'Oh, cool!' Darcy says, typing. 'The kids loved that last time.'

I am brave enough (and pissed enough) to ask how this all works and I am blown away by the answer. The kids bring in canned goods and the fire truck comes by to pick everything up, with the children helping to load the truck. Then it goes off to deliver to a homeless shelter just outside town.

And that's not the end of the fundraising ideas; every single store in Westmont seems to be involved in helping the community by donating the proceeds to local charities: the local art shop hosts an art exhibition of kids' paintings, which parents (each kid's own presumably) can bid for; Westmont cinema offers discounted tickets to particular kids' movies; and the very pub we're sitting in makes up wine hampers for a charity auction at Thanksgiving.

Despite the odd (frankly ludicrous) fundraising idea offered up by Nina (yoga with animals), everyone listens to each other carefully, and nobody puts anyone down. Of course, some voices are louder than others – Sakura being the most opinionated – but she is also willing to listen to others and easily accepts when someone disagrees with her. The more the women swap ideas around, the more admiration I have for them. They lift each other up through lively debate, rather than put each other down, all of them united in their goal to enhance the lives of others through the power of community spirit.

I feel a bit ashamed that I had no idea the PTA could achieve so much. The closest Tania Henderson came to helping others was by lecturing them on calorie count every time she spotted someone with a sausage roll.

Darcy turns to me and asks me if I have any fundraising ideas to suggest.

'We're curious to see how things are done back in London,' she says, smiling encouragingly.

Shite.

'Erm, well, I was involved in the bake sale last year,' I say, feeling utterly lame.

Try as I might, I can't think of anything else to say. I wasn't involved in the Christmas or Summer fairs because I was shunned by the Organics when the whole blowing-the-head-teacher thing got out, so honestly, I've done nothing to help the school or indeed the local community. There are dozens of thriving communities in London, but Woodvale isn't one of them.

I open my mouth and close it again, feeling the blush rise to my cheeks. But then Darcy, clearly sensing my discomfort, steps in.

'Hey, guys, we have totally put Saoirse on the spot!'

Lots of noisy apologies follow and I wish I could redeem myself, but honestly, what can I say?

'Some of us find fundraising ideas from our jobs,' Nina says kindly, clearly trying to be supportive. 'I run my own beauty business, for instance, so I offer up a collection of products for the raffle.'

That sparks off a whole flurry of conversation about finding inspiration from jobs. The more I listen to them, the more inadequate I feel. They all seem to have really high-powered jobs: divorce lawyer, engineer, software developer, lifestyle magazine editor, beauty business owner... Even Darcy has a high-flying job as a management professor at a top New York university, as does her husband, all of which they manage to balance with looking after five children.

I shrink down in my seat and take a deep gulp of my wine, hoping against hope that the spotlight doesn't land on me again. But of course, it does.

'So, what you do, Saoirse?' Sakura says, politely.

Jesus, there's nowhere to go from here. I'm just going to have to bite the bullet. So, I tell them I'm a ghostwriter-turned-author and then I tail off because there's not much else to say. To my utter shock everyone starts speaking at once.

'Wow, a writer! How cool!'

'What books have you written?'

'We've never met a ghostwriter or an author before!'

'Have I read anything of yours?'

I am blown away by their enthusiasm and feel suddenly extremely self-conscious. In all my years of being a writer, I have never received this sort of reaction.

Buoyed by their enthusiasm (and by now three large glasses of white wine and a beer), I decide to tell them about the book. Isn't this what Harriet has been on my case about? Telling everyone I meet? Building word of mouth before the book comes out next January?

'Where can we buy it?' Darcy says, instantly.

'Well, it's not out yet, but I have a few early copies that I can hand out,' I say.

Everyone at that table wants a copy.

My heart sings. A week ago, I had nobody to give the book to other than Bea and Jen and now I have a whole group to help spread the word. Harriet will be delighted with me!

'You could be our school writing ambassador!' Sakura says, her eyes flashing with excitement.

I don't know what that means.

'That's a great idea!' Darcy chimes in. 'You could give writing talks to the fifth-grade kids about being an author. You could even have your book launch in Bodie's Book Shop!'

I don't know what to say.

'Hey, it would also be amazing if you could take a look at the content I post on the school website,' Nina chimes in, her green eyes sparkling. 'My spelling and grammar is barely middle-school level.'

I smile at her honesty – I would never have the confidence to admit that weakness in front of a group of women without feeling like a total failure, but she states it with no shame.

Despite being three sheets to the wind, I still hesitate. I have never volunteered for anything before. What if I cock it up? They all seem so organised, confident and capable. A flashback of the disastrous bake sale pops into my head. I'd be terrified of letting the side down.

'Will you think about being our writing ambassador?' Darcy says gently, clearly picking up on my hesitation.

I tell them I will definitely think about it. Then I beam at everyone and promise again to give them each a copy of the book, until something serious occurs to me.

'Listen,' I say, putting down my glass of wine. 'There's a lot of swearing in the book.'

They exchange puzzled glances.

'So?' Darcy says, looking at me, eyebrows knitted.

'Well, I don't mean to generalise but I'm not sure if Americans are into swearing,' I say, hoping I haven't offended them. Still, though, I have to be careful – so far not one person has sworn in this meeting. Not even me, which is frankly shocking given the amount of booze I've just consumed.

Roars of protest follow. Darcy's voice is the loudest.

'Of *course* I swear!' she says indignantly. 'I have *five* kids and a husband who still hasn't learned the kids' soccer timetable, or how to take out the trash.'

The others giggle and tell similar stories about family life, not a trace of fakery among them. I look around the room, smiling at all these new faces: kind faces. People who will go out of their way to help others; people with busy lives and huge jobs yet who still find the time to volunteer; and by the looks of it, not an Organic in sight. A feeling of pure exhilaration fills my chest. Maybe, just maybe, I have found my American tribe.

24

I'm convinced Anna has a hangover radar because she always seems to jump on my bed when I'm a little worse for wear. Still, I can't be too cross with her especially when I've woken up with a glow after last night's surprisingly successful PTA meeting. I reach up and gently take her little hands in mine, pull her down, and cuddle her close.

David walks in and smiles at the pair of us.

'Well, how was last night?' he says. 'I didn't even hear you come in.'

Jesus, he must have been out cold because I definitely remember tripping over the coffee table, swearing noisily and then shushing myself.

Anna wriggles out of my arms and mutters something about 'boring grown-ups' and leaves the room in search of her iPad.

I fill David in.

'So, is it official?' he says. 'Are you now a member of the PTA?'

Oh god, am I? After the swearing discussion, we drank more wine and to be honest, the details are pretty sketchy after that. I remember walking home with Darcy, who filled me in a bit more on kindergarten and Anna's new teacher, Miss Garcia, who sounds as though she's as close to a Disney princess as you can get, which is music to my ears. Anna will adore her. I have a vague memory of emphatically telling Darcy to *wait right there* at the front of the house while I ran back to grab the four remaining copies of my book (just about remembering to keep one back for myself) for the other PTA members to share around *just in case* I miss them at the school gates. Then I remember Darcy telling me that there was no pressure to join the PTA as a writing ambassador, and then me saying exuberantly, 'Try and stop me!'

So much for thinking about it.

'Yes,' I tell David. 'I suppose I am officially on the PTA.'

He gives a low whistle and shakes his head.

'Never thought I'd see the day,' he says, sitting on the bed.

Me neither.

'Just make sure you don't go giving oral sex to the head teacher in this particular school, OK?' he says, his eyes twinkling.

I give him my best withering look.

'The head teacher's a woman,' I say.

His eyes take on a dreamy look.

'Oh, grow up!' I say, throwing a pillow at him.

Honestly, men are so bloody predictable.

* * *

After breakfast I treat myself to an Anna-free walk down to the seafront, gazing wistfully at the giant 'closed' sign at the entrance to the beach. To be honest, the whole area is a bit disappointing – there's no coastal walk to speak of as the giant houses take up most of the space, but there is a very pretty gazebo right at the water's edge, which I sit in for a bit, enjoying the warm sea breeze and the sun's reflection on the sparkling water.

When I return to the pool house, feeling slightly less hungover, I spend the rest of the day trying to get organised for the week ahead. David is off to Washington, D.C. tomorrow but it's only a short trip so he will be home at the weekend, which is a relief. He trots off to get some groceries, while I check Google Maps to find a place to buy school supplies. I find a shop called Stan's Stationery Store just across the road from the pub and although it's Labor Day, thankfully Stan's is open even if the beach isn't. I've never had to buy school supplies before because Woodvale Primary provided everything, so this is the first time Anna will choose a pencil case. It turns out the novelty of this is immense and she chats merrily all the way to the store about what type of case she will have – apparently it will not be pink because pink is too 'girly', which is the first I've heard of it given that she has been a pink fanatic since she was able to talk.

We push open the door to the shop and an elderly gentleman with a neatly trimmed white beard and round metal glasses greets us warmly, introducing himself as Stan Beckerman, he then personally takes us around the large store and addresses Anna the whole time, which I love. Finally, we have everything we need and we thank him and leave the shop.

As Anna is on such good form, I decide to chance a longer walk and lead her down the main street, pleased to find that Fletcher's Flowers, with its pretty pink-and-white-striped awning, is also open. On impulse, I decide to go in. I'm pretty sure there is a vase in one of the kitchen cupboards and it would be a treat to have some beautiful flowers on display. Besides, I'm keen to meet the man the PTA mums were talking about – the one who delivers bouquets every week to the mysterious (and, by the sounds of it, cantankerous) woman living in the main house.

The shop is small with exposed red brick, and the walls are covered with wooden shelves displaying vases of every colour and size; several tables in matching wood are laden with stunningly arranged bunches of flowers. The scent is intoxicating.

A small, clean-shaven man in his mid-thirties, wearing slim-fitting beige shorts and a pec-defining red T-shirt, smiles at Anna as we walk in. She gives him a little wave.

'Hi there!' he says.

I tell him very deliberately that we've just moved into the neighbourhood and I'm looking for some flowers to add a bit of colour to the living room.

'Any particular colour?' he says.

'Not pink!' Anna replies, shaking her head.

He laughs, gives her an army-style salute and deftly picks out a stunning bunch of purple and white flowers interlaced with stems adorned with delicate leaves.

'What about this one?' he says, lowering them to Anna's level for approval.

Anna nods primly, giving it her best *they'll have to do* sniff.

'So where have you moved to in Westmont?' Fletcher says casually, taking my card.

I stifle a gasp as the price flashes up: $95 for a bunch of flowers – I'm not telling David; he doesn't like flowers at the best of times.

'The pool house on Astor Avenue,' I say weakly as he hands my card back to me.

His dark blue eyes grow wide and his jaw drops.

This is it – this is where I get the gossip.

Then, quick as a flash, he plucks a single yellow rose from a large display in the corner and pops it into a silk-lined, black presentation box, tucking a small white envelope right in the bottom, before slotting a clear plastic cover in place. He holds out the box towards me with both hands.

'Can you please deliver this to the big house?' he says, with a pleading look in his eyes. 'Her name is Beth.'

Beth. The recluse has a name!

But still, I'm reluctant to take the box. If Fletcher's been getting short shrift every time he attempts a delivery, I doubt if I'm going to receive a better reception.

'I haven't met her yet...' I say, but his eyes only get bigger and more puppy-like so I cave and take the box from him. I promised Bonnie, after all.

'Thank you!' he says, a big smile of relief and satisfaction flashing across his chiselled features.

I decide to drop the school supplies and our flowers at home before braving the still-shuttered house. The minute Anna and I walk down the lane towards the pool house, I sense that something's off. I look around quickly trying to pinpoint what it is. Then it hits me: the pool is covered up. Anna may not have braved the water since that first attempt a couple of days ago, but I still have great plans for that pool. A rush of irritability washes over me. Why has this happened? Is this Kelly the realtor's work?

Then from somewhere behind me I hear the unmistakeable sound of a door clicking. I turn my head towards the large, glass-panelled back door, and notice the shutters flicker. I bet any money that it's Beth who has covered up the pool – and without even asking us first. The cheek!

Indignant now, I grab Anna's hand and march towards the back door, rapping smartly on one of the glass panels, but there is no movement inside. Well, I'm not having it – I know she's in there. So, I walk quickly around to the front of the house, sprint up the steps and ring the bell, once and then several times. The shutter to my right opens sharply before shutting again. I know she's there watching. Well, she can bloody well come out and face me.

I knock again. Nothing happens. No more movement. I'm not giving up. Didn't Sakura say that she only opens the door for deliveries? So, I cup my hands to my mouth and shout 'Delivery!' as loudly as I can. The door opens so quickly that I jump a little in fright. And suddenly there she is – Beth, the mystery woman, standing on the doorstep in nothing but a huge, green-and-white-striped, fleecy dressing gown and fur-lined slippers, her barely-there light-brown eyebrows knitted in a furious frown.

'What. Is. It?' she says, spitting out each word staccato-style.

It takes a second for me to recover, not just because her appearance has been so sudden, but also because she is entirely different to how I had imagined her. Although her pale complexion is fierce, the rest of her is absolutely tiny – almost bird-like in her fragility and small-boned-ness. My mother would describe her as someone who you could 'snap in two' or who could 'do with a good decent bowl of porridge'. Her light-brown hair is pulled back into a tight ponytail, which accentuates the creases on her forehead and the pointiness of her features, giving her an almost skeletal look. Her hazel eyes are shadowed by dark bags. It's hard to put an age on her – her tiny frame suggests she could be in her twenties but her worn features indicate that she's older – maybe more like mid-thirties. I open my mouth to answer her, but Anna gets there first.

'We brought you a yellow flower,' she says, sliding the box from my hands and holding it out towards her.

The woman shifts her gaze from me for a moment and looks at Anna as if just realising she is there.

'Thank you,' Beth says, her hazel eyes softening as she takes the box from Anna.

'Oh!' I say, surprised, momentarily forgetting my irritation. 'You're English.'

She snaps her head back towards me and gives me an *and what of it* look.

Although she's not exactly encouraging conversation, I am nothing if not persistent. Sensing some common ground, I intro-duce myself and Anna as the pool house residents, and tell her that my husband is also English, and babble on about living in London until her impatiently raised eyebrows force me to stop.

Then her eyes drift to the box and her expression hardens again. *Jesus, whoever is sending her these flowers every week is wasting their time, and their money*, I think.

She suddenly takes a step back and grabs the door handle.

I take a step forward.

Not so fast.

'The pool seems to have been covered over,' I say, crossing my arms for maximum impact.

'The pool is only for use during the summer months,' she says flatly.

For fuck's sake: first the beach, now the pool. Has nobody in Westmont ever heard of cold water swimming?

Then she slams the door in my face.

25

It's Anna's first day at her new school today and I can safely say I'm
more nervous than she is. David's already left for his work trip but
judging by his response this morning, I doubt if he'd be much reas-
surance anyway – 'Anna will be fine – it's just another school.' He
was similarly underwhelmed when I told him about my altercation
with Beth, reasoning that I could have left the flower box on the
doorstep to avoid the terse exchange and called Kelly about the
pool cover situation – which by the way, according to him, is standard when the seasons change. I find it annoying when David is
being so reasonable about everything.

'Come on, sweetheart,' I say, patting the couch. 'Let's get your
runners on.'

'Ready, Mummy!' Anna says, springing off the couch.

Today, Anna has chosen a strangely subdued outfit (for her),
rejecting all the usual blingy, pink tutus and reverse-sequinned tops
to opt for a pair of sky-blue leggings and a plain purple T-shirt. Now
that she's gone off pink, I'm going to have to replace half her
wardrobe.

When we arrive at the school gates, I am surprised to see all the teachers lining the pavement holding up signs for classrooms. It looks as though the kids walk towards the teachers, who greet them and direct them towards a particular entrance: the older kids go through one gate while the younger children go through another. I spot Darcy in the distance surrounded by three small blonde whirlwinds dressed in the same soccer kit, all shouting at once – presumably the triplets. She has her hands on her hips and is gesturing to them animatedly to keep it down. Much as I'd love to say hello, I know better than to interrupt a busy mum who is trying to tame her excitable children.

I'm not totally sure but it doesn't look like the parents are supposed to go into the playground to drop the children off. My heart flutters. This is one of the best things that has ever happened to me. No hanging around the playground; no painful minutes wasted trying to make small talk with people with whom I have nothing in common. Just a pure drop and go. But then a less happy thought crosses my mind – how am I supposed to meet any of the parents of the kids in Anna's class with this set-up? Much as I enjoyed meeting the PTA members the other night, I would really like to have at least one pal in Anna's class.

My eyes land on the sign for kindergarten and I move through the chatting swarm of adults and kids to introduce myself and Anna to the teacher.

Darcy wasn't wrong – Miss Garcia couldn't be more approachable with her jet-black shiny curls, soft, dark brown eyes and wide mouth. Her face lights up when she sees us. I open my mouth to introduce us, but she surprises me by cutting me off.

'Saoirse and Anna! Welcome!' she says brightly.

How does she know who we are? Then I twig – I bet it's The Firm working its magic again. They've probably sent her everything about us, including our photos, food preferences, and sleeping positions.

She holds out a hand towards Anna, and Anna takes it immediately. Jesus, *I* feel like taking it.

Then Anna gives me her best *laters* flick with her other hand and my heart sings in relief. She's clearly not going to throw a fit at the gates, so I give her a quick kiss on the head, suddenly feeling a bit watery-eyed.

'She'll be fine, Mom,' Miss Garcia says, her eyes full of sympathy.

I nod, and thank her, taking in a big gulp of air.

'Come and see me twenty minutes before collection today,' she says. 'I understand Anna has already completed a year of school in London, so maybe we can talk more about her learning. I'll meet you right here.'

I nod and she gives me a warm smile, before turning her radiance back to Anna and leading her in through the entrance. My heart heavy, I turn towards home when a child's voice behind me stops me in my tracks.

'Stop pulling me, Mommy!'

I look around quickly to find two little girls who look very alike in every way apart from the colour of their glasses (one blue, one red) being propelled along the path by a very skinny, heavily made-up woman with flowing, fresh-out-of-the-hairdresser highlighted blonde hair. Both children are dressed in the same outfit – white T-shirt emblazoned with the name of an expensive brand and blue denim shorts. As they draw closer, I notice their mother is dressed in exactly the same thing.

'We're not that late,' the other child whines.

The mother grits her teeth and pulls them through the kindergarten entrance.

'God almighty, will you just get in!' she says crossly.

My heart skips a beat. I can't believe my luck. There's an Irish mum in the same class!

I fiddle with my phone for a bit, trying to look busy and important, and wait for the mother to emerge. She strides out a few minutes later, and I arrange my face into a Miss Garcia-like smile. There is nothing better than meeting a fellow Irish person, especially when you're in a different country. Let the bonding begin!

But she doesn't seem to notice me. Instead, she whips out her phone, the black leather phone case dotted in little white diamonds, holds it high above her head, the kindergarten sign just behind her, and shoots a mega-watt smile before pressing the button. Then, frowning, she taps for a bit before doing the same thing again. I look on in astonishment, wondering why anyone would want to take a selfie outside a school. Still, it could be worse – she could have a selfie stick.

'Hiya!' I say, seriously getting my Irish on.

She stares at me and raises her eyebrows in a *do I know you?* sort of way.

Maybe she hasn't picked up on the accent.

'Howerya!' I try again, seriously stereotypical Irish now.

She looks me up and down slowly, and I start to feel really self-conscious. I haven't exactly given much thought to my appearance today (or any other day for that matter) and I have just thrown on a pair of my comfiest loose jeans, a bright-pink T-shirt and a hoodie, which could do with an iron. My hair is up in a messy ponytail and I am entirely make-up free.

Still, I press on. She's Irish.

'I'm Saoirse.' I smile.

I mean, if she still hasn't cottoned on to the accent, then the name is surely a dead giveaway – my name couldn't be more Irish.

'My daughter Anna started kindergarten today,' I add.

She purses her full lips, tosses her hair, and says, 'I'm Brigitte. This is the first day for my girls too.'

'Is it?'

She nods, staring at me like I'm a bit thick. But I am at sea for two reasons: firstly, her accent has changed from a fairly pronounced Dublin accent to something that sounds distinctly more Californian; and secondly, the intonation of every statement is a question: as in 'I'm Brigitte? This is the first day for my girls too?'

'Where are you from?' I say, thinking that maybe I have misheard the accent.

'I'm actually from Dublin in Ireland?' she says, pronouncing 'Dublin' as 'Doblin'.

Any money she was born Brigid.

Every part of me is desperate to cry out, 'Are you?' but I manage to resist it.

'Me too,' I say brightly.

She nods and her eyes grow glassy.

'Whereabouts?' I say.

She drops her heavily mascara-d eyelids and looks at her silver watch bracelet.

OK, so she's not giving off the friendly vibes, but she's Irish, for god's sake – we must share a friend or a distant relative in common at the very least. But then again, she is probably about ten years younger than me, so maybe not. As she's made zero effort to answer my previous question, I decide to take a different tack.

'How long have you been in Westmont?' I say.

'Three months? My husband, Joe Williams, is an actor so we move around a lot? His movie is shooting in New Jersey at the moment?'

Never heard of him.

She taps and slides, and holds her phone up to my face. It is a magazine shot of a tanned man in his late forties, all silver and pepper hair, nose a little too long, not much of a chin. He looks like George Clooney's slightly-less-blessed-in-the-looks-department younger brother. 'He's gorgeous, isn't he?' she says, looking at me searchingly.

Shite. That one is an actual question and not one I'm thrilled to be asked.

'Mmm hmmm,' I manage to mumble.

In any case, who flashes up a photo of their husband to a complete stranger and asks them to confirm how handsome he is?

'So, do you know anyone in our class?' I say.

She wrinkles her nose and shakes her head. I can't help but feel she thinks she's too good for the likes of Westmont.

'I met a lovely group of PTA mums the other night...' I begin.

Her eyes darken instantly.

'I actually hate the PTA?' she says, venom creeping into her voice. 'They're just a bunch of interfering do-gooders?'

Jesus – that's a pretty strong reaction. But then I realise with a flush of shame that I had a similar opinion of the PTA before I spent time with them. I open my mouth to defend Darcy and her crew, but she cuts me off the second I start talking.

'Are you on Insta?' she says.

I nod, aware that this is the first question she has asked me about myself. I'm only on Instagram because Harriet has made me sign up to social media to promote my book. I've done bugger all on it so far, mostly because I'm waiting for my mother to do it all for me. She's way more savvy on social media than I am.

'I'm like a marriage influencer? I have almost fifty thousand followers?'

My head snaps up. She's an influencer. Exactly the type of person Harriet tells me I need to help promote the book. Imagine the sales I might get if she posted my book on her account! But a marriage influencer – what does that mean?

'Do you post about your experiences as a mother too?' I say, trying to see if there is an angle for my book.

She nods quickly.

My heart leaps. Thank Christ I popped a copy of my book in my bag when I left with Anna this morning. The only one left.

'I wrote a book about motherhood, which is being published next January. You might like a copy to read,' I say, digging into my bag, taking it out and offering it to her. I feel enormously self-conscious but the support from the PTA group has given me the boost to put myself forward.

She frowns a little before reaching over to grip it with her perfectly manicured nails and pinches it by the spine, letting it dangle a little, in the way you might pick up a dead mouse by the tail. The expression on her face is pure weariness. To be fair, she probably gets people begging her to promote stuff all the time, but still. We're both Irish.

'Maybe if you like it, you could post something on your social media? It's my first book so I need all the help I can get!' I babble.

She sighs with a vague 'hmmmm' but at least she puts the book in her oversized designer handbag.

Then she looks back at me.

'You can follow me at #PerfectWifeHappyHusband?'

Oh Christ.

Not only is she an uptalker – someone who ends every sentence with an upward inflection – but judging by her Instagram name, it sounds as though she is a smug wife and therefore most likely to be a smug mum. I can feel the breath catching in my throat as it suddenly occurs to me that, Irish or not, Brigitte could be as unbearable as an Organic.

'In fact, my husband is even happier now because I'm expecting another baby?' she adds, patting her entirely flat stomach.

'Wow! Congratulations!' I manage. 'Is it twins again?' I add, thinking of Darcy's situation.

She gives me a dark look.

'Odette and Cosette are not twins? They were just born super close together?'

Christ – two kids born less than twelve months apart in the same school year; that's a seriously small age gap.

'So, I suppose you get lots of comments about Irish twins?' I say, recalling the slang expression for babies born less than a year apart, hoping she'll see the funny side.

She doesn't.

'I actually think that's a really offensive stereotype of Irish culture?' she says.

Then she shifts the strap of her expensive bag onto her shoulder, shoots me a hard stare and stalks off.

I bite my lip. Trust me to offend a successful influencer who now has the only remaining copy of my book. She's going to slaughter me online.

Sick to my stomach, I look up Brigitte's Instagram page as soon as I get back into the pool house. Her latest photo is the one I saw her take outside the school less than an hour ago.

Devastated to drop Odette and Cosette off for their first day of kindergarten – so many tears (me!). Home now to retouch my make-up before calling my gorgeous husband Joe to tell him all about it!

Plus about a thousand hashtags.

I scroll down – forty-five comments so far, all telling her how fabulous she looks and that the first day is always sooooo hard and what an amazing couple they are and so on. I wouldn't mind but by the looks of things she couldn't have given less of a shite about dropping her kids off on their first day.

My heart sinks into my boots as I scroll through her previous posts. Her mummy fakery is only the half of it: most of it is tips on 'how to keep your man happy', including one particularly popular post that advises women to create a sex diary to chart the number of times they have had sex with their husbands – that way they will be able to avoid the dreaded sex drought, the worst thing a wife can do to her husband. There's also plenty of chat about how women can keep the marriage alive through cooking recipes in the 'a way to a man's heart is through his stomach' vein, and how LAT couples rarely last because the man is bound to cheat without regular sex. That last one strikes a particularly unpleasant chord. Is she trying to say that LAT couples like me and David won't survive? I feel an angry flush rise to my cheeks. How dare she comment on other people's relationships? Who the hell does she think she is?

I can't understand how fifty thousand people like this drivel. It's like we're back in the 1950s. This is the problem with Brigitte, the Organics and anybody else for that matter who posts this sort of nonsense on social media; it makes the rest of us women feel like if we don't 'pay enough attention' to our darling husbands, we're all failing as wives and mothers; that we should be doing better, even though most us are just about keeping our head above water.

I bite the inside of my cheek crossly. Fifty thousand followers or not, I don't want my book to be associated with anything Brigitte-related, particularly when she's spouting this sort of nonsense, but then again, I can hardly ask for it back.

I contemplate telling Harriet about my blunder, but I can just hear her voice in my head: 'There's no such thing as bad publicity, Searcy!'

I disagree. Brigitte is bound to hate my book; it rails against mummy smugness and fakery both in real life and on social media. What if she posts a nasty review? I grab a glass of water and sip it, trying to get some perspective. By the lack of interest she displayed earlier, Brigitte probably won't even touch my book again, let alone read it.

I hope.

* * *

When I arrive at the school before collection, Miss Garcia is already waiting for me. She beams at me and I can't help it; despite the last few hours of nail-biting about Brigitte and worrying about how Anna is coping on her first day, I smile back. She leads me through the entrance into a hallway covered in kids' drawings and paintings, before guiding me into an empty classroom decorated with giant letters of the alphabet, more paint-splattered pictures, four tables of different colours with small children's chairs, and a rainbow-coloured rug on the floor. She pulls out one of the small chairs at the orange table and gestures that I do the same. I sit down on the hard plastic, my knees up to my chin, and wait for her to begin.

She starts by reassuring me that Anna has had a wonderful first day, which is a huge relief. I smile and tell her that I am happy to hear that but then she props her chin in one hand and says something that blindsides me.

'How does Anna feel about her literacy?'

God, what do I say to that? Well, she has yet to discover the joy of reading and writing... But does she really have any feelings about it? Of course not – she's five. So, I take a chance and tell Miss Garcia that Anna feels fine about her literacy. She nods seriously as if I've said something deeply profound.

'That's great to hear!' she says with a little clap. 'Because here at Westmont Elementary, we want every single child to feel good about their learning. Is that the same approach Anna's school took in London?'

Well, let's see, at Anna's last parent meeting, her teacher Miss Bridges told me that Anna could 'step up' her reading and 'make more effort' with her phonics, to which I responded: 'She's five.' That conversation got us both precisely nowhere. Rather like this one.

After a few more minutes of Miss Garcia filling me in on the school day and what the kids will be doing over the course of the year, she claps her hands and rises. I do the same, thighs burning at the effort of rising from such a low seating position. I thank her as she walks me back towards the school entrance.

'Hello there!'

I turn around to find Darcy smiling with her impossibly white teeth. I am so happy to see her.

'Anna happy going in this morning?' she says.

I tell her about my chat with Miss Garcia and she nods and says: 'That's great!' at every opportunity.

'Hey, I handed your book out to the PTA mums this morning!' she says, giving me a little nudge. 'They have promised to pass it on when they have finished.'

I thank her warmly. At least the rest of the books are in the right hands.

'I'm going to start mine this evening,' she says.

My heart flutters a bit. God, I hope she likes it.

She must notice the nervous expression on my face because she says, 'Listen, Saoirse, you have achieved something that millions of people would love to do, but can't. You must be so proud. I can't wait to read it.'

A lump forms in my throat – what a gorgeous thing to say. It means even more after my altercation with Brigitte earlier. I think about confiding in Darcy about the whole sorry incident, but part of me thinks it's a bit soon in our blossoming friendship to be slagging off another mum, so I decide to leave it until I know her well enough to have a judgement-free, good old-fashioned gossip over a bottle of wine.

Just then the kids start flooding out. Darcy waves goodbye and heads towards the bigger kids' entrance as I eagerly scan the group of little people for my Anna. Then I spot her firmly clasping hands with another child.

My heart fills to bursting. It looks like she has already made a new friend. Then my mouth drops open. I really should have seen this coming. The child she is so happily clinging on to is one of Brigitte's daughters. Of course she is. This is not the first time Anna has gravitated towards children whose mums I can't stand, and I imagine it won't be the last.

'Hiiiiiiiii!' I say shrilly, bending down to give Anna a hug and a kiss, trying to mask my panic.

'This is my new bestie, Odette!' Anna says, giggling and swinging Odette's arm.

Odette wriggles out from Anna's grip and throws her arms around her.

'I LOVE you, Anna!' she says, showering her with kisses.

I can't help but smile at the pair of them. Despite my reservations about Brigitte, Odette seems like a sweet kid.

Cosette appears and gives Anna and her sister a glare that could curdle milk.

Three's a crowd.

Then Cosette walks briskly towards Odette, and says right into her face, 'You're a big eejit!', an Irish-ism that I imagine she picked up from her mum, and punches her hard in the arm. Odette squeals and starts to cry.

'Stop giving out to me!' Odette says, tears running down her face.

Anna looks up at me, eyes wide, and whispers, 'What does "giving out" mean?'

'It means that she doesn't want her sister to tell her off,' I clarify.

Anna nods and then gasps when Cosette punches her sister squarely in the arm again.

The last thing I want to do is interfere in sibling fisticuffs, so I look frantically around for Brigitte and finally see her walking slowly towards us, her eyes glued to her phone. The second Cosette spots her mother she opens her mouth and starts to scream. That old chestnut – pretending that she's the innocent one. I've seen that scene play out in the playground more times than I can remember.

Brigitte finally looks up and rushes over to Cosette, stroking her hair and asking her what's wrong.

'She punched me!' she says, pointing to Odette.

I forget about not interfering. I'm not having that.

'It was actually the other way around,' I say, giving Brigitte my best comedy non-judgemental grimace.

But she ignores me and continues to cuddle Cosette while shooting dark looks at her other daughter. Odette doesn't react at all to the injustice that's just occurred, and it strikes me that this obviously isn't the first time she's been unfairly accused.

Brigitte straightens and pulls a packet of carrot sticks out of her bag and hands it to the two of them.

I have a bag of pretzels for Anna.

Then to my surprise, Brigitte leans over to me while the girls are munching and says, 'Cosette is actually seeing a feelings doctor?'

I glance over at Cosette, who is kicking her foot dangerously close to Odette's ankle and think that it's not a feelings doctor she needs, it's a good...

'Ouch!' Odette says, hopping around, clutching her ankle.

'Can we have a playdate together, Mummy?' Anna says, through a mouthful of pretzels.

The last time Anna did this to me it involved Heath Henderson, Tania Henderson's son. Now, as Tania and I both hate each other, we actively avoided this playdate by making all the excuses we could come up with. I'm hoping Brigitte and I can come to a similar arrangement, but she surprises me by doing the opposite.

'Where do you live?' she says, briskly tapping on her phone.

I am completely nonplussed and too caught off-guard to make any excuses, so I tell her.

'You live in the pool house?'

She says it as if I've just told her I live in a house made of shit and vomit. I bet she lives in one of those mansions along the seafront.

I nod.

'Wow! Must be so cosy?'

Now I'm really regretting not making an effort to avoid the playdate.

Odette, who has clearly had enough of her sister, suddenly lashes out and the pair of them fall to the ground, writhing around on the pavement. I can't say I blame her.

Time to go.

I wave the bag of pretzels at Anna, and she walks over to me, beckoning to me with one hand.

'I don't like Cosette,' she whispers, spraying crumbs into my ear.

I know, I think, straightening up. *You picked the right sister*. I take her hand and give a vague wave towards Brigitte, who is busy trying to separate her two children.

Then just as we're walking away, she calls over to me.

'Saoirse! I'll drop the girls over to you after school tomorrow?'

If only that was an actual question. Then I could say no.

Shite.

I'm not doing tea.

27

'But why do both sisters have to go to you? Clearly Anna is friendlier with one of them more than the other, so why are you being landed with the pair of them?' Bea says in her most indignant voice.

I take a deep gulp of wine, delighted Bea understands why I am so wary about the playdate tomorrow. I called her at work as soon as Anna got back from school, desperate to fill her in on Anna's first day. *This is the kind of conversation I would have had with David if he was around*, I think with a pang. I've spoken to him today on the phone and filled him in about Anna's first day and meeting the dreadful Brigitte, but it's not the same as having a good laugh about it over a bottle of wine. I miss him.

'I know!' I say vehemently. 'Why does she have to drop both girls off when only one of them seems to be friends with Anna? It's ridiculous!'

'Because she wants to get shot of them both so she can have the afternoon off to post more smug photos of her perfect husband and kids on Instagram.'

I bet she's right. Brigitte's latest post is neck-deep in fakery. She must have calmed the girls down enough to take a picture of them outside school after Anna and I left because there they are posing under a tree with the comment:

Missed my angels sooo much today but so happy they had such a great day at school! Now home to Zoom Daddy to tell him all about it.

'Why don't you just cancel the playdate?' Bea says.

I've thought about it, but the truth is that I'm worried if I piss her off too much she's going to post horrible things about my book. But I fib and tell Bea that Anna is excited now and there's no way I'll get away with it, to which she replies, 'Do it once and don't accept a return invitation. That way you won't get stuck in this awful play-date loop.'

Agreed.

'What's the latest with Tom?' I say.

'Saoirse, I am still in the office and unfortunately cannot disclose that level of information,' she says in her strictest school-marm voice.

I giggle, although I'm also surprised she is in the office this late. I glance at my watch: it's almost 7.30 p.m. over there. Normally, Bea is strictly a nine-to-five sort of person. I bet she's going on a date.

'He's behind you, isn't he!' I tease.

She lets out an impatient breath and whispers, 'Beside me, actually!'

I tut. No getting the gossip out of her now then.

'However,' she says, back to her normal voice. 'Ryan has just announced his engagement to Adriana.'

My stomach jumps. Ryan and Adriana have been seeing each other for over a year now, but I didn't think it was that serious. Then I catch myself. Why do I care what Ryan does or does not do?

'What does Harry think?' I say, taking a deep swallow.

'Oh, he's fine about it.' Bea yawns. 'He loves her. It sounds like she spoiled him rotten that time he was staying in her place in Manhattan, and I've had the odd chat with her too. Seems like a nice girl even if she is practically a teenager.'

How can she be so blasé about it? Harry's going to effectively be getting a new stepmother, but when I say all this, she just laughs.

'She's only twenty-one. Ryan tells me there's no wedding date on the horizon as yet.'

I breathe out in relief and immediately hate myself for it.

'Speaking of weddings, any news from Jen?' she says.

Grateful for the subject change, I tell her that Jen and Dee have been WhatsApping and Jen reckons she's found the perfect wedding dress in a tiny bridal boutique in Dublin. What I don't tell her is that during this exchange, Dee has been giving all sorts of 'advice' to Jen about marriage, in the 'don't do it!' vein. I know a lot of it is meant in jest, such as 'Don't let him get his feet under the table when the ring goes on your finger!' but some of it is a little too close to the bone: 'Sure, marriage is over-rated anyway – you only need to look at the rising divorce rates to know that!'

I haven't said anything to Jen about it, and knowing her, she will take it all with a pinch of salt, but things are clearly not perfect at home for Dee. What she needs is a good holiday. I make a mental note to drop her yet another message about coming to visit us. All attempts so far have been batted away with more rants about Sean's incompetence around the kids. Still, I'll keep trying.

Bea moves on to gossip about school – apparently, Caroline, Tania Henderson's second-in-command, is attempting a coup for head of PTA for next year as they have fallen out over whether it is best to serve vegan or gluten-free cookies at the next bake sale.

'It's major handbags at dawn in the playground,' Bea laughs.

Although I am delighted to be out of the toxic school politics, I am also sad to be missing all the daily gossip. Bea and I would have been halfway through a bottle of white by now.

I tell Bea about Darcy and the PTA mums and my 'writing ambassadorship' and she is both surprised and pleased for me.

'That's the way the PTA should be run,' she says. 'Kind, welcoming volunteers who support each other and the local community. It's a shame Tania and her cronies can't do the same.'

Cheers to that! I think.

Then I fill her in about Beth but instead of enjoying the salacious gossip, Bea says something that makes me think.

'Well, it's her prerogative to keep herself to herself. Maybe she's going through something you don't know about. You've just spent the last few minutes telling me how admiring you are of the West-mont community spirit. Perhaps you should show her a little more kindness. She might shut the door in your face again, but at least you will have tried.'

God, she sounds just like Bonnie the other day, who said pretty much the same thing.

Oh, fine. I suppose they're both right.

I'll give it one more go, but if she slams the door in my face again, I'm done.

28

This has to go down in history as the worst playdate ever. Odette and Cosette have been in our house for less than an hour and all hell has broken loose. Anna is proudly showing the girls her wobbly tooth, to which Cosette has tartly responded, 'There's no such thing as the tooth fairy.'

Odette nods in agreement, albeit reluctantly.

Anna immediately looks at me for confirmation. 'Tell her, Mummy!'

Shite.

Before I can respond, Cosette stomps over to me, arms firmly folded over her yellow dress with black spots – the same dress as Odette.

'The tooth fairy is a lie!' she pronounces with all the conviction of a courtroom lawyer.

Anna's eyes start to fill.

OK, technically Cosette is right but there are very few years left of the magical stories phase and there's no way I'm going to take those away from Anna now.

'Of course, there's a tooth fairy!' I say, with a high-pitched giggle. 'Now, who wants a snack?'

But I'm not going to be let off that easily.

'It's YOU taking the tooth from under the pillow and replacing it with a coin,' Cosette says, eyes glittering, pointing at me with a stubby finger.

'Sure, why would I do that?' I shrug. 'I'm fast asleep all night.'

Cosette shakes her head angrily. '*And* you're Santa Claus too!'

What? Don't you dare bring Santa into this. That's seriously crossing a line.

'I am *not* Santa Claus,' I say sternly.

I am so cross that I almost believe it myself.

'AND you're the Easter Bunny,' Cosette says, stamping her foot.

Anna turns to her, quick as a whip, and says, 'There's no such thing as the Easter Bunny.'

She's right there. I was never raised with the Easter Bunny when I was growing up in Ireland and I haven't bothered with it for Anna either.

Anna and Cosette glare at each other before Odette blessedly breaks the ice.

'Come on!' Odette says. 'Let's go and look for Luna in the garden!'

The three of them race out the door, whooping, as if the stand-off never happened.

I flop down on the couch, shoulders loose with relief. I've managed to dodge that bullet, but the seeds of doubt have been planted in my little girl's head all the same. Bloody Cosette.

My eyes fall on the gift that Brigitte dropped off with the girls earlier. It's a massive, cone-shaped plastic bag of popcorn tied with a red ribbon, which takes up most of the coffee table. A red-and-white-striped label hangs off the ribbon, which says *Playdate*

Popcorn! in fancy black lettering, and in smaller letters: *unsalted.* Jesus – what's the point of unsalted popcorn?

I heave myself up off the couch and head to the window to keep an eye on the three girls. They have indeed found Luna and I can tell by the quick twitch of her tail that she is not impressed with the unwanted attention, so I rush out of the door intending to tell them to lay off. But just as I'm approaching them, Cosette reaches over and pulls Luna's tail. Luna springs up and twists around, blindly lashing out with one paw, scratching Anna. Anna screams and immediately covers her face.

I let out a roar and race over to her – convinced she has lost an eye. I throw myself on the ground in front of her and gently prise her hands from her face. There is a nasty, deep scratch on her right cheek and it's dripping with blood. Christ. What if she needs stitches? I have no idea what to do. Once again, I am reminded of how useless I am in an emergency.

'Can I take a look?' a woman's voice says from somewhere above my head.

I look up and let out a little 'oh' of surprise to see that it's Beth, still in the same huge dressing gown as before, half-bending towards Anna, her features crinkled in concern.

I hesitate.

'Don't worry. I'm a doctor.'

I look at her in surprise – judging by her cranky behaviour last time, I wouldn't exactly have put her in the caring profession. Ninja assassin maybe, but doctor, no.

'What kind of doctor?' I say. She could be a doctor of philosophy for all I know.

'Obstetrician,' she mumbles and then works her mouth a bit as if she hasn't said the word in a long time.

I nod and shift a little to make room for her on the grass.

She kneels down in front of Anna.

'Anna, I'm Beth. We met the other day. I'm going to pop back to the house and get my first aid kit and I'll be right with you, OK?

Anna nods tearfully.

I cuddle Anna while we wait, trying to get my head around the fact that the unpleasant woman from the other day has turned into a helpful doctor.

Beth soon reappears with a first aid kit, opens it deftly, takes out a tube of antiseptic cream and a packet of gauze pads, and presses one against the wound. Anna stares at her, mesmerised.

After the bleeding has stopped, she applies the cream, talking to Anna softly the whole time.

'No stitches,' she says, turning to me, snapping the lid back on the tube.

Thank Christ.

'It's better not to cover the wound; makes cleaning it easier,' she adds. Then she explains how to protect the cut from infection, and I try to take everything in even though I'm still feeling a little wobbly.

'Thank you,' I say, my voice still trembling.

She gives me a curt nod, waves to Anna and turns to leave.

'Do you fancy a coffee?' I say on impulse. After all, anyone who is willing to help a small child can't be that bad.

Beth turns her head and opens her mouth, but I don't get to hear whatever she says next because it is interrupted by a high-pitched screech.

Brigitte.

'I called you and called you but you didn't even answer!' she says, striding over the grass in gold flats. She is wearing the same outfit as her daughters, save for a huge, patterned handbag emblazoned with enormous silver capital letters from an exclusive brand that even I recognise. The bag sways violently in one hand as she marches towards Odette and Cosette, who are still busy trying to torment Luna despite everything that has happened to Anna.

I start to apologise but she cuts me off with a hard glare.

'My phone is in the pool house,' I try again, 'because Anna had an accident.'

And it was your *daughter's fault*, I feel like adding.

Brigitte glances at Anna, the livid cat scratch clearly evident on her cheek, and then looks at her watch.

She couldn't give a shit.

'Come on, girls, we have to go home. Your dad wants to Zoom from the ski chalet in Aspen.'

She glances at me, then at Beth, before flicking her hair as she says the word 'Aspen', presumably to let me know how rich she is. I'm not impressed – what's he doing in Aspen in September? Surely, it's not the ski season.

Beth looks on impassively. Frankly, I'm surprised she's stuck around. I'd be off like a shot if I was her.

'Mummy – I want a snack!' Cosette says and tugs at Brigitte.

'No – we have to get home!' Brigitte says, heaving her huge bag back onto her shoulder, lips tight.

But she has underestimated Cosette's sheer determination to get what she wants. Cosette lifts her feet off the ground, launches into a giant leap and wrestles the bag from her mother. It tilts a little, and out falls my book onto the ground.

My heart gives a little jolt. I immediately reach down to pick it up and hug it close.

'I've scanned it and it's really not suitable for my brand?' Brigitte says, with a sniff.

Then she turns on her gold flats, grabs both girls firmly by the hand and marches down the path, Cosette screaming the whole way.

I feel my mouth drop open. The cheek of her! She has 'scanned' my book? Well, good riddance!

I turn to Beth, ready to instigate our very first bitching session but she is not looking at me. Her gaze is firmly on the book I'm clutching, her mouth set in a thin line. Then Anna pulls on my hand and tells me she needs the loo. By the time I look up again, Beth is gone.

29

My phone goes just after I kiss Anna goodbye at the school gates the following morning. No sign of Brigitte, thank goodness – grateful as I am to have my book back, I am still seething over yesterday. Brigitte may be Irish but clearly that's the only thing we have in common.

I take my phone out of my bag, surprised to see Harriet's name flash up. The last time I talked to her, a mugger grabbed my phone. I emailed her since to explain what happened but typically, she didn't respond.

'Searcy, hi,' she says in a way that indicates she resents pleasantries. 'I'm calling to see if you received the copies of your book.'

A wave of irritation rushes through me. I told her I had received the copies in the same email that I mentioned the mugging. The email she clearly hasn't read.

'Yes, I have,' I say as evenly as I can manage.

'I hope you have given them to people to read and review,' she says.

'Yes, I have,' I say. 'Actually—'

But I don't get any further.

'And don't forget to keep an eye on your author website,' she says in a lecturing voice. 'Readers will want to know more about you and post their thoughts after they have read your book.'

I can't remember the last time I checked my website, let alone did anything with it.

'Will do!' I say as confidently as I can.

'Oh and Searcy? Take no notice of the comments section. Death by a thousand cuts as they say.'

What?

Then she's gone.

Oh fucking hell, I think, tapping my phone quickly to access my website, my heart racing. And there it is: one comment by 'Anon-Mum' written in the white comments box just below the cover of my book.

Got an early copy of this book. Don't bother – it is totally shite.

My chest tightens and my stomach rolls over.
Brigitte.
The bitch.

* * *

Later that evening, I'm still mulling over the horrible comment on my website when my phone buzzes with a text from David.

Put your glad rags on – we're going on a DATE this weekend!

I reply, mystified:

Has someone hijacked your phone?

David doesn't do spontaneous. Well, not since we had Anna anyway and responds:

Very funny.

Where are we going then?

It's a surprise!

Suddenly I feel tingly. A night out is exactly what we need, especially after spending so much time apart. I ask him a few more questions about the big date but he is teasingly secretive about it. The only thing I can get out of him is that we're going to Manhattan.

I bet he hasn't thought through the logistics.

I text:

'So, what about a babysitter?'

'Can you check to see if Darcy's daughter can do it?'

Mia! Of course. I'll text Darcy and hope that Mia is free.

Then feeling all warm and fuzzy, I press the call button and fire more questions at him about date night, but he is disappointingly tight-lipped. So, I give up and fill him in on yesterday's drama: Luna scratching Anna, Beth coming to the rescue, Brigitte's dismissal of my book, and the nasty comment from AnonMum on my website.

'So, you think AnonMum is Brigitte because it contained the word "shite" and she's Irish?' he says.

'Yes!' I say. 'Brigitte is the only one who I've butted heads with since I got here. It has to be her.'

David blows out some air. 'Saoirse – I know it hurts, but it might not be Brigitte.'

'What do you mean?' I say.

'Well, technically it could be anyone,' he says.

'But there are only ten copies out in the world!'

'Right, but Jen sent a copy of your book to your mum, right?'

'Yes, but she's hardly going to be slagging it off, is she?' I say, tutting. 'She'd be more than happy to say it to my face.'

In fact, she has read it and texted me to say that she enjoyed it, but a little less swearing wouldn't hurt.

'No, your mum won't be posting nasty comments about your book online,' he says, with a little impatience in his voice. 'But knowing her, she will have passed your book to half of Ireland.'

Christ.

The man has a point.

30

I wake up on Friday tired but still buzzing from the second bottle of wine the night before. After David and I discussed Brigitte-gate, he called back after Anna went to bed and we ended up chatting on the phone for hours. Without Anna interrupting us every five seconds, I was able to truly listen to him, hear how work was going – about his colleagues, the people he has met. Everything. Well, everything apart from where we are going on Saturday night. He was still tight-lipped even though he had raided the hotel mini bar and was as tipsy as I was. We ended the call shortly after one of us suggested phone sex (I think that was me) and then laughing uncontrollably because we would both be hopeless at it.

Still, as I make Anna's breakfast, I feel a sense of anticipation I haven't experienced in a long time. I'm going on a date! I texted Darcy about Mia last night and she replied with a thumbs up emoji so now all I have to do is break the news to Anna.

As soon as I tell her, her little hand flies to the scratch on her face. It's not as livid as it was and a dark scab has started to form, which hopefully won't leave a scar. I watch her carefully, ready to say something if she starts picking at it, but she merely touches it and drops her hand again.

'Is Mia an influencer?' she says, in her most serious voice.

'Erm, I don't think so,' I say, curious at this line of questioning.

Her face falls. 'Is she a gamer?'

I search my fuzzy mind for any hint of Mia being a gamer and can't come up with anything, so I just say, 'No.'

Anna sighs and her shoulders drop. I have disappointed her. A light bulb goes off.

'BUT! She is amazing at doing hair,' I say, thumping the kitchen table as if I am pressing the buzzer on a quiz show panel.

Anna brightens. She loves getting her hair done – the more complicated the style the better.

Buoyed by the promise of a new hairstyle, Anna chatters happily all the way to school, exploring several options that she has apparently spotted on various YouTube channels. I swing her hand, feeling happy and determined to push all thoughts of Brigitte and that nasty book review to the back of my mind. David's right – I bet my mother has set off a chain reaction in Ireland by passing on my book to all and sundry. The chances are I will never know who it is – likely some jackass having a bit of 'craic'.

Anyway, David and I are going on a date! I might even treat myself to a new top from one of those posh boutique shops on the main street.

I give Anna a quick cuddle goodbye and immediately bump into Darcy, who thrusts a copy of the PTA schedule in my hand.

'Take a look at this when you have time,' she says. 'Oh, and Saoirse? I loved your book – it made me laugh and cry.'

'Thank you!' I breathe, feeling the goosebumps prickle all over my skin.

Then she tells me she has a lecture to give to some 'lazy ass' students and races off.

I tuck the sheaf of papers into my bag and turn towards the high street, my heart full.

Fletcher from the flower shop, who is busily arranging vases in the front window, waves a cheery hello as I pass by. The chances are I will never buy flowers from him again given the price of them, but it's lovely when someone you don't know very well makes the effort to greet you. Then the same happens when I catch the eye of Stan Beckerman from the stationery shop, who gives me a big wave and I wave back. Gosh, everyone is so friendly. I feel like I'm in an episode of *Gilmore Girls*.

When I reach the boutique, I pause to look at the window display, dithering as to whether I should go in or not. The truth is I am a hopeless shopper – I tend to shop out of necessity rather than enjoyment and I really have no idea what suits me or not at this stage in life. Still, the weather has a distinct chill in the air that tells me that autumn is very much on the way, so I should really be finding something to match the weather when I go out on my big date with David.

I'm still hemming and hawing when the door suddenly opens and Brigitte comes out laden with shopping bags. She is wearing a beige blouse with big, puffed sleeves and some high-waisted, pleated, grey cotton trousers. I'd look like a bag lady in that get-up but, of course, she looks fabulous. Still no sign of her baby bump.

I take a deep breath and attempt a mature *let's keep it civil* half-wave, but she looks straight through me. At least I think she does but I can't tell exactly because she is wearing big, black, square sunglasses, which I'm sure are the height of fashion but only make her look like a robot.

She drops her bags down with a sigh, blocking the entrance into the shop, and spends a couple of moments rooting in her bag. I look at her, mystified. Has she not even noticed that I'm waiting to get into the shop?

Just as I am making moves to get past her, she brings out her phone with a flourish. Then she roots in her bag again and tuts. The giant robot eyes swivel towards me.

'Saoirse – I've left my selfie stick at home and I need a photo of me with all these shopping bags outside this boutique. Can you take a picture?'

What? The nerve of her. After the way she behaved when she came to pick up Odette and Cosette, I can't believe she's asking me for a favour. But before I can say anything, she thrusts her phone into my hand, lifts up all her shopping bags to shoulder level and does a sort of *ta da!* pose.

'Make sure you stand well back so you can get in the name of the boutique,' she instructs.

I am so stunned that I actually do it. God, I'm a wuss. She examines the shot carefully and gives a small grunt of approval. No 'thank you', however. Then she starts typing furiously. Despite my outrage, I am curious to see what she's posting.

'What's all this for, then?' I say.

Her fingers pause and she tuts a bit, cross with the intrusion.

'Oh, this boutique is one of my sponsors? I'm basically saying that it is shopping heaven for N&P mums?'

I haven't the faintest idea what she's talking about. Clearly taking in my puzzled expression, she tuts impatiently and says, 'You know? New and pregnant mums?'

Well, there you go, N&P mums it is. Now I feel really down with the social media brigade. I look at the shop front doubtfully, taking in the autumn collection of neatly dressed mannequins adorned in slim, wool, pencil skirts and shiny, satin blouses. Presumably these clothes come in bigger sizes but personally my nerves wouldn't take wearing anything that expensive, not to mention impractical around a newborn. I wouldn't even do it now with a five-year-old. I say all this in a jokey way to Brigitte and she pushes her sunglasses up onto her hair and frowns. Her eyes are pure flint.

'Actually, mums deserve to treat themselves and look good?'

For their husbands, you mean? I add silently.

I take a deep breath to quell the rising anger before replying, 'I totally agree, and mums who have lots of money and a nanny can probably afford a shop like this, but most people can't.'

She wrinkles her nose.

'Well, my followers don't want to see me covered in kiddie crap, hanging around in a tracksuit, do they?' she says, her Dublin accent more apparent now she is riled.

'Maybe they do!' I say, with a slight shriek to my voice.

I am dangerously aware of climbing too high on this horse, but I can't seem to stop myself. 'Maybe some of your followers would like you to show them a bit of authenticity rather than trying to sell them an impossible fantasy.'

She takes a step towards me, her mouth in a grim line.

'Look, Saoirse –my husband and I are a brand? We're a business, OK? It's our mission to sell dreams of the perfect family life? One false move and we lose our sponsors and then the whole enterprise collapses. It's bad enough that...'

Then she stops abruptly and her eyes suddenly water.

'I have to go,' she says shakily.

She stalks off, her bags swishing violently against her perfectly toned legs.

I stand there open-mouthed, stunned at this surprising display of emotion. Clearly all is not well in her perfect world, which makes it even more frustrating that she's blasting 'everything is rosy in the garden' posts over social media.

Feeling a bit deflated after the confrontation, I am in no mood for shopping, so I decide to head home. Just as I'm approaching the main house, I catch sight of Beth's tiny figure hauling some rubbish bags towards some giant bins in the front of the house. I call out to her and give her a wave.

'Hi,' she mutters, her mouth clenched as if the word itself is torture.

Then she turns on her heel and marches straight back into the house. All right, that's the last time I attempt to be friendly.

I let myself into the pool house and sit down on the couch to check my text messages. My heart skips a beat: Harriet again.

Ignore this one too.

Shit. I log into my website and there it is – another horrible comment staring at me in black and white.

I would on my HOLE recommend this book.

Jesus Christ. This can't be a coincidence. It's got to be Brigitte – I've had a go at her and she's upset. This is her revenge.

But before I jump to conclusions, I should really talk to my mother first. I send a text asking her to call me when she's free and spend the next few minutes trying to focus on the PTA material that Darcy handed me. My role as writing ambassador is more comprehensive than I thought – it kicks off next week with an author visit to the school to explain to the fifth grade the difference between an author and a ghostwriter; then I'm to read with different year groups every week and edit all the PTA news and events on the Westmont Elementary website. I chew nervously on the edge of my thumbnail – mostly I am worried about messing up. Still, though, after so many months of doing very little in the way of work, it feels good to be useful again.

By the time I finish checking out the Westmont Elementary

website – Nina's not wrong; her grammar could do with a bit of a polish – it's close to 11 a.m. My phone rings.

'Hi, Mum,' I say.

'Is Anna OK?' she says instantly.

'Erm yes,' I say, confused. 'Why?'

'Well, I got your text just there and I had a bad feeling that something happened to Anna.'

I flop back against the couch. Trust my mother to panic when there is absolutely no reason to.

'Anna's fine,' I say. 'Well, apart from the cat scratch on her cheek.'

I regret the words as soon as they fly out of my mouth.

'WHAT?' she screeches. 'Mother of God. Did you get her a tetanus?'

'No!' I say. 'It turns out Beth, who lives in the main house, is a doctor so she took a look and said it wasn't a serious scratch. It's healing already.'

She huffs for a bit.

'Well, I should hope so,' she says eventually. 'That cat should be on a lead. I'd say this Beth was delighted that you didn't sue her for gross negligence – they're all into that over there.'

'*Anyway,*' I say, trying to move the conversation forward. 'I have something to ask you.'

'Go on.'

I take a deep breath. 'Did you pass my book on to anyone else after you read it?'

'I did!' she says, with conviction. 'I gave it to Miguel to read.'

Oh bloody hell. I have never imagined a man reading my book, let alone my mother's special friend who I have yet to meet.

'And then when he finished it, I passed it on to Jen's mother, who I met on the beach shortly afterwards. Do you know she's got very scrawny? Probably all the stress of Jen's wedding next year. I'd say now that she's worried sick Liam won't turn up at the altar after the stunt he pulled last year. Mind you, it's awful pressure being the mother of the bride too—'

I prop up my head with one hand and sigh. It feels very weird thinking that my best friend's mum, who has known me since primary school, has my book. Still, so far, it cements my case against Brigitte.

'Right – so it's just Miguel and Jen's mum,' I say, cutting her off.

'Ah no, Saoirse!' She tuts, annoyed that I have interrupted her. 'Jen's mum passed it on to Sheila from the newsagent, and then she gave it to Moira who does the readings at Mass. Did I tell you Moira's daughter is having another baby? That'll be number six now if you can credit it.'

I can't help letting out a small groan.

'Anyway, people keep approaching me to tell me how much they like it,' she says with a hint of pride in her voice. 'It's going around like wildfire, Saoirse. I'm a local celebrity!'

I shake my head slowly. Despite my investigations, I am no further along in finding the culprit. I just need to let it go. Then she asks after David, so I tell her that David will be home this evening and we're off on a night out tomorrow night.

'And who will be looking after my beautiful grandchild?' she says.

'A local teenager. Her name is Mia.'

Silence.

'Well, I hope she's not going to be bringing her boyfriend with her "to make out" or "go to second base" or whatever they do in some of those American films.'

Christ.

'Anyway, Saoirse, I can't be spending all day chatting about teenagers. Miguel will be here soon. We're off for a walk.'

'Well, I hope he keeps his hands to himself!' I say lightly.

'Honest to God, Saoirse. You're as *juvenile!*' she says.

Then she hangs up.

I lie back on my bed and think for a moment. Now that I know my book is being passed around Ireland, I really have no evidence at all that Brigitte is the culprit. I just need to leave it all behind and toughen up.

My phone pings in my hand, breaking me out of my reverie. I lift it up and immediately smile. It's a blurry photo of the Eiffel Tower sent to the WhatsApp Group I share with Jen and Bea that looks as though it has been taken through a window. The caption says:

Paris baby!

My stomach turns over. Not just because I'm jealous that Jen is in Paris (I am, obviously) but because I miss her. Much as I've enjoyed meeting Darcy and all the other PTA mums, there is really nothing like your friends from home. Before I can think of a response, a text from Dee pops up.

Fuck off, Jen. I'm here bra-less because Niamh has chucked a bowl of milk over me and I haven't had time to do the laundry. You'd think my lazy arse of a husband would do it, but no. He's too busy listening to a vitally important podcast. Lay down rules with Liam BEFORE you get married and laminate them. Don't let him take the piss!

The phone rings in my hand.

It's Jen.

'What the fuck is wrong with Dee? I'm fed up with her warnings about Liam. Jesus – I've lived with him for years! We've already had the rows about the washing-up, whose turn it is to do the shopping, and screamed at each other over mismatched socks. I could seriously do without her input.'

'I know,' I say quietly. 'But she's not thinking straight. She's absolutely knackered. I can't imagine how hard it must be to cope with two young kids.'

Jen is quiet for a moment.

'OK, I'll stop whinging about her,' she says, blowing out some air. 'How are you doing over there?'

I tell her about the negative comments on my author website, my confrontation with Brigitte and how I suspect she is the culprit.

'But then, of course, my mother tells me my book is doing the rounds in Dublin, so it could be anyone,' I finish.

'Hang on a second,' Jen says. 'What's Brigitte's last name?'

'Williams.'

'Jesus – you've been scrapping with Brigitte Williams?'

Then she roars laughing.

I am speechless for a moment.

'What? Do you know her?' I say when I recover.

'Half of feckin' Ireland knows her, Saoirse,' she says, giggling. 'She's known as the Irish Kardashian. And by the way, she's plain old Brigid Murphy.'

I bloody knew it.

According to Jen, Brigid comes from quite a poor background, dragged herself up, and became an air hostess with an exclusive airline. She met her husband, Joe Williams, seven years ago when she was working in first class and they have been together ever since.

'The tabloids are always pitching her story as rags to riches,' Jen says. 'Like *Pretty Woman* – being swept off her feet by a handsome prince, which is bullshit obviously as she had a decent job, could clearly fend for herself, and it's not like she grew up in some sort of prostitute or drug den. But the tabloids love to make out that she's been rescued from the type of flats that have horses going up and down in the lifts. As far as I know, she lived in a fairly working-class area and her father was a builder who had a gambling problem and gambled away his clients' money. He bankrupted his business and brought shame on the whole family by ending up in prison.'

Wow. Seeing her now, it's hard to imagine Brigitte as being 'plain old Brigid' from Dublin.

'So basically, she's hooked up with a wealthy actor, escaped Ireland, and totally reinvented herself,' I say.

'Precisely. And now she and Joe are the poster couple for the perfect marriage and family,' Jen says, making gagging noises, 'which is fine if you're into that "keeping your man happy" shite spouted by those women's magazines we grew up with in the nineties.'

God, I remember those magazines well – the ones with 'How to know what your man is *really* feeling', and 'Happy sex life – happy man' and 'Why your man will never cheat on you again' plastered in big colourful letters across the front page. All of them putting the fear of God into us impressionable teenagers that we had to behave in a certain way to attract and keep a boyfriend.

'Of course, Liam quotes Brigitte all the time just to wind me up,' Jen continues. 'Like he'll come home from work and I'm lying on the sofa looking like a bag of shite, and he'll say something like, "You know Brigitte says that we men are very visual, so you need to glam yourself up if you want to hang on to me."'

I laugh. I may not have totally forgiven Liam for letting Jen down last year, but he certainly knows how to get a rise out of her.

'So, you don't think it's Brigitte posting the comments on my website?' I say.

'I think you're too small fry for her,' Jen replies. 'She wouldn't waste her time on you.'

She probably has a point. Who the hell am I? If she wasn't a school mum whose daughters happened to be friendly with Anna, I wouldn't be on her radar.

We spend a few more minutes chatting about her wedding plans – 'Honestly, Saoirse, my mum is having heart failure about being mother of the bride; she's gone on a no-carbs diet to trim down and she's driving me mental!' – before we say goodbye.

Just as I'm getting off the bed, my phone pings. It's David.

I can't wait to run my tongue over your firm nipples on date night tomorrow.

Eeeew.

I text him back quickly:

Text sex also banned.

Plus vomit emoji.

He sends back another one with a laughing emoji.

Thought you'd like that one!

I laugh but more out of relief. Thank Christ we're not exploring sex texting. It'll be a miracle if sex happens at all after a night of rich food and wine...

31

I wake up on Saturday morning to the sound of David having a chat with Anna just outside the bedroom door. David got in late last night so we haven't seen much of each other yet, but we can always make up for that later, because tonight is date night!

Yawning lazily, I reach for my phone on the bedside table and text Jen and Dee about my big date in Manhattan with my LAT husband. Then I head to the bathroom to take a long, indulgent shower, taking full advantage of the fact that I am no longer the focus of Anna's attention. As it's a special occasion, I decide to wash my hair with the 'good' shampoo before slathering myself with some body moisturising cream I stole from the fancy hotel I stayed in with Jen and Bea.

Then I wrap my wet hair in a fresh towel, turban-style, clothe myself in a robe, and pad back towards the bedside table, intending to dig my hairdryer out from the drawer. But the flashing of my phone stops me in my tracks.

The first text is from Jen:

Way haay! Date night! Go on ya good thing!

I let out a giggle. Then I stop when I see the one from Dee:

Ah Jaysus, rub it in why don't ya. It's bad enough me stinking of baby shite without you banging on about your glam life!

She accompanies her message with a laughing emoji but even so, I can tell she's not happy. On impulse, I send her another text.

Come over then, woman, and we'll do the glam thing together!

But she sends the usual text back about not wanting to leave the kids with their incompetent dad. I sigh. I know she's going through a hard time but as Jen said, it's almost like she doesn't want anyone else to have fun either.

Anyway, I think, reaching for my hairdryer. *Nothing is going to bring me down today.*

* * *

'So, I think that's everything,' I say to Mia when she arrives on the dot of 6 p.m., having just filled her in on Anna's bedtime routine (non-existent when a babysitter is over) and her love of all things hair-related.

'OK, sounds good!' Mia says, flicking her long, shiny, black hair and flashing me a radiant smile. 'Come on, Anna,' she says, offering her hand. 'Let's go to your room and try out some hairstyles.'

Anna, who has been glued to Mia since she arrived, happily places her hand in hers and off the pair of them go without so much as a backward glance.

'Let's leg it in case Anna changes her mind!' David whispers, his body already halfway out the front door.

I grab my bag and follow him quickly. I doubt if Anna will even notice we're gone but once we're both outside on the street, we glance at each and smile, simultaneously breathing a sigh of relief.

'Come on, then,' he says, taking my hand. 'Let's paint this Big Apple red.'

I laugh and give his hand a squeeze. I can't remember the last time we held hands as a couple. We walk quickly to the train station, me pestering him to spill the beans about the surprise he has planned for tonight and him being firmly tight-lipped.

The train rumbles into the station and we find a seat easily, chatting all the way to Grand Central. As I'm listening to him telling a funny story about a work colleague, I am reminded with a jolt how much I love him. The laughter lines at the corners of his eyes, the way his grey-streaked hair bobs a little when he's enthusiastic about something, how his dark brown eyes light up in amusement. He may have a few grey shadows under his eyes from yesterday's journey, and he is a little heavier around the middle (thanks to all those work lunches and hotel meals) but there's no doubt he's aging well. The story comes to an end, and I laugh, lean over and give him a kiss.

He kisses me back and to my absolute surprise slips in the tongue.

'Bloody hell!' I say, retreating. I can feel my face reddening. 'We're on public transport!'

'Well, I just felt like giving my gorgeous wife a proper kiss for a change,' he says playfully.

By the time the train chugs slowly into Grand Central, we're in the kind of mood where we're both laughing at absolutely nothing. And we haven't even had a drink yet.

My mood plummets as soon as we hit the crowds in the station. Westmont is so quiet that I'd forgotten how noisy and intimidating large numbers of people could be when they're rushing to get to their destination.

'You OK?' David says into my ear, clutching my hand tightly.

I nod and take a few deep breaths, focusing on the brightly lit exit ahead. My heart starts to slow as soon as we're outside in the cold night air. David holds out an arm and a yellow taxi slides up alongside us. He opens the door and I slowly climb in the back.

Then he hands a slip of paper to the taxi driver before settling beside me.

'Couldn't risk you overhearing where I'm taking you!' he says, grinning.

Damn it.

'I mean technically we could have walked but I didn't want to start off the date with you feeling anxious.'

I shoot him a grateful smile. My heart rate has just about slowed to normal and I'm relieved we don't have to negotiate the fast-walking commuters to get to our destination – wherever that may be.

Less than ten minutes later, the driver comes to a halt. David hands him a decent tip and he drives off happy.

I raise my hands at David, who has a mischievous look on his face, and say, 'Well?'

'Look up!' he says, waving his hand towards the buildings lining the sidewalk.

I look up and into view comes the majestic form of the Empire State Building.

Hang on a second...

'Yep, you're finally going up the Empire State Building,' David says, grinning. 'Surprise!'

My eyes water. I can't believe he's remembered. Then he produces a couple of tickets from the inside pocket of his jacket and hands me one. It says VIP on it.

'Courtesy of The Firm,' he says with a wink.

They may be getting their pound of flesh by sending my

husband off on long business trips, but I can't deny the perks are unreal.

To my mind, there is nothing better than an opportunity to skip a queue and this queue is a real doozy, snaking all the way down the street: a forty-five-minute wait at least. It's one of the reasons why I never took Anna. There's no way she would tolerate standing still for that long.

'Shall we?' he says, crooking his arm.

'We shall!' I laugh, looping my arm through his.

A few short minutes later and we're past the hordes and in the glass elevator, my head light with the speedy upward momentum. The doors glide open on the eighty-sixth floor and we step out onto the observation deck, making our way through all the other visitors towards the huge windows to gaze in awe at the view in front of us. It's hard to take in the sheer scale of the Manhattan skyline on the ground – but up here it is visible in all its glory, the inky night sky lit up by thousands of twinkling lights shining brightly from row after row of buildings.

'It looks so peaceful from up here,' I breathe.

'I know,' David says, pressing his head against the glass. 'It's a stunning view.'

'Thank you for bringing me,' I say, taking his hand. 'I've always loved Manhattan and I really value this reminder after everything that happened when we lived here.'

We stay there for a bit longer and then David leans back, glances at his watch and says, 'Right! Time for the next surprise.'

I am full of questions on the walk back to the elevator and he ignores every single one of them.

'But I will tell you one thing,' he says, as we step out of the elevator into the lobby. 'I toyed with continuing the whole tourist thing by taking you on a horse and cart trip around Central Park but—'

'—my bladder wouldn't have been able to cope with it,' I finish for him.

That jolting movement would have me off that cart and peeing in the bushes in a nanosecond. *Thank you, childbirth.*

'Well exactly,' he says. 'So, instead I'm taking you somewhere where we can eat in private, and which has a toilet less than three metres from the table.'

'Sounds perfect!' I say happily.

Honestly, the man has thought of everything.

Not long after, we're whizzing our way in a taxi. This time David has told me where we're going: the East Village, but he knows he's on safe ground because out of the few times I've been to New York, I have never explored this side of Manhattan. The taxi turns in to a side street and pulls up outside a brightly lit diner, and to be honest, I'm a little disappointed. Don't get me wrong – I love a diner and would munch on burgers and hot dogs all day long, but I guess I would have preferred something a little more romantic for the first real date we've had in months.

But still, as he's gone to so much effort I jump out of the taxi, plaster a grin on my face and say, 'This looks great!'

David bursts out laughing as he pays the taxi driver.

'You think I'm taking you to a diner for a romantic date?' he says, spluttering as he gets out of the car to join me. 'How could you think so little of me!'

I laugh too, but more out of relief than anything else. Still, I am a bit puzzled about where he's taking me. Apart from the diner, the street looks pretty much abandoned – shuttered buildings, broken paving stones, and graffiti everywhere. But it's hard to feel apprehensive with David's warm hand nestling in mine and I follow his lead with confidence. It occurs to me for the first time in ages that there's nobody I trust more. It's easy to lose sight of that when we're apart for days or weeks at a time. If there's one thing that this LAT situation has taught me, it's how important it is to have these moments.

Although I would be lying if I said that my trust in him didn't waver just a little bit when he leads me around the back of the diner through some giant bins. It looks like the perfect location to shoot a crime scene for a detective show. Just as I'm about to ask him if there's any chance we might have the wrong place, he exclaims, 'Ah, there it is!'

There's what? I think, trying desperately to focus in the darkness.

He tugs my hand and we walk quickly now towards a black vintage phone hanging off the wall. Before I can say anything, he picks up the receiver and holds it to his ear.

'It's David. I have a booking for 8 p.m.,' he says confidently.

He nods once and replaces the handset.

'David – what is this place?' I say, mystified.

'You'll see!' he says, clapping his hands.

I can't help but smile back. This is the impulsive side of David that I haven't seen since we moved here – it was one of the reasons I fell for him all those years ago. Suddenly there is a loud rattle and part of the wall starts to move, revealing a woman in her twenties, with short cropped blonde hair, dressed in skinny black jeans and a black T-shirt that says *Hidden Dining Genie*.

'Welcome to Hidden Dining Genie!' she says with a big smile. 'I'm Megan. Follow me.'

I shake my head at David. What is going on?

We follow her down a flight of narrow stone steps and come out into a tiny, dimly lit room. There is a small bar on the right-hand side and a single table laid beautifully with a sparkling white table-cloth, crystal wine glasses and expensive-looking silverware.

I look around rapidly and spot the sign for the toilets at the back of the room. We are the only people here. No queues. This is one of the happiest days of my life.

'Please have a seat,' Megan says, waving her hand towards the table. 'I'll be back soon with your drinks.'

Then she walks off behind the bar.

David opens his mouth but much as I'm dying to hear what he has to say, my bladder takes priority.

'Hold that thought!' I say, making a beeline for the toilets.

When I get back to the table, David greets me with a smug smile on his face.

'Spill!' I say in my most demanding voice, settling myself into the seat.

He bursts out laughing.

'OK, I'll tell you now. This is a place that recreates the best meals you've had in the past. You just call up a couple of months in advance, give them a menu, and then they will recreate it as best they can. They even let you taste-test it before they serve it. That was the reason I was home so late last night. I had to race from the airport to test the meal before tonight.'

My mouth drops open. I can't believe he has gone to this much effort.

'So what are we...?'

But Megan is back with a bottle of wine and we wait while she pours the delicious, ruby-coloured liquid into the crystal-cut wine glasses and rests the bottle on the table. Then she disappears again.

'Cheers,' David says, his eyes twinkling in the flickering candle-light as he raises his glass towards mine.

'Cheers!' I echo as we clink glasses.

Then we both take a sip and the wine is perfect – light and silky smooth.

'Take a look at the label on the bottle,' he says, grinning.

I frown a little. I never check a wine bottle label. The fact that it has alcohol in it is more than enough for me. But I decide to humour him, so I squint at the label, trying to focus on the writing in the dim candlelight. Then I let out a little squeal.

'Oh my goodness!' I say, covering my mouth.

David's eyes sparkle.

The label says *David and Saoirse's wedding wine.*

'This is a recreation of our wedding meal?'

David bursts out laughing.

'No way!' he says. 'The only good thing about our wedding meal was the wine, which is why I've chosen it for tonight.'

I can't pretend I'm not relieved. My mother is still going on about how tough the lamb was at our wedding dinner.

Megan appears again with a large platter and I peer at it closely before letting out a proper scream. It's tapas – exactly the same ones we ordered during our very first date together in a tiny Spanish restaurant in Borough Market in London. I take in the gorgeous display of little parcels of chorizo and calamari, interlaced with prosciutto and Iberico ham, accompanied by a bowl of glistening olives and a pile of scrumptious-looking crusty bread.

'Oh my god, this is amazing!' I say, leaning over the table to give him a kiss.

He grins at me in return.

'Honestly, David, I can't believe you have done all this,' I say, my eyes starting to water again. 'You're up to your eyes in work; you're travelling all the time. How the hell did you have time?'

David's eyes grow soft and he reaches across to take my hand.

'Listen, Saoirse – it's been mad since we got to New York. We've barely done anything together. This year was supposed to be an adventure for the two of us, but it hasn't worked out that way. It looks like going forward I'll still be travelling loads, but I miss you and all this time apart has just reminded me how important it is to spend quality time together – starting tonight.'

My eyes fill up. We have spoken about how much we miss each other, and I have to admit I'm relieved he's finding it as hard as I am.

'I also want to talk about how we can spend more time together as a family,' he adds. 'So, I've booked us into a hotel in Washington, D.C. for October half-term. We're going to rent a car and drive there.'

I let out a screech that causes Megan's mega-watt smile to slip just a little, but I don't care.

'David, I don't know what to say.' I blink away the tears.

'Saoirse, I love you and I miss you and Anna, and I know it's horrible being apart for this length of time, but we can and will make it work.'

And for the first time since we moved to New York, I know he's right. LAT couple or not, we will get through this together.

We spend the rest of the delicious meal excitedly chatting about D.C. and other possible weekend road trips we could take. By the time we finish every delectable bite plus a second bottle of wine, we are both stuffed and pleasantly tipsy. We struggle with the giant, stunning display of gelato but manage to make some headway before we admit defeat.

'So, how are you taking me home?' I say to David teasingly as we climb slowly up the stairs towards that mysterious door. 'Helicopter? Limousine? Private jet?'

'Just plain old taxi, I'm afraid.' David smiles.

'Fine with me!' I say, sliding my hand into his.

32

David flew out to South Carolina last night and my chest hurts from missing him. But that's not the only thing that hurts. My stomach could also do with a rest after a weekend of sheer decadence. After our magical evening out, David rose early on Sunday morning and picked up some scrumptious bagels from the Westmont bakery. Then he cooked eggs benedict for lunch, and a fabulously creamy pasta dish for dinner. Anna was also in flying form thanks to the extraordinarily patient Mia and her magical hairdressing skills. Apparently, they experimented with quite a few styles before Anna settled on a bog-standard French plait, which she insisted on sleeping in so she would have curls the next day. She spent most of Sunday swishing her curls from side to side, stopping at every opportunity to check herself out in the mirror in the bathroom.

I would go so far to say it was the perfect weekend – apart from one thing. Another negative comment on my website. David had gone into my site to delete all of them (I'd had no idea you could do that as I have zero technical prowess) and discovered another negative one-liner.

Maybe if this author could string a sentence together, this might be a decent read but…

'Fuck whoever it is,' David said. 'Pure jealousy.'

Today, I need to get myself together because I'm giving my first writing talk to the fifth-grade pupils at school. While Anna ponders the pros and cons of swapping me for Mia (it turns out there are no cons) on the way to school, I try to settle the nerves in my stomach. I've never addressed a classroom of ten-year-olds before. I just hope I can hold their attention.

Anna waves me away distractedly as we approach the school entrance, her gaze on a little boy with blonde hair and brown eyes who could pass for Harry's brother. He spots her too and races over to give her a hug. I hope this is the beginning of a blossoming friendship – preferably one that takes Anna's mind off Brigitte's daughters.

As I turn away, I spot Darcy coming towards me with a big smile on her face. I say a quick goodbye to Anna and take a few steps towards Darcy. I am keen to thank her once again for letting us borrow Mia on Saturday night, but I am completely cut off by Brigitte, who barges straight into me.

Bags of shopping fly everywhere.

'Oh for god's sake?' she spits out, surveying the contents on the ground. I notice that it's mostly make-up, still in boxes – gifts from more sponsors probably. Any money there'll be a post on Instagram soon with tips such as 'how to apply make-up to make you more sexy for your man'.

Darcy rushes forward, crouches down and immediately starts to gather everything up off the ground and back into the bags. She's so nice. She probably doesn't even know Brigitte – desperate as I am, I have so far restrained myself from slagging her off to Darcy, although I bet that even if she did know her and hated her, she'd still get down on her hands and knees to help. She's just one of life's decent people. Now, of course, I feel obliged to do the same. I'm just about to bend down to help when Brigitte does something to make me spring back up to attention.

'Get your hands off my stuff,' she spits out.

Holy God.

I look at her in horror but her hard stare is firmly fixed on Darcy's crouched figure.

How could she be so rude?

Darcy sighs heavily as she straightens up and hands her the neatly packed bags. Brigitte snatches them from her and strides away, her nose firmly in the air.

'What the hell just happened?' I say to Darcy.

She gives me a searching look and then shakes her head a little.

'I guess she's just having a bad day,' she says, shrugging her shoulders and attempting a smile.

Bullshit.

'Hey! Aren't you giving a talk to the fifth graders today?'

Crap. With everything that's just happened, I have completely forgotten about my first job as writing ambassador. I tell Darcy I'll check in with her later and give her a quick wave. Then I rush through the gate for the senior part of the school and follow the signs towards the fifth-grade classroom. The kids have clearly been well briefed by their teacher, Mr Adamos, because they greet me in unison the second I walk through the door. Hot Mr Adamos introduces me to the class and then takes his toned body and sexy, flashing black eyes to the back of the classroom, telling me to 'take the floor'. Feeling beyond self-conscious, I take a deep breath and dig into my bag and take out two books: one I have ghosted, and my own book.

'Does anybody know what a ghostwriter is?' I say, in the most animated voice I can muster.

Twenty pairs of wide eyes stare back at me for long moments until a boy with Justin Bieber hair and rosy cheeks raises a tentative hand.

'Do ghostwriters write books about ghosts?'

That's a fair question and one I have never considered before. I praise him for asking such a great question and he beams. My heart lifts – look at me! Educating young minds.

That is until I fill the class in on the much less exciting truth and notice many pairs of eyes glaze over. In a drastic effort to keep their attention, I decide to split them in twos for a bit of role-play: one of them playing the part as the ghostwriter, interviewing the other, who is playing the client.

Mr Adamos joins me for this part and we both assist the pairs if they get stuck. Mind you, they don't need much prompting given that most of the 'clients' have chosen to be either gamers or influencers and are more than happy to be interviewed about their avatars, private servers and fictional YouTube channels.

To my surprise the time goes quickly and I can't help but feel a sense of pleasure when each pair reads out their interviews to the whole class, uplifted by the smiles of pride on their faces as they receive thunderous applause from their classmates when they finish.

When it's time go, Mr Adamos walks me to the door and suggests that I come back the following week to give the kids some feedback on their writing and I surprise myself by replying with an enthusiastic yes. I never thought it would be this fun being in a classroom.

As I walk home through the crisp, cold sunshine, admiring the vibrant autumn colours on the trees lining the perfectly manicured streets, I feel a sense of contentment. In Darcy, I have found 'the one' friend at school; I'm living in a beautiful, quiet area surrounded by friendly people who will do anything to help their community and I'm keeping busy by volunteering with the school and helping out with the PTA. I'm doing things I never would have done back in London and I'm really enjoying it. And even though David and I aren't together full-time, we have plenty to look forward to. I still miss my mum and my friends in Ireland, not to mention Bonnie, Bea and even Rose, but I am determined to make the most of the time we have left.

* * *

I am in such a good mood when I reach our street that I give Beth a little wave when I see the shutters flicker at the top of the house. She probably won't even notice but I'm glad I did it all the same. Much to Fletcher's delight, I have taken over the weekly flower delivery, too, but I don't knock on Beth's door any more; I just leave the box on the doorstep. So, she wants a quiet life – who can blame her?

Bonnie would be proud of me with my newly discovered empathy towards my fellow human beings. Then I remember how Brigitte behaved towards Darcy. That rude, pretentious, fake bitch.

Maybe I haven't come that far after all.

I let myself back into the pool house, put on a wash, tidy up the bedrooms and, when I'm finished, I reward myself by calling Bea.

As usual, she answers on the first ring.

'Saoirse, fucking hell, I was just thinking about you,' she says.

Harry shouts something in the background.

'Harry, if you don't like Mummy swearing, you can go into another room,' she says sternly.

I giggle, loving the way she is not remotely apologetic for swearing in front of Harry.

'Honestly, he's become so evangelical lately,' she says exasperatedly. 'Keeps ratting out all the other kids in school for using the "f" word. Anyway, he's gone off in a huff, so I'm all yours,' she says.

I work out the time over there. Almost 4 p.m. Bea usually goes into the office on a Monday.

'Are you working from home today?'

'Technically yes, but really I'm here because Harry had a school workshop this morning that he desperately wanted me to attend.'

'What workshop was it?'

'Papier mâché.'

Christ.

There is nothing like the messiness of creating something out of newspaper and glue, surrounded by hyper kids to put a real dampener on the day. Frankly, I'm shocked that Bea agreed to it – normally this is the kind of thing she would have sent her nanny, Maria, along to.

'Maria's off sick today,' she adds, as if reading my mind.

'How was it?' I say.

'As dreadful as you might imagine,' she says, yawning. 'Tania going around telling everyone how gifted Heath is and how she's mortified she hadn't spotted it earlier. And how it actually makes her think her younger kids could be gifted, too, as they are behaving exactly the same ways as Heath did at that age, etc.'

Ugh.

Still, I remind myself, I'm not there, I'm here and I've had a surprisingly enjoyable school experience of my own, which I share with her.

She whistles slowly when I finish.

'Saoirse – you've changed,' she says in a teasing voice. 'I never thought I'd see the day that you would volunteer for anything PTA-related, let alone enjoy it!'

'I know!' I say vehemently because I can hardly believe it

myself. 'But the PTA is different over here. Everybody is so kind and supportive – not like the Organics.'

'Aha!' Bea says. 'Well, in that case I'll spread the word that you're going to initiate a take-over when you get back from New York. That'll definitely put the shits up Tania Henderson and her Lycra-clad minions.'

'Don't you dare!' I say, laughing.

Then Bea asks about David and I fill her in on our fabulous weekend together, starting off with the magical Hidden Dining Genie night, and she 'ooohs' and 'aws' in all the right places and says how romantic it must have been.

Speaking of romance...

'What about you and Tom?' I say. 'Did you get up to anything romantic?'

She blows out some air, says nothing, and does the same thing again.

'Listen, Saoirse...' she says, her voice wavering a little.

My chest tightens. Oh god, what's wrong? Have they broken up? Poor Bea.

'Tom's asked me to move in with him.'

What?

I almost drop the phone. I did not see this coming.

'Oh, that's great news!' I say, relieved. 'I thought you were going to tell me you'd split up!'

'I haven't agreed to it yet. I told him I'd think about it.'

Fair enough. I can understand her hesitation. They may have worked together for years but they haven't been together that long and, of course, it will be a big change for Harry...

'Saoirse, Tom lives in southeast London.'

My stomach flips.

Surely... she can't be...

'It's a beautiful house – recently inherited from his grandmother. My place is obviously tiny and we wouldn't be able to afford anything bigger around here.'

I open my mouth and close it again.

'Also, his house is close enough to good schools and it wouldn't be much more of a commute for Maria, so...'

I find my voice.

'So, hang on a second – you'll be moving to the other side of London and switching schools for Harry?' I say, trying to keep the tremble out of my voice.

'Erm, well yes, but I haven't really made any decisions yet. To be honest, I really wanted to talk to you about it first,' she says softly.

My stomach rolls over.

'Do you love Tom?' I say, in a small voice, hardly wanting to hear the answer because if she says 'yes' I will lose her forever.

'I do,' she says.

My eyes start to water.

'Listen, Saoirse – we will still see each other even if I do move, right? I'm not letting you go that easily! Besides, you seem to be a lot happier over there now. You might never come home!'

Suddenly I feel furious. How dare she move across the other side of London and put Anna's best friend in another school? Just because I feel more settled here doesn't mean I'm not counting down the days until I'm back in her house getting pissed and swapping stories about parenting fails, relationships and everything else life throws at us. How could she do this to me?

But of course, I don't say that because I'd sound like a needy, emotional nutcase, so I take a deep breath and do something far worse instead.

'You said you wanted to talk to me about it before you made up your mind,' I say, more sharply than I intended.

'Yes, I would value your opinion,' she responds, her voice coldly formal.

I can sense the tension through the phone lines, but I forge ahead anyway.

'The truth is I'm not sure it's a great idea.'

'Oh,' Bea says.

She sounds disappointed but I don't care. It's for her own good. And mine.

'I just think it's a bit soon to be moving in together,' I continue. 'You haven't been a couple that long. You don't want to rush into something and then regret it.'

Then I drive home the final nail in the coffin.

'It wouldn't be fair on Harry.'

Silence.

'You're probably right,' she says, after a long moment. 'I don't want to rush into anything, and it would be a lot of change for Harry, even if he does love Tom.'

My stomach collapses in relief – she's not moving yet. I have persuaded her to stay in Woodvale – for now.

I should feel relieved, but I don't.

I just feel like the worst friend anyone could ever have.

Then Harry runs in shouting for a bag of crisps, so we hurriedly say our goodbyes. I slowly place my phone down on the kitchen table and burst into tears.

33

I keep myself as busy as possible over the next few weeks to take my mind off Bea and her potential move to the other side of London. Our weekend to D.C. at the end of October half-term was certainly the diversion I needed. As predicted, Anna couldn't have given a shite about the White House, or the Washington Monument or any of the museums for that matter, but she did have fun on a carousel that she could have gone on anywhere in the world.

I'm so ashamed of what I've said to Bea I don't even tell David, reasoning that he'll only say things like, 'It's southeast London, Saoirse – not the ends of the earth!' and I can't bear it because although I know he'd be right, I can't visualise Woodvale without my best friend down the road.

So, I've been distracting myself by being at the school every single week helping the kids with their reading and writing and encouraging them to read their essays aloud to the class. I have also been spending a lot more time with the PTA members swapping new fundraising ideas for Thanksgiving over drinks at Westmont Tavern.

Maybe they're not my friends for life; their lives are so insanely busy that there isn't really time to have meaningful conversations, but they're well-meaning and kind. And more to the point, they have been hugely complimentary about my book and passed it on to their friends to read. It's a similar situation with some of the mums I've met from Anna's class – always smiley and willing to lend a hand but they have busy lives, too, and there's not much room for building forever friendships.

Out of all the PTA mums, Darcy is the one I have spent the most time with, whiling away pleasant hours sipping coffee at her enormous, walnut dining table under the huge dark wooden beams of her bright, rustic kitchen, the piles of scattered football kits, sports bags and other detritus in each corner hinting at the chaos wrought by a family of seven.

Her husband, Bill, quietly spoken, pleasantly plump, wanders in and out with a permanently puzzled expression on his face as if trying to figure how he ended up here in the first place. Darcy reckons he is still stunned from the arrival of the triplets eight years ago.

Despite our growing friendship, it's not the sort where we tell each other everything and it's refreshing to start from a point where our life experiences coincide. However, I do tell her about the Organics and how militant they are in the PTA, and she is gratifyingly appalled. I also told her about exiting the class WhatsApp group (I didn't explain why – Darcy seems too sweet to be able to handle blowjob-gate) because of all the judgement and she told me she is fundamentally against WhatsApp groups. This is why she insists on Westmont Tavern gatherings.

One afternoon, she shared one of her own experiences of being judged, which really made me think. Last year, she was offered an opportunity to guest lecture at a university in China for six months. Bill had done same thing the previous year and loved the experience. Although she was worried about leaving the kids for that long, Bill actively encouraged her to go. Mia and Mason were already pretty independent, and they would hire a nanny for the triplets. When she told friends and family about the trip, everyone was really supportive apart from one family member who was openly critical about her decision to leave her family.

'Do you know the thing that killed me the most?' Darcy said, shaking her head slowly. 'It was the double standards. Bill had made the same trip and not one person said anything to him about "abandoning" his family.'

She was right. Mums get all the flack. In fact, her story reminded me of all the crap Brigitte peddles online about standing by your man, but before I had a chance to raise it, Mia's twin, Mason, wearing the type of messy mohawk that he's seriously going to regret when he looks back at pictures of his youth, slumped into the kitchen mumbling about a burger, and the moment was lost.

* * *

A few short weeks later, and it's Thanksgiving. I'm up to my eyes organising food drives for the local food bank, not to mention mucking in at school helping the kids make Thanksgiving headbands, despite my protests at the last meeting (I am neither artsy nor craftsy, but Sakura talked me through every step until I got the hang of it), sorting out the wine hampers for the annual charity auction, and judging the kids' Thanksgiving poems.

Last night, David and I had a particularly hilarious time at the Thanksgiving charity auction at Annie's Art Shop bidding for Anna's picture of herself holding hands with a turkey. It's fair to say we overpaid but it was worth it just to see the look on her face when we presented it to her afterwards. It was also a great opportunity for David to meet Darcy and the PTA mums properly and he seemed to really hit it off with Darcy's husband, Bill.

This is our first time celebrating Thanksgiving and I really enjoy the festiveness of the occasion. Mind you, I think it's fair to say that Anna doesn't quite grasp the concept: her teacher laughingly told me that when she gave a smooth rock to each of the kids and asked them to paint what they were grateful for, Anna wrote 'iPad' when everyone else wrote 'Mom', 'Dad', 'God' or 'Jesus'. At least David and I know where we sit in the pecking order.

As it was just the three of us, David cooked a pared-down version of a Thanksgiving dinner and the turkey was juicy and delicious. Even Anna tried it – and rejected it – but at least it looked good enough to try.

Between all the school stuff, Anna and Thanksgiving, I don't have much time to dwell on what happened with Bea, but an uncomfortable feeling settles in my stomach every time I lie in bed at night.

Bea and I have spoken since that conversation weeks ago, but it hasn't been the same and I don't know how to make it better – it's so hard to discuss anything emotional through a screen, so I force the issue out of my head and try to focus on the next bit of madness in the calendar.

Christmas.

34

'Now, how cold is it over there? I'm wondering if I should be bringing thermals.'

My mother's trip over here is just a few weeks away but she's already in full packing mode.

'It's cold but there's no snow,' I say, glancing out the kitchen window. 'I'm not in thermals.'

Far from it in fact. A mere dusting of snow has fallen so far in December, much to mine and Anna's disgust. David and I rented a car when he was home over Thanksgiving weekend and headed to the outlets to spend a fortune on snow boots, industrial winter gloves and massive padded coats but wearing them would be seriously overkill in this weather.

'But would it be icy?'

'No.'

'Because the last thing I need now is a fall on the ice. That's how Patricia who used to own the flower shop broke her hip when she slipped and fell on a patch of ice in Manhattan years ago.'

'You can't blame New York for that!' I say, exasperated. 'She could have had a fall anywhere.'

'Ah, but didn't she end up with an astronomical hospital bill at the end of it? Sure, I can't afford that on a teacher's salary.'

God Almighty. Talk about catastrophising.

'It's not icy and you're not going to break your hip,' I say, resting my forehead in one hand.

'Now, the next thing I need to ask you is...' she says, carrying on as if I haven't spoken. Still, I'm grateful for the subject change – *any* subject change.

She chatters on about Christmas presents for Anna – 'Now you know I like to travel light, Saoirse, so I won't have room for any of those giant dolls in my suitcase, so I was thinking of packing some dolly outfits instead.'

I tell her that Anna will be delighted with anything dolly-related and she seems satisfied with that.

'And what will I get for David?' she says. 'Men are awful difficult to buy for.'

For the umpteenth year in a row, I tell her not to get anything for David. Jesus – even David and I don't give each other gifts any more. We'll just treat ourselves to an Anna-free night out when all the hype has died down. But more to the point, my mother's gifts to David are always wide of the mark. Given they are both into tech and cooking, you'd think she would come up with something practical like a cookbook or new earbuds for his phone, but despite my heavy hints, she gets him woolly hats in off-putting brash colours or paisley-patterned grandad slippers in the wrong size, or novelty Christmas socks. But still, she insists on getting him something, so in a panic I tell her (again) to get him a cookbook, realising my mistake as soon as the words are out of my mouth.

'What! The weight of it in my suitcase!' she says as if I have told her to pack an elephant in there. 'I'm not going to be dragging a cookbook halfway across the Atlantic, Saoirse!'

Then she huffs for a bit.

'I'll get him some socks.'

'Grand,' I say, sighing, another battle lost.

'What does Miguel eat?' I say, because I'm already terrified about how we're going to manage Christmas dinner with the limited space available. Still, David has assured me that it won't be much more work than Thanksgiving dinner.

'Ah, don't be worrying about Miguel – he's not fussy. He'll eat anything. Mind you, the turkey won't be the same, will it?'

'Why not?' I say, mystified.

'Full of hormones,' she says.

Christ.

'And what will be the sleeping arrangements?' I say carefully.

I've been wanting to ask this for a while but given that she's been extremely quiet about their relationship, I'm slightly nervous about the answer.

'We have three bedrooms so it's up to yourselves,' I continue.

Silence.

'Ah sure, you wouldn't want to be changing all those sheets. Just pop us in the one room.'

'Grand so.'

I bloody knew they were an item. But still I am eager to move on before my mind has the chance to conjure up traumatic images of my seventy-two-year-old mother shagging an elderly Spanish man, so I ask her what they would like to eat when they come off the flight – their flight lands at 3.30 p.m. so they should get to us by around dinnertime.

'Just something light,' she says, which tells me nothing.

By the time I get off the call, I am exhausted and she's not even here yet.

35

The weeks leading up to Christmas fly by in a whirl of Christmas-themed school events. My job is general dogsbody – wrapping and delivering gifts to families in need as part of 'angel giving', hauling the more manageable Christmas trees from Fletcher's Flowers to local families, and arranging plates of mini doughnuts and muffins for the annual Breakfast with Santa event. I love every second of it. From the faces of the kids when Santa (Stan from Stan's Stationery Store) ambles into the school canteen for the Breakfast with Santa event, to the warm responses from the locals when I deliver their Christmas trees; and the glow I feel when I've finished wrapping the last gift for a family who can scarcely afford to celebrate this year. I drop the yellow rose on Beth's doorstep every Friday, giving her a wave whenever I see the shutters move, hoping that one day she will feel like coming out into the world again.

In fact, I have been so caught up in the Christmas whirlwind that I have semi-forgotten that my book is coming out in a few short weeks – New Year's Day, according to a typically curt email from Harriet. But that's not all – she has also been demanding details of a book launch, which I'm supposed to organise myself. Months ago, at that first PTA meeting, Darcy suggested launching the book at Bodie's Book Shop, but I haven't explored it any further even though I've met Bodie – a jovial man in his late fifties – several times. The truth is, although I've tried my best to move on from the negative comments on my website, and none have popped up since early December, my confidence is still shaken. What if the people who have said they like it are just being kind? What if it is slated when it is finally released into the world?

So, I make the decision to celebrate at home instead with David, Anna, my mum and Miguel. We will pop open a bottle of champagne and raise a toast there.

That'll be enough.

* * *

It's the day before Christmas Eve and even though I'm frantically trying to get everything ready for Miguel and my mother, who are arriving in three hours, I am on top of the world. David is home for starters and busy putting up Christmas decorations with Anna. I've gone to town this year, and tinsel and twinkling Christmas lights hang everywhere. As space is limited, our Christmas tree is about Anna's size, and stands in one corner of the living area. It's the first real one we've ever had (David doesn't 'do' pine needles but is strangely fine with it given that he's not here long enough to be picking them up).

Anna has plastered the tree with her own tinfoil-based 'tasteful' creations and frankly it's a total shambles, but she loves it.

David switches on the next set of garish Christmas lights and Anna and I oooh and aaah, while David folds his arms, smiling in satisfaction at his handiwork.

'How's the soup coming along?' I say.

David has decided to greet the visitors with gazpacho and some freshly made crusty bread – it's not exactly a winter soup, but it's a nice gesture to Miguel's roots. But there's no time to think about that because there are still presents to be wrapped: a navy and white silk scarf for my mother (she likes to 'smarten up' her 'good coat' with a decent scarf for Mass every Sunday), and a pricey bottle of whiskey (it's a bit of a punt as we have no idea if he even likes whiskey) for Miguel.

By the time 6.30 p.m. comes around, I finally feel as if we're semi-organised for the visitors. David rented a car for the week and left a couple of hours ago to battle the traffic to pick my mum and Miguel up from the airport. Anna has spent the last fifteen minutes with her face pressed up against the window. Excited as I am to see my mother, I am a little apprehensive about meeting Miguel. Jen has made me promise to text her as soon as he walks through the door. She's desperate to know what he's like.

Anna gives a sudden squeal, runs over to the door and pulls at the handle.

'Nana's here!' she says, her little cheeks flushed with anticipation.

I quickly walk over to the door and flick the lock and Anna races outside into the dark, the only glow coming from the Christmas lights I made David hang over the door. I hang back a little, smiling as Anna throws herself at my mother, who laughs and drops to her knees to give her a big hug. An elderly man stands next to her, his gaze firmly on Anna, his soft-brown eyes crinkling in amusement. A light grey, well-maintained beard covers the lower part of his face, something that surprises me given my mother's 'never trust a man with beard' stance. Mind you, he has a fine head of grey hair, which probably makes up for it in her book. His skin is tanned but not as dark as I would expect – I imagine the Irish weather has beaten all the colour out of him.

Fair play, Brenda, I think. For a man in his seventies, he's pretty easy on the eye.

He catches my eye and gives me a wave, walking towards me with his hand outstretched.

'Hello, I'm Miguel,' he says, in a gorgeously smooth Spanish accent.

His hand is warm and dry. I look into his twinkly brown eyes set underneath thick, grey, bushy eyebrows, and decide immediately that I like him.

'How was your flight?' I say.

He throws a quick glance over his shoulder and leans a bit closer.

'It was bleedin' dreadful,' he says, his eyes wide.

I burst out laughing. The last thing I expected to hear was this distinguished-looking Spanish gentleman throwing around a rude Irish-ism.

'She doesn't like to hear me swearing,' he whispers, jerking his head in the direction of my mother.

'Me neither!' I say, delighted we already have something to bond over.

My mother, finally free of Anna's death grip, walks over and throws her arms around me.

'Saoirse! Finally!'

Then she promptly releases me with a sharp 'Jesus!' and looks down at the ground. I follow her gaze and spy Luna brushing against her leg.

'What in the name of god is that thing?'

'It's OK, Nana,' Anna says, reaching down to stroke Luna's soft head. 'It's just Luna the cat.'

My mum narrows her eyes at Luna and says, 'That thing should be in a stable.'

Miguel bends down and joins Anna petting Luna.

'Hola, Miguel. I'm Anna!' she says.

My mother glances at me in surprise. I give a shrug in response. I had no idea Anna was going to greet Miguel in Spanish.

'Oh, you know *español!*' he says delightedly.

'Just a few things I picked up from *Dora the Explorer*, you know?' she says.

I try to stifle my giggles. Good on her – who says TV isn't educational?

'Well, I'm very happy to meet you, *princesa*,' Miguel says, pausing his stroking of the cat to offer his hand to Anna. She takes it instantly and works it up and down.

'That means "princess", right?' she says, with her head cocked to one side.

'*Sí*,' Miguel says, smiling.

Anna gives him a serious nod.

David appears with two cases, one in each hand. My mother's not wrong – the pair of them have packed lightly.

'Come on – let's get you inside and get a drink into you.'

'Great stuff!' Miguel says, rubbing his hands. 'I have a real thirst on me.'

I smile again to myself. What kind of English has my mother been teaching her students?

I lead the way into the pool house, Miguel behind me, Anna clinging to my mother's hand, and David at the rear, still clutching the cases. I close the door as soon as everyone is inside, and David takes drinks orders (whiskey for Miguel – hurrah! A white wine spritzer for my mother – 'Now, plenty of sparkling water, David – I'm not great with alcohol after a long flight'; apple juice for Anna, and a large glass of wine for me). While I give my mother the 'grand tour', Miguel goes to the kitchen to give David a hand, which makes me like him even more. I'm not great with guests who expect to be waited on hand and foot.

Anna, clinging to my mother, leads her into each room, chatting happily the whole time. My mother gives her trademark 'hmm', so I know she is not completely impressed with the pool house. I'm not in the least bit surprised – she did the same when she visited me last year in Ireland when I was staying in the all-glass, architectural, structural phenomenon The Cube.

'It's a bit Mickey Mouse, isn't it?' she says, looking around Anna's bedroom, hastily tidied from earlier. Then she knocks on the wall between the room and the bathroom.

'Paper-thin walls.' She tuts. 'A small gust of air could blow away the whole place.'

I don't say anything. What's the point?

Then David calls us in for drinks and we make our way back into the living area, where Miguel has already settled on the couch, shoes off, a large tumbler of whiskey in his hand. He reaches over to the coffee table, grabs the glass on the table and hands my mother her spritzer.

'There you go, my love,' he says, casually.

My whole body grows warm as if this small moment of intimacy is somehow catching. I am so happy my mum has found someone after so many years of being alone. But judging by her nervous glances at me and the blush creeping up her neck to her cheeks, she doesn't seem too happy. Oh, for goodness' sake. It's clear as day they are a couple.

She finally lowers herself beside him, Anna instantly balancing herself on her knee while I walk into the kitchen to help David with the snacks.

'So, what does your mum think of the place?' David says with a glint in his eye.

He knows damn well my mother is never backwards in coming forwards with her opinions, especially when she visits somewhere new.

'Paper-thin walls, apparently,' I say, rolling my eyes.

'Well, at least it'll make her think twice about shagging Miguel while they're here,' he whispers, grinning.

I punch him in the arm and down my wine in one gulp and head back to the living area with a newly filled glass.

'So, Miguel – how did you two lovebirds meet?' I say, perching myself on the edge of the couch, already feeling a little tipsy.

I can't resist teasing her – they're so obviously together that she can't honestly expect me to ignore it, but going by the daggers she's giving me, I'm guessing that's exactly what she wants me to do. Luckily, Miguel has no such reservations.

'When I moved to Ireland a few years ago, I already had some English – bits and bobs – but I wanted to learn more, so I went on Google and up popped your mother's classes.'

'My classes are in the top ranking now on the Google,' my mother says, clearly willing to swallow her mortification to impart this essential information.

'Great!' I say, with more enthusiasm than is strictly necessary.

'So, I walk into the class and there's Brenda and I think to myself, what a good-looking woman!'

'Ah, stop,' my mother says, tutting, but I can tell by the fresh blush on her cheeks she is delighted with the compliment. Then she flashes another nervous glance at me, but I ignore it.

Anna, who has been watching with great interest, suddenly pipes up.

'Nana, is Miguel your boyfriend?'

My mother's eyes widen. She opens her mouth and closes it again. I glance at Miguel but he is busy taking a long sip of his drink.

'Ah, go way out of that!' my mum says, rolling her eyes at Anna. Then she starts to give Anna the tickles – a classic distraction method.

Finally, Anna has asked the question on everybody's lips, but we still don't yet have an answer. What on earth is going on between my mother and Miguel...

36

David nudges me awake the morning of Christmas Eve and I can't honestly say I'm pleased to see him. Far too many drinks were consumed last night – mainly by me. My mother and Miguel took it easy with the wine, pleading jet lag, and although David indulged a bit, he certainly didn't inhale as much as me. The meal went well enough – the only hitch being when my mother put her gazpacho in the microwave to heat it up.

'Jesus!' she exclaimed, mortified, when Miguel gently reminded her that gazpacho was best served cold. 'I'm such a dose! It must be the jet lag.' Never one to fully own up to an error, she followed this with a barely audible, 'Sure, who'd be eating cold soup in the middle of winter anyway.' But we all ignored her and tucked in – apart from Anna, who just had the bread and a few olives.

Miguel generously pronounced the soup the best he'd had outside Spain, which delighted David. The conversation flowed easily – thankfully, Anna seemed to have forgotten about Miguel and my mother's relationship status and we spent most of the time chatting about their plans for their week. My mother, desperate 'not to get under your feet', has booked a few sightseeing trips in

Manhattan, including Anna in one or two of them, which we are all happy about as it will give David and I some time alone together.

Then, as we were collecting the dishes, Miguel announced he was off to bed, my mother quickly following him after tucking Anna in.

'What time is it?' I say groggily.

'It's 9 a.m. I got up at 7 a.m. to make breakfast for everyone but your mum and Miguel were up earlier with jet lag, and they already helped themselves. They went for a wander with Anna to blow the cobwebs away.'

I rub one hand roughly across my eyes.

'Oh god, sorry. I should have been up earlier. Too much wine!'

Then a feeling of dread washes over me.

'Did they say where they were going?'

'No, just that they wanted to explore the area. Your mum had Google Maps out and everything.'

Oh Christ. If I know my mother, I know exactly where she's headed. And I'll never hear the end of it.

* * *

'I just can't get over it! They close the beach for nine months of the year, and then you have to *pay* a fortune for the remaining three months? There's barely any coastal path because of the big houses being built right up to the edge. You can't even walk along it! Absolute disgrace, isn't it, Miguel?'

I don't say anything. In fact, apart from sitting in the seafront gazebo now and then after school drop-off to breathe in the salty air and stare at the waves, I've spent very little time by the water since we moved here, especially since the weather turned cold.

Miguel, who has been busily munching on a scrumptious Spanish omelette that David whipped up for lunch, nods his head in agreement while simultaneously giving me a wink. I grin back. Clearly, he knows my mother well enough not to get involved in one of her rants.

'And I wouldn't mind but that beach is *tiny*! It must be bursting at the seams in the summer,' she says, tutting. Then to my relief, she takes up her fork and resumes eating her omelette.

Nevertheless, I am keen for her to see Westmont High Street later on, which looks even more magical now the Christmas lights are ablaze. Every shop window has been decorated with colourful tinsel and gorgeous baubles, some of the awnings lit up with projected images of Santas, elves and sleighs. This evening, Westmont Tavern is holding an outdoor mulled wine event and all the parents from school will be there so Anna will have plenty of kids to play with. I suggest to my mum and Miguel that we go, and Miguel's face lights up.

'That sounds deadly!' he says with a little clap.

I'm really warming to Miguel – and not just for the Irish-isms. He's such an easy guest. So enthusiastic about everything and, more to the point, brilliant with Anna.

My mother frowns. 'What about midnight Mass?'

Ah, shite. I've forgotten about Christmas Mass. I don't even know if there is an evening Mass here on Christmas Eve or where the nearest Catholic church is for that matter.

'Ah, we can go tomorrow morning, Brenda,' Miguel says, reaching over to pat her hand.

My mother stares at his hand on hers for a second, darts a furtive glance at me, and snatches it away as if she's been burned.

'Grand,' she mumbles, spearing a piece of potato and letting it dangle on her fork before slowly placing it in her mouth.

I look at her and shake my head. What is going on? They're clearly mad about each other. One thing's for sure, I'm going to let the mulled wine do its work tonight and get the truth about her and Miguel once and for all.

* * *

It's not yet 6 p.m. on Christmas Eve but the street outside Westmont Tavern is alive with people, Christmas music and the sweet smell of mulled wine. Staff from the tavern have dressed up in Christmas costumes and are busy doling out fresh cups of mulled wine from huge silver trays under the twinkling lights of a giant, meticulously decorated Christmas tree. Anna is especially delighted to receive a cup of orange juice from Tinkerbell and is hotly debating with Miguel whether Tinkerbell is really part of Santa's posse.

David has spotted Darcy and her husband Bill and a few of the PTA mums, and they also seem to be having an animated discussion together about something.

I hang back a bit with my mother, who has been uncharacteristically quiet since lunch. She didn't even give me a lecture for coming out tonight without a woolly hat, which, given her determination to 'wrap up' in layers for the cold weather, is very unlike her.

I watch her sipping her mulled wine and wonder if she's tipsy enough yet to spill the beans about her and Miguel. But before I can broach the subject, her eyes widen and her mouth falls open.

'Jesus, it's yer one!' she hisses, clutching the sleeve of my padded coat.

'Who?' I say, mystified.

'The one taking selfies over there!' she says through gritted teeth, jerking her head violently towards the giant Christmas tree.

Puzzled, I glance over and instantly sigh. It's Brigitte dressed in a white faux-fur coat, her small bump causing the coat to stand out a little from her otherwise slim frame, her blonde hair twisted in ringlets, a sparkling silver tiara on her head. Odette and Cosette are dressed as little elves, both wearing resigned smiles.

Ever since Brigitte's shocking behaviour towards Darcy, I have made a point of not making any effort with her at the school gates, and judging by her dismissive attitude towards me, she feels exactly the same way.

There's no sign of her 'amazing' husband, Joe, but no doubt she will be treating her followers to a wide range of Christmas-themed, overly saccharine photos hand-feeding 'her man' a bit of turkey from their 'perfect' Christmas dinner. Anything for the brand.

'It's Brigitte Williams,' I say in a low voice.

'Jesus, it is!'

Then she punches me fairly painfully in the arm.

'And why in the name of God would you not tell me that you knew her? Sure, she's HUGE!'

It never occurred to me to tell my mum about Brigitte. Deep down, I still haven't ruled her out as the one who's been leaving nasty comments on my website. If my mother even got a whiff of my suspicions, she'd be over there like a shot, all guns blazing to defend my honour.

'I'll say hello anyway,' she says, straightening her shoulders, nose in the air.

Oh no! I should have seen this coming. My mother can't resist approaching celebrities if she spots them – not because she admires them but because she is 'every bit as good as them' and has the absolute right to have a chat if she damn well wants to. I grab her by the sleeve but it's no use – she shakes off my hand, leaving me no choice but to follow her.

'Hello there!' my mother says, giving Brigitte a big wave.

Brigitte lowers her selfie stick and looks my mother up and down, the camera-ready smile slipping off her face. Now that they have been set free, Cosette and Odette immediately start fiddling with the lights on the Christmas tree.

'I'm Brenda – Saoirse's mum,' Mum says, pointing at me unnecessarily.

Brigitte frowns at me, then looks back at my mother, before taking a deep breath.

'I'm Brigitte?' she says.

My mother glances at me with a puzzled expression.

'Yes – you are Brigitte,' she says slowly.

I try to stifle a giggle. My mother has clearly not come across the uptalk affectation before.

'I know I am?' Brigitte responds, with more than a touch of irritation in her voice.

'Well, I think we've established who you are,' my mother replies in a voice that brooks no argument.

'Honestly?' Brigitte huffs.

My mother glares at her for a moment, and then she turns on her heel and strides off back to where we were standing before. Without daring to look in Brigitte's direction, I follow her quickly.

'Jesus Christ,' she mumbles, taking a big sip of her mulled wine. 'Is she an *imbecile*?'

I try to explain to her charitably that some people naturally have that inflection in their voice but she's not having any of it.

'Pretentious is what it is,' she says. 'It's bad enough that she's lost her Irish accent but she's also changed her name from Brigid to Brigitte. I always thought Brigid was a good solid name.'

'Hmmm,' I say, desperate to change the subject.

I glance at Mum and her eyes are sufficiently glazed enough from the mulled wine for me to ask the question that's been on my mind for months.

'So, what's the story with you and Miguel?' I say carefully.

Her cup drops from her lips and her eyes immediately begin to water.

Oh no. What have I done?

'I'm sorry,' I say, rubbing her shoulder. 'I didn't mean to upset you. It's just that you're obviously more than just friends and I don't know why you're keeping it a secret. He's mad about you!'

She drops her shoulders and shakes her head.

'It doesn't matter if he's mad about me, Saoirse,' she says, through a little hiccup. 'Miguel is married.'

37

The freezing, salty wind whips through my hair as my mother and I huddle closely together on the hard seats in the wooden gazebo by the waterfront. After her big revelation about Miguel, I have managed to persuade her to take a walk with me somewhere quiet where we can talk privately. David, who came over just after my mother's confession, took one look at her and, without saying a word, immediately replaced our empty cups with full ones. Planting a kiss on his lips, I told him to keep an eye on Anna while I had a quick walk with my mother. David told me that Darcy had mentioned a Christmas carousel over the other side of town that he and Miguel could take Anna to, and I flashed him a grateful smile, loving him for not asking any questions, and knowing just what to do.

'Jesus, you should have brought a woolly hat,' my mother says, her hands clutched around her half-empty cup of mulled wine, her gaze firmly towards the sea.

These are the first words she has uttered since we left the festivities behind and I'm choosing to ignore them.

'So, Miguel is married,' I say softly.

'He is,' she says, her voice resigned. 'And I knew it too. He didn't hide anything from me. At first, he was just a student and I was his teacher. But then he asked me out for coffee one day and we became friends. I wasn't looking for romance – far from it, but I suppose you could say that we grew close, and then I realised that...'

Her breath catches in her throat.

'That you were in love with him,' I finish for her, gently.

She takes a moment to gather herself before answering.

'I suppose,' she says.

Then she straightens herself and turns to look at me.

'Now, he was the one who declared himself first, Saoirse. I didn't go chasing after him,' she says.

I bite the inside of my cheeks to keep a straight face, grateful for the dimness of the gazebo. As if I care about who made the first move.

'Anyway, he told me all about his wife back in Spain. They have been living separate lives for years – they even have their own apartments.'

'Why didn't they get a divorce?'

'Apparently, she's very religious. He's been trying to persuade her for years, even before he met me, but she won't budge.'

She puts her cup on the wooden table and pulls her coat tightly around her, her expression pained.

'I just never thought I'd be the other woman!' she says suddenly.

'You're not the other woman!' I say, exasperated. 'The man is separated from his wife. He's not cheating on anyone. The only issue is if you want to get married.'

'Well, that would be the right thing to do,' she says stiffly.

'Sure, the pair of you are in your seventies!' I say, spluttering. 'What's the point? Just enjoy yourselves.'

She is quiet for a moment and then reaches across and takes a long slug of her drink.

'You see, when we first became close, I told Miguel about my vow.'

'What vow?'

'The same vow I made to your father. Not to have relations until the wedding night.'

I can't help it – the wine splutters out of my mouth, spraying the front of my coat.

'Ah Jesus, Saoirse, will you get yourself together?' my mother says, reaching into her coat pocket and bringing out a packet of tissues. She spits on one and dabs at the liquid furiously, like I'm a small child who has dribbled her dinner down her front.

'That coat will have to go straight in the wash when we get back,' she says grimly, putting the sodden tissue back in her pocket.

'Never mind my coat!' I say.

She takes a deep breath and looks out towards the sea again.

'Well, when your father died, I made a vow to myself that if I was to meet anyone new, I wouldn't have relations until we were married.'

'But why?' I say, mystified.

'Listen, I've turned myself inside out about this situation, Saoirse. I am an upstanding member of the community. I help out at the church. People respect me.'

'So, you're worried about the local gossip?'

She folds her arms and purses her lips. 'Do you remember the scandal with Betty and Jim last year?'

'Is Betty the one who was sexting a bloke from a dating website, then split up with Jim and got back together with him afterwards?'

'Hmm,' she mutters, clearly cross that I have infringed on her storytelling. 'Well yes, but the whole town was buzzing about it.'

You were buzzing about it, I think.

'And you don't want people to be saying the same things about you and Miguel,' I say.

She turns to me, her eyes glistening. 'It's not just the local gossips, Saoirse. I was also a bit worried about what you would think about me and Miguel. I didn't want you to think that I had forgotten your father. Because I haven't! Not a day goes by when I don't say a prayer for him.'

Is this why she has been so reluctant to talk about Miguel? Because she was worried about how I'd react? My heart breaks a little.

I take her cold hand in mine.

'Listen, Mum. I was so little when Dad died that I don't have the memories to miss him. But yours are sacred and they will never leave you no matter who you're with. All I want is for you to be happy. I'd be delighted for you both if you moved in together and enjoyed the rest of the time you have with each other.'

She nods and squeezes my hand.

Then Mum takes a deep breath and says the words I will never be able to unhear for the rest of my life.

'I've been having urges, Saoirse,' she whispers.

And if that isn't enough, she qualifies this with: 'Sexual urges.'

Why is she telling me this?

'Now, I haven't been with a man in *that way* since your father, and I suppose if I am to break the vow, I'm a bit nervous about having relations with Miguel.'

My empty cup starts to crack in my other hand.

'Now, it's not like we haven't explored that side of things. We have been sharing a bed sometimes and Miguel would be great at the stroking but—'

Enough.

'Listen, Mum,' I say, swallowing. 'It's natural to feel apprehensive but I think you and Miguel need to spend more time in the bedroom and chat about what you both feel comfortable with.'

'Do you think so?' she says, brows furrowed. 'It's just that when I was with your father it wasn't the *done thing* to be having that kind of conversation, you know?'

I will get through this.

'Well, Miguel seems to be an open person, and I'm sure once you get to know each other better, you can work out what's best.'

'Well, maybe I'll have a go.'

I don't want to think about what this means so I just give a quick nod.

The wind is really cutting through me now, and my ears are starting to burn. I can see my mother shivering, despite her thermal layers.

'Come on – we'll head back,' I say, rising to my feet.

She gets up slowly, grabbing my shoulder to steady herself. It's only then I realise how pissed she is.

I put my arm around her waist and guide her out of the gazebo. As we reach the footpath, she turns and looks searchingly into my eyes.

'Do you think Miguel is a catch?' she says, with a little wobble in her voice.

'I think Miguel is a fucking ride!' I say decisively.

Jesus, I'm a bit pissed myself.

Bad language or not, this sends her off into hysterics that last the whole way back to the high street and on towards the twinkling fairy lights in the distance.

38

The days between Christmas Day and New Year's Eve are the happiest I've had in a long time. Christmas Day was a particularly hilarious affair, starting with a champagne breakfast courtesy of everybody's new favourite guest, Miguel. By midday, we were all pretty tipsy, apart from Anna, and nobody remembered to put the bloody turkey in the oven on time. Which is why we ended up eating at 9 p.m. instead of the planned 4 p.m. We had pizza out of the freezer to keep us going until then. Still, Miguel has proved to be a fabulous sous-chef and he and David have bonded over their love of fresh ingredients.

My mother has also been in flying form. Ever since our chat in the gazebo, she has become more relaxed around Miguel, even going so far as to accept a peck on the lips from him on Christmas Day, without so much as glance in my direction. Good on her. It has been an absolute joy to see the pair of them so happy together.

Anna was in her usual Christmas Day state – a combination of overjoyed and overwhelmed with all the presents. Bonnie sent her (yet another) giant doll, which she immediately called Luna, together with a gorgeous handmade card, with 'LOVE ANNA' printed in giant swirly writing on the front, each letter decorated with an intricate design of tiny red hearts and flowers. Of course, Anna barely even looked at the card, but I immediately tucked it away in Anna's bedside drawer as a keepsake. It's too pretty to lose.

When I thanked Bonnie over Zoom for Anna's gift and card, she told me, blushing, that she had made it herself. Not for the first time, I think there is still so much we don't know about Bonnie. She also told me that she's working over Christmas keeping a few lonely, elderly people company. Staying in rent-a-friend mode, she commented on Beth and how lonely she must be on her own over Christmas, but this time I was one step ahead of her. I had popped a note through the door to Beth on Christmas morning, inviting her to join us for drinks, but unsurprisingly she didn't respond.

David called Rose in the morning to wish her a happy Christmas and he got short shrift – apparently, he had called right in the middle of the Christmas lunch she had prepared for her golf crew. David just about managed to thank her for Anna's present before the line went dead, leaving him staring at his phone, shaking his head in amusement. Two minutes later, Rose texted David, curtly reminding him to send photos of Anna to show her dinner guests. Rose and I have too much history to be best friends, but I know there's a heart of gold behind that gruff exterior.

The only thing that put a bit of a dampener on the day was my call with Bea. There was no denying the stilted nature of our conversation, and with all the chaos of the Christmas dinner preparations in the background, not to mention the horrendous noise of the remote-controlled car Anna had received as a Christmas present from Rose (of all people), there was no opportunity to have a proper chat. Still, I have made a promise to myself to talk to her after Miguel and my mother leave. Screen or no screen, I need my best friend back.

I didn't manage to get to talk to Jen or Dee but we shared

messages. Jen, fed up with her mother's constant worry about the preparations for her wedding in April, had scarpered to Barcelona with Liam for the week, and was sending over photos of the pair of them outside the sights, pulling crazy faces. Judging by her dark mood, I had half-expected Dee to send a rant about how useless Sean was at helping her out at Christmas, but to my relief, she actually sent a lovely family picture, everyone smiling madly in front of their twinkling Christmas tree. Maybe things have finally settled down.

* * *

The days have passed quickly and today is New Year's Eve, although we've decided to stay in. There will be fireworks down by the water's edge but, as my mother says, 'There's nothing to stop us from looking out the window.'

She is particularly keen to stay in given that she has 'walked the feet off herself' going to see all the sights in Manhattan, an activity even more exhausting with Anna in tow, although my mother claims she was 'good as gold' during their trip to the Statue of Liberty.

Following a lazy day of eating meals made by both David (turkey soup) and Miguel (turkey pie), we flop on the couch in the evening with a glass of wine.

At 10 p.m., my mother gets to her feet, yawning. 'I can't be bothered staying up until midnight,' she says. 'Sure, isn't tomorrow going to be a big enough day!'

'What's tomorrow?' I say, puzzled.

I thought she had said she was going to spend the day packing in preparation for the trip back to Ireland the following day.

She looks at Miguel, eyes wide in panic.

What's going on?

Miguel pipes up. 'Oh, I'm taking Brenda out somewhere for dinner tomorrow. One last hurrah before we head back to Dublin.'

He looks at her with such tenderness that my heart melts for them both.

The pair of them say their goodnights while David and I stay up for another glass of wine and to ring in the new year. When the ball drops in Times Square, David clinks glasses with me and says, 'Happy New Year, Saoirse. The year of your wonderful book!'

39

'Right so! We're all off for a walk!' my mother announces with a touch of hysteria in her voice shortly after we have tidied up lunch.

I look at her curiously. She has been jittery all morning – dropping the breakfast cereal all over the floor and screeching like a banshee when she spied Luna sitting peacefully outside on the bathroom windowsill – 'Jesus, I thought it was a burglar!'

After staying up late last night, I could do with a quiet afternoon, but before I know it, we're all bundled up in our coats and heading towards the town, Anna swinging happily between Miguel and David.

'I thought we'd be going towards the sea,' I say to my mother, as we enter the high street.

'What kind of walk would you be getting out of that?' she says, tutting. 'Not a coastal path to be found.'

I walked into that one.

Our little group comes to a halt.

'We're here, Mummy!' Anna says, clapping her hands.

I squint up at the shop sign.

It's Bodie's Book Shop.

David walks over to me and grabs my hand.

'Look!' he says softly, pointing towards the shop window.

My hands fly to my face. I can't believe what I'm seeing.

The entire window display is made up of dozens of copies of my book set against a gigantic poster of the front cover, everything delicately backlit in a sea of twinkling white and gold fairy lights.

'Happy book launch day!' David says, gently removing my hands from my cheeks.

My mother, David and Anna embrace me in a group hug while Miguel steps back to take a photo. I'm completely in shock.

'As if we'd forget about your big day,' my mother whispers into my ear before pulling away.

So that's why she's been so nervy. Dinner with Miguel, my eye!

'Congratulations, Mummy!' Anna says, her arms still flung around my legs.

Tears start to roll down my face. All those years dreaming of seeing my book in the window of a book shop and the moment is here at last.

'But how?' I say, when I finally get my voice back.

David steps back and smiles.

'All credit goes to Darcy,' he says. 'She was hellbent on throwing you a book launch, so she got together with the other PTA mums and organised it for you.'

I stare at him, open-mouthed.

'So, I guess we'd better not keep your fan club waiting,' David says, guiding me towards the front door.

My what?

Then he flings open the door and a sea of familiar faces yell in chorus, 'Happy book launch day!' My breath catches in my chest as I try to take it all in. All the PTA mums are there, and a few mums from Anna's class, plus Fletcher from the flower shop, Annie from the art store, Carrie from the cupcake shop, Stan from the stationery store; the list goes on... Darcy approaches me with a giant smile on her face.

'I can't believe you did all this,' I say, giving her a hug. 'You're amazing!'

'Just enjoy it, Saoirse,' she says.

More people come and congratulate me; those who have already read it tell me again how much they loved the book, and there's so much warmth and kindness in the room that I can't help but feel overwhelmed.

'Drink?' a man's voice says behind me.

I turn around and see Bodie, a wide smile on his face, balancing a tray of champagne flutes.

'I'd love one!'

After a sip of champagne, I thank him profusely for allowing us to hold the book launch in his wonderful shop.

'Pleasure, my dear,' he says, and wanders off to the waiting group, who eagerly take glasses of their own.

Darcy whips the glass out of my hand and says, 'You can have as much champagne as you like after the book reading.'

What?

'Yes, that's right. You're going to do a book reading for all these lovely people who have come to support you and your book.'

A moment of panic rushes over me. I've never given a book reading in my life.

'Just start from the beginning, Saoirse,' Darcy says, her eyes warm and reassuring.

Before I have chance to gather myself, she links my right arm with hers and propels me towards the shop window, positioning me underneath the giant poster. She plucks one of my books from the display and thrusts it into my hands.

A hush falls on the small group and my stomach starts to flutter.

I open the book with trembling hands and falter when the words come into view.

An image of the last negative comment I read about my book flashes into my mind ('This book is SUCH a bag of shite'). My armpits start to prickle. Then a little voice pipes up.

'Read, Mummy!'

I look up from the page to see Anna in David's arms, waving at me, her eyes alive with excitement. David catches my eye and gives me a smile and a quick nod.

So, I start to read, stumbling a little at first, but I begin to lose myself in the words – the ones I crafted well over a year ago now – and for a few minutes, I forget where I am. Then I reach the end of the chapter and stop. There is a moment of silence before the clapping begins and before I know it, another glass is pushed into my hand. Before I can go and mingle, Darcy grabs me and firmly directs me towards the back of the shop where a small table and chair have been set up.

'This is where you sign the books,' she says, gesturing towards the chair.

I sit down in a bit of a daze, trying to capture the preciousness of the moment. With shaky hands, I start signing the books, trying to remember to smile at each person, to thank them for coming to the event. The queue grows longer as people I don't even know wander in, clearly curious about the activity going on. By the time I have finished signing the last book, my face is tight from smiling. But as I watch the last person go to the desk to pay Bodie, I feel utterly elated. These are real people paying for something I wrote and, whatever they may think of it, surely that's a bloody great achievement in itself.

Darcy is the last of the guests to leave. I stand up and give her a warm hug.

'Did you have fun?' she says.

'It was the best!' I smile. 'You are amazing.'

'Enjoy the rest of the day!' she says, giving me a little wave as she walks out the door.

She is one of the kindest people I have ever met. What on earth does Brigitte have against her?

As much as I've loved every second of the launch, I can tell that Anna is starting to feel the pressure of behaving herself for such a long period of time and is now attempting to climb up the ladder attached to one of the bookshelves.

Time to go.

As I step out from behind the desk, David pops out from my left, through a door I hadn't noticed before, his forehead creased.

'Everything OK?' I say, puzzled.

'Fine!' he says, his voice taking on a curiously high pitch.

Then he points at the chair I have just vacated.

'Sit back down for a minute. You have one more customer left.'

I look around the empty shop. Apart from Bodie, my mother, Miguel and Anna, there is nobody else here.

'Okaaay,' I say, lowering myself slowly back onto the chair.

David throws me a nod of satisfaction and disappears back through the door again. I hope to God this is quick because even from my position at the back of the shop, I can see Anna with one foot on the ladder, her stubborn 'Why not?' leading my mother to respond with a flustered, 'Because you'll break your neck, Anna!' But then David appears again all smiles and claps his hands and announces: 'Time for hot chocolate!' and before I know it, Anna has scrambled off the rung of the ladder, taken hold of Miguel's outstretched hand, and they're all waving goodbye.

'See you at home, love!' my mum calls over.

Now it's just me and Bodie.

What's going on?

Then I hear the sound of heels and I whip my head around and jump out of my chair so quickly that it falls backwards onto the floor.

Because there in front of me with a tentative smile on her face is my best friend, Bea. I rush over to her and hug her close, breathing in the glorious perfume scent of her.

'You didn't think I'd miss your first book launch now, did you?' she whispers into my ear.

Somewhere in my peripheral vision, I see Bodie quietly leaving through the front door, but I barely register it. I just can't believe she's here.

I draw back and try to blink away the tears, noticing she's as watery-eyed as I am.

'How did I not see you?' I say.

'I had to hide in Bodie's office and peep through the crack in the door,' she says. 'Harry spent Christmas with me, but he's been with Ryan for the last few days. I didn't want Anna to spot me and make a fuss about Harry not being here. Ryan was supposed to drop him back to London tomorrow but when David messaged me about your book launch, I knew I couldn't miss it, so I took the first available flight and here I am.'

My heart swells with emotion.

'I'm so sorry,' I burst out, the tears falling freely now. 'I should never have tried to talk you out of living with Tom. I was just worried you wouldn't be in Woodvale when I got back.'

Her face starts to crumple.

'No, Saoirse – you were right. I was rushing into things. I don't want to leave Woodvale. It's just that I was worried that you might not come back at all.'

'How did you come to that conclusion?' I say, wiping the tears from my face.

'Well, I know you had a rough start, but ever since you've moved here, you've just sounded so settled. You've made new friends, found a new calling at the school, and really been involved in the community. Even Anna has settled in beautifully. And I know you've had a few unpleasant encounters with that fake cow Brigitte, but aside from that you're building a wonderful life here.'

I stare at her, mouth open.

'And I know there is an option for The Firm to extend David's contract when the year is up,' she continues. 'So, when Tom asked me to move in with him, my first instinct was the same at yours: it's too soon in the relationship; too much change for Harry. But the happier you became the more I started to wonder if there was any point in me staying in Woodvale if you decided to stay on here.'

My eyes fill again. I don't believe this – each of us dreading the thought of living in Woodvale without the other. I feel like doing a little jig but instead I take a deep breath, throw my hands in the air and shout: 'Well, of COURSE, I'm coming back to Woodvale!'

Bea's shoulders immediately relax.

'Are you sure?' she says.

'Hundred per cent,' I say firmly.

Her face breaks out into a wide smile.

'And what about you?' I say. 'Are you moving in with Tom?'

She sighs and folds her arms.

'I love him, but I've told him I need more time. In any case, if I do move in with him, I'm telling him I want to stay in Woodvale. There's no way I'm moving to the other side of London now I know you're definitely coming back!'

'Too bloody right!' I say, my heart singing.

She nods for a moment, pushes her glasses to the tip of her nose, and says in her most decisive voice, 'Well, that's settled then.'

And just like that, I have my best friend back.

'When are you heading back to London?' I say, full of grand plans to whisk her off to Westmont Tavern for a few catch-up drinks – that's if it opens on New Year's Day.

'Tonight,' she says, grimacing. 'Ryan is meeting me with Harry at JFK and we're heading back to London.'

I'm disappointed that she can't stay longer but so happy she was able to come at all.

The door clicks and Bodie walks in, his bushy eyebrows raised in enquiry.

We should really get out of the poor man's shop.

Bea and I say our 'goodbyes' and grateful 'thank yous', and head out into the icy air – my head still in the clouds, but this time, the high I'm feeling is not from the champagne: it's because Bea, my best friend for life, is right by my side.

40

After a fabulous Christmas, the unforgettable experience of the book launch, and the surprise visit from Bea, I half-expected the January blues to set in, especially as David has been away in San Francisco for most of the month. But here I am on a freezing but crisp late Friday evening on the last day in January settling into a bottle of red, feeling in better spirits than ever. Thanks to the book signing, I can't walk more than a hundred yards before someone stops me to tell me how much they enjoyed my book. Bodie has sold out of his copies and has ordered more. Harriet is, for once, pleased with me because the online sales are rocketing thanks to my mother's sterling efforts on social media. I now have a small number of carefully curated followers – not even remotely close to Brigitte's numbers, but a good start nonetheless.

My mother has also been brilliant with the tips – sending me suggestions of other mums to follow on Instagram and persuading me to do the odd (terrifying) live-video reading excerpts from my book.

Each time a comment pops up on my website, I brace myself, but thankfully the feedback has been mostly positive (apart from the occasional complaint about the level of swearing) and I haven't received anything as vicious as the comments posted before.

Just as I'm contemplating a third glass of wine, my phone starts to buzz. It's David.

'Listen, Saoirse, have you been watching the news?'

I scoff at this. David knows that I avoid the news whenever I can, mostly because it makes me cry.

'There's a pretty serious snow storm heading towards New York.'

Oh, fab! Anna will be delighted. Apart from a tiny flurry, there's not been so much as a scattering of snow since winter started and she's desperate to build a snowman.

'They're predicting at least seventeen inches of snow and strong winds. I'm just a bit worried about the pool house withstanding the storm.'

He's such a worrier.

'The pool house seems solid enough,' I say.

He sighs. I can just picture him running his hand through his soft, dark hair.

'It may be pretty solid, Saoirse, but it's over twenty years old. I noticed a small crack in the skylight in the bathroom and I meant to call Kelly about it but it totally slipped my mind.'

'I'm sure it's fine,' I say, walking over to the front window and peering out into the darkness.

Everything looks completely still; the only movement is Luna as she slinks by the edge of the covered pool.

'I just wish I was there,' he says.

Me too. Not because of the storm but because I miss him – three and a half weeks is a longer stint than normal.

'Maybe you and Anna should go to Darcy's for the night,' he blurts out.

What! I glance at my watch. I'd rather risk storm damage than wake up Anna this late and drag her out of bed, let alone disturb a busy mum with five kids at home.

'We'll be grand, David!' I insist, taking a big gulp of wine.

He sighs. 'OK, but promise me you'll call Darcy if you're worried.'

I promise and he calms down a bit.

Honestly, I think as I polish off the last of the wine. Between my mother banging on about the 'paper-thin walls' and David worried about the bathroom skylight leaking, it's any wonder the pair of them agreed to stay here at all.

* * *

I am unceremoniously aroused from my wine-induced slumber by a sharp jabbing in my right cheek. I immediately swat it away, too deep in exhaustion to care what it is. And then a familiar and impatient voice causes me to sit bolt upright.

'Mummy!'

'What is it, Anna?' I say, trying to focus my groggy eyes on her little frame standing by the bed.

I squint at my bedside clock. It's just gone midnight.

'Well,' she says conversationally, as if late-night chats are something that happen fairly regularly, 'there's loads of snow in the bathroom.'

Shiiiiiiit.

I leap out of bed and the coldness hits my face like a ton of bricks.

'Mummy, where are you going?' she says, as I switch on the light.

I rush over to her, lift her up, tuck her into bed and cover her up with my heavy duvet.

'Just stay here where you're nice and warm, OK? I'm going to take a quick look.'

I pad next door to the bathroom, shivering with every step, and I gasp as soon as I reach it. The entire tiled floor is covered with lumps of powdery chunks of snow intermingled with shards of glass. A freezing, howling wind hits the back of my neck. I look up and throw my hands to my mouth; there is a great big hole where the skylight used to be. The crack in the glass must have weakened it so much it has caved in from the weight of the snow. I don't know if the rest of the building is sturdy but I'm sure as hell not hanging around to find out.

I race back into the bedroom, fling open the wardrobe, grab all the snow gear we thought we'd never use, and throw it on the bed. I start dressing quickly, not pausing to remove the labels.

'What's happening, Mummy?' Anna yawns, peeping out from under the covers.

'Anna – I'm going to help you get dressed in your snow gear and then we're going to leave the pool house for a little bit,' I say, trying to keep my voice as calm as possible.

As soon as she's dressed, I grab my phone from the bedside table, tapping at it quickly with numb fingers. Unsurprisingly, given the lateness of the hour, Darcy doesn't answer.

Anna watches me with big eyes.

'Where are we going?' she says, hopping around a little in her red snow boots.

I look at her and sigh.

'We're going across the road to wake up our friends and ask them if we can stay in their house for tonight,' I say, grabbing her hand and leading her to the front door.

Then, taking a deep breath, I heave the door open, and we set out into the storm.

41

I clutch Anna's gloved hand as tightly as I can as we crunch our way down the side path, and bow our heads against the freezing, howling wind, half-blinded by the thick snow flying directly into our faces, before finally emerging on the footpath in front of Beth's house. At least I think it's the footpath because at the moment everything is covered in a thick, fluffy, white carpet.

I take a step to cross the road to Darcy's house but Anna doesn't budge.

'Mummy, look!' Anna shouts.

I peer through the flying snow to follow her gaze and just about make out a dark shape moving towards the steps leading up to Beth's house.

'It's Luna, Mummy! And she must be freezing. We have to help her!'

That bloody cat.

'Don't worry, Anna!' I roar. 'Luna will be fine!'

Just then a wailing sound penetrates the air as Luna starts mewing plaintively.

A light flashes on.

'Beth's up!' Anna shouts happily.

Before I can stop her, she breaks free, lifting her legs high to climb up each step. I follow her as quickly as I can but by the time I get to the top of the steps, she is already ringing the bell.

The door flies open and Beth appears with a scowl on her tiny little face. She is wearing the same huge, fleecy, dressing gown and fur-lined slippers as she always does. I shiver as a blob of snow from the roof drops onto my head and down my back. Luna races straight in the door and Anna rushes in after her.

Beth glances at Anna shooting past her, opens her mouth and closes it again. I try to apologise but the roar of the wind is too loud, so I just end up walking into the house myself, intending to find Anna as quickly as I can before heading across the road to Darcy's.

As soon as the door closes, I apologise to Beth for disturbing her and quickly explain what happened to the pool house. Then I tell her I'll be out of her hair as soon as I find Anna, my eyes scanning the expansive, wooden-floored hallway, wondering where she's disappeared off to.

Beth's face remains impassive throughout this exchange and then she points at a spot behind me. I turn around to find Anna sitting at the bottom of a huge staircase with Luna on her knee. Well, that's not strictly true – as Luna isn't far off Anna's size, half of her big furry belly is on Anna's legs while the rest of her is splayed out on the wooden step. The sound of Luna's purring is like an engine idling at a traffic light.

'Anna seems happy. You can stay here for a bit if you like,' Beth says, hugging her dressing gown tightly across her frail body.

'Oh!' I say.

Maybe it does make sense to stay here rather than wake up a peacefully slumbering family.

I thank Beth and walk quickly towards Anna, cajoling her into letting Luna go so I can take off her coat, gloves and boots. I just hope Beth lets us stay until it's light again and we can call the agency to get the skylight fixed. Beth motions me towards a coat rack just to the left of the front door. I take off all my gear and hang everything as neatly as I can. Then I turn to face Beth, intending to reassure her that we won't be in her way, but then the bell rings.

Beth jumps a little before shooting me an accusatory look, but I raise my hands at her in reply. I'm as clueless about who this can be as she is. I watch her walk slowly to the door and open it just a crack.

'Thank CHRIST!'

The door suddenly jerks wide, the momentum on the other side forcing Beth backwards. Within seconds the hallway is filled with three more people – one big, two small, all of them dressed identically in startlingly white, designer snow gear.

My mouth falls open in shock.

Beth shuts the door quickly, crosses her arms, her tiny face pinched and white with fury.

'What the hell are you doing here?' she says, raising her voice above the din of Odette and Cosette greeting Anna.

Brigitte glares at her, her nose bright red from the cold, her lips a startling shade of blue.

'I'm actually in labour?' she says.

Then she doubles over and starts to moan.

* * *

Beth and I exchange horrified glances while Brigitte pants and groans. Cosette and Odette, completely oblivious to their mum's discomfort, race off up the stairs with Anna (a petrified Luna running in the opposite direction) as if they have been best friends all along.

When Brigitte finally straightens, I ask her how on earth she has ended up here.

'I started feeling the contractions about an hour ago?' she says, grimacing. 'So, I called the ambulance but there's a tree down across one of the highways. They have to clear it first. So, when I heard they weren't coming, I threw the snow gear onto the girls and got into the car, hoping the highway would be clear by the time I got there.'

Wow.

'How did you manage to drive with the contractions, let alone during a snow storm?'

'With great difficulty?' she mumbles. 'I had to stop every few minutes and then the snow got so bad I couldn't see out the windscreen any more? So, the girls and I had to walk? Then I saw the lights on here and, well, here I am.' She sighs bitterly.

'And where were you going to go in the car?' I say, mystified.

'The hospital!' she says, rolling her eyes. 'I was hoping the tree would have been cleared by the time I made it to the main road. I have to get there before the baby arrives?'

Beth, who has said nothing since her angry outburst at Brigitte, suddenly turns on her heel, crosses the hallway and disappears into a door just to the right of the stairs.

'There is NO WAY in hell I'm having a baby here. I'm booked into the most exclusive hospital in Manhattan. The place is like a feckin' five-star hotel. All the celebs have their babies there. I've been posting about it to my followers for months.'

I can't help but notice that her Irish accent is back in full force – childbirth is a real leveller.

But before I can respond to this tirade, the doorbell rings.

I open it quickly, praying that, by some miracle, a crew of paramedics have somehow tracked her down and are waiting to whisk her off in an ambulance. But when I fling it open, it's not the paramedics at all.

'Darcy!'

I am so happy to see her.

'Saoirse!' she says, her face already dark red with the icy cold even though she's barely walked any distance at all. 'I was on my way to the bathroom and I noticed a missed call from you. Then I spotted all the lights on here. Such a crazy storm. Is everyone OK?'

I usher her in and shut the door behind her. Beth reappears in the corridor, phone in hand, and stops dead the moment she sees Darcy.

Her face twists. I know what she's thinking – not another bloody unexpected guest.

'What the FUCK is she doing here?' Brigitte screeches suddenly, pointing directly at Darcy.

A bubble of anger surges through me.

'Brigitte,' I say sharply. 'I know you're in labour, but you have no right to speak to Darcy like that.'

Darcy looks at me and back to Brigitte. Her face softens.

'Oh, honey, you're having a baby!' she says, her huge, pale-blue eyes filling with tears.

'Don't "honey" me!' Brigitte says fiercely, and then stops as her face crumples in pain.

'There's a fallen tree on the highway; the ambulance can't get through,' I say to Darcy, helplessly.

Darcy fixes a determined expression on her face and crosses towards Brigitte.

'OK, Brigitte, I'm going to keep trying the ambulance but first I'm going to take off your coat. Then I'm going to settle you in the living room.'

Her voice is calm and measured, just as it is when she's directing the volunteers at school events. Thank Christ one of us is keeping a cool head because my legs are like jelly. Emergencies are not my forte.

Brigitte tries to push Darcy's hand away, but she's no match for Darcy's sheer tenacity and, in no time, she is coatless and being shepherded across the hall towards the open door Beth used earlier.

I follow quickly and watch Darcy as she settles a groaning Brigitte on one of the couches in the spacious living area, all the while talking to her in a calm, measured voice, asking her when the contractions started, how far apart they are and so on. Brigitte stays stony silent but allows Darcy to take her boots off all the same.

It occurs to me that I haven't seen Anna in some time, so I trot quickly up the stairs only to find the three of them in a large bedroom, which must be a guest room, judging by the sparseness of the furnishings, tucked into the massive bed, eyes glued to a wide-screen television hanging off the wall.

'Your mum's going to be OK,' I say to Odette and Cosette, but they don't as much as glance my way. Well, at least they're not worried. Keeping them out of the way is probably the best thing for them until the ambulance arrives.

It better arrive.

I walk quickly down the stairs and back into the living room. Brigitte is lying sideways on the couch with a large blue cushion between her legs, facing away from Darcy, who is sitting on a cushioned stool in front of her.

There is no sign of Beth.

Brigitte's legs clench and she lets out a small groan.

She may not be my favourite person but I can't help but feel desperately sorry for her. Going through labour with Anna was no joke and it wasn't too long before I was begging for the epidural.

Darcy starts to fuss around her, propping her up with more cushions while Brigitte mumbles at her to 'feck off'.

Then something horrifying occurs to me.

'Jesus – what about Joe?' I say. 'Does he know?'

Brigitte stiffens and turns her head towards me, her mouth set in a grim line.

'Ask *her* where Joe is!' she says, narrowing her eyes at Darcy.

I turn towards Darcy but she looks at the ground.

'Darcy, what's going on?' I say, dismayed to see her unflappable composure slip.

Oh god, please don't tell me there's something going on between her and Joe. I can't bear it. Darcy rakes her hands through her short blonde curls and takes a deep breath.

'Saoirse – Joe is my twin brother.'

42

Brigitte goes through two more contractions (and a lot more swearing) in the time it takes for Darcy to explain what happened between her and Brigitte. Apparently, just before we moved to Westmont, Darcy found out through mutual friends that Joe was cheating on Brigitte – not only was he cheating on her, but he had moved his new girlfriend into their place in Aspen. Reasoning she had a right to know, Darcy told Brigitte the minute she found out and by the sounds of it, Brigitte well and truly shot the messenger.

'She never liked me,' Brigitte says to me with tired eyes, panting from the effort of her last contraction.

'That's not true,' Darcy says calmly. 'I felt protective over you the second I met you at the wedding.'

'Bullshit,' Brigitte mumbles.

Darcy sighs. 'He's never been faithful. When he told me about you, I tried to make him promise not to mess up this relationship. Then when Odette and Cosette came along, I felt more reassured. I knew he was working away a lot, but I was pretty sure he wouldn't risk everything by cheating on you.'

'Well, he did,' Brigitte says through a bitter laugh.

The thoughts swim in my head.

'So why were you so cross with Darcy when she told you about Joe?' I say.

Brigitte stares at the ceiling.

'I just didn't want to believe it,' she says. 'I thought I had done everything right. He wanted me to be the perfect wife – someone who would wait on him hand and foot. He also had a penchant for the California sun-kissed look and was obsessed by French movies. So, I put the whole thing together and created Brigitte.'

Darcy looks like she's about to throw up. It must be awful to find out that your brother is even more of a knob than you thought.

'I reinvented myself for him. The entire brand is based on our perfect marriage and family life. A life I had never experienced before I met Joe.'

Then she turns her head and looks at me, her eyes suddenly ablaze.

'Without him, I have nothing – no brand, no followers, no sponsors – nothing. And when you come from nothing, Saoirse, that's the last place you want to end up.'

Jesus, not only is she selling a lie, but she is living a lie.

But then a memory of Jen telling me how Brigitte's father had ended up in prison after gambling away his clients' money pops into my head and a wave of compassion washes over me. Who could blame her for reinventing herself after going through all that?

'Deep down, I knew Darcy was telling the truth, but I hated her for it, and I lashed out at her on social media.'

Oh no, what did she say? I look at Darcy, but her head is lowered.

'Last year, Darcy went on a six-month work trip to China,' Brigitte says, her eyes full of shame. 'And I lambasted her for it on Instagram: "What kind of mother leaves behind her five kids and husband for that length of time?" I fed off the negative comments, hoping she would spot it and feel as hurt as I was.'

I remember Darcy telling me about this particular judgement from a family member – I just had no idea it was Brigitte she was talking about.

'I'm so sorry, Darcy,' Brigitte says, her eyes filling.

Darcy raises her head and nods with a half-smile. God, she's such a good person. I'm not sure I would be quite as forgiving. Actually, hang on! If Brigitte is so willing to wreak revenge on Instagram, what's to stop her from posting nasty comments on my author website? She could be AnonMum after all! I have to find out. But then Brigitte has another contraction and the moment is lost.

Darcy starts to rub her back and this time Brigitte lets her.

When she has recovered, Darcy leans over her and tenderly strokes her forehead.

'Divorce him, shut down the brand, and get out of this situation,' Darcy says softly.

'I can't,' Brigitte says, rubbing her eyes.

I think for a moment.

'I agree you need to get shot of Joe, but maybe you don't need to shut down the brand,' I say slowly. 'Maybe you could rebrand. Dump all the perfect wife and mummy shite plus the worship-your-husband stuff that's set the women's movement back by about a hundred years and go back to being yourself.'

She gives me a dark look and turns to Darcy.

'I can't divorce him; I signed a prenup. I'll end up with nothing.'

'No, you won't,' Darcy says quickly. 'I happen to know the best divorce lawyer in town and between her and the emotional black-mail I'm going to lay on Joe, he's bound to give you a fair deal.'

I presume she's talking about Sakura, the divorce lawyer, one of the PTA mums. With her on Brigitte's side and a fired-up Darcy to boot, the man has no chance.

Brigitte's eyes light up, before fading away just as quickly.

'I can't,' she says, letting out a small sob. 'I have the girls to think about. They'll be so upset if we split up. And what about this baby? How the hell am I going to cope?'

Darcy leans forward. 'I know the girls will be upset but it'll be worse for them if you get back together. You'll never forgive him for the betrayal and they'll pick up on that tension. And I'll help out and give you a hand with the girls and the baby.'

'I'll help out too,' I say. 'I can take the girls after school to give you a break.'

'And don't forget about the PTA mums too,' Darcy adds, smiling. 'You forget that you're part of the sisterhood here whether you like it or not.'

Brigitte offers Darcy a half-smile but then her face collapses again and she hunches up her legs and moans.

Beth suddenly rushes in, waving her phone. She's been gone so long I've almost forgotten about her.

'They've almost cleared the road,' she says breathlessly.

I lock eyes with her and motion for her to come into the hallway. She glances at Brigitte's hunched figure and twists her hands together.

'Listen, Beth,' I say in a low voice as soon as we step out into the hallway. 'I'm no expert, but it's clear that her contractions are coming closer together. I don't think she's going to make it to the hospital.'

Beth's eyes widen in fear.

'Beth – you're an obstetrician. You're the only one qualified to deliver this baby safely.'

She shakes her head violently.

'I can't,' she whispers, dropping her gaze to the floor, her hands bunching into fists.

I take her gently by the shoulders, feeling how thin she is under the folds of thick material.

A terrible moan echoes from the living room.

'Beth – please!'

But she steps away from me and starts tapping violently on her phone.

'I'm trying the ambulance again,' she says, her mouth set in a defiant line.

I stare at her for a moment but I can tell by the set look on her face that her mind is made up.

Jesus – what are we going to do?

I hurry back to Brigitte, whose forehead is now glistening with sweat, and ask her if she needs anything.

'Just a fucking ambulance, thanks,' she says wearily.

Then she heaves herself onto her arms and shoots me a weak smile.

'By the way, you can call me Brigid.'

43

I don't know what makes Beth change her mind but the next thing I know she's at Brigitte's side, holding her hand, talking in a firm but reassuring voice.

'Brigitte. I'm a doctor. If the ambulance doesn't get here in time, I can deliver this baby for you. You and the baby are going to be just fine.'

Brigitte stares at her with hollow eyes and whimpers but thankfully remains calm. I don't think she has the energy left to protest.

Beth signals to Darcy and me, and the three of us step out into the hallway.

'I'm going to deliver this baby when the time comes but I'll need your help.'

'Anything you need,' Darcy says instantly.

Then both pairs of eyes look at me.

'Me too!' I say.

Although by helping I hope they mean looking after the kids, rather than the disposal of the placenta, for example. I'm about to tell Beth all this when the blessed roar of ambulance sirens fills the whole house.

Beth rushes towards the door and opens it just in time for the paramedics to crash in. Within minutes, Brigitte is on her feet, sobbing in relief, wrapped in blankets, being supported by a burly man in a navy puffa jacket on one side, and Darcy on the other.

At the door, Brigitte turns to me.

'My girls!' she says.

'I'll take care of them, don't worry!' I say.

She shoots me a grateful look just as Darcy links her arm through hers.

Then, because I can't let it go, I quickly call out, 'AnonMum!'

It's now or never.

Brigitte narrows her eyes at me. 'What?'

'Nothing! I just said, "Good luck, Mum!"'

It wasn't her. She might have been putting on an act all these months, but nobody is *that* good an actor.

And then they're gone.

I look around for Beth but she's nowhere to be seen. A wave of utter fatigue washes over me as I tread slowly upstairs to check on the girls. The TV is still on but the three of them are fast asleep under the covers. I switch off the TV and tiptoe out. What a night.

I walk slowly down the stairs, yawning as I go. There is no sign of Beth, who has probably gone to bed herself, so I decide to try for a snooze on the couch, leaving my phone on a high volume in case Darcy texts me with any baby news. Before I nod off, I text David to fill him in on the night's drama, hoping he won't be too worried when he wakes up. Then I lie down and immediately fall asleep.

* * *

I awake to the sound of my phone beeping. My eyes feel like they are stuck together. When I finally prise them open, I realise it is still dark. I grab my phone and squint at the time. It's just gone 6:30 a.m.

I've been asleep for less than two hours and I feel like death. But I perk up instantly when I see the message. It's a photo of a beautiful little baby all wrapped up in a luxurious-looking pink baby blanket. Fully awake now, I eagerly read the message from Darcy:

Made it in the nick of time. Mum and baby all well.

I yawn extravagantly. Switching on a side light, I swing my sleepy legs off the couch and pad quietly across the dark hallway towards a narrow corridor that I'm guessing must lead to the kitchen. I root around in one of the cupboards to find some coffee and turn on the kettle. Luna comes sidling into the kitchen, mewing and rubbing against my legs. With everything going on, she probably hasn't been fed in a while. I search all the cupboards for cat food but there's nothing, so I settle on giving her a bowl of fresh water.

I'm on my second cup of coffee when I hear footsteps. I pop the kettle on again, figuring Beth must be awake and might like something hot. Her slight figure appears in the doorway, and she stops dead when she sees me, her face pale and agonised.

'Hi, Beth,' I say tentatively. 'Would you like a cup of—'

But I don't get any further because she leans against the doorframe and bursts into tears.

44

It's been ten minutes since Beth broke down and I'm almost in tears myself. I've managed to persuade her to come into the kitchen and sit down but she is still heaving and sobbing at the kitchen table. I tried throwing an arm around her, but she shrugged me off, so I made her a cup of hot milk, figuring that might settle her down, but when I put it in front of her, she looked at it without seeing it.

I tell her the news about the baby's safe arrival, but this seems only to make her cry harder. So, in the end, I sit back in my chair and wait until she's ready.

Finally, her chest stops heaving and her breath slows. She looks at me with red-rimmed eyes and shakes her head.

'I'm sorry,' she whispers.

'No need to be sorry,' I say firmly. 'It's been a long, crazy, stressful night.'

She breathes a heavy sigh. 'Oh, it's not just tonight – it's every-thing. It was... it was so hard being around a woman in labour again.'

She starts to cry again and this time I go over and wrap her in a hug and she doesn't push me away. When her sobs have subsided, I take the chair beside her and hold her hand.

She takes a long shuddering breath. 'I've always wanted to bring babies safely into the world, and I've always wanted babies of my own. I just took it for granted that I'd marry and have a family, you know?'

She sniffs and puts her head in her free hand.

'So, I did marry Jonas, the man I loved, and the first thing we did was try for a baby... and nothing.'

My heart goes out to her. David and I were so lucky to conceive Anna quickly. It's such agony for women who struggle.

'Months went by, and then we both got tested. We were both fine. So we kept trying and trying. Procreation sex – really beats the romance out of a relationship – and still nothing.' She gives a bitter laugh. 'We tried IVF, of course, but that didn't work.'

'Well, sometimes it takes a few tries,' I say gently, thinking of a few mums I know back in London who have been through it.

'We did eleven rounds of IVF,' she says, her eyes filling again. 'Bankrupted ourselves. Jonas begged me to stop after the first few, but I was so determined. My hormones were a mess and I was heart sick every time there was bad news, but I couldn't bring myself to stop.'

I can't imagine the pain of wanting something so badly and the crushing disappointment when it doesn't happen over and over again.

'After the last of our savings ran out, I started taking it out on Jonas. I couldn't help it – I hated both of us for not being able to get pregnant but I also knew I couldn't live the rest of my life without holding my own baby in my arms.'

She bites her lip.

'Work was hell, too. Imagine delivering all those babies,

witnessing the joy on their mums' faces when I knew I would never be able to have child of my own.'

God, now I know why she was so reluctant to help Brigitte deliver her baby. Even eventually offering must have taken a huge amount of courage.

'And don't get me started on all the commentary from other mums: eat this food, take that vitamin, do this exercise... as if I haven't done everything I can to conceive. One mum even had the cheek to tell me I was too thin to carry a baby. I just felt like a total failure,' she says, her eyes filled with pain.

I'm not having that.

I fold my arms and lean forward.

'Look, being unable to conceive is not a failure – you did everything right. This is something that happened *to* you. You are not to blame – for any of it.'

She sighs and bites her lip.

God, all these months living here alone, suffering.

'You've been dealing with this all on your own,' I say, squeezing her hand.

'I couldn't face talking to anyone. I just wanted to get as far away as possible from Jonas and work, and my life back in London. I needed to shut out the world. When my dad told me the house was free, I grabbed the opportunity to come here – a place where nobody knows me. The only thing I brought with me was Luna. My dad's happy for me to stay here rent-free as long as he gets some income from the pool house.'

'What about your mum?' I say.

Because if I was her, I would definitely need my mum in my life at a time like this.

'My mum?' she says, releasing my hand. 'She's the last person I'd talk to. Do you know what she told me after the eleventh round of IVF failed? She...'

But then her face closes over and she looks away.

'Do you know what? I'm not going to talk about her because it makes me too angry.'

Fair enough.

'Well, someone's obviously been thinking about you,' I say tentatively. 'Those yellow roses certainly come as regular as clockwork. Are they from Jonas?'

She blows out some air.

'No, they're not from Jonas. We aren't in touch,' she says shortly.

I can sense when it's time to keep quiet.

Suddenly, she gets to her feet.

'I think I need to put my head down,' she says, rubbing her eyes. 'I haven't been able to sleep yet.'

I rise quickly. 'Listen, Beth, I'm so sorry for everything you've been through...'

Then I clasp my hands to my mouth as a terrible thought occurs to me. No wonder she looked so horrified when she spotted my book on motherhood. That's the last thing she needed to see. I say this to her and she shoots me a sad look.

'I'm sorry for the way I reacted. It's just that any reminder sets me off...'

I wave my arms violently in a *no, don't worry!* sort of way, and she gives me a small smile.

'Thanks for listening, Saoirse.'

I give her another hug and draw back quickly when I feel an unmistakeable sensation against my right leg.

Beth looks at the big mass of fur and smiles fondly. I can't believe she brought Luna all the way from London.

'She's hungry,' Beth says, biting her lip.

'Oh, I'll feed her,' I say. 'I've already given her some water, but can you point me in the direction of the cat food?'

'There's a few tins in the pantry,' she says, pointing to a slim, white door right at the back of the kitchen.

She gives me a little wave as she leaves, and I wave back, tired but happy I have finally made a connection with her. Then, with legs like lead, I push open the pantry door, trying to avoid stepping on Luna as she weaves in and out of my legs, clearly sensing the prospect of food ahead. I find a big tin of the stuff in the first cupboard I open and swear out loud when it catches on the white plastic bag next to it, spilling a pile of small white envelopes on the floor.

I mutter a few 'fuck sakes' and get down on my knees on the tiled floor and try to sweep everything back in, but then Luna comes along and starts to paw at one of the envelopes as if it's a mouse, so I grab it from her, annoyed. As I do so, the envelope flips over, exposing two words, each letter neatly embellished with hearts and flowers. My stomach drops and my mind races, trying to take everything in.

Because I've seen that writing before and I know just who it belongs to.

* * *

I return to the kitchen, my head swimming both from the shock of what I have just seen and from the sheer exhaustion of the night. With trembling hands, I make myself another cup of coffee, grateful for the peace and the chance to think things through. As the dawn light streams into the kitchen, I make up my mind. Nobody is going to hear about this discovery until my suspicions are confirmed.

David calls in a panic at 8 a.m.

'So sorry, Saoirse – bloody Wi-Fi went off in the hotel when I was asleep and I only got your message now. Are you and Anna OK?'

I'm not sure how I manage it, but I keep my voice as steady as possible and fill David in on one of the most bizarre nights of my life. I focus on discovering the connection between Darcy and Brigitte, and the dramatic rush to the hospital for Brigitte to deliver her baby, but I don't say too much about Beth. That will come later. He reacts in all the right places and then asks about the pool house and when we can move back in. I reassure him that I will call Kelly as soon as the office opens.

'I'd love to get an early flight back today, but everything is booked out,' he says, his voice full of frustration.

'You'll be back tomorrow!' I say, tutting. 'We're fine. Stop fussing!'

We sign off with a few 'love yous' and I put down the phone carefully. I know I am right not to discuss my suspicions with him.

Not before I know the truth.

45

The rest of the morning passes by in a hive of activity and I'm grateful for the distraction. Anna, Cosette and Odette raced into the kitchen just after I spoke to David so I've fed them, warned them not to be too noisy for fear of waking Beth, and plonked them in front of the telly in the living room with a vat of popcorn (I don't care how early it is; it's keeping them quiet). None of them has asked to build a snowman, thank Christ, even though it's the perfect weather for it. I look out the back window, marvelling at the idyllic snowy scene before me. It feels like days ago that Anna and I battled through howling, icy winds.

The doorbell goes just after 9 a.m. and I hurry to answer it, hoping it's the people coming to repair the skylight as I've already left a message for Kelly. When I swing it open, I'm surprised to see Darcy standing on the doorstep, dressed head to toe in ski gear, and holding a massive oval-shaped dish covered in tinfoil.

'When did you get back from the hospital?' I finally manage, as she thrusts the dish into my arms.

'About an hour ago,' she says. 'I just popped back to pick up Cosette and Odette. It's about time they met their little sister.'

'Come in, come in!' I say.

'It's a frozen lasagne by the way,' she says, as I close the door behind her. 'Thought you could do with some home cooking after the night you had.'

Jesus, only Darcy could stay up for an entire night and be thoughtful enough to still deliver a lasagne.

I throw a quick glance towards the stairs but there's no sign of Beth and I'm glad she's still sleeping.

Darcy walks over to the living room and peeps in before returning again.

'They seem happy!' she says.

I nod – I've lost count of the number of times I've refilled that popcorn bowl.

'Have you seen Brigitte's Instagram?' she says. 'There's huge hoo-ha over it.'

I look at her, puzzled. Darcy digs deep into the pocket of her padded waterproof trousers, taps a few times, and hands me her phone. I gasp. The photo of Brigitte is far from flattering. I mean, she looks fine for a mum who has just given birth, but it doesn't look like she's used any of her usual forgiving filters.

My darling followers. I had another baby girl in the early hours of this morning and I couldn't have done it without the help of the sisterhood. Darcy, Saoirse and Beth – you are all total legends. #mumpower. P.S. It was quick but bloody painful!

I smile. Good on her. She's finally being real. But there's more.

For the last few months my husband Joe and I have been living apart. We plan to divorce. I was so terrified of losing everything – my husband, my livelihood, and this brand – that I pretended everything was normal. I'm so sorry I let you down. But I hope you guys can forgive me. I'm going on an Insta break now while I take care of my little one, but I will be back soon with a new, fully rebranded, better, authentic me.

Wow! I can't believe she has taken my advice to give her Instagram a big makeover.

I scroll down through the comments from her followers and apart from the odd nasty comment along the lines of, 'Can't believe you lied to us!', plus about a dozen followers who've vowed they are going to unfollow her, the response has been overwhelmingly positive. I hand the phone back to Darcy, feeling a bit dazed.

Then Anna comes rushing out of the living room waving yet another empty bowl, and Darcy skips into action, gathering the girls, who are finally excited about seeing their baby sister.

I lead Anna into the kitchen with the empty bowl, intending to find something else to compensate for the popcorn, but before I can have a proper root around the cabinets, my phone pings. It's David texting me to let me know that he will fly back from San Francisco to New York tomorrow.

My stomach flips over. I need to have all my facts straight before he arrives.

As soon as we're back in the pool house again, I'm making a Zoom call.

46

The workmen showed up just after Darcy left and worked at speed. As there has still been no sign of Beth, I pop the lasagne in her freezer and scribble a note with my number. Anna and I walk into the pool house just after midday. Apart from the fact that it's freezing cold, you would never think there had been any damage to the house at all. The skylight has been replaced and the bathroom thoroughly cleaned of all snow and glass. I turn on the heating and tell Anna to stay in her snow gear until the place warms up. She yawns in return. She's been quiet since the girls left and I'm sure she's as wrecked as I am.

She mumbles 'iPad' and heads for her bedroom. When the place starts to warm up, I pop her in her pyjamas, and tuck her into bed with her iPad. I'll be in for it if she falls asleep at this hour but I can't see how I can keep her up all day after such a crazy night. Besides, I don't want her to overhear the conversation I'm about to have. I kiss her on the forehead and she grunts, already lost in her world of avatars and mythical creatures.

Then I walk slowly into the living room and sit on the couch

with my phone. I tap into Zoom, find the contact and press 'call'.
She answers immediately.

'Saoirse! I've been so worried! David has been texting me about
the snow storm. Is everyone OK?'

I take a deep breath and try to keep my voice as calm as
possible.

'Hi, Bonnie,' I say.

* * *

I hate seeing anyone cry, let alone a woman in her mid-sixties, and I
hate having this conversation over Zoom because if I was with her
now, I'd be giving her a hug. Despite my attempts to comfort her,
Bonnie is inconsolable.

'I'm so sorry,' she says, for what seems like the fiftieth time. 'I
should have told you Elspeth was my daughter.'

It's only when she says it out loud that I realise how obvious it
all was. How could I not have seen it before? Bonnie firmly guiding
us to rent this place; her regular enquiries about the mysterious
person living in the big house; and, of course, the final clue on the
envelope I discovered in Beth's pantry: two words written in the
same swirling script that so perfectly matched Anna's Christmas
card from Bonnie, but instead of 'LOVE ANNA' it said 'LOVE
ELSPETH'. Elspeth – a Scottish name that perhaps Beth adapted
herself. But why hasn't Bonnie mentioned her daughter before?
Doesn't David have a right to know his half-sister is living on our
doorstep? Anna's aunt.

I wait until Bonnie has recovered and then ask her these questions as calmly as possible. She takes a deep breath and starts to tell
her story.

'After I gave David up for adoption, I didn't think I would ever
have another child. But then when I was approaching thirty, I had a

one-night stand with Mike, an American artist who was exhibiting some of his paintings in Cornwall. We exchanged numbers but I hadn't intended on seeing him again. That's until I found out I was pregnant. I called him immediately and he urged me to keep the baby. There was nothing between us – no love or romance, but we still managed to make it work; he'd fly over from New York to Cornwall to see Elspeth a couple of times a year and I'd do the same in reverse.'

'So, you've been coming to Westmont for decades?' I say.

'No – I've only been a couple of times when Elspeth was very young,' she says. 'But when she turned two, Mike moved to San Diego. He became quite successful and kept the house in Westmont and rented it out. Mike recently agreed to let Elspeth stay in his house for a bit. Thought the break would do her good.'

'And that's where we come in,' I say.

I have so many more questions, I don't even know where to start.

She nods, her eyes red-rimmed.

'Why was Beth so upset with you?' I say.

I mean I know Beth had a terrible experience trying to conceive but I can't imagine gentle, kind Bonnie deliberately hurting anyone, let alone her own daughter.

'Because I told her about David and how I gave him up for adoption,' she says, her eyes welling up again.

That knocks the stuffing out of me.

'She didn't know that you had a son?' I say, aghast.

'I never told her when she was growing up,' she says, her eyes pleading. 'It was too painful. I never thought for a second that I'd see David again. I had intended to tell her when she was older, but the moment just never came. I didn't even tell Mike until I was reunited with David last year. Then I knew I couldn't put it off any longer.'

Jesus Christ. I'd be bloody livid if I was Beth.

'Not only was she furious with me for not telling her about David before, she was outraged that I had given my baby away when she was having such a hard time conceiving. She accused me of being cruel and heartless and told me she would never forgive me.'

Bonnie breaks down again and my mind starts to whirl.

'Why didn't you tell David any of this?'

'I couldn't!' Bonnie almost shouts. 'Beth was too angry to hear me out. She said she wanted nothing to do with David or his family. After all the years he spent wondering why I gave him up, how could I turn around and tell him he had a half-sister who didn't want to know him? I couldn't hurt him like that. I was desperately hoping she would change her mind, but she still won't take my calls.'

What a bloody mess.

'So, if Beth didn't want to know about us, then why on earth did you push us towards renting this place?'

Bonnie swipes a hand across her eyes. 'It was an impulse, I suppose. When Mike told me Beth was moving to Westmont and then you mentioned you were having a hard time settling in Manhattan, a lightbulb went off in my head. I knew Beth was in a bad emotional state, and even though she spoke to Mike now and then, I was desperate for someone to keep an eye on her. I knew she wouldn't see me if I flew over there and Mike was so busy with work in Hong Kong. I thought if you were living in the pool house, you could check on her, and I suppose in my wildest fantasies, you might even become friends. That way, it would be less of a shock when she found out who you and David really were.'

That was one hell of a risk.

'What if I'd never found the envelope?' I say.

'Whether Beth came round or not, I had planned to tell you and

David when you returned to London,' she says quietly. 'I wanted to do it in person.'

I believe her.

'And the weekly flowers I've been delivering?' I say, suddenly feeling exhausted.

'Yellow roses are a symbol of friendship and caring. I used to buy her a single rose whenever she was going through a hard time. She's not just my daughter, Saoirse, she is my best friend. I love her and I miss her so much. I know it appears as though I manipulated you into this situation, but as her mother, I'd do anything to protect her. David too.'

That does it. Now the pair of us are crying. Despite keeping Beth a secret all this time, I can't help but feel desperately sorry for both of them. I would move heaven and earth for Anna and, regardless of how badly Bonnie has handled the whole situation, I can't blame her for trying to do the same. In a weird way, she has done us a favour – without the move to Westmont, I would never have met Darcy, joined the PTA, or experienced the sheer pleasure of being part of a vibrant community.

But even so, there's no denying this latest revelation is going to be a shock for David.

'How am I going to tell David?' I say.

'You're not going to tell anyone anything,' she says, drawing herself up. 'I am.'

'But—'

'It's my mess, Saoirse, and I'm going to fix it.'

She looks so determined that I just nod. She's right – it will be better coming from her. Then she tells me she is going to call David now, and afterwards she'll try to contact Beth. If Beth won't speak to her, then she'll ask Mike to break the news. Either way, everything will be out in the open within the next twenty-four hours. Beth will find out who we really are, and David will find out he has a half-sister. I say goodbye, and head to the kitchen in a daze, open a bottle of wine, and carry the glass back into the living room. I flop down onto the couch and raise the glass to my lips with trembling hands. If Beth rejects David then she will be throwing away a relationship with Anna. And if she does, despite everything she has been through, I'm not sure I'll be able to forgive her for it.

47

'What? So, you're trying to tell me that David has a half-sister?'

I rub my eyes with my free hand. Clearly two glasses of wine, on top of a sleepless night, has impaired my judgement. It's been two hours since I spoke to Bonnie, and I haven't heard a thing from David. I imagine they're still talking everything through, but the waiting has been unbearable. I don't even have Anna to take my mind off things, as she conked out an hour ago. So, when my mother called for an update on the snow storm, I was grateful for the distraction, although I'm regretting telling her the latest news now.

'Yes,' I say, trying to stifle a yawn. 'She's Anna's half-auntie.'

'Yer wan with the cat the size of a bear?'

'Yes,' I sigh.

She's quiet for a bit then.

'Jesus, between Beth, Darcy, Brigitte and the new baby, it's like *Days of Our Lives* over there.'

'Mm hmm.'

'Now, I wouldn't be too fond of the name Elspeth,' she says thoughtfully. 'Do you think that's why she calls herself Beth?'

'I have no idea, Mum,' I say, taking a deep swig of my wine.

'Ah well, it'll be great for David to have a sibling, and Anna will only be too delighted to have another relative to make a big fuss over her.'

'I know – I'm just a bit worried about how David will take it,' I say.

'He'll be grand after the initial shock – from what you've told me about Bonnie, she didn't do this out of badness. She was trying to protect him.'

I hope she's right. I don't tell her my other fear – that Beth might still reject him.

'Anyway, I ran into Jen's mother at Mass the other day – stick thin – and she was telling me she's finally reached her target weight for the wedding. I mean, did you ever!'

Despite the abrupt subject change, I can't help but smile. My mother can't understand why anybody would change their appearance so drastically for something as 'trivial' as a wedding day.

'Then she asked me if I was going to bring a plus-one to the wedding, which hadn't occurred to me...'

Of course, this has occurred to her. This is just her way of asking me what I think.

'Oh, you should definitely bring Miguel,' I say.

She sighs. 'Well, I didn't say anything to her at the time, but I've been giving it some thought...'

Drumroll please.

'And I think it's time for me and Miguel to *go public*.'

She says this so gravely that, despite the stress of the day, I have to stifle a giggle.

'You should absolutely go public,' I say, trying to match her solemn tone.

'Well, no doubt there'll be many a raised eyebrow, but I'll just have to style it out,' she sighs.

I let out a squeak of laughter. I can't help it. She's not generally one to use phrases such as 'style it out'.

'Honestly, what's the matter with you, Saoirse? Are you pissed or something? Don't think I can't hear the slurping over the phone. Sure, it's barely 4 p.m. over there!'

And I don't know whether it's the wine, the hysteria from the night before, or worrying about David, but I start to shake with laughter. Then David's name flashes up on my screen and I stop dead. I hurriedly tell her I have to go and press the answer button, my heart jumping out of my chest.

'Hi, David,' I whisper.

'Hi,' he says, his voice hoarse.

Silence.

I can't imagine how he's feeling after everything he's been through. But on the other hand, I can't cope with too much silence without rushing to fill a gap, especially after half a bottle of wine, so I bite my tongue and count to sixty in my head. I'm in the fifties when he starts to speak.

'So, apparently I have a half-sister,' he says quietly.

'Yes,' I say softly.

Every part of me is screaming to give him a hug.

'I understand Bonnie's reasons,' he says, voice full of pain. 'But god, I wish she'd been straight with me from the start.'

'I know,' I say.

'I mean, maybe I could have handled it if she'd told me I had a half-sister who didn't want to know. Of course, it would have hurt but...'

'David, I agree with you, but remember that Bonnie doesn't know you as well as I do. She was just trying to protect you from any more trauma. I don't think she managed the situation well, but I do think she did everything for the right reasons.'

He sighs.

Then a thought flashes through my head – something that hasn't occurred to me before.

'Do you want a relationship with Beth?' I say.

This whole time I've been terrified of Beth rejecting David, but what if he doesn't want to get to know Beth either?

'Of course I do!' he almost snaps.

Then he immediately apologises.

'It's OK,' I say.

Frankly, I can't believe David's keeping it together at all. His head must be in shreds.

'In fact, maybe I'll call over there when I get home tomorrow. Bonnie has just texted to tell me that Mike has arranged a call with Beth this evening. She'll know everything by tomorrow.'

'I would give her time, David. She is still vulnerable and may not be in the right emotional state to deal with a reunion.'

Then I fill him in about Beth – her heartbreak over her failure to get pregnant, the breakdown of her marriage, and the destructive impact of this on her job as a doctor *and* her relationship with Bonnie.

'OK,' he breathes. 'Maybe I'll give her some time to approach us.'

Then he lets out an animalistic groan.

'My head is wrecked, Saoirse!' he shouts.

'I know, I know,' I say soothingly. 'I just wish you were here so we could talk it through properly.'

Late tomorrow afternoon seems too far away.

'Me too,' he says quietly.

'I love you,' I whisper.

'I love you too.'

Then he ends the call.

Suddenly I don't feel like drinking any more. I get up slowly, gather up the bottle and glass and tidy everything away in the kitchen. My head is swimming. I don't think I could bear it if Beth hurts him. For one mad moment I consider calling her, but then I instantly change my mind. What am I going to say? 'Hey, half-sister-in-law, please don't hurt my husband!'

No – if she wants a relationship with David and our family, then she's going to have to make the first move.

48

I yawn for what feels like the millionth time and put a couple of slices of toast in front of Anna. It's only 6 a.m. but it could have been worse given she fell asleep so early yesterday. I, on the other hand, tossed and turned for most of the night, my mind swirling with thoughts of David and Beth.

I sit at the table with Anna, watching her inhale her toast with unusual speed. I'm not surprised she is so hungry – she skipped dinner yesterday, after all. I can't eat yet: the desperation to see David has made my stomach churn. I cross to the living room window, open the curtains and spot a flicker of light coming from Beth's kitchen. She knows everything now and I would give anything to know what she's going to do next.

* * *

The day crawls and I spend most of it checking my watch, willing the hands to go faster. Thankfully Anna has been an angel and spent a good chunk of the afternoon staring at a screen. I don't have the energy to feel guilty about it. And then at last there is the sound of a key in the door and David steps in, a large suitcase gripped in one hand. His eyes are bloodshot and his expression weary. Anna rushes out and David's face immediately lights up. He picks her up in his arms and holds her close.

After a few moments she squeaks for him to let her go, then runs back towards her room as quickly as she's arrived. The smile fades from his face as I walk towards him. I throw my arms around him, feeling the roughness of his unshaven chin prickling my skin, breathing in the scent of aircraft mixed with the woody aroma of his aftershave.

'Come on,' I murmur, leaning back to look into his eyes. 'Let's unpack and get you settled in. We can talk later.'

He kisses me lightly on the lips.

'I think I'll shave and shower first,' he says, running a hand over his stubble.

As he walks off towards the bathroom, I wheel his case towards our bedroom to make a start on the unpacking. Anna races towards me with a face full of urgency. 'Snack!' she says. Shaking my head wearily, I tell her to help herself from the kitchen cupboard. I've given up monitoring the snack situation at this stage.

But I barely unzip the case before I hear a high-pitched screech. I sigh heavily and walk quickly down the corridor, rounding the corner into the living room.

I clutch my chest in surprise because standing just inside the front door, her tiny frame swamped in her massive dressing gown, the same scruffy slippers on her feet, is Beth. And she looks absolutely petrified.

* * *

I am so shocked to see her that the only thought I can process is that Anna has opened the door by herself – something I have repeatedly warned her not to do. But when I reprimand her, she just shrugs.

'Beth isn't a stranger, Mummy,' Anna says, throwing her arms around Beth's waist. 'Are you, Beth?'

Beth's eyes fill with water, which she blinks away quickly. Then she gets down on her knees in front of Anna, takes her little hands in hers and says, 'No, I'm not a stranger, Anna.'

Relief surges through every part of my body, because in that moment, I know that my worst fears are not going to come true.

Anna cocks her head on one side and says, 'Did you bring Luna with you?'

Beth smiles and shakes her head.

Anna frowns and instantly wriggles away. Giving Beth her best *laters* wave, she trots off towards her bedroom. Clearly Beth isn't such an attractive prospect without the massive ball of fluff in tow. Beth slowly gets to her feet and darts a furtive glance over the top of my head.

'David's in the shower,' I say. 'But he'll be out soon.'

She nods and bites her lip.

'I saw him get out of the taxi earlier, so I thought I'd...'

She falters then, hands clasping and unclasping, her complexion growing paler by the second.

I offer her a coffee, but she shakes her head. There's so much to say yet I know I'm not the one to say it. The sound of a door clicking punctuates the silence. Beth's eyes widen. She shifts a little.

'Don't go!' I blurt out, terrified she'll leave. I know what a huge step it must have been for her to come over here, how nervous she must be, and I can't bear the thought of her bottling it.

'I won't!' she says, almost crossly.

'OK, sorry,' I say.

The silence falls again and it's too much for my nerves.

'This is a bit awks, isn't it?' I say, and immediately feel like a knob.

Beth raises her eyebrows at me and then her head turns sharply at the sound of light footsteps. My heart thumps in my chest, and although instinct tells me I should probably warn David that his half-sister is waiting for him, my feet are well and truly planted to the ground.

And before I know it, David is standing at the entrance to the living room, with a towel around his waist, his hair sparkling with droplets. He lets out a puzzled 'Oh' when he spies Beth. Unlike me, he's never met her before.

Beth crosses the living room quickly, her slippers making soft thuds on the floor.

'David, I'm Beth,' she says, through a shuddering breath.

Then she holds out her small, trembling hand.

David stares at her and then slowly takes her hand as if in a trance.

Beth closes her eyes for a second and swallows deeply, the tension falling from her face. It occurs to me that she's been as worried about David's reaction as I have been about hers. She clears her throat and offers him a hint of a smile.

'Actually, my real name is Elspeth, but I never liked it...'

David just stares at her, still clutching her hand, and she continues to look directly into his eyes as if her gaze alone will give him the strength he needs to respond. It works.

'You know, Bonnie wanted to call me Magnus,' he says slowly.

And then the pair of them break into huge smiles at the exact same time, while I look on, my heart unable to cope with the emotion of it all, hot tears cascading down my cheeks.

49

'So, if Beth is my half-auntie, does that mean that I half own Luna?'

David catches my eye and grins. Trust Anna to try to capitalise on the situation. It's been a week since Beth and David met and, as things are going so well, we have decided to fill Anna in on the good news.

'I suppose you would be entitled to some kind of shared owner-ship under the circumstances,' David says, using the kind of corporate speak he tends to trot out when he's under pressure to say the right thing.

Anna turns to me, puzzled.

'The answer is yes,' I say to her, and she squeals and wraps her arms around me.

'I'm off to find *my* cat!' she says and races out the door into the back garden.

'Well, that was easy!' David says, smiling.

I smile back, delighted to see him so happy. After meeting Beth, David demanded a week off and The Firm, although disgruntled by the short notice, conceded. No doubt they will get their pound of flesh, as my mother calls it, when he returns to the office on Monday. But still, it's been worth it.

* * *

David has spent every day with Beth. For the first couple of days David saw her in her house but in the end, he managed to persuade her to leave the house and go out in public. Granted, they deliberately stayed away from the high street, seeking out quiet pathways to take long walks, each of them eager to get to know the other after all these years. Despite the eight-year age gap, they like the same music and love the same types of food. They have also bonded over their shared domestic quirks including the colour-coded tea towels organised by function. Beth is the only other person I've heard of who does this.

The best news, though, is that Beth is finally talking to Bonnie again. I am so happy for them and hope that they will eventually end up as close as they were before.

So far, I have deliberately kept my distance from Beth, wanting to give her the time she needs to bond with David. In any case, I have plenty to occupy me. Brigitte (I still can't call her Brigid) is home from hospital with her as yet unnamed baby – 'I'm going to ask my followers for some name choices' – and has us all run ragged. I'm in charge of picking up Cosette and Odette after school every day and giving them their tea before dropping them back. For the most part, it's not been too traumatic, but no matter what way you look at it, three five-year-olds in the house is no picnic. Mind you, it could be worse – I could be Darcy, who is practically a live-in unpaid nanny, changing nappies, doing all Brigitte's shopping, and taking the baby out in the pram. All this on top of her job and trying to manage her own five kids. But it doesn't stop there: Darcy has also teamed up with Sakura, PTA mum and divorce lawyer extraordinaire, to browbeat Joe into cutting a fair deal for Brigitte in the divorce.

When I hint to Darcy that she might just be overdoing it (and more to the point, Brigitte just might be taking the piss), she shakes her head vigorously.

'I'm just so happy that she is back in my life and that my kids get to know their cousins properly after all this time.'

And when I see her eyes light up like that, I know she really means it. Inspired by her selfless nature, I send what I hope is a meaningful text to Bea, Jen and Dee, about the life-changing power of forgiveness.

Instantly, I knew I shouldn't have bothered.

Jen:

Ah Jesus, Saoirse. Are you on your feckin' deathbed or something?
Save the preaching for Sunday Mass...

Bea:

Wow! Someone's on the happy pills.

In fact, the only person who seems to take my text seriously is Dee, whose life, judging by her more recent texts, seems to have calmed down a bit. Her reply is simple but thoughtful.

Dee:

I think that's a lovely thing to say about forgiveness and I couldn't agree more.

Jen then ruins it by responding:

Bloody hell, get the pair of you to a convent and be done with it!

Still, I don't care what they say. I've learned that even the most hopeless of situations can improve through the goodness of people, and that's a lesson I am determined never to forget.

* * *

David goes to pack for his work trip tomorrow, so I grab a jacket and walk out into the freezing February sunshine, scanning the garden for Anna. It doesn't take me long to find her hunched down on the frosty grass, stroking Luna with a look of pure adoration on her pink little face.

'I'm stroking *my* cat, Mummy!' she says, beaming at me.

'Great!' I say, as sincerely as I can.

Much as I love to see her so happy, I can't help but feel a bit concerned. I know there's a few months to go yet before we return to London, but she's not going to be thrilled about leaving 'her' Luna behind.

The back door flies open, and Beth appears dressed in a gorgeous, fluffy, yellow jumper and a pair of black leggings. Her hair, which is usually severely tied back in a ponytail, is falling in gentle waves around her shoulders. She waves at me, a warm smile across her face.

'Saoirse! Do you have time for a coffee?'

I glance at Anna.

'Anna can come too!' Beth says, clearly noting my hesitation. 'Luna has some new toys!'

Anna is up like a shot and in through the door before I have a chance to put one foot in front of the other. The truth is, I'm a little nervous. Now that Beth has bonded so quickly with David, I feel under even more pressure to do the same.

'Come in! Come in!' she says cheerily, throwing the door wide open.

I walk quickly towards her beaming smile, wondering how this could be the same person who slammed the door in my face not so long ago. She leads me through the utility and into the kitchen.

The first thing that catches my eye is a small white wheelie suitcase, positioned on one of the kitchen chairs.

I can feel my face falling.

'You're leaving,' I say.

She glances at the case and then back at me, her eyes wide.

'Yes, I'm flying out to the UK to see Mum,' she says. 'It's time we made up in person.'

Wow.

'That's amazing news!' I say, pulling her in for a short hug.

She embraces me before drawing back.

'It was David,' she says simply. 'Listening to him over the last few days made me realise that if he can forgive her for her past, then I should too.'

Then she shakes her head as if she is annoyed with herself.

'All these months, I've been making it all about me. How could she have given up a baby when she knew I wanted one so badly? Why did she not tell me earlier? I just never really thought about what she had been through. Then the other day, when I finally opened up all those little envelopes...'

She takes a deep breath as if to gather herself.

'I feel terrible about ignoring them. I presumed the notes would be her begging my forgiveness and I wasn't ready for that. But they weren't like that at all. They were about me – little lines reminding me of my strength, resilience, courage – and how I needed to forgive myself.'

She lets out a shuddering breath.

'And the more I read, the more I knew she was right. I've been blaming myself for not being able to conceive – something that I thought every woman "should" be able to do – and it's been eating me alive. I can't go on like this – thinking that I'm a failure and lashing out at everyone around me.'

I walk over to her and give her another hug.

'I'm so glad you're going to see your mum,' I say.

She hugs me back tightly and then pulls away a little.

'And I'm so glad I met you, David and Anna,' she says, smiling warmly.

Then she shakes her head a little as if coming out of a dream and says, 'Goodness, I haven't even offered you a cup of tea or coffee! Come and sit down at the table.'

I sit down on one of the chairs at the table and watch as she bustles around the kitchen, marvelling again at how much things have changed since I met her. And although it's wonderful that things are coming together, I can't help but feel a bit sad that Beth is leaving so soon. I had been hoping Anna and I could spend some time with her. But when I say this to her, she looks back at me and smiles.

'You're not getting rid of me that easily,' she says. 'It's only a week. Then I'll be back here for another few months.'

I let out a squeal.

'That's great news!' I say.

'Then it'll be back to London again,' she says, smiling.

Beth in London. This is fabulous news.

I do have one more question, but I don't know if we're at the stage in our friendship for me to ask it.

'You've gone all quiet,' she says, setting two cups of tea carefully on the table before flopping down on the chair beside me.

I decide to go for it.

'What about Jonas?' I say.

She sighs. 'I have to talk to him. I don't think we will ever get back to where we were, but we need to put the flat on the market at the very least. I just hope we can part on good terms.'

'And work?' I say.

'I'm going to see my boss when I'm back in London to talk about next steps. I've been given the year off, so I don't have to make my mind up just yet, but despite everything, I miss it. I know I froze when you asked me to deliver Brigitte's baby—'

'—But in the end, you overcame your fears and found the courage to get back into doctor mode,' I finish for her. 'If that ambulance hadn't arrived in time, I have no doubt you could have delivered that baby safely.'

She nods slowly and looks thoughtful for a moment. 'I can't really explain what happened. I think it was her pain that jolted me into action – it forced me to remember why I became a doctor in the first place. Then all my instincts kicked in and I couldn't resist any longer. I had to help.'

'I'd say you're a brilliant doctor,' I say, patting her on the arm.

She throws me a shy smile. Then she takes a sip of tea. 'I ran into Darcy with Brigitte's baby in the pram when I was coming out of Fletcher's Flowers yesterday.'

Wow! Beth venturing out to the high street? She has come a long way.

She must notice my surprise because she tells me that she was keen to apologise to Fletcher for slamming the door in his face so many times when he was trying to deliver Bonnie's flowers.

'It's not just Fletcher. I feel so bad for the way I've behaved to everyone around here. I considered everyone a threat but now I see that everyone was just being kind.'

'And how were you when you saw Brigitte's baby?' I ask, knowing how difficult it must have been for her.

She folds her arms across her fluffy jumper. 'You know, that's the weird thing, I didn't feel anything. Obviously, I thought she was gorgeous but I didn't feel the usual pang of emptiness.'

'You're healing,' I say softly.

'I hope so.'

Then she darts a nervous glance at me.

'I was wondering if you could do me a favour,' she says.

'Anything.'

'Would you mind taking care of Luna for the week? I can leave you the house keys.'

Anna's Christmases have all come at once.

I tell her that's no problem and she smiles.

Luna stalks into the kitchen, her tail very firmly in the air, Anna in hot pursuit. When Beth tells Anna that Luna is all hers for the next week, Anna actually climbs up onto Beth's knee and sobs with happiness. Beth rocks her back and forth, hugging her close, and kissing her on her wet cheeks. My heart swells. She is already part of our family.

As we head out the door, she tells me that she'll be over soon to say goodbye to David. I give her a quick hug and tell her I can't wait to spend more time with her over the next few months.

My phone pings just as Anna and I walk back into the pool house with a text from my mother. Apparently, Miguel has been approved as her 'plus one' for Jen's wedding. She is officially 'going public'. With everything that's been going on lately, I have unconsciously pushed the most important event of the year to the back of my mind. Jen's wedding will be here before we know it.

IRELAND

50

It is early on the morning of the wedding and Jen, David and Anna are still fast asleep in Bea's mum's glass architectural miracle, The Cube. I'm standing on the clifftop, my feet brushed by swathes of coarse, wavy grass, gazing at the churning Irish sea, breathing in deep lungfuls of the salty sea air. It may be mid-April but spring has certainly not yet sprung in this corner of southeast Ireland. The wind whips my face, but I am in no hurry to go back inside. With the inevitable wedding chaos, this is bound to be the most peace I get all day.

I exhale in satisfaction. It may be grey and blustery but it's the perfect weather to blow away the last vestiges of jet lag. We flew from New York to Dublin a couple of nights ago and stayed with my mum, before driving down here in our rental car yesterday evening. Mum is driving with Miguel a bit later, timing her arrival for the beginning of the ceremony at 2 p.m. – 'I don't want to be around for all the build-up,' my mother said fussily. 'I just want to *arrive*, you know?'

I know exactly what she is planning – to swan down the aisle with Miguel on her arm to make a point in front of Jen's mum and

Betty-from-the-beach that she's 'going public' with her new man. Still, I say nothing: I need to keep on Mum's good side as she and Miguel have offered to take Anna back to their hotel tonight, giving David and me the very rare chance to really let our hair down.

As I watch the waves crash along the shore, the memories wash over me one by one. It's hard to believe that the last time I was at The Cube, I was going through such turmoil. Not only had I been convinced that David was having an affair, but I felt I was failing at everything: my marriage, parenting, my job. But now, standing here, I feel reborn. Like all the troubles of the past have just melted away.

Although we have spent great chunks of the year apart, David and I are stronger than ever; Anna seems to be growing out of her meltdowns and I'm enjoying her company more every day; thanks to the PTA crew, my career is also on the up. Madison, one of the PTA mums, used her connections in the magazine world to get me an interview with a major parenting magazine, and the publicity has really driven sales. Much to my relief, there has been no more negative commentary on my website, and even Brigitte has announced my book as 'The Motherhood Bible' on her freshly rebranded Instagram account (CallMeBrigid: my life as a fabulously fashionable single mum) to her legion of followers.

Now that Brigitte has dropped the 'throw yourself in front of a bus for your man' angle, I'm delighted with the post. She might not be posting pictures of herself looking knackered with baby vomit down her front, but she's a lot more authentic than she was before. Even her Irish accent is making a comeback.

Beth has also been wonderful at spreading the word, by constantly recommending my book to everyone she meets. My heart leaps whenever I think of her. Ever since she came back from visiting Bonnie in London, we have seen each other almost every day.

When David is home, she comes over for dinner or babysits

Anna for us when we go out. Anna is besotted with her auntie and loves the fact that Beth brings Luna with her when babysitting. Beth has also started coming with me to meet Darcy and Brigitte for coffee now and then.

After much cajoling, Bonnie has finally accepted David's offer to fly her over to visit us in May. She's going to be an emotional mess when she sees David and Beth together – even now, she can't stop tearing up over Zoom whenever she calls David and me. I'm happy for her – this is the family reunion she has been desperately longing for.

I'm so lost in my reverie that I jump when I feel a sharp tug on my coat sleeve. I look down to see Anna, the strong winds rendering her features almost invisible as strands of brown hair whip across her face. It takes me a moment to realise she is still in her pyjamas and entirely barefoot.

'Where's your dad?' I say, puzzled.

I'm pretty sure David wouldn't let her go into the freezing cold without anything on her feet.

'He's popped out to buy some bacon and eggs for breakfast.'

Last night Jen mentioned wanting an Irish breakfast to 'line her stomach before all the boozing' and David must have remembered.

'Come on, Mummy!' Anna says, pulling at my sleeve impatiently. 'Jen is having a connip-shit!'

A fit of giggles rises up in my chest.

'I think you mean "conniption".' I laugh, bending down to give her a hug.

I take Anna's soft little hand in mine as we start walking back through the elegant, white wedding marquee, which had been constructed before our arrival, sparse apart from a pale peach carpet covering the floor, and in through the sliding glass doors that lead into the kitchen.

'Why is Jen having a hissy fit?' I say to Anna. 'It's hours until the wedding.'

'She says her big fat arse won't fit into her fancy wedding knickers,' Anna replies gravely.

Shite.

Unlike me, Jen is into her lingerie and she was thrilled to be gifted a gorgeous set from an expensive brand for her wedding night, courtesy of her TV crew. She mustn't have tried on the knickers before today.

I slide open the glass doors and a warm blast of air instantly eases the burning sensation in my cheeks. Anna slides the door closed, letting out a huge sigh.

'I'm just fed up waiting for Harry to get here!' she says, raising her eyes skyward.

God love her. She's been asking for Harry ever since we arrived in Wexford yesterday.

'I know it's frustrating, Anna,' I say, stroking her wind-tangled hair, 'but Harry will be here as soon as the wedding ceremony starts at 2 p.m., OK?'

Anna glares at me and then stalks off towards the living area, muttering something about being late for a YouTube Live event.

She's not the only one tired of waiting. I had hoped that Bea would have stayed here last night too, and it's not just her I am keen to see. The truth is I am *dying* to meet Tom – the man who has broken through her tough, no-nonsense shell to capture her heart.

But Bea refused the invitation to stay over the second I suggested it to her: 'Number one: there's only two bedrooms so there's no room for us. Number two: no bride needs two hyper children running around on the morning of their wedding. Number three: you and Jen should spend the night together before her big day.'

Much as I was disappointed Bea wouldn't be joining us, I could understand her reasons, and she was right, it was a lovely evening with Jen last night. David tactfully took Anna off for a pizza in the village, giving Jen and me a chance to cosy up on the couch together for a decent heart-to-heart over a couple of glasses of dry white wine.

I was concerned about the wedding jitters, my mother's voice ringing through my head: 'After what that Liam did to Jen last time, I'd be terrified of him not showing up!' But last night Jen seemed completely content, doling out strict instructions for me to rescue her if Betty or any of her mum's other friends cornered her at any point, and proudly showing off the stunning diamond-encrusted silver eternity ring her husband-to-be had given her the day before. In fact, forget about being 'jilted'; her only concern was Liam rocking up to the ceremony 'hungover to bejaysus' from getting shite-faced in the hotel room he was sharing with his best man – 'I swear to God, Saoirse,' she said, her eyes flashing from below her perfectly shaped eyebrows, 'if he turns up tomorrow with blood-shot eyes and stinking of stale booze, I'll feckin' murder him.'

I'll murder him too.

I leave the kitchen and turn in to the first bedroom on the right. Jen squeals when she spots me and I'm not surprised. Apart from a seriously uncomfortable-looking pale pink corset covering her upper body, she is entirely naked.

'You've nobody with you, do you?' she says, frantically grabbing a heavy blanket off the back of an armchair and swinging it swiftly around her bottom half.

I shake my head, my gaze landing on the chaos in the bedroom. Piles of half-open tubes and lipsticks litter every surface, and torn packaging is strewn across the sheets of the unmade bed.

'Oh, good!' she says, dropping the blanket, her eyes wild. 'Look at the state of this!'

She grabs a pair of delicately laced, cream, silk knickers off the bed and steps into them, pulling them up her enviably toned, bronzed legs before coming to an inconvenient halt just at the point they reach her thighs. She straightens up again and puts her hand on her hips.

'See?' she says, her face pink with frustration.

'Right, they don't fit, but surely you have another pair you can use.'

She shakes her head miserably.

'I don't. All my fancy stuff for the honeymoon is back in Dublin.'

That makes sense. The newlyweds are going back to Dublin tomorrow before flying out to the Maldives the following day for two weeks of sunshine and romance. She looks at the mess on the bed dolefully.

'I'm not wearing me holey pants on my wedding day, Saoirse,' she says.

I open my mouth.

'And I'm NOT going commando.'

I close it again.

Then she looks at me with a glimmer of hope in her eyes and says, 'Do you have fancy knickers I can borrow?'

I raise my eyebrows at her, slightly irritated that after over three decades of friendship, she still doesn't remember that I'm strictly a big, comfy pants kind of girl. Even if I did have fancy pants, they'd be swimming on her. She is tiny compared to me.

Defeated, she rolls the knickers off, steps out of them, and then asks me to tie the loose strings on her corset to make sure that it at least 'bleedin' fits'.

It does. Thank Christ.

'Where am I going to get a decent pair of knickers?' she huffs, as I work my way through unclasping all the tiny hooks.

I think hard.

'What about Dee?' I say.

Jen half-turns her head. 'Do you think?'

'I don't know, but it's worth asking,' I say, finally reaching the last hook.

Jen carefully takes off the corset. I take a satin robe off the back of the door and she shrugs into it.

'Her arse would probably be the same size as mine,' Jen says, chewing her lip.

'Grand, I'll give her a shout now, so,' I say, pulling my phone out of my jeans pocket.

I've been meaning to have a quick chat with Dee before the wedding mayhem started. Like Bea, I texted her trying to persuade her to come for drinks last night but she cried off, saying she wanted to be as well-rested as possible for today. I text Dee and give her a rundown of knickers-gate and she immediately texts back and tells me to come over to scan her knicker collection.

I tell Jen and her face relaxes. 'OK, fab. Just no thongs – I can't have anything going up my arse-crack on my wedding day.'

I laugh and head off to check on Anna. I find her on the couch, glued to her iPad.

'I'm off to Dee's house for a bit,' I say loudly. She nods in a vague way and I make my way towards the front door.

David appears in the hallway, a plastic bag hanging off one wrist.

'Breakfast!' he says, turning around and grinning at me.

My stomach growls – I haven't eaten yet today and I would kill for a proper Irish breakfast, but Jen will *kill* me if I don't sort out the knickers situation pronto. So, with huge regret, I tell David to get cracking on breakfast and that I'll be back as quick as I can.

'Right. Knickers – Dee's house – breakfast. Got it,' he says, passing me the car keys as I head out.

* * *

Dee's house is on the other side of the village, so I drive right through the centre, past McGowan's pub – memories flooding back of the drunken nights I spent there with Dee and Jen last summer.

I pull up alongside a smart-looking, semi-detached bungalow at the side of the road and switch off the engine. I do a quick calculation in my head – Dee's little boy, Conor, must be four now, and his angelic-looking baby sister, Niamh, must be close to two.

I walk towards the front door and press the bell. Dee opens it within a few seconds and I smile. It's so good to see her after all this time. She looks well – the short pixie haircut she was sporting the last time I saw her is now a chic bob, which perfectly frames her delicate features.

'Come in, come in!' she says, gesturing at me violently. 'The house is a shit-hole, by the way.'

I tut at her as I follow her inside. Honestly, why does every mother say the same thing when you go around to their house? I couldn't give a shite about the mess – all I want is a cup of tea, a chat, and a place to plant myself.

She leads me into a living room full of comfy, over-stuffed couches, knitted throws and colourful, mismatching cushions – exactly the décor I would have gone for in our house if David hadn't insisted on museum-chic.

I settle myself on a sofa between two bright-orange cushions decorated with cartoon elephants while Dee stays standing, twisting her hands together, offering me tea, coffee and everything else under the sun. I look at her curiously but she won't meet my gaze. Is it my imagination or does she look nervous?

I refuse everything because I need to see her knicker collection and get a pair back to Jen as soon as possible.

But before I can say this, she sits down next to me.

'Where are the kids?' I say, looking around, thinking that it's suspiciously quiet for a house with two young children.

'Sean has taken them to the supermarket,' she says.

Wow – I'm impressed. I never would have gone near a super-market when Anna was that young. And on a Saturday too. I tell her this and she clasps her hands together.

'A lot has changed over the last few months,' she says quietly.

Then she looks away for a moment. When she looks back, her eyes are full of tears.

'Oh no! Dee! What's wrong?' I say, rubbing her arm.

She looks down at her hands and heaves a big sigh.

'Ah, look, I wasn't going to say anything until after the wedding... even now I don't know how to explain what happened, but I have to try,' she says, her voice wobbling.

I squeeze her arm, feeling totally helpless, and also guilty. Clearly something terrible has happened while I've been in New York. I should have checked in on her more.

'OK,' she says, taking a deep breath, furiously swiping the tears from her eyes. She shifts a little to face me and straightens her shoulders.

'Just after you left for New York, things got really bad between myself and Sean. Niamh still has me up almost every night and Conor is a relentless ball of energy, and I was struggling to get from one end of the day to the other. I took it all out on Sean, who, although working crazy hours himself was, in hindsight, trying his best to help. But in my emotional state, nothing he did was good enough – the way he prepared food, folded the washing, how he dressed them.'

This is exactly how David and I were when we first had Anna – sniping at each other over the tiniest things.

'Could you not get any help with the kids?' I say softly, because this is the one regret I had as a first-time mum – being too proud to ask for help, worried I would be judged if I didn't do it all by myself.

'Sean constantly suggested it. His mum does the odd bit of

babysitting anyway, but I didn't want to her think I couldn't cope. Of course, now I know she would have loved to spend more time with them, but at the time, I was too full of rage, exhaustion and paranoia to think straight.'

'So, what happened?'

She sighs. 'What happened is that I started drinking – and more than my usual "reward" glass of wine after the kids went to bed. Soon I was sinking a bottle of wine a night. Sean begged me to stop but I accused him of wanting to take away the only comfort I had in my life.'

Jesus.

'I was horrible to him, Saoirse,' she says, her voice cracking. 'I told him I hated him and I wanted him out of my life. On the worst nights, I fired any object I could lay my hands on at him. I was completely out of control.'

'You've been through hell and back,' I say, putting an arm around her.

She rubs her forehead with one hand.

'Things came to a head one afternoon in early December when I tried to get into the car drunk,' she says, her face screwed up in pain. 'Thank Christ the kids weren't with me. But if it wasn't for Sean, I would have driven away in that state. It was the wake-up call I needed. Sean took me to see a therapist – something he had been suggesting for months. I meet her twice a week now and it's the best thing I ever did.'

'Ah, that's brilliant, Dee.'

Good on her. There is so much stigma around therapy but I am a firm believer in the power of ranting to a non-judgemental stranger. I tell her this and she gives me a weak smile.

'Yes, she is amazing. Thanks to her I have been able to share my feelings honestly and openly with Sean, which has brought us closer together. Now the kids are with Sean's mum three days a week and for the first time since they were born, I feel like I have the freedom and the confidence to go back to work – at least part-time.'

'That's fantastic, Dee!' I say, giving her a warm squeeze.

Much as I know she loves her children, everyone needs something for themselves.

Then she shoots me a haunted look.

'Saoirse – I wish I could tell you that's the end of it, but it's not.'

Then she rises slowly from the couch and walks out of the room.

My phone pings.

Where are me knickers?

I have been so caught up in Dee's story, I have totally forgotten about my original mission. I text Jen back quickly, and tell her to keep her knickers on, to which she responds seconds later with the middle finger emoji.

Dee returns, holding a laptop. She sits down next to me, positions it on my knee and flips it open. I frown at the screen, puzzled. It's my author website.

'Why are you...?' I say.

She reaches across and taps a couple of keys. An image of the comments page pops up, and then the penny drops.

Oh my god.

She hangs her head, heaving agonised sobs, but this time I don't move to comfort her. I am completely numb. For so long I pointed the finger at Brigitte but all the time it was Dee who was 'Anon-Mum'. I feel like I have been punched in the stomach.

'Why?' I whisper.

'I am so sorry, Saoirse,' she says, raising her head, her eyes pleading. 'I was in such a bad way and I was lashing out at everyone. It seemed like all my friends were having the time of their lives and I was trapped in this awful cycle of sleep deprivation, parenting and endless hell. You were on a trip of a lifetime to New York – a place I'd always wanted to visit – and you had this amazing new book out... I was so jealous. Jen had a fabulous wedding to arrange, and here I was trapped in a boring, humdrum routine. I was surrounded by family but I'd never felt so alone. So, one day back in September, I received your book from Jen in the post and I was torn apart with jealousy. I didn't even read it; instead, I got drunk and set up a fake email account and began posting negative comments on your website. And I'm ashamed to say I got a buzz out of it. The fact that I could behave that badly without anyone finding out felt like the most control I had over my life at the time.'

I'm desperately trying to understand where she's coming from, but how could deliberately hurting someone you care about feel good? Those comments knocked my confidence so much that I didn't even want to have a book launch, not to mention that horrible, lingering feeling in the pit of my stomach that someone was out to get me. I could never have guessed in a million years that that 'someone' was a close friend.

Dee takes my hand. 'Part of my treatment involves apologising to the people I have hurt when I was out of control. Saoirse, I would be furious in your shoes, but please think about forgiving me. And for the record, I read your book recently and loved every single sweary word.'

I look dumbly at her hand in mine. Part of me wants to shake it off and scream in her face, while the other part wants desperately to find a way to forgive her. At the moment, I can't seem to do either.

The pinging of my phone cuts through my swirling thoughts.

'Knickers,' I blurt out.

Dee nods quickly and disappears out of the room again.

I reach for my phone with shaking hands but it's not Jen. It's

Bea, saying she's at Heathrow and will be in touch when they leave Dublin Airport. Christ, it's 9.30 a.m.; I've been here almost an hour. Jen will kill me if I don't get back soon. I rise to my feet just as Dee re-enters the room with a small bag.

'I've put the best ones in there,' she says in a small voice, handing me the bag. 'Tell Jen she is welcome to choose whatever pair she likes.'

I take the bag quickly and move towards the door. Now that I have found my legs again, I just want to get the hell out of here.

As I pass her, she touches my arm.

'I'll stay out of your way at the wedding,' she says. 'The last thing I want is to make things awkward for you.'

I brush past her, open the front door with trembling hands and walk quickly out to the car. Keen as I am to get away, once I'm in the car, I take a few deep breaths, waiting for the nerves to settle before starting the engine. Dee stands in the doorway watching me, the look on her face so distressed that I almost feel pity for her.

Almost.

* * *

When I feel calm enough, I drive back to The Cube slowly, forcing my mind to focus on the road. It's only when I have parked in the drive that I allow myself to think.

Dee. Of all people. I know we've only spent a bit of time together since we met a few years ago right here in this village, but I thought we had a bond, and we've always kept in touch. I had come to see her as someone I could trust. How the hell could she do this to me? I root around in my bag for a tissue and wipe my tears away quickly. I need to put my game face on. The last thing I want is to ruin Jen's big day.

A knock on the window makes me jump and my stomach

collapses in relief when I see it's David. I press the button and lower the window.

'What's wrong?' he says immediately.

I try to shake my head in a *sure, I'm grand* sort of way, but it's no good. I start to sob and he hurries around to the other side of the car and before I know it, he's sitting in the passenger seat holding my hand. I tell him everything and he listens without interrupting.

When I have reached the end of my tissues, he nods thoughtfully.

'Listen, Saoirse. This is a real shock and I know how awful and betrayed you must feel.'

I DO feel betrayed.

'But people don't act like themselves when they're going through trauma. I mean, look at Beth. She spent months shunning Bonnie and everyone else who came near her because she blamed herself for not being able to get pregnant. And look how badly Brigitte behaved towards Darcy to conceal the fact that her marriage was in trouble.'

I know he has a point. Loneliness and desperation can make you do stupid things, especially when you don't have the right support. Look how quickly I went downhill after I was mugged in Manhattan. It didn't take long before I was drinking too much, comfort-eating, too paranoid to leave the apartment. But unlike Dee, I didn't lash out at those I was supposed to care about.

'It hurts,' I say, feeling fresh tears fall down my cheeks.

'Of course, it does!' he says, releasing my hand to brush the tears away from my face. 'And I'm not saying you should forgive her straight away, but it took a huge amount of courage to confess. She could have said nothing.'

Deep down, I know he's right and although a huge part of me desperately wants to slag her off to Bea, Jen and Mum (my mother would seriously dine out on this one), something is stopping me. If the last few months have taught me anything, it's the power we all have to dig deep and forgive.

I explain this to David and he wraps his arms around me.

'Proud of you, Saoirse,' he says.

I hug him back. I'm proud of me too.

'Jesus Christ!'

David and I spring apart.

It's Jen – hair wild, wrapped in the same dressing gown she was wearing when I left her earlier, although this time there is a drizzle of what looks to be egg yolk down one lapel. My stomach grumbles again. I seriously need to eat something. Jen's face is a colourful display of pink and green eye shadow and orange blusher. I detect the work of Anna.

'Would the pair of you stop fondling each other and help me get sorted for my feckin' wedding!'

I start apologising and she stares at me, eyes narrowed.

'Why are your eyes all red? What's wrong?'

'PMT,' David says instantly.

Fair play. The man has been trained well.

I hastily grab the bag of knickers and shove them through the window at her. She snatches them from me with the eagerness of a heroin addict and I watch with bated breath as she roots through the bag. Then she brings out a pair of beautiful, cream, lace and satin pants, holds them against her crotch and smiles.

'These will do,' she says.

Thank Christ.

David and I scramble out of the car and walk quickly with Jen towards The Cube.

'Anna give you a hand with the make-up, then?' I grin.

'Wouldn't take no for an answer,' she says, marching straight towards the bedroom. 'Now let me try on these bloody knickers before the marquee people arrive. Christ – Nora the make-up woman and Mary the hairdresser will be here in an hour.'

David catches me by the waist in the hallway and wraps me in a big hug.

'Let's try and put all this behind us, get shite-faced, and dance badly enough to traumatise Anna well into her teenage years,' he says as he pulls back.

I kiss him and smile into his kind, brown eyes.

'Agreed,' I say. 'But for the love of god give me a bacon sandwich first.'

51

It is well into the evening of the wedding and so far, the day couldn't have gone any better. Despite knicker-gate, Jen looked the very picture of serenity as she walked down the aisle in a simple but elegant, fitted, strapless, ivory dress that showed off her perfect figure in exquisite detail. Her hair had been expertly arranged in a fabulous up-do with tendrils of curls framing her meticulously made-up face. Contrary to Jen's (worst) expectations, Liam showed up looking fresh and clear-eyed, and despite my misgivings about him, I couldn't help but shed a tear during the vows – the pair of them looked so in love.

He'd better not cock this up.

Anna, in a pale-mint, pleated playsuit with delicate ivory roses sewn onto the neckline, carried out her flower girl duties beautifully – scattering rose petals carefully and very seriously down the aisle. I had one anxious moment when Harry raced into the marquee just as Jen reached the altar, quickly followed by a harassed-looking Bea dressed in a satin tailored suit in a stunning shade of peach, with heels to match, and a tall, slim, entirely bald man wearing black, thick-framed glasses, in a soft grey suit and navy tie. The man jerked forward to catch Harry before he got too far up the aisle and firmly directed him by the shoulders into the back row. I noticed Bea flashing him a grateful smile as she pulled a wriggling Harry onto her knee.

Tom.

I must admit, I hadn't pictured Tom this way. It sounds shallow but compared to Ryan, Tom isn't model material, but then again why would she want a Ryan again after everything he did to her? As my mother always said: 'Get the rock stars and the bad boys out of your system in your twenties and find yourself a serious fella in your thirties and forties – because it's the geeks who make the best husbands in the end.'

I watch Anna now from the back of the marquee, where the music isn't as loud, dancing her heart out to a Taylor Swift song under a giant glitter ball, spinning Harry around, a huge smile on her face. Thanks to Nora, the make-up artist, Anna (at her insistence) looks like one of those kids from those American beauty pageant programmes – plastered in heavy make-up and looking about twenty-five years old.

But I can't complain – she's been an absolute star today. Not only was she quiet and attentive during the ceremony but she has also been a great little helper to the bride – fetching Jen's lipstick from the bedroom when Jen needed a touch-up before the drinks reception and staying alert during the fairly tedious wedding speeches.

The marquee company has done a fantastic job transforming the space for every stage of the wedding. The rows of gold, velvet chairs adorned with fresh Calla lilies set out for the ceremony were replaced with gorgeously dressed round tables adorned with huge floral arrangements of cherry blossom, and a smart buffet bar was set up along one side, overflowing with gourmet-style fish, chips and burgers. The perfect food to soak up all the alcohol. Now all the tables have been removed to make way for a gleaming, white, vinyl dancefloor, huge glitter balls and artfully placed lights that glow different colours to the beat of the music played by the energetic DJ in one corner.

'Ah, look at the pair of them,' my mother says, smiling. 'Still best pals.'

My heart fills up. It won't be long now until we're back in London for good and Anna and Harry can play to their hearts' content.

'Champagne?' a waiter offers and I take one eagerly.

I've held off on drinking too much until now in case Jen needs me for bridesmaid duties, and I wanted to keep a clear head and a calm mind for when I saw Dee again. She turned up at the ceremony, her skin looking paler than normal against her knee-length, bright-yellow dress. My mother, of course, was the first one to point this out (along with her relieved mutterings about thanking the Lord and heaven itself for Liam showing up) by whispering: 'Ah, very few people can get away with that shade of yellow. It draws colour from your face.'

I greeted Dee when our paths crossed on the way to the loos later and she gave me a tentative smile in return. I didn't see her much after that, but during the drinks reception I noticed she was drinking orange juice. Thankfully, Jen was too caught up with well-wishers to notice Dee slipping away before the dinner. One day soon, when I'm ready, I will call her and we will put all this behind us.

But, for now, Dee is gone, the formalities are over, and I can finally have a proper drink.

'I won't!' my mother says, fluttering her hands at the waiter, and he moves away.

She leans into me conspiratorially. 'Jesus, I'll be *floothered* if I have another one.'

I laugh and give her a hug.

'Well, you look fantastic!' I say.

And I mean it. She is wearing a gorgeous pale-pink, short-sleeved, calf-length dress trimmed with ivory lace that accentuates her small, neat figure.

'Ah, Miguel picked it out for me,' she says with a hint of pride in her eyes.

'Where is Miguel?' I say, conscious of the fact that, apart from greeting him earlier, I've barely set eyes on him.

'He's outside chatting to Jen's mum and a few of the others,' she says.

Jen, in a genius move, organised a covered, heated outdoor area for the oldies to save them from the booming music.

'I'd say he's a bit of a hit,' I say, nudging her.

She purses her lips.

By the set of her expression earlier walking in with Miguel, I think she expected more of a reaction from Jen's mum and her pals, but there wasn't so much as a sucking-in of breath – merely warm smiles and nods. I'd say after all her agonising, it's been a bit of an anti-climax for her.

'You're looking great yourself,' she says, scanning her eyes up and down my turquoise, strapless, floor-length dress that Brigitte chose for me from the boutique in Westmont, having left the baby, Charlotte – the name most voted by her Instagram followers – and her other kids at Darcy's house. To be honest, I'd thought I would never find a dress, given the extent of the 'well-intentioned' commentary from Brigitte whenever I had the misfortune to exit the changing room. But after conceding that this dress didn't make my boobs look as 'floppy' or my hips too 'child-bearingy', I agreed to buy it before checking the price, favouring the damage to my wallet over any further destruction to my confidence. But on the positive side, as the boutique was one of her sponsors, Brigitte redeemed herself by getting me a whopping discount.

'I suppose I should go and rescue Miguel,' Mum says. Then she points a warning finger at the champagne glass in my hand, and says, 'Don't be drinking too much of that stuff. You'll have a head on you tomorrow.'

I smile as I watch her walk slowly towards the exit, swaying a little as she goes.

The champagne tray passes by again and I swap my empty glass for two full glasses.

'Ah, champagne handcuffs!' a gruff voice heckles.

I turn around, balancing each glass in one hand and grin.

It's the groom himself, tie off, shirt collar unbuttoned, and by the flush in his cheeks, a little worse for wear.

'Too right!' I say, taking a big swig. I'm starting to feel tipsy already.

'Get it down you, girl,' Liam says emphatically, draining half his pint glass.

We clink glasses.

'Ah, it's been a great day,' he says, his eyes growing soft. 'Isn't Jen just a stunner?'

His eyes are so full of love that I can't help but smile.

But still. As her best friend, it would be remiss of me not to have 'the chat'.

I neck the rest of the champagne feeling the bubbles of confidence growing. Then I take a step towards him and look him directly in the eye.

'Listen, Liam, I'm delighted for you both, but if you ever, and I mean *ever*—'

'Jesus, I know!' he says seriously. 'I fucked up, Saoirse, and I know I am the luckiest man alive to be married to her now. I will never ever hurt Jen again.'

I narrow my eyes and give him a menacing *too right you won't, mister* stare, just to be sure.

'Good enough,' I say, and I clink my glass to his and we both drink steadily.

'Where is the beautiful bride anyway?' I say, looking around.

'Last I saw her, she was doing shots with Bea in the kitchen,' he says.

Christ, I'd better head there quick-smart. I'm under strict instructions to protect her from being *that* bride – the one who pukes all over her wedding dress and passes out on the dance floor.

I head straight for the kitchen, catching sight of David in deep conversation with Tom, and I can't help but feel delighted at the thought of a bromance brewing. I collared Tom at the drinks reception and I love him already – he may be quietly spoken, but he has a wicked, dry sense of humour that makes him instantly likeable. I gave Bea my stamp of approval, to which she replied, 'Good! Because I'm keeping him!'

It doesn't take me long to spot Jen and Bea – the pair of them sitting at the kitchen table in the corner, a half-empty bottle of vodka and a couple of full shot glasses between them. When they see me, they both roar.

'Siddown! Jen says, violently pulling out a chair, mascara smudged, eyes dancing.

I turn to Bea, ready to exchange a *look at the state of Jen* glance but, judging by the glassiness of her stare, I'd say she is about the same degree of hammered.

Christ.

'Where'sh my hush-band?' Jen slurs as I sit down wearily on the chair.

Bea gives me a lopsided smile and says, 'She hasn't seen him since the first dance.'

Then the pair of them burst into giggles.

Water, I think. *They need water.* Just as I'm about to get up, Bea shouts suddenly.

'STOP!'

Jen jumps and she curses in a distinctly un-bridelike manner.

'Saoirse! Get yourself a glass!' Bea shouts.

'Good idea,' I say, reasoning I can get those two pissheads some water while I'm at it.

Just as I'm about to move off, Bea grabs my arm.

'What time is it?' she says in an urgent whisper.

I glance at my watch – there's no point in telling her to look at her own watch.

'It's just gone 10 p.m.,' I say.

Bea's mouth drops into a hard frown.

'That asshole was supposed to pick Harry up half an hour ago!' she says, tutting.

What's she talking about? Harry's staying with her and Tom in the hotel tonight. Unless...

A cold shiver runs through me.

'Bea,' I say sternly. 'What asshole?'

She says the name I was dreading.

'Oh, just Ryan,' she says.

Bubbles of anxiety swirl around my stomach, and suddenly I feel very sober indeed.

Jen turns to me, mouth open.

'Shiiiiiiit,' she says, pointing not so subtly towards David, who is chatting animatedly to Tom.

Bea clasps her hand to her mouth.

'Oh, don't worry, Saoirse – Ryan's under strict instructions to wait in the car. Adriana will come in to collect Harry.'

Thank god. I know it's been almost two years since Ryan kissed me in the park, and David and I have moved on, but let's face it: the last thing anyone wants is for their ex-crush to come face to face with their husband. Still, I'm cross Bea hasn't mentioned it before now and I tell her so.

'I'm so sorry – I only found out this morning. Adriana had a make-up gig in Dublin, but Ryan was supposed to pick up Harry from the hotel tomorrow. Anyway, the job finished early so he asked if he could drive down and pick up Harry this evening. I agreed because I thought it would be a chance for Tom and me to have a lie-in tomorrow.'

Jen pats my hand. 'David won't see Ryan. It's all grand, Shersha,' she says, in a soothing slur.

Sod this babysitting. After the Ryan scare, I need a proper drink.

I grab a shot glass from the kitchen cupboard, head straight back to the table, sit down and pour myself a shot of vodka. Then another. The warm liquid races to my stomach and to my head. I'm just considering pouring a third, when Bea looks at me, wide-eyed.

'Have you seen Harry recently? I need to get him ready.'

I sigh heavily. I can tell that she's in no fit state to be dealing with small children.

'I'll go,' I say, my head starting to buzz.

David calls to me just as I'm on my way out of the kitchen.

'Are you OK, Saoirse?' he says.

His forehead is glistening with the effects of booze, and his gaze is a little unsteady, but I'm glad he's letting off steam.

I blow him a kiss and Tom pretends to catch it, and David and Tom dissolve into giggles. Jesus, I must be the only one at this wedding who isn't utterly annihilated.

* * *

I make my way out into the marquee, scanning the dance floor for Harry and Anna. I crack up when I spot the pair of them dancing in a circle, each of them holding hands with Miguel and Liam, who, despite being fairly hammered, seems to be holding up better than his wife. It's not going to be easy breaking up the party. Grown-ups first. I put a hand on Miguel's shoulder and he whips around, releasing Anna's hand to give me a warm hug.

'Howerya, Saoirse!' he shouts, his eyes merry.

I'll never get tired of his Irish-isms.

'Where's your drink?' Liam says accusingly, pointing at my empty hands.

Before I can respond to either of them, Miguel's expression suddenly transforms into one that can only be described as shock, and Liam's mouth drops open. Both of them are staring at a fixed point behind me.

I freeze. I know the signs. I have seen the very same reaction before on the faces of both men and women.

Ryan.

Shit.

'Jesus,' Liam breathes, his pupils dilated.

Here we go.

'Deadly,' Miguel says, shaking his head slowly.

Oh, for goodness' sake.

'Are you seeing what I'm seeing?' Liam says, nudging Miguel heavily.

'I am,' Miguel breathes.

'Looks just like...'

Just spit it out. Yes, yes, Ryan is a dead ringer for Ryan Gosling – blah de blah.

And then, in perfect unison, they both say something completely unexpected.

'... Gisele.'

What?

I whip round and notice that the entire wedding party is staring in the same direction. But it's not Ryan standing at the side entrance of the marquee; it's a tall, lithe, tanned, willowy creature with blonde-streaked hair flowing down her shoulders to frame the type of perfectly symmetrical facial features that could only belong to a professional model. She's dressed simply in a pair of dark blue skinny jeans and an off-the-shoulder, white, cable-knit top, and she is absolutely breathtaking. This must be Adriana.

'Jesus, Saoirse – I don't know who she is, but we need to get yer wan Gisele out of here pronto,' Liam hisses in my ear. 'Talk about upstaging the bride.'

Oh god. He's right. Jen will go mental if she sees Adriana. As gorgeous as Jen is, she's no match for a twenty-something, super-model doppelganger.

'I'll handle it,' I say briskly.

Booting someone out of a wedding for being too gorgeous may not fall under the remit of bridesmaid duties, but for Jen's sake, I'm damn well going to do it.

I lean down and whisper into Harry's ear that Adriana is here to pick him up.

'Not going!' he says, stamping his smart black shoes.

Anna saves the day.

'Right, Harry – it's late. You're off!' she says bossily.

Then Anna takes Harry firmly by the arm and gazes up at me, eyebrows raised.

'Where to?'

'Erm, over there,' I say, pointing at Adriana.

She pulls Harry behind her with some force and he trips along after her, sulkily.

I follow them, reasoning that an adult should probably be involved somewhere along the line.

'There y'are now!' Anna says, half-pushing Harry towards Adriana.

Adriana immediately crouches to her knees and envelops him

in a hug.

'Harry! My love!' she murmurs into his ear.

Her voice is smooth and gorgeous.

Harry resists for a moment and then his shoulders relax and he hugs her back. I'm impressed; it's not easy to get a five-year-old boy out of the sulks.

She straightens up and beams at me.

'I'm Adriana,' she says. I introduce myself in return, and before I know what's happening, she's embracing me like a long-lost friend. She smells like all the flowery meadows in the land. I'm tempted to ask her what perfume she uses but I'm afraid she's going to tell me that it's her natural scent, and there's only so much perfection I can handle. Then she kisses me on both cheeks with her gorgeously shaped lips before pulling away. Looking at her now, I don't know why she's not a model rather than a make-up artist – it seems like the obvious career choice.

'I am sorry we are late,' she says. 'I don't like being late.'

Then she leans in and whispers, 'Ryan had trouble fixing the cover on the convertible. He was upset. Sometimes, Harry's dad can be a bit of an asshole.'

Her frankness catches me off guard and I burst out laughing.

She stands back, gives me a cheeky grin and an exaggerated shrug, then turns to Harry.

'Let's go, my darling,' she says, taking him by the hand.

It occurs to me that Harry hasn't a thing with him for bedtime, but when I tell her this, she just waves me away.

'No, no – you stay and enjoy the party. Send my love to Bea. We'll be fine, won't we, Harry?'

Harry nods, calmer now, and the two of them walk slowly towards the exit.

What a surreal moment. Meeting Ryan's new woman. And much as I'd love to hate her, I don't. She seems absolutely lovely and far too decent for a ratbag like him. Still, maybe she will keep him on his toes.

Anna yawns loudly. I take her by the hand, intending to find my mum to tell her that Anna is flagging, when suddenly she lets out a loud yelp.

'Mummy!' she says, looking at me with big, panicked eyes. 'Adriana forgot Harry's iPad!'

Oh shite. Harry won't be happy when he discovers his favourite toy is missing.

'I don't think we'll have time to look for it,' I say, turning back towards the exit. 'They'll be in the car by now.'

'But it's here, Mummy!' she says, dropping my hand.

Then she's off, weaving her way across to the other side of dance floor, and before I know it, she's back with Harry's iPad and a big smile on her face.

'We were taking videos of each other dancing.'

She thrusts the iPad into my hands.

'Go on! Give it to him!' she says, giving me a little push towards the side exit.

I hesitate. The last thing I want is Ryan coming in here to get it, and Bea will not be happy if her planned lie-in with Tom is interrupted by a call from Ryan tomorrow. So, I take a deep breath and step out into the dark night, walking as quickly as I can down the gravelly driveway in my impractically high, cream, satin shoes. My heartbeat quickens when I spot a red convertible parked with its lights still on. I throw back my shoulders and march quickly across the tarmac. I'll pass the iPad through the car window – I barely have to see him.

But just as I'm getting closer, the door on the driver's side flings open, releasing the sound of wailing and Ryan steps out, wearing a V-necked, navy and white, knitted, cricket sweater and dark blue jeans.

He slams the door and runs his hands through his dirty-blonde hair. His eyes fall on me, and his eyebrows shoot up in surprise.

I take a deep breath and brace myself as he starts walking towards me – waiting for my stomach to flip, my mind to cloud with his sheer gorgeousness, the same reactions I've experienced ever since we first met. He comes to a stop opposite me. His naturally olive-toned skin has clearly been touched by the summer sun, giving him a deep tan that accentuates his sparklingly blue eyes.

I look into his blue, blue eyes, and they twinkle back, but the only thing I feel is a huge wave of clarity. I finally see him for what he is – a beautiful man who I once fantasised about when I was extremely vulnerable. In that moment, an almost unbearable rush to see David washes over me.

'Here,' I say sharply, pushing the iPad into Ryan's hands.

Our fingers make contact and again I feel nothing. No flutters, nothing.

'Thanks,' he says, stepping back. 'Harry's going crazy in there.'

He gives me the sort of crooked smile that would have made me go weak at the knees before, but not now.

'No worries,' I say.

Then I turn around on my satin heels to leave but I need to say something first.

'Adriana's sound,' I say, nodding my head towards the car.

He follows my glance and smiles. I hope for her sake this is the real thing. Then when our eyes meet I give him an even harder look than the one I used for Liam earlier.

'Don't fuck this one up.'

The smile drops from his face, and he raises his hands in a surrender gesture. Then I whip round and walk as fast as I can to find David.

I don't turn back once.

52

'Jesus Christ! It's bloody freezing!' Jen screams, racing away from the shore, wedding dress scrunched in one hand.

It's testament to how drunk we all are that we have agreed to moving the party to the beach. It's midnight and only the stragglers remain: me and David, Bea and Tom, and Jen and Liam. The menfolk have stacked all the remaining booze in the shelter used by the local swimmers and have wisely remained there, chatting, while the three of us have foolishly decided to expose ourselves to the elements. Although we're all in our big winter coats, they're no match for the biting chill of the Irish weather.

My mother left an hour ago with an overtired Anna, who burst into tears when she was told the party was over but recovered quickly when Miguel promised to bring her to the hotel pool in the morning.

'Well, what did you expect?' Bea says, frowning at Jen, huddling close to me on the picnic blanket Tom discovered in one of the bathroom cupboards and had the good sense to bring down.

'It's the Irish Sea! It's Baltic at the best of times!' I add.

Jen throws herself down, wrapping her coat around her and

tucking her damp, sandy feet under the soft folds of her wedding dress. She looks at us in an accusatory way.

'Who's hiding the champagne?'

I shake my head at her, wondering how she can possibly manage to drink after the state she was in earlier. But she has (after much persuading) taken a break, been pumped full of water and coffee, and now appears to have a second wind. I tell her I'll head to the shelter and grab a bottle and some glasses.

My feet are bare and, despite the chill, it feels fabulous to set them free on the cool sand after being stuck in tight shoes all day. As I scrunch my way towards the shelter, I am relieved to find all three of the men in fairly good shape – even Liam has sobered up enough to string a sentence together.

They stop talking as soon as I approach.

I bet they're gossiping about Adriana. Liam wasted no time in telling Tom and David all about her but, thankfully, Jen wasn't in hearing distance at the time.

'It's all right, lads,' I say, sighing, stepping onto the hard stone surface of the shelter. 'Adriana's a stunner.'

Their faces visibly relax.

'So's the fiancé, Ryan, apparently. Jen mentioned to me before that Harry's dad is often mistaken for Ryan Gosling,' Liam whispers. 'But apparently this Ryan has an American accent whereas the real Ryan Gosling is Canadian.'

If Liam had an ounce of social awareness, he would notice that Tom has started to wriggle uncomfortably, David has shifted his gaze towards the sea, and I am trying not to make eye contact with anyone.

Jesus, get the hint, Liam. I doubt Tom wants to hear about how gorgeous Bea's ex-husband is, and David definitely doesn't want to hear it. But Liam, in his pissed-up state, doesn't notice a thing and just keeps blathering on about what a good-looking couple they make, and on and on.

Enough.

'Listen, Liam,' I say in a warning voice. 'Don't go on about Adriana when Jen is only sitting a couple of yards away.'

He immediately clasps one hand over his mouth.

'Jesus,' he says through his fingers. 'You don't think she knows, does she?'

Of course Jen knows a supermodel type turned up to her wedding. How could she not? The whole place was buzzing about it. In the end it was Jen's mum who broke the news to her in a way that mothers do to protect their daughters:

'Jen – a young girl did pop in to collect Harry, and now she'd be good-looking enough, but she wouldn't be a *patch* on you.'

And then Bea, who was clearly feeling guilty about Adriana's show-stopping entrance, added, '*And* she has cankles.'

It wasn't true but her comment left Jen relatively pacified.

I reach down and grab a bottle of champagne and three plastic wine glasses before straightening up. I take a couple of steps towards David and plant a big kiss on his chilly lips.

'Woah! Get a room!' Liam says, grinning.

I spin around and give Liam the finger.

'*You* get a room!' Tom says to Liam, laughing.

Liam's face falls for a second and then he shakes his head quickly.

'Ah, nobody has sex on their wedding night anyway,' he says, somewhat defensively.

Nobody says anything (although I'm inclined to think he's right).

'Come on, the lot of you,' I say bossily, waving the bottle of champagne at them. 'Join us in finishing off the last of the booze.'

Liam's face brightens, Tom and David grab a couple of six-packs, and the four of us tramp across to Bea and Jen, who are practically entwined in each other in their efforts to keep warm.

Liam pulls Jen onto his knee, Tom wraps his arms around Bea, and the pair of them look so fondly at each other that I wouldn't be surprised if I was hunting for another fancy dress sooner rather than later. David sits behind me, cuddling me into him, and that's where we stay, six of us squeezed together on a far-too-small picnic blanket, on a beach in southeast Ireland in the middle of the night, freezing but too busy drinking, laughing and gossiping to notice. I sink back further into David's embrace, and sigh in contentment, savouring these precious moments of love and friendship, never wanting the night to end.

ACKNOWLEDGMENTS

Ten years ago, we moved to New York (Manhattan and Westchester) for a couple of years when our eldest daughter was just nine months' old. I had planned to revisit the Big Apple while writing this book, but unfortunately Covid put a stop to that. As first-hand research (and a gloriously spendy shopping trip!) was out of the question, I badgered friends and family living in the US to help refresh my memories of life in NYC.

Hugely grateful to Loryn Amso for her wonderful insights into community life, volunteering, and elementary school, ex-pat Clair Grayston for giving me a highly entertaining refresher course on living in Manhattan, and Julie Siler and all her mum pals in the New York suburbs for sharing their different experiences too. Needless to say, all inaccuracies are my own.

I would also like to thank my agent Bea Corlett for getting me this far, my editor Sarah Ritherdon, who I often think must live inside my head, Nia Beynon for her enviable patience, and the rest of the brilliant Boldwood team.

Endless gratitude also goes to Cathy Kelly, the doyenne of

women's fiction, for continuing to support my novels and for always lifting me up with her warmth, kindness and enviable wit.

And of course, a special mention goes to the cheerleading team in Ireland – all the friends and family back in Dublin, particularly my mother who is as determined as ever to spread the word far and wide.

Finally, another massive thank you to all the fabulous readers from all over the world for continuing to support my books. It goes without saying that I couldn't do any of it without you.

BOOK CLUB QUESTIONS

1. What do you make of the power dynamic between Saoirse and David when they decide to move to the US for David's career?

2. What did you think about Emma Murray's descriptions of living in New York?

3. Do you think Emma Murray captured the experience of ex-pat parenting well?

4. How important do you think it is to 'find your tribe'?

5. Do you imagine Saoirse and David staying in the US or will they head back to the UK?

6. What did you think about the different experiences of living in the city as compared to living in the US suburbs?

MORE FROM EMMA MURRAY

We hope you enjoyed reading *Winging It*. If you did, please leave a review.

If you'd like to gift a copy, this book is also available as an ebook, digital audio download and audiobook CD.

Sign up to Emma Murray's mailing list for news, competitions and updates on future books.

http://bit.ly/EmmaMurrayNewsletter

Have you read *Time Out*? Discover the first laugh-out-loud instalment of Saoirse's story.

ABOUT THE AUTHOR

Emma Murray is originally from Co. Dublin and moved to London in her early twenties. After a successful career as a ghostwriter, she felt it was high time she fulfilled her childhood dream to write fiction.

Visit Emma's website: http://www.emmamurray.net/

Follow Emma on social media:

- facebook.com/EmmaMurrayAuthor
- twitter.com/murrayemma
- instagram.com/emmamurrayauthor
- bookbub.com/authors/emma-murray

ABOUT BOLDWOOD BOOKS

Boldwood Books is a fiction publishing company seeking out the best stories from around the world.

Find out more at www.boldwoodbooks.com

Sign up to the Book and Tonic newsletter for news, offers and competitions from Boldwood Books!

http://www.bit.ly/bookandtonic

We'd love to hear from you, follow us on social media:

facebook.com/BookandTonic

twitter.com/BoldwoodBooks

instagram.com/BookandTonic

Lightning Source UK Ltd.
Milton Keynes UK
UKHW041857301121
394885UK00002B/360